North Pole Inc.

A Novel

Davy Pepperidge

Nonprofit Project:

North Pole Inc. is a nonprofit project. Contributions to the author's tip jar are appreciated and accepted at www.NorthPoleInc.net (he has spent considerably on coffee and scotch while writing). Revenues or contributions made in excess of project costs will be sent to charity or used to print more paperbacks for donation.

Disclaimer:

This book is a fiction (as it takes place in the North Pole), and is a non-profit book that utilizes numerous sources, including facts and ideas not protected by copyright, and uses various ideas in limited substantiality, protected by Fair Use. Names, characters, places and events in this book, even those based on real people, are either products of the author's imagination or are used fictitiously.

To

My Friends & Family who inspire me,
My Mom who encourages me,
And my Dad,
His insights about the workings of the world,
and the curious nature of money and people.
Rest in Peace, Dad.

I love you all.

ACKNOWLEDGMENTS

This book would not be possible without the ideas and writings of many thinkers and storytellers. The most influential to this book being David Harvey (Seventeen Contradictions and the End of Capitalism), the Semiotext(e) Intervention Series (which Glenn Beck once described as "evil"), notably Christian Marazzi (The Violence of Financial Capitalism) and Maurizio Lazzarato (Governing by Debt and The Making of the Indebted Man), among other academic giants of the past and present, like Karl Polanyi, Joseph Schumpeter, Dr. Nicholas Shaw, David Graeber, and the grandfather of capitalist critique, Karl Marx. Please follow along or reference the "Notes" section in the back of the book to see how these concepts were woven into the story and dialogue. Oh – and the book wouldn't be possible without Christmas, Santa Claus, Elves or the North Pole. So, thank you Jesus!

"Criticism may not be agreeable, but it is necessary. It fulfills the same function as pain in the human body. It calls attention to an unhealthy state of things."
– Winston Churchill

1 - WOODEN HAND

A toothache, the only thing holding Willie back from a perfect morning. Even for elves, too much of any other sweet thing can become destructive. Funny how something so delicious can morph into an aching agony, and if left untreated, can lead to the rotting of the tooth itself. Even a sugar lover, like Willie, knows that the fleeting sugar high doesn't compare to the importance of keeping a healthy tooth in his mouth.

Willie rides Ursus, his fun-loving pet Polar Bear, quickly down the lively cobblestone streets of the North Pole. On some streets, the snow fluttering down after being swooshed high into the air is the only evidence of their passing. Escaping a day of school is exciting, but the thrill of riding his fluffy white bear full speed amid the madness of rush-hour gives Willie a much-needed escape.

Willie, a 13-year-old redhead, is skinny and a bit fidgety. His athletic display as a skilled Polar Bear rider is at odds with his awkward ways. He has no real friends, minus Ursus, but he's kind and adventurous in his own way. You wouldn't know it at first, but Willie Maven isn't your typical elf. Something always seems to prevent him from fitting in. He's the kid that gets pushed around the schoolyard and doesn't know how to fight back, not yet at least.

His parents allow him to skip school today but what he cannot escape is his need for acceptance.

Ursus with Willie slow to a haughty prance before turning a corner, rendezvousing with Willie's proud parents, James and Lucy Maven. His parents are chicly dressed and effortless in their ways as they are in their style. Funny how opposite they are next to their son. They're a couple of the times but with respect for tradition, knowing how to rock a modish pair of shades with the pointed elf hats of centuries past.

James and Lucy are cut from the same cloth, but James has an air of pride, or maybe it's over confidence he's inherited from his father. He embraces the privileges his family receives as basic rights. But Lucy doesn't rest on her laurels, or last name. To her, respect is to be earned day in and out, every day. And unlike James, she exerts her cutting intelligence only to uplift and inspire the many elves in her life, through patience, good listening and generosity.

In a more obvious way, they're different in that James has curly strawberry blonde locks that bounce up and down with each stride. His hair is parted on the side, as is traditional, and sprouts outward, ever so charmingly from underneath his hat before it curls up onto the brim of his hat.

Lucy's snow-white complexion contrasts beautifully against her flowing, shiny black hair. The ever-reflecting sheen gives her a radiant quality. Her level headedness and purity of spirit matched with James' fire for life makes them such a compelling pair—as lovers, parents and heads of the Maven Workshop.

There's an undoubtable charisma and benevolence to them, and they're fed up with the harassment Willie gets back at school. So, they're giving him a day or two away from the hostilities by taking him to their famous family workshop. Willie hasn't visited since he was a tiny elf-ling. Perhaps this time around he can really appreciate it, they hope.

The Maven Workshop is one of the North Pole's longest running and historically enriched workshops. It has a rare and lasting legacy for excellence, innovation and craftsmanship. There are many workshops that produce all kinds of toys for Kris Kringle and the Christmas Mission, but few, like the Maven Workshop, prove themselves repeatedly, always keeping top talent and prominence.

Willie's doesn't get out often, so James and Lucy are excited to have their boy with them for the workday. It's a good chance to remind Willie he has much to be proud of as a Maven.

The family navigates through the chaos of the North Pole morning commute, crisscrossing past rambunctious markets and vendors, filled with lively smells of freshly baked pies and roasted chestnuts the permeate the cool breeze.

Distractions within downtown are ample, not only because of the flow of elvish characters but through the immense architectural beauty and precision of the cityscape.

Homes and offices are comfortable and consistent, while most buildings are slim, high and deep, reminiscent of the pastel neighborhoods outlining the canals of Amsterdam. Their uniformity of size is contrasted with their stylistic individuality, with striking bell-shaped neck-gables, dual entrances, elegant cornices and moldings. The façades further differentiate the homes, promoting quirky features like sculpted draperies and garlands. They are often stylized with monograms of the traditional family occupant, with statues of honored family ancestors and hieroglyphic-like depictions of the splendors of Christmas past.

The cityscape is sprinkled with public spaces and areas for recreation, including various fields, trails and racket courts. The meticulously manicured parks and intimate gardens which surround the outer walls of *Santa's Hermitage*, Santa's palatial compound, are filled with the likes of pine trees, mistletoe and poinsettias, all arranged in a Zen-like order.

From high on Ursus' back Willie views Santa's Hermitage through the closing gates of the Redcoat Guardhouse, the true entrance of the grounds. Meanwhile, the Hermitage's decorative faux-entrance, false in that it's heavily guarded and cannot be entered, has a dominating presence. It brushes up against the city Square, which is also the city center, next to the Belief Meter and surrounded by tall, slender administrative buildings, many of which could be easily confused for Swiss cathedrals or clocktowers.

The Hermitage is the beating heart of the North Pole, where Santa lives and conducts all official business with his handpicked ministers. It's surrounded by high walls, looming towers, tall turrets and ramparts that interconnect the various castles and structures. It's best described as a mishmash of Moscow's Saint Basil's Cathedral, with colorful, bulbous, onion-shaped domes, crossed with various combinations of the Louvre, featuring gothic flying buttresses and Romanesque semi-circular arches, in a combination of eclectic, awe-inspiring modernism that fascinates and delivers an overwhelming sense of grandiosity. One's presence on the grounds either lifts the spirit or fills it with intimidation. But perhaps that depends if you're a guest or a prisoner?

High above the locked doors facing the Square, in what's known as "*Santa's Tower,*" Santa's luxurious penthouse, complete with a fanciful balcony that faces the Square. It's where Santa delivers his annual "Christmas Eve Address" to all elves. On the lucky, rare occasion, an elf may be in the right position of the square to spot Santa sitting behind his desk, holding court, or doing whatever else the fat magic man does.

Yet the prominent central structure of the complex is a massive, opaque, glass-like spherical achievement called "*Santa's Sphere.*" Surrounding it are impressive towers of various heights and sizes standing asymmetrically through the grounds. Twisting domes and improbable shapes adorn the penthouses, while a mix of vivid colors and intricate patterns decorate the exteriors.

Willie takes a long last glance into the Hermitage until the massive iron doors close with a *thud.*

"The North Pole in all of its glory. There's nothing like it." James says with a smile.

Willie is drawn to the sight of Santa's Tower. There's something about it that draws him in, perhaps it's grandeur? Or more metaphysically, a feeling of dense gravity, like a black-hole, that pulls him. Strange how the very sight of the tower makes him feel as if he's already been there, or perhaps fated to go there? He equates his lingering sensation to the strange feeling of déjà vu, but unsure if it's related to experiences already lived or yet to come, or both, or neither. Even so, the sight makes Willie grin.

James can read his son's face like a book, pleased with Willie's excitement in high office and the responsibility that comes with it. James knows his son has a good shot of getting in Santa's administration if he puts his mind to it, because unlike most elves, the Maven name carries a lot of weight, politically, economically and socially.

"Maven" was made famous by Santa through the indoctrination of the Maven Workshop. In fact, honoring a family with their own workshop is the highest honor Santa bestows. The privilege is strictly reserved for the most talented and productive families, rewarding their fruitful, loyal and consistent service. With that, the Maven family is known for producing generations of talented craft-elves, artists and inventors, all highly valued in Santa's everlasting Christmas Mission.

Santa, aka Kringle, and his various administrations have awarded the Maven's along with about one percent of families, designating them "Workshop Society." With the honor comes beautiful workshops and associated privileges, allowing the families the freedom to pursue their own endeavors while steering the creative projects of their workshops. This leaves them to imagine, push limits and come up with the next best fun, exciting and advanced generation of toys. The newest and best toys going to the best-behaved boys and girls at the tip top of Santa's good list.

With that, the Mavens have great expertise and skills through their generations of elite education. That and through the fact that they've grown up in Workshop Society itself. They're the best at what they do, born and bred for it. Although they come from families that have inherited workshops, they feel that they've earned their special status because it's impossible to point to anyone more qualified. Even in the North Pole a meritocracy is under-developed. The privileges the Maven's and all workshop families enjoy through their status are immense. So much so that Santa provides for their every need and awards them luxuries based on workshop productivity, performance and inventiveness.

Essentially, Workshop Society reproduces the next generation of workshop leaders. Santa has designed it so that Workshop Society almost never intersects with Factory Society, where the other ninety-nine percent of elves exist. Santa believes it best to have Factory Society work as hard as the founding ancestors of Workshop Society.

Through an immense spirit of hard work paired with some breakout toy, imaginative production processes, or new method, is how the work-shoppers earned their special status in the first place, at least according to legend, and Santa. There's no strict system for how a factory family gets promoted to Workshop Society, except they must somehow prove themselves as exceptional. However, Santa only elevates a handful of families per generation.

Yes, factory elves can afford the luxuries of Workshop Society, if only for the rare occasion, granted they figure how to meticulously save their wages, paid in sugar cubes.

Meanwhile in Workshop Society there are no wages. Just

status. Those working at workshops are trying to earn their own workshops. Those that own workshops are doing their best to hold onto them. It's a never-ending game. Nonetheless, the whole of Workshop and Factory Society must be at work in their various roles to fulfil Santa's Christmas Mission.

Back on the morning commute, James and Lucy navigate past the occasional red station post. They're crewed by the Redcoats, Santa's police force, armed with candy cane clubs as solid as a baseball bats. The Redcoats are dressed in their signature red wool uniforms and swanky black hats. They're big and broad, all with oversized arms and chests. They're obedient elves, trained like attack dogs, and certified through their own militaristic Redcoat Academy. Redcoats work to maintain the order while keeping the two societies segregated. With Redcoat posts on the corners of the posh boulevards, the work-shoppers prestigious existence is effectively enclosed.

Willie, James and Lucy soon arrive at the Maven Workshop, a building unique because of its simplicity. It's reminiscent of a noble's barn, colored in firehouse red with the name "Maven Workshop" in green, with big rounded letters and elongated curves outlined in shiny gold-leaf. The font is appeasing in an elegant and catchy way. Although the workshop is miniscule in outward panache it is impressive, measuring up to a city block long and wide, while standing a dozen stories high.

Before they enter, Willie takes one last look in the sky searching for Santa's sleigh, as young elves do. What a sight it is, to catch a glimpse of Santa in aerial splendor.

"No fat man yet, young Maven." An elf blurts out. It's Sticky, the family's longtime senior manager. Some jelly drips from his donut onto his crinkly chin.

"Just a fattening elf." James jokes.

"Good one, Sir." Sticky chuckles back in his primed and proper way. "I deserve that, I do."

Sticky slides open the front doors, exposing the sounds of production in the background. Sticky's sons, his five junior apprentices collectively known as the "Ickles" appear.

Rickle, Tickle, Bickle, Smickle and Hickle, assist Willie off Ursus and escorts the Mavens down the foyer. The foyer is complete with a runway-like red carpet, polished pinewood dressers and full-length mirrors. The Ickles act as a service entourage, changing them into practical work clothes and grooming them perfectly for the day ahead.

The Ickles have laser like focus and determination. They stand ready for any task as their efforts and obedience are derived from loyalty, a sense of duty, history, and the hope that they'll seriously be considered for their own workshop in the not so distant future.

Walking through the foyer they pass richly detailed portraits of Maven ancestors. You can tell they're related by their rosy, dimpled cheeks. The painters having emphasized their callused hands as to express the pride they have for working with them. Smile lines off the corners of the mouth are common, so are a touch of wrinkles on the forehead in between the brows, as running a workshop is stressful, and pointy ears to boot. The portraits are a prideful display of Maven lineage going back generations. There's an allure to this family. They're proud of the North Pole just as the North Pole is proud of them.

Between the grand portraits are joyous old photos of the workshop teams. Centrally hung are the black and white shots of historic Mavens surrounded by apprentice and master craft-elves alike. They're jubilant images. Like elves raising their glasses of eggnog in a toast, along with images and memories of kissing, dancing, singing and celebrating Christmas.

Not unintentionally the biggest photo is of James and Lucy with Santa Claus himself. It's a funny and ecstatic image. Santa, a magic man of colossal stature, holding a toy gun in the air as if he were a cowboy, shooting wildly into the sky without a care in the world. Kringle's other arm is wrapped around James and Lucy who look up at him, beaming with pride.

Willie pays specials attention to the last photo on the wall. It's of James, a younger elf at the time, victoriously displaying the

Wolves Cup to a wild crowd that hoist him up at the finish line. An image of sheer and visceral joy having captured the moment perfectly.

Next to the photo is one last rich family portrait. James in the center is posed proudly, hoisting the brilliant Wolves Cup trophy. It shines in his one arm along with a jubilant Lucy, holding both baby Willie and Ursus tenderly in the other. It's significant because the Wolves Cup goes to the winner of the annual Wolf Sledding Race, a contest that pins up-and-coming heads of workshop against one another in a primal way.

The Wolf Sledding Race acts as a metaphor for elvish strength and excellence. The sleigh drivers must navigate the dangers of the course, earn the respect and obedience of their wolves, cope with the treacherous blizzard conditions, and maneuver the dangerous mountaintop racecourse. It's a test of bravery, skill and endurance as racers must control and rely on their alpha wolves, while the race helps Santa discover his alpha elves. As evidenced by the Wolves Cup, James, Lucy and Willie belong to elite company, even among the one percent of Workshop Society.

"About that time, boys." Lucy blurts, waving the team to follow her as Willie arrives by her side.

"Watch and learn today, maybe hands on tomorrow." She tells Willie.

He nods, smiling back before pushing the door open, entering...

The workshop floor. They're greeted by buzzing, clanking, and sand-papering, all of which serve as a second cup of coffee. The Mavens oversee several teams of elves, each team working on their own toys and projects. Willie wipes his eyes as the room fills with a light haze of fresh saw dust that smells of fresh pine. James greets every elf on the floor by name, he knows all of them.

The floor of the workshop is old-fashioned but runs like clockwork, with the collections of shiny polished tools all neatly organized and placed. Every work station is precisely designed with its own flavorful characteristics.

James jumps in and teaches a team of woodworking

apprentices a new technique, giving a master tutorial in manipulating a dual axis radial arm saw. The secret is simple, guide it with firm hands, delicate touch and an intuitive sense of creative awareness.

Willie enjoys watching his father teach the enthused group. They respect him immensely, and in some ways, love him. James reintroduces Willie to the team, he shakes their hands candidly and is reminded of what it feels like to be respected. Next, James takes Willie aside and strolls with him through the bustling floor.

"Stay present, consider your breathing, notice how your body and emotions are affected by the elves around you. Notice how you affect them, and elevate your alertness." James says.

Willie slows his pace and focuses on his breath.

"Good." James smiles. "Now let's take an attentional posture, *bare attention.*"

"What's attentional posture?"

"The awareness of what's happening to us, and in us, at the successive moments of perception. We are going to try to open your mind. Not by trying to change anything but by observing your emotions and body the way they are."

"Ok, I'll try." Willie stumbles.

"Pay attention to what you're experiencing. Separate your reactions from the raw sensory events and take in the bare facts. Allow things to speak for themselves, as if seen for the first time, and distinguish your reactions from what is creating them."

Willie steadily breaths, gathering his sensations, feelings and thoughts.

"It will take practice, but working within this posture culminates in a state of choiceless awareness, where the 'observer' and 'the observed' are no longer operational. Bare attention removes self-consciousness and permits the kind of spontaneity that enable us to reach for the highest levels of our potential, of our creativity."

"I'd like to do that, to be a craft-elf, like you."

James laughs to himself. "I'd like that too."

He pulls Willie aside, secretly observing Sticky at work. He gets on a knee and whispers to Willie, "Watch Sticky, he's immersed in focus. Not only is he enjoying the process, but living within it. You see, to embrace challenge and strive for beauty and meaning are the highest pursuits of our work."

Willie observes Sticky and other elves fully absorbed in their activity. They seem to lose track of space and time, focused in as if their lives depend on their quality of effort.

James whispers more, "An apprentice must not only master a technical skill, but through doing so learn consciousness. Every elf has an obligation to create to the best of their ability, and expand their mind. The obligation is spiritual and material. It's the responsibility of every elf to fulfill. One day you will fulfill it, my boy, one day."

"I'd like to." Willie smiles at his Dad.

Later, James and Lucy host the daily team luncheon, consisting of a delightful spread of cinnamon buns and snicker doodles. They enjoy the sugary desserts, which elves depend on for healthy functioning, however over-indulgence has negative consequences, like Willie's toothache. James digests his cupcake before asking his favorite question, "What's new today?"

Everyone jumps at the opportunity to share ideas, sketches, blueprints and models for all types of toys, games and inventions. This is their favorite part of the day as they debate designs, share insights and let their imaginations run wild. It's often the most creative and liberating part of the process.

Even with more progressive attitudes the Maven Workshop tends to draw traditionalists and those who enjoy creating with their hands. This isn't true of all workshops—some are focused more on science, others on mechanic tinkering, and so on. Beyond woodwork, the Maven Workshop is also one of the North Pole's strongest think-tanks for game design and innovation, responsible for classics like Battleship and Chinese Checkers, contrary to human folklore.

The work-shoppers are efficient specialists in the morning and creative generalists in the afternoon. The breaking of routine and the destruction of the mundane is a core concept, so the latter half of the day is devoted to ingenuity. Many ideas are scrapped while others are twisted, but the best are built upon and fleshed out.

Near the end of the day Willie helps Nickle and Tickle paint an elaborate model of the North Pole while James and Lucy plop down for a break. Sticky delivers them coffee and a copy of "North Pole Daily" - the most popular paper in town. There's no news coverage or interaction with the outside world, the whole society is isolated minus Santa, only he knows what happens in the outside world, unless he informs some of his deputies. James raises an eyebrow reading the headline "Belief Meter Up Ten Percent." An impressive figure.

Lucy, always skeptical of the news, wants to confirm it for herself. She peers out the window to spot the towering BELIEF METER, just outside the Square. It stands several stories tall and is reminiscent of a giant thermometer with an oversize clock face at its top. It looms over the Square, while its numeric display dictates the very eb-and-flow of all productive activity in the North Pole. Supposedly it measures the collective level of belief in Santa Claus, the North Pole and Christmas - across the spectrum of humanity.

"It's going to get busy." She says as she snags the newspaper cover from James. With a sense of angst.

James attempts to lighten the mood and smuggles the sports section to Willie, the main article glorifies the contenders of the upcoming annual Wolfsled Race. Willie already fantasizes winning it.

James gazes at another headline, "Sugar Supply Stable," and breathes a sigh of relief.

Not only do elves depend on sugar for their diet, it's also the only energy source of the North Pole. Everything from factories and workshops to schools and homes, depend on a specially modified and processed sugar molecule for power.

In essence SUGAR *POWERS* the NORTH POLE, so THE NORTH POLE *RELIES* on SUGAR and SANTA *COLLECTS* THE ENTIRE SUGAR SUPPLY. No, he's not eating those treats and goodies that children leave him on Christmas Eve, he's BRINGING THE SUGAR BACK TO THE NORTH POLE in his magic sack, not only for the production of Christmas but for the *SURVIVAL* of the North Pole.

Further, SUGAR CUBES are used as a means of exchange in Factory Society. It's a fickle currency because it dissolves, breaks apart and is easily reduced to dust. Accordingly, most factory elves use their sugar quickly to satisfy their daily dietary needs, putting them in a constant demand for sugar, giving them a constant need to work.

Meanwhile, sugar is important in Workshop Society because it's used for energy. The more energy the workshops have for mechanic and electric processes the better their workshops perform. So, an available sugar supply is important for them too, even if they're provided with all the sugar they can eat in a lifetime.

In theory, Santa's need to expand Christmas is unlimited because human demand is unlimited. According to Santa the force of the infinite is the force that drives growth. But really, it's his insatiable appetite for power and worldwide fame that's the real force expanding Christmas. Santa's ambition and seemingly divine mission requires the maximum output of energy that the North Pole can produce. Everything is built around this effort, and James and Lucy, like most elves who helm the workshops, have an intimate understanding of this dynamic between sugar, productivity, and the Belief Meter, which corresponds to Santa's ability to extend the scope of Christmas. The more sugar that's available the more Santa can expand Christmas and reinvest in the North Pole. So, the goal is to have at least enough sugar to keep the North Pole supplied for another year. Because of high demand the entire society stays on the brink of sugar solvency, a continuous stressor for Santa and everyone else.

Soon it's the end of the day as the team comes down from their rush of ideas. They file their scribbled notebooks and schematics as they spend their remaining hours calmly hand painting and polishing the completed toys. Before they leave the team thoroughly sweeps and dusts the facility until it's spotless. Everything is back in its place and ready for a fresh start tomorrow. They all pop one last sugar cube and the Mavens bid their work-shoppers adieu with sincere gratitude. Meanwhile, Willie's had a thrill and feels like he grasps what it means to be a Maven.

"I want to come back tomorrow." He requests.

Sticky jumps in, "We'd love to have you back, young Maven."

Willie packs up and changes. He smiles once more at the fascinating workshop before turning to step outside and climb atop of Ursus. He sticks his arms out wide and catches a gentle breeze as a flurry of snow and a gust of wind propels them into the busied city streets. James and Lucy catchup and leap upon Ursus, joining Willie as they gallop through downtown.

Soon they climb the hill of their ritzy neighborhood before arriving at their cozy home. It stands three stories high and rests on top of a hill above the city. The small family of three settles in and lights the evening candles as a warmth emits. Lucy brushes Ursus, making him *purr* with a relaxed and soothing hum.

"Sparkling cider! To celebrate Willie back in the ol' family workshop." James jeers.

"Cider on the roof, so we can spot Kringle!" Willie snaps excitedly, grabbing his pair of binoculars.

They climb the spiral staircase and pour hot cider, spiced with cinnamon, before getting comfortable on the observatory-like deck. They huddle close, tight and warm until Ursus barrels up the stairs then plops himself down. He snarls up behind them. With Ursus at their backs Lucy, James and Willie recline into their pet polar bear, slipping into his soft, pristine white fur as it wraps around them like a snug blanket.

Here they lay between two dazzling planes of existence. The metropolis of the North Pole sparkling below, and the shining stars of the galaxy above. In comparison, the infinitesimally small family feels at one with this everlasting sea of existence. Gazing up with awe and love, they know they're a small node within an endless universe. This sense of the infinite brings them immense joy. It's an oceanic feeling shared between them, providing an unbounded oneness with everything. For them it becomes impossible to imagine any other reality that might be better than this one, at this moment, right here and now.

They further recline into Urus' fur and stare higher into the heavens. Though they want to freeze this moment they absorb the beauty of it, because it's precious, fleeting, and must come to pass.

Willie points at something, about to speak, but realizes it's a shooting star, "Not Kringle." He sighs.

"Maybe he doesn't always like the attention of flying over the Pole? Maybe he prefers the cover of night over the mountains?" James suggests.

Willie stands and shifts to a less familiar view, aiming his binoculars above the rigid *Artic Range*, a vast and treacherous series of mountains, each elevation seemingly larger than the next. He stares into the dark sky and scans, glancing high into the atmosphere as something unusual catches his eye.

"What's that?" Willie asks.

Lucy playfully takes his binoculars and looks out with a smile, which morphs to a baffled and worried state. She hands the binoculars to James. It's something he's never seen before either - a giant black and red, oval shaped balloon airship. A TWISTED CROSS flagrantly illuminates its side. It floats steadily across the sky and over the ocean with a blatant sense of self-importance.

James puts the binoculars down and holds his family tight. His heart beats quicker with fear. "Whatever it is I'm sure Kringle knows all about it." He tries to reassure them.

The next morning Willie is back in the Maven Workshop having a one-on-one with Sticky. He's wearing a pair of safety glasses as Sticky lectures on and on about the plethora of tools at their disposal. Sticky grabs a Handsaw, the most iconic and reliable tool of the workshop, and shows him the basics.

It's mind-numbing to young Willie, as Sticky lectures and demonstrates all the different saws in great detail, methodically going down the list of Hacksaws, Japanese Saws, Coping Saws, Jigsaws, Circulars Saws, Table Saws, Band Saws, Milter Saws, Oscillating Saws and the alike. Sticky is putting him to sleep.

"Did you get that, young Sir?" Sticky asks.

Willie sleepily nods in appeasement.

"Very good, I'm going to get more wood so you can try. Just sit still and don't touch *anything!*"

Willie slips further into boredom waiting for Sticky who's been gone for a little while. He notices a giant, half done, life size wooden carving of Santa Claus leaning against the wall, ominously staring right back at him. If only Santa had eyes it'd look a lot less creepy. To carve the eyes the Oscillating Saw should do the trick, Willie thinks. After all it has a precise vibrating blade that can maneuver the confined space without issue. He picks it up, turns it on and carves into Santa's blank eyes.

Willie's impressed with himself, it's working. It's even fun as he shaves down the wood creating a funny, bulging set of eyes on the wooden Kringle bust. He takes a step back to admire his contribution and gets a good laugh.

But the saw in his hand is still on and as he takes another step back, TRIPPING on the cord...

Losing balance and FALLING, Willie drops the saw as to instinctively use his hands to catch his fall. But just before impact the path of the bouncing saw, buzzing at 20,000 rotations per minute meets with his wrist and ZIPS THROUGH IT like a warm knife through butter. The clean slice leaves his hand half attached to his wrist as *blood gushes* onto the floor.

After a moment of shock Willie lets out a torturous SCREAM that echoes through the halls of the workshop. Everything stops. He faints as the emergency lights flicker. Sticky rushes over as Willie passes out in the puddle of his own blood.

The next day Willie wakes up, he's back home in bed with James and Lucy passed out in rocking chairs by his side. Sweat runs down his forehead. He goes to wipe it but sees how *his hand is gone*. In its place... a metal stub with a detachable *wooden hand* screwed in. He cries at the lifeless sad nub, tears pouring realizing he's lost his dominant hand. His mind races wondering if he'll ever be a craft elf, feeling robbed of his dream and future.

The next week Willie is back in school, crouching into his desk as if hiding. His teacher, Mr. Pinwheel, takes notice.

"Good to have you back, Mr. Maven, I hope you've enjoyed your vacation." The class laughs on cue.

"I didn't take a vacation." Willie replies.

"You seem to have forgotten how to take notes." Pinwheel utters.

"It's not that I've forgotten, I just don't know how."

Mr. Pinwheel laughs. "Come again, Mr. Maven? You're slow, but not that slow."

"How does one write with this, thing?" Willie reveals his wooden hand, shocking Pinwheel along with the entire class. He detaches and fumbles over it, showing how fake and useless it is.

Axel Kendal-Crink grabs the wooden hand and tosses it over Willie's head to his friend Clyde Holly, making Willie scramble for it as they play catch, like monkey in the middle.

Axel, broad shouldered and belligerent, sports a sharp buzz-cut and an inherent arrogance that's ingrained to his core.

The teasing proceeds even as Axel's younger sister, Renee, the cutest little button of an elf, attempts to intervene.

"Give it back!" Renee demands.

But the boys carry on.

Renee is an inherent sympathizer of Willie. She's always disgusted when the strong take advantage of the weak, and has an innate will to defend those who cannot defend themselves. Willie looks up to her, they share a connection until the embarrassment is too much for him to bear.

"Keep it." Willie says, giving up as he sheds a sudden teardrop. He wipes it away hoping no one saw, but Renee did, and she's devastated as he escapes the classroom.

Willie returns to his empty home with Ursus solemnly trekking behind, able to sense his pain. He goes to pet Ursus but realizes his hand is still nothing but a nub.

Lucy and James return to find Willie depressed in bed.

"School is the most wretched place." He cries. "I just want stay home. *Let me stay home*, please."

James and Lucy share a glance of sorrow before she nods approvingly.

They all embrace in another tight family hug. Ursus joins in too, lovingly trapping them all within his fur. Willie cracks a faint smile, certain anything will be better than school, uncertain about everything else.

2 – WOLF SLEDDING

Three years later, it's 1945. Crowds of excited elves dressed in their finest threads fill the stands at the starting line of the annual North Pole Wolf Sledding Race. The air is thin at the mountaintop where they all await to greet their brave champions. It's an event mainly for Workshop Society, but it's easy to point out the small crowd of factory elves who've saved everything for the privilege to attend.

The racecourse runs around the mountain-tops of several treacherous heights of the Artic Range. At the starting line the caged wolves *howl* with wrath, eager for release. It's like dog sledding but exponentially more dangerous. It's a time-honored tradition where the workshop leaders of tomorrow seek to make a name for themselves today. In the North Pole there are few things more sacred than honoring ancient customs and one's house.

Over the generations the races have become a battleground for great rivalries, a test of smarts, strength and strategy. It's also a proud reminder that creatures small in stature can tame the ferocity of the powerful and unruly. Not just control, but harness and transform it into an act of grace and beauty. It's a reminder to push oneself to the edge, and that great things can be accomplished in the face of danger.

It's a closed loop track so the starting line is also the finish. The course bends around various curves of the mountain range, making it important to get the inside position as to avoid the cliffs on the outside.

The rowdy crowd humbles as a color guard of trumpeters march forward, outlining both sides of the starting line with the three sets of wolf-sleighs set in between. The wolf-sleighs mimic Santa's sleigh, with four pairs of wolves in a straight column formation, and a ninth wolf, the alpha, in front leading the pack.

Behind the official's tent awaits Willie, now sixteen years old, tall and still lanky for an elf. He's trained hard, even earning himself a layer of athletic muscle although he doesn't fill out his frame. He's an elf on a mission to prove himself. If he can't build because of his hand at least he can race with his hook. And through being homeschooled and sheltered he has a growing urge to show up all those kids who bulled him back at school. He wants to show them how tough he is, even if he's missing a hand.

Not only is the wooden hand they once tossed around gone for good, in its place is a proper multi-purpose hook. He's learned to embrace it and even show it off. He's not nervous about his hook but he is about the race. With pressure mounting he tries to puff himself up and fight through the nerves, eager to make a statement.

Willie's huddled by James and Lucy. His mom trying to calm him, holding his unsteady hand.

"You don't have to do this." She insists.

"I'm just cold." He replies, hand and hook still trembling.

He looks her dead in the eye with reassurance. James grabs Willie's hand and warms it between his.

"No fear, Willie."

"No fear." He whispers back.

At the starting line the trumpeters let out a regal welcoming for the Master of Ceremonies, Sir Louie Kendal-Crink, the patriarch of the esteemed Kendal-Crink house and right-hand elf to Santa Claus himself. He arrives in the finest and warmest red and green threads, decked out in proud ceremonial garb. Although his outfit is graceful, he himself is not. He's short, even for an elf standards, crotchety and irascible. He has a rigid stride and swings his arms with firm and deliberate gestures. The stress of his duties has corresponded with the complete loss of hair on his head, sporting a shiny bald dome underneath his tall yet cushiony hat. But like his hat, he too possesses much panache in that he carries himself with a level of confidence that's only second to that of Santa.

With the sudden passing of his wife many years ago, Sir Louie half-filled the void by devoting himself to his career. In his mind, to compensate for that most horrific loss, he's vowed to never lose again, at least in any professional pursuit. That doesn't mean he's immune from losing, but with his extreme focus and value on winning he's become a horribly sore loser, susceptible to bursts of madness if his thirst for a daily victory isn't quenched. Thus, the seriousness of his mission cuts to his core, making him an expressive elf, leaving deep creases and heavy-set wrinkles imprinted upon his face. To him, his duties are sacred obligations, and his efforts to them far outweigh any fatherly responsibility. This often means Axel and Renee go about as they please while Sir Louie labors. His career is his religion, his meaning, and anything that comes in way of it must comply or be steamrolled. Santa likes him as his chief lieutenant because he knows how to get things done, and to Santa, that's all that really matters.

Next to this most intense elf is his daughter, Renee, older now and tomboyish, but still coming into her own splendor. She accompanies him to the podium. They're so different from one another that they're similar in being extreme. Nonetheless they're bound by blood. Like her father, she's on the petite side. More interestingly, she too has a boundless energy for the things she cares most about. Right now, that's reading and literature. Also like him, she spends much time in his private library with a collection of books that Santa has stolen amid his Christmas misadventures.

While delivering presents, Santa, having glanced at more than a few intriguing titles, often finds his curiosity piqued. He figures it best to bring the knowledge back home for his chief minister. Their exclusive access to the many novels, encyclopedias and non-fictions remain privileged and restricted to anyone else but Santa and Sir Louie (and Renee, through her curiosity and thievery). Yet once her father gifted her with "A Christmas Carol" she became an addict of Dickens, ever since she hasn't ceased visiting his secret library. Nor has she stopped stealing his books, building her own contraband collection.

But their differences are countless, and most unlike her pugnacious father she's trying to blend into the background, feeling conflicted about her brother Axel and Willie facing off. Renee still hurts for Willie. In her heart she's always held a tiny fire for him, although she has a funny way of showing it in that she doesn't at all.

Sir Louie takes to the platform as the trumpeters quiet. With great charisma he proclaims "Welcome to the great Wolf-Sled Race! What a great day it is to be an elf!"

The elves roar back with exhilaration.

"What a great tradition to honor all elf-kind! Today we honor those willing to risk it all, those racers willing to take their lives to the edge of possibility, who inspire us with their courage and valor. By the power invested into me through Kris Kringle, I have the great honor of introducing our three champions to you now!"

The crowd loses it as the trumpeters' salute and burst into a war cry of a tune.

"From the proud Silversmith Workshop, please welcome Rebecca Jensen-Gin!"

Rebecca is tall and slender, standing at a height of five foot six inches. She approaches the sled confidently and bursts into a hop, skip and flip, landing perfectly with her hands on the sled handles before twisting and landing on her feet like a vaulter. She's a beautiful athletic freak. Rebecca settles into the sleigh ready to go.

"Next, from the long line of toy tinkerers, it is my pleasure to introduce Willie Maven!"

Willie steps forward and gives a brief wave to the crowd. He spots his Mom, Dad and Ursus among them, and gives them one last reassuring nod as he marches to his sled. He's scrappy looking, like a stray, but if he has one notable strength it's that of sheer determination. Willie arrives at his sled and wraps his hook around the handlebar before punching his fist into the air, rallying the crowd.

He catches Renee smiling at him. He's never had a striking girl look at him like that. Willie remembers it was her who stood up for him all those years ago. He smiles in remembrance but shifts back into focus. He closes his eyes then reopens them to concentrate dead ahead at the powder keg of a wolf pack awaiting to explode. They're angry, aggressive and ready to run the race of their lives, just like him.

Sir Louie takes an extra moment for the crowd to quiet using the lurking silence to build suspense.

"And last but not least, from the Kendal Keep at Kringle's Hermitage and the workshop of Crinks, please welcome my very own son, Axel Kendal-Crink!"

The crowd goes wild as Axel takes to the starting line. Willie notices Renee's enthusiastic cheer for her brother. Axel's grown now too, since he's last taken Willie's wooden hand. He's become the golden boy of the North Pole, sporting a prominent muscular chest, dark flowing locks, square jaw and a smile that could melt a glacier. His uniform is fashionable as it is aristocratic, aerodynamic in design, but also light and insulating. The teen girl elves of the crowd drown out the others with their high-pitched jeers as Axel relishes in the attention, exuding excellence. Born into pride and privilege, this is an opportunity to defend his family's status and build upon his own. It's good PR at least and represents an opportunity to set himself apart from his highly competitive peers at the Redcoat Academy, especially those itching for government and ranking Redcoat positions like himself. Willie watches the young celebrity take to his sled next to him.

"Didn't expect to see you here, Maven." Axel says. "Nice hook."

Willie doesn't reply. He knows Axel is coming after him, but both guys should be more worried about Rebecca.

The three champions stand ready at the starting line as the sun peeks through the clouds, the rays gleaming brightly against the Arctic mountain before them. The reflecting light makes the opaque ice-walls of the track glisten, almost blindingly, while the wolves and crowd howl. The intensity of the moment heightens, compounding the pressure upon itself in an ever-loudening tension as the three racers await the trumpets to sound.

Willie takes a glance at his hook. "No fear," he whispers one last time.

Sir Louie counts "Three, Two, One," the trumpeters burst aloud as the cage doors come crashing down with the wolves thrashing into action.

Rebecca earns a quick lead and makes a beeline to the inside wall on the first turn. Her maneuver sharply cuts off Axel as if directing her wolves to trample his. Axel's taken by surprise, realizing this is no longer a gentleman's sport, and like his father, he has no qualms about winning by any means necessary.

The passage rounding the first turn is only wide enough for two sleds. Willie, trailing, is forced to slam down his brake lever while Axel speeds to advance a whole sled length ahead – but as Axel catches Rebecca he's forced to the outside of the turn dangerously close to the cliff's edge, while Willie shifts inward toward the wall following Rebecca's smoothly paved tracks.

Willie's wolves line up behind Rebecca as his alpha snarls and snips at Rebecca's heels. He tries to direct his alpha to a split between the emerging space widening between Rebecca and Axel. As his alpha leans in toward the opening Rebecca *kicks* his alpha wolf square in the face. The alpha stumbles, jolting Willie's sled and forcing his face to *smack* against the handle bars, breaking his nose in one quick *snap*.

But he's quick to recover as is his wolf, both with blood spilling from the nose. Then, as if within a hallucinogenic flash, Willie sees his red noised alpha transformed into Rudolph, and lets out a primal *cry*, rallying his pack to fight harder as they glide through the turn and head towards a stretch of open trail. He shifts his weight directing the pack to take advantage of the small space dividing Rebecca and Axel.

Willie's alpha, now invigorated with focused anger, exploits the narrow gap and dashes to take the contested ground as his sled consistently gains. The blood ridden alpha bullies the beta wolves of the opposing sleds, creating enough space for Willie to push through as the three sleds become locked in a *dead even heat*.

In unison the three racers rapidly ski down the open course but the trail ahead funnels into a narrow cave wide enough for just one sled—but no one backs down.

Rebecca makes a move trying to ram her sled into Willie's, but she doesn't have enough inertia. The maneuver inspires Axel to do the same as he SLAMS into Willie with a powerful BASH, nearly knocking him off – but he clings on with his hook.

Half knocked off Willie struggles to regain balance, but the impact of the collision has caused his sled skis to loosen, causing them to rattle back and forth flimsily. He tries to make a quick repair but Axel sees the distress and leans outward to create even more space between the two... before rapidly transferring his momentum back inward—about to devastate Willie by ramming him with twice the force.

Amid rebalancing Willie recognizes the threat and thrusts against the break-lever with the full force of his weight as his sleigh *screeches* viciously against the ice like nails against chalkboard—just as Axel's sled swings past Willie's alpha and *collides* into Rebecca with a CRASH. It's an instant scene of destruction - dislodging Axel and Rebecca, sending them airborne before *skidding* across the icy snow in a violent high-speed tumble before disappearing somewhere in the powder.

Silence endures.

Willie breaths heavy—having braked perfectly with nothing but open track ahead. It's a prime opportunity to seize victory, but after a moment of contemplation he steps off his sled and searches for his opponents.

He explores the immediate area around the flipped and half buried sleds as the wolves' struggle to dig themselves out. With much digging of his own he soon finds Rebecca and then Axel, they're about fifty yards apart, lodged deep into the snow and struggling to move. He rushes to un-bury them. They're shaken but catch their breath and thank Willie. They walk back to patch up their sleds but Rebecca hobbles with the excruciating pain of a broken leg. Willie tries to help her walk but she only grows more frustrated.

"I'll be fine, Maven." She balks, pushing him away. He gives her some space as she hangs her head low. "The race is yours, take it." Rebecca orders. The surrender more painful than her leg.

Axel reluctantly nods in agreement as he dusts off his damaged sled, "Well played, Maven." He snickers. Willie accepts their defeat with a humble nod of understanding.

"Cross the finish line." Rebecca says.

"I will."

He steps back onto his sled but struggles to free the break-lever that's become wedged deep into the layer of ice that covers the ground beneath the snow. Axel smells an opportunity in his struggle. It takes Willie an extra moment but he frees it, and takes one more glance at Rebecca and Axel limping about, arduously attempting to put themselves back together. With some guilt Willie pulls back on the rope of the wolf harness and orders his pack forward, through the dark subzero cave.

As Willie disappears into it, Axel grimaces to himself, realizing he still has some fight left.

Willie exits the cave and cautiously continues around a sharp turn. In the midst of the turn he gazes into the cave and doesn't see either Rebecca or Axel, as a sly smile forms on his face, almost in disbelief that the Wolf Cup is within his grasp. With a calm determination he steers his sled through the final leg of the course.

But as if a bullet through a barrel Axel shoots out of the cave in a frenzy, his speed several times quicker than Willie's pace.

"Faster, Faster, Faster!" Axel screams as his momentum crescendos.

Willie spots him in dismay, on the prowl and gaining on him quick. He shouts to his wolfpack forcing them into the awkward position of accelerating through the final and most dangerous turn of the course.

Axel shifts his sled into top speed while Willie's pack further accelerates. It's clear Willie is in trouble with his rickety sled rattling intensely. As he loses momentum it's Axel who claims the pivotal interior position at the beginning of the final turn with a powerful burst forward. As they travel through the turn they progress wider and wider outward, forcing Willie further and further to the exterior, *nearing the ledge.*

Steadily the turn hits its climax and most extreme angle as Willie screeches, holding on with all of his might to keep his sleigh on the track. He pushes his wolves to an excruciating max acceleration, only a hair away from an endless fall but meters from a magnificent victory.

Lucy and James, terrified, spot Willie swinging around the corner as the crowd jeers. Within a moment Willie and Axel are locked neck and neck. But the physics of the situation force Willie to hang on for dear life as the momentum of Axel's sleigh inches Willie *ever wider*. In the heat of the moment their eyes meet and teeth grit as the outer ski of Willie's sled hangs off the cliff. Willie knows he's in dire danger and pleads to Axel, *"Pull in!"*

Axel's tries to give an inch but his dense muscular weight works against him through the apex of the final turn, having no ability to fight the g-forces that have taken control, forcing Axel's sled to dig further against Willie's, pushing the outer ski of his sled even further off the ledge.

Willie barely hangs on, fighting the forces of motion with all his might.

But it's not enough—and within a flash Willie's outer ski drifts over the cliff as the bottom of his sled CRASHES against rock, jolting Willie off the handle bar sending him *FLYING*.

The body of his sled drags along the cliff edge, scrapping and sparking against the minerally rock before bouncing back onto the track with the sled tumbling wildly, tossing the wolves with it.

Axel is in shock as he crosses the finish line as the victor. Willie's wolves follow just behind with the battered sled on its side, *empty*.

Ursus, from his elevated position and stuck on a chained leash - ROARS as he spots Willie HANGING ON with his one hand to a jagged rock. He dangles from the cliff, with miles of free fall and puffy, misting gray clouds below.

James and Lucy sprint to the cliff's edge. Willie's grip loosens as he tries to dig in with his fingertips, hanging onto the mountain face about ten feet below the ledge.

"Hold on son!" James yells as he arrives with Lucy, who tries to focus amid the tears streaming down her face.

Axel arrives at the scene while the rest of the panicked crowd trailing in the distance.

Thinking fast, James instructs Axel, "Hold my legs, and I'll hold my wife!"

Axel abides, planting his trunk like legs deep into the snow. He holds James by his boots with his body curving *over the cliff* toward Willie.

After a deep breath, Lucy climbs over James and he grabs her boots, forming a chain as they slowly descend down the cliff side. Within moments they're fully extended but it's still not enough with Lucy's hand mere inches from Willie's hook, his arm already reaching up as far as possible.

"Willie, baby, I need you to grab my hand. Do it now!" Lucy urges.

He attempts to swing his hook into his mom's hand, but he's centimeters away on every exhausting attempt. Tears form in Willie's eyes with death evermore imminent.

"I'm sorry, Mom."

"Stop that, get my hand! You can do this!"

James gives the very last inch he can as Axel's feet *slide* closer to the ledge.

Willie locks eyes with his mother and gives her a nod, knowing these next few seconds are his last chance. He inhales, and with a sudden burst of energy he *pivots off the rock becoming airborne and extends his hook upward to his maximum reach.*

Lucy jolts forward and *catches Willie's by the hook!*

"I got you, baby!" She shouts in a joyous frenzy.

Willie gets his other hand around and locks in a firm grip with his mother.

The chain of four connect, but as they dangle Axel fights for his stance, *sliding* ever closer to the ledge while the other elves rush to the scene, still seconds behind.

"Pull up!" James begs.

But Axel can't do it.

Lucy senses James' panic and feels them slipping. "Climb up my back, Willie, before it's too late!" She orders.

Willie hesitates but abides, climbing and making his way up the chain, but they proceed to slip...

"Hurry Willie!" She yells.

He gets his forearms and elbows up on the ground but sees how Axel is just inches from the ledge himself.

But Willie finds the strength to LIFT HIMSELF UP AND ONTO THE GROUND - while Axel is still fighting but losing his footing and grip.

They regain some ground as Willie rushes to pull Axel, who pulls James, who holds a dangling Lucy. There's a glimmer of hope as they try their best to pull and pull, until...

SLIP!

Willie goes sliding, accidentally tripping Axel who's instantaneously dragged to the ledge with his *torso hanging over the cliff.* Willie fights with all of his might, lifting up as hard as he can against all of their hanging weight.

But they're too heavy, and they're slipping, making Willie skid ever so persistently and inevitably to their deaths. The crowd remains too far away, still no one to help except for a quick young elf named Gabriel Star, a Factory Society fan who's enticed by wolves. Little Gabriel latches onto Willie and pulls, but his puny stature hardly makes a difference in their losing fight against gravity.

As precious moments linger it's clear that no progress can be made. It becomes obvious to James and Lucy that if they try to hang on all of them will fall to their fate...

"We love you, son." Lucy says.

"We'll always love you." James reassures.

Then James shifts his glance to Axel.

"Let go." James says plainly.

If he doesn't, they'll all fall, but Axel doesn't abide.

"Axel, it's time." James says.

"Axel, don't!" Willie screams.

But with his strength depleted, within that moment Axel RELEASES his grip and is pulled back up onto solid ground...

As James and Lucy *fall into oblivion*, descending into the everlasting white abyss below.

Willie holds a silent stare into the nothingness of the clouds beneath, then caves into anguish.

Ursus arrives next to him, having broken free of his chained leash, groaning with scorn. The crowd arrives and stands quietly around the boys and bear, not knowing what to do but gaze as Ursus snarls against Willie, tears flowing without control.

Renee steps forward from the crowd and offers Willie a hand, but he pushes her away. Ursus helps him up instead, softly biting into his jacket, pulling him to his feet.

He's barely able to stand, until Ursus kneels down allowing Willie to climb on his back before they hobble off. And they tread through crowd then down the mountain, alone in the world.

3 – DROWNING GERMANS

It's dark and cold as Willie and Ursus are soaked and exhausted, tottering home through the slush of the city. They arrive in their familiar neighborhood. Willie stops and longingly peers through a neighbor's window, watching the family smile and banter as they share stories over dinner. His gaze lingers for a moment too long as he turns back to the shadows before being noticed.

Arriving home, Willie takes a deep breath at the front door. He hesitates, not wanting to enter or accept this dark, quiet house as his own. He leans against the door and dreams of his parents preparing dinner, hearing their voices in his head as if it were all a bad dream. But the silence inevitably lingers, until Ursus remorsefully rumbles, reminding Willie he's still here for him. Ursus nuzzles against him before raising up on his hind legs to give him a big slobbery lick.

Willie can't help but smile back, if only for a second, and they enter the empty home together. He paces amid the stillness, and realizes life isn't tragic because it's wretched, rather it's magnificent and overwhelming, and that's the whole of tragedy.
Without beauty, love, or danger, it would almost be easy to live. His realization that life is absurd is not an end point, instead, it may be a beginning. With his new hunch he slowly accepts the absurdity of everything, and a quiet revolt ignites within him.

With a sense of love, Willie tenderly lights a couple of candles, each illuminating a sentimental family photo. Unlike the proud portraits at the workshop, these are more personal and revealing. Everyone appears relaxed, fun-loving and at peace as a small family. Willie takes a moment to appreciate each image, welling up as he stares and remembers those fine days.

He wipes his eyes and gets Ursus a fresh salmon from the ice box. He stands there, observing Ursus eat before he pours himself a pint of eggnog. With his mug in hand he climbs on top of the bear and ascends the stairs to the roof. The winds are churning, swirling the snow and sleet.

Willie gives Ursus a gulp of eggnog and together they

overlook the whole of the North Pole, seeing it glint through the blur of the storm. To Willie, star gazing with his parents feels like yesterday. He closes his eyes and transports back to that moment, sensing the presence his parents' souls' surrounding his own. He holds onto that sensation as long as he can, until it dissipates as if blown away by the icy wind. He reopens his eyes and returns to this disappointing reality, unable to shake the sensation of an endless pit widening within his gut as a depression deepens.

The next morning Willie and Ursus are passed out on the kitchen floor. They're surrounded by empty, foamy eggnog pint-glasses and sticky salmon bones sprawled about. Both are deep asleep until a loud *knocking* on the door wakes them - it's Sticky along with the rest of the Maven Workshop crowded behind him. Willie and Sticky stare sadly at each other until Sticky jumps at him with a hug.

"The funeral is today, Sir." Sticky informs him.

Later, Willie rides atop Ursus following Sticky and the Maven Workshopers until they arrive at the grand funeral. To Willie's surprise the event is full of excessive pageantry. The sheer size of the crowd in the stands is impressive, but he remains stuck in another world, spaced-out and unable to shake his guilt.

Once the ceremony begins Sir Louie Kendal-Crink provides the opening words and introduces a series of respected eulogizers composed of workshop leaders and esteemed families, all sharing their highest compliments and warm stories of James and Lucy, and their goodness.

But through his fog of emotion Willie takes notice to one thing - the absence of Santa Claus. If the fat man really cared then why isn't he here? Willie wonders amid his daydream.

"Last, some words from their son, Willie." Sir Louie announces, catching Willie off guard. With jitters he accepts the podium. He tries to straighten himself up...

"I have taken them from you. I have taken them from myself. I

31

have taken them from Kris Kringle, wherever he may be..."

The crowd gasps collectively as Sir Louie pants, almost in disbelief. He's called out Santa - this doesn't happen in the North Pole.

"Christmas will never be the same, nor will the North Pole." Willie concludes. He stumbles back to his seat, leaving the crowd silenced.

Later at the reception, Willie shakes hands and accepts niceties out of obligation. Sir Louie approaches and embraces him.

"I'm so sorry, my dear boy." Sir Louie says.

Willie's not sure how to reply as he watches Axel in the distance goofing off with Clyde Holly and his friends from the academy.

"Axel is devastated."

"He sure looks it." Willie mocks. "But he did what he had to do to win, right? It's a race, I get it."

"Pardon?" Sir Louie jolts, like Santa he's not used to being challenged.

"You're excused."

"I know it's been difficult for you, Willie, being homeschooled and all."

"What does it matter to you?"

"Let me refer you to a proper school, we can have you admitted to the Academy at once. Axel can take you under his wing. Once you finish your education, you can run the Maven Workshop or manage any workshop you choose."

But instead of considering his offer Willie is distracted by Axel and his friends cackling about. He wants nothing to do with their pretentious clique. Their outward snobbery and condescendence are clear, solidifying his view that the world around him is a deeply perverse one.

"To hell with your son, and these fake elves with their fake condolences...To hell with this place and to hell with Kris Kringle!" Willie shouts, causing a scene.

"You don't mean that." Sir Louie asks.

"I've never meant anything more."

Sir Louie leans in. "We'd never allow someone who doesn't know the craft or hasn't graduated from an academy to head a workshop. You don't have the temperament or the skills, and now you don't have the parents. Hell, you don't even have the hands. You can't even carve wood!"

Willie angrily grasps Sir Louie, pulling him close.

"You have one second to put me down, boy." Sir Louie orders, but Willie only gapes more intensely into his eyes.

"I'm my own elf, I don't need your pity." Willie says, grasping Sir Louie even tighter.

"I wish I were wrong." Sir Louie gasps. "But the one day you've spent in the workshop was rightfully your last. It's not everyone who cuts their hand off first day on the job."

Willie drags him as close as he can, eye to eye, staring with a burning hate, on the verge of smashing Sir Louie's face in—something that might as well result in a death sentence. Sir Louie's Redcoat body guards rush forward but he signals them off as he and Willie hold their stare.

"Look at yourself, boy. Ask yourself if this is this the elf you want to be?"

Willie pulls him harder nearly choking him. "And who put you in charge?"

"Kris Kringle."

Willie deflates almost instantly, defeated in a realization that it's true. There's nothing else to press as he releases Sir Louie and pushes him aside.

"Thanks for this grand networking event and superb lecture, what a spectacular way to celebrate my parents' demise." He says to all watching. "Long live the North Pole!" He yelps contemptuously before grasping a pint of eggnog and slugging it down in front of the bewildered crowd.

"Kringle won't save you." Willie says before taking one his last giant swig.

He grabs Ursus by the harness and leaves. On his way out he spots Renee looking at him from across the garden. He knows she's had her eye on him, but she turns away from his gaze.

Willie returns to his empty home, sleeps, drinks, sleeps, and drinks some more as the days turn into weeks. The newspapers stack up on his front door. He picks one up, the headline describes Sticky's promotion to head of the Maven Workshop, and he goes back inside for more even more eggnog.

As time passes Sticky grows more concerned and re-arrives at the Maven home. He knocks and knocks until Willie opens it, still inebriated and stumbling over himself.

"If it isn't ye ol' Sticky elf, head of ye ole' Maven Workshop," Willie slurs.

"I know you don't believe me, Mr. Maven, but the whole of the North Pole feels for you, Sir."

"Sir? Hah! It seems you're the boss now, ol' Stick." Willie says with a smug drunken grimace.

"I need you to listen, Sir, really listen this time. They want you back, out and about, in school or in the Christmas effort. Maybe back in the ol' 'shop? I can teach you properly this time, really."

"Ha!" Willie blurts sardonically. "The Christmas Effort, and oh, and the workshop? Look where the Christmas Effort got you, ol' Stick. A career apprenticeship? A lifetime of production orders? An existence of making brat kids toys they'll inevitably dispose of and forget!"

Sticky is lost for words.

"I take that back ol' Stick, the Christmas Effort has gotten you far, it's gotten you my workshop, hasn't it? Well played old elf, well played!"

"Willie, please if you'll -"

"If nothing else, you can toil away there until the day you drop dead on the production floor. That'd be your preferred demise, I'm sure."

Sticky takes a moment to compose himself. "The honor of working for your parents was the best thing that's ever happened to me."

Willie takes this in, finding it sad because he knows it's all Sticky has ever had, neglecting his own family to the point of his wife leaving him. Still his boys joined him at the Maven Workshop as it's the only place where they could spend any time together.

"I hope the North Pole treats you differently, I really do." Willie says.

"It's treated me well, Sir." Sticky jolts back. "Has it not done the same for you?"

Willie takes a deep breath.

"Has it?"

A silence lingers between the two.

"Axel didn't kill my parents. Kris Kringle didn't kill my parents, but the traditions of the North Pole did. Wolf Sledding? What kind of sick sport is this?"

"A proud tradition, Sir. One that your family has dominated for generations. You should feel honored..."

"Really?!"

"Why yes, Sir."

"My parents are dead, and for what? My honor?"

"You raced for your honor and that's noble, but they've perished in an accident."

"But it was my race Sticky, it should've been me!"

Sticky throws his arms around Willie and breathes deeply, trying to get him to do the same.

"There will always be a place for you at the Maven Workshop, Sir." Sticky says. "Always."

Willie appreciates the words, but he lifts his arm and displays his hook - holding it up high and inspecting it, cognitive of all its shortfalls.

"I think not, ol' Stick." Willie says with a lasting sense of despair. "They tell me I have to go back to school, to enlist in one of their academies. I won't do it."

Sticky stares at the hook, heart breaking, then lunges into him with a one last hug, holding onto each other in a true embrace.

"I will change this place Sticky. I don't know how, but I will, believe me." Willie whispers.

"I hope we'll get to work together again, one day, Sir."

"Me too." Willie gently replies.

Sticky nods and makes his way out, leaving Willie alone, standing there, holding his own wobbly balance. Ursus makes his way over. He senses Willie's gravity. They stare and share their sorrow once more...

Until Willie is enlightened by an inspired idea. "Let's find 'em, boy."

Ursus snorts with approval as Willie wipes his eyes and experiences a sense of purpose for the first time in weeks.

The elf/polar bear duo journey through the streets of all the way to the fringe of the civilization. They stop at the edge of the great icy plain to stare up at the intimidating Artic Range. It takes some scouting but Willie spots the mountaintop racetrack high in the distance. He looks into the valley beneath the summit, knowing the frozen bodies of his parents are still up there, becoming mummified somewhere in the snow.

The grandeur and beauty of the mountains gives Willie some solace, finding it a fitting resting place for his parents in that they're reunited with nature, and one day will become the very fabric of the great mountain itself. After a moment they take the first steps to cross the plain toward the range. As they climb the mountain the snow picks up, becoming more and more aggressive the higher they advance.

Willie has Ursus stop halfway up. They scan, looking around, but there's still nothing. Just more snow, rock and ice. Nothing but whiteness and gray in every direction.

They continue higher, stopping periodically, scouting and searching, but still nothing.

Finally, they're back before the finish line of the track. But it's as if the snow and winds have erased everything except the past. The racetrack itself is barely recognizable, without a single footprint or a sled mark intact.

Tensely, Willie and Ursus approach the ledge. They hold each other tight and lean out to peer into the abyss, trying to spot bodies.

Yet still...*nothing.*

Just a desert-like void of snow, with shades of white and gray, forever.

They step back and fall onto the ground. If it wasn't clear before it is now, Mom and Dad are gone. There's nothing left to do but accept this, and move on.

But instead of going back down the slopes they slowly push higher and *dangerously higher.* Going up the mountain without a shred of fear, until they finally reach the summit. They take a deep breath and together ROAR with all their pain.

As a moment of catharsis settles, they catch their breath and soak up a view of what seems like the entire world. From this amazing vantage point they overlook the North Atlantic Ocean and all of its icebergs scattered about like clusters of tiny floating islands. It's the first time Willie or Ursus have laid eyes on the great Atlantic. Few elves have ever come this far, and they cherish the incredible sight with a smile, until Willie spots a horrific sight on the horizon...

A massive ship on the water.

It's like the airship he spotted as a kid - dark, mechanic, intimidating. Like the airship this sea-ship also carries the emblem of the TWISTED BLACK CROSS on its side.

But the ship isn't moving across the horizon, it's SINKING into it, descending into the subzero waves.

He squints his eyes, watching the catastrophe unfold as packed lifeboats fall into the freezing ocean. People—yes, HUMANS, jump from the deck of the sinking vessel into the water.

The lucky ones climb aboard lifeboats while the unlucky drown or freeze to death, their bodies turning dark blue as they submerge below the waves.

Willie takes in the horror, but has a visceral instinct to help even at the risk of his own life. Without realizing it, if he can save any of these people then he might be able to forgive himself for not saving his parents. The intensity of his feeling overwhelms him, and he *clenches* his grip to Ursus' harness.

"That way boy, *fast!*" He yells as they charge down the mountain.

4 – SANTA'S TOWN

Willie and Ursus barrel down the mountain to where the icy slopes hit the ocean. Between the cliffs lies a narrow cascading hill that meets with the Atlantic, acting as the only possible landing site for the 100 or so lifeboats filled with freezing Germans. There's a few thousand in all, trying to navigate their boats through the floating icebergs to make their way ashore. The boats are equipped with only two oars, making it tedious for many to fight the tide. The first boats beat Willie and Ursus to shore. Willie approaches and realizes he may be the first elf in generations to see humans in the flesh, not to mention these humans have never seen an elf before.

But Willie and Ursus don't flinch, running straight to the ledge of the ice as they pull the nearest boats in. Ursus uses the strength of his bite, gripping the lifeboats with his sharp teeth and dragging them in as Willie extends his hand to the nearest human, a well-built man in his late-30's.

The man is more athletic figured than broad, with his blonde hair and a passionate energy that reminds Willie of his father. There's a charm to him. Even amid the scene of panic it's as if he's some kind of Ubermensch, with a vibrant aura radiating a powerful confidence, knowing exactly what to do next. He is very much in touch with his inner life so much so that he seems on the cusp of self-actualization. That, or maybe he's just a superb actor. In this man's mind it's as if everyone is already dead and that the world has already come to pass – which makes every moment of his existence so special, empowering him.

As the two beings make eye contact the man is captivated by all of Willie's elvish features. After a prolonged moment of confusion, the man accepts Willie's hand and is pulled onshore. Willie notices how the charisma of the man's demeanor is at odds with his deep-set eyes which carry a worldly gravity, as if he's seen and done things very few have ever seen or done.

The man speaks quickly and directly in German until it's clear Willie can't understand, so he switches to English in a breeze.

"Where is this, who are you?" The man asks fluently,

sounding almost as if he were a proper Englishman amid the small hints of a high German accent.

"The North Pole, I'm Willie Maven." Willie says as he pulls more and more Germans on shore.

The man is spinning inside, confused, anxious, but finally lets out a wide grin, "So, it's true, the North Pole is a real, elves and all."

"Of course it is, Santa couldn't do it without us." Willie states.

The man engages Willie with all of his attention and introduces himself as *"Klaus Mauser"* and shakes Willie's hand enthusiastically.

Klaus returns to action with Willie, frantically helping the masses of desperate Germans ashore. Many possess a sense of survivor's ruggedness, which mixes in a funny way with a layer of privilege that's tangible just beneath the surface.

Another athletic man of action hops off a boat and pulls people off one by one with Willie and Klaus. Without a blip Klaus announces to Willie, "Meet *Otto Becker*, my right-hand man."

"Introductions later, eh?" Otto spits amid the scene, with a sharper German accent than Klaus'. After pulling a boat ashore Otto shake hands hurriedly, only pausing for a moment with the realization that Willie is an elf.

Otto is lean, pale, gangly. Far less welcoming than Klaus. He's a little slick and slippery, and doesn't make much eye contact, making him seem inherently cold, or perhaps just inherently German, with a logical or and even pessimistic mindset to match.

Individually, Klaus and Otto are opposites, but when Otto's shrewdness is paired with Klaus' dynamo energy, the mixture results in a compatible balance. When united, these two are a force to be reckoned with. However, you can always tell them apart, as Otto wears exclusively black opposed to Klaus' colorful attire and their laughs are especially distinct. Otto cackles like he's gasping for air compared to the hardy, full-body chuckle of his counterpart, and Otto has a thin lippy smirk compared to Klaus's full toothy display.

More Germans arrive on the snowy beach and huddle in groups to keep warm, all staring at Willie in Ursus in action. They're shocked with their existence and impressed with their valor. They gaze at Willie and quickly realize he's their only hope in this remote, icy corner at the top of the world.

Klaus checks his pocket radio but there's no signal, only the sound of static fizz as he twists the knob back and forth until he gives up, concealing it back in his jacket pocket. Willie spots a lifeboat in the distance, it's drifting further out, not rowing and without oars. Willie points out the situation to Klaus and Otto, who jump into an empty lifeboat and make their way out. After a minute it becomes obvious that they won't be able to catch them.

Ursus senses the tension and Willie gives him the go-ahead to attempt to save them. The bear daringly splashes into the ocean and swims out, surpassing Klaus and Otto's boat before getting straight to the drifters. The Germans on the lifeboat toss out a lifesaver which Ursus snags within his bite, and pulls the boat to safety.

As Ursus and Willie pull in that final lifeboat the crowds of survivor's cheer, earning not only admiration but their love and respect.

The refreshing sense of jubilation is a feeling Willie hasn't felt in a long time. It's comforting, reminding him of his parents and the good ol' days. But he restrains his feelings of excitement out of respect for those who just lost their lives at sea.

Klaus and Otto return ashore, drenched, shaking and shivering as hypothermia becomes a concern. Willie realizes there isn't a moment to spare. He hops on Ursus and shouts *"Follow me!"* at the top of his lungs. The Germans gaze in awe at this sight of this feisty elf riding on top a polar bear. With very little hesitation the masses follow Willie and Ursus up into the mountains.

Klaus and Otto run to join Willie, struggling but walking confidently just behind him in a display of support for their elf guide. As Willie ascends the climb he looks to Klaus and Otto, sharing an unspoken trust. Then the trio face toward the unforgiving mountain terrain ahead as Willie fuels their confidence, moving once again with purpose.

Almost a day later the caravan of German survivors led by Willie arrive at the outskirts of the city. With excitement workshop and factory elves alike rush to streets, watching the tattered mass of frost-bitten Germans stammer behind Willie and Ursus.

The crowds start small, but a few hundred elves turn to thousands. Soon tens of thousands of elves line the streets and help the most desperate looking of parades. The Germans move at a crawl, near frozen with icicles formed in their hair and whiskers. The elves with their giving nature offer blankets, warm cookies and hot chocolate to the struggling people.

But the gifting is abruptly halted as the Redcoats *barge* onto the streets. They viciously push the elves further back while standing their ground, creating a barrier that prevents them from reaching the Germans. The confusion and chaos of the Redcoats against the crowd gives Willie pause, but the Redcoats don't stop the march of German refugees, actually they clear a path for them direct to Santa's Hermitage. Willie knows where to go, and as the Hermitage comes into sight, he looks up at the tallest spiraling tower and spots Sir Louie beaming down at him.

Willie and the Germans are barely able to hold themselves up as they arrive at the grand gatehouse of Santa's Hermitage. They're welcomed by a battalion of Redcoats. With a loud cry from their commander they point their candy-cane clubs straight at them. The battalion quickly breaks formation and encircles the mass of Germans. Once they're surrounded the Redcoats forcibly guide them through the grand doors. Willie and Ursus are still upfront led by the security escort. Willie's baffled by the move – thinking he'd be rewarded, given a hero's welcome by Santa. But with a Redcoat's club resting on his shoulder it's exactly the opposite.

As they march inside the Germans stare in wonder at the massive iron doors, every inch covered in ancient elvish hieroglyphics, telling the Christmas story in an elaborate, cryptic way. Klaus presses his hand against the finely chiseled symbols until a Redcoat *slaps* his hand down. The entrance of the Santa's Hermitage intimidates, and gets the Germans sweating with a sense of doom.

The nerves and lingering danger vibrate through Willie's body but he's on a mission to save these people. His sense of confidence gives the Germans a small glimmer of hope on the ever-darkening path as they're guided through the intricate maze of hedges and ivy-covered walls that wrap around skyscraping towers. They travel over a series of bridges above powerful glacial river rapids until the path goes from dim to absolutely dark, then turn a corner and meet with a *blinding* white light.

It's Santa's Sphere, and might as well be the center of the universe. The opaque glowing Sphere is as wide as the Titanic, shinning bright with light bouncing off of its fine crystal in all directions. Without a sound the Sphere opens as a solid sparkling mineral staircase peels back from within it, connecting the Sphere with the ground below. Ursus and Willie make the brave first steps into the structure as the Germans follow, climbing the glistening staircase and slowly filling the massive spherical hall.

The staircase rescinds upward then blends into the wall behind them, closing the entrance off entirely as the Redcoats organize the Germans into neat rows while they bringing Willie and Ursus to the front and center.

Willie is ordered off Ursus as the Redcoats scurry around the group, completing a surrounded formation with militant precision. The battalion moves to uniformly stand at attention with a sudden CLANK of their candy-cane clubs against the crystal floor. The room becomes absolutely silent, eerily so. But Willie knows what to expect as a band of trumpeters arrive, while Santa's Executive Ministers, made up of a few hundred bureaucrats, proceed inside and make way for the illustrious Sir Louie.

In a moment of exact coordination, the band erupts with a Christmas melody, creating a grand welcoming until they suddenly stop, and the whole room goes silent once more. Within the pristine quiet a floating platform descends from the top of the dome, carrying none other than *SANTA CLAUS* himself.

"HO, HO, HO." Santa belts in a sinister tone.

Santa, with a powerful and proud demeanor, stands poised with perfect posture. He wears a primed red velvet suit complete with an elaborate series of shining medals that cover his heart like a decorated general. His stern expression is derived from his status as an unchallenged semi-deity, the possessor of god given magic which he alone controls and flaunts.

But Klaus knows this type well, and picks up on his blind spot immediately, realizing Santa's brashness is his greatest vulnerability. The fact that Santa believes he's unchallengeable is the thing that makes him an easy target, if Klaus needs to turn him into one...

Santa's floating platform descends to just a few feet off the ground. He leans in and stares into the crowd of humanity, shaking his head in disgust, overwhelmed with agitation.

"Willie Maven!" Santa breaks the silence with him booming voice. "Step forward."

The commanding echo vibrates through the room as Willie cautiously steps up, shaking in his boots.

"I'm told it is you who have led these German's here." Santa booms.

"I have, Sir."

Santa's patience falls short as his anger heats to a boil.

"And do you know these Germans are Nazi's? You drag this scum to our sacred North Pole, the only refuge for elf kind." Santa jabs. "Do you even know what a Nazi is, elf?"

"No sir." Willie mutters.

"Well I do! They endanger all of us when you could've just let them die!" Santa yells.

"I only know they're humans, and as elves we're to respect all of humanity."

"But you're ignorant, elf! That's why I, *thee* Santa Claus, deal with humanity *alone*. It's my great responsibility and you're undermining me of it! You will apologize."

"I will not." Willie says, surprised in his own gut reaction. He bites his tongue as Santa fumes and realizes he needs to explain himself.

"What did you say?"

"We elves don't know what Nazi's are, or anything outside of the North Pole. If we're ignorant it's because you've made us so!"

Santa isn't use to this tone from an elf, but pulls back his anger, huffing deeply. He needs to provide the illusion of proper justice. Sentencing these humans to death without good reasoning would leave the masses of elves dangerously confused.

"Your ignorance blinds you, elf. And since you love them so much it will be you who defends them in my court."

Willie's trembling worsens, this isn't what he's expected.

"And never have I seen an elf disdain his family's great workshop, piss on generations of his ancestors and throw his own future down the drain so deliberately and disrespectfully as you, *Willie Maven*."

Willie stands there blankly, taking it.

"Sir Louie Kendal-Crink shall represent the North Pole prosecution. A trial shall take place here in one week's time. No further distractions from the Christmas Mission are needed, this shall be dealt with expeditiously." Santa blurts before turning his back. But he realizes he isn't done, and turns to look at Willie, locking eyes as if seeing through him.

"And Maven, now that you're without a workshop you'll learn what Factory Society is all about." Santa grimaces.

Willie continues to stare, unsure what to make of it.

"This is my town, elf. *Santa's Town*." He says dismissively. "You're excused." He adds as several Redcoats snatch Willie away. But before he's dragged off...

"Thank you, Willie." Klaus says.

"I'll do my best."

Ursus is thrust into a heavy chains and pulled by a dozen Redcoats, just behind Willie's escort.

The staircase silently peels back as Willie hears Santa order, "to the Fortress with them!" Then ascends up and away on his floating platform.

CLANK – the Redcoats clubs hit the ground marking the conclusion of the session.

Willie glances back, watching the Germans being round up and put into chains. With their forced escort Willie and Ursus are dragged through the maze-like grounds as Renee spots them from high on her tower balcony.

Soon Willie and Ursus are unshackled and kicked onto the street while the Germans are locked up in the Fortress prison.

Willie dusts off and pets Ursus gently around his roughed neck. He contemplates the impossible task of being a defense lawyer in the court of Santa Claus. It will be a kangaroo court, and feels like he doesn't stand a chance.

As he wracks his mind, he spots Renee running toward them. But as she nears the grand iron doors close shut with a loud and echoing *clunk*.

5 - GIFTWRAPPING

It's early in the morning, Willie's barely slept with his mind racing. His sheer exhaustion has him nearly passed out until an expeditious, annoying *knocking* at the door pumps his adrenaline. It's two Redcoat's drumming with increasing irritancy. Willie tests their patience until he arrives. He stumbles over to the funny-looking duo—one stocky and plump, the other tall and hunchbacked.

"Willie Maven?" The Redcoats question simultaneously.

Willie nods, bothered and staring back in confusion until the Redcoats burst aloud in laughter.

"You workshop brats crack me up." The hunchback spouts.

"Never thought we'd be knocking on the Maven's door, yet here we are." The plump one chuckles.

"And here you are, totally inept." The hunchback slings.

"Kind of sad yet still very funny." Plumper admits.

"I don't understand, what do you want?" Willie asks.

The hunchback leans in, further stretching forward his already extended neck, "Now that your last name no longer carries any official weight..."

"And Santa has revoked the rights and privileges of your workshop status..." Plumper adds.

"You are to report to a factory position!" Hunchback announces with a sense of revenge.

"But I'm already tasked with a court case." Willie states.

The Redcoats burst in laughter.

"You need to work for the Christmas Mission, that doesn't count."

"Okay, then I'll just work for Sticky. I can start tomorrow."

Willie suggests.

"Unfortunately, you're unqualified for that." Hunchback interjects.

"What do you mean? It bears my name. The Maven Workshop."

"You don't meet the minimum requirements for workshop participation." Plumper explains.

"But I'm a Maven." Willie tries to remind them, and himself.

"You're unqualified, boy, and Santa's revoked your workshop rights."

"What disqualifies me?"

"Well, you have no professional degrees or any real workshop experience or internships."

"You're not enrolled in the academy."

"You lack respect for authority."

"The list goes on!" Plumper yaps.

"But I have a hook-hand." Willie jokes. "Everybody loves hook-hands."

"Funny guy, huh?" The hunchback sniffles. "Don't quit your day job."

"I don't have one."

"You're about to." Hunchback states.

"Welcome to the 99%, Maven." Plumper adds with a wink.

Willie can hardly believe it, then it hits him, his identity has become permanently altered and his social status officially reduced to nothing. The Redcoats snicker as Willie's eyes well, full of disillusionment and uncertainty. He trembles as the Redcoats throw their arms around him and start listing off potential factories to send him;

"Paintbrush factory?"

"Not a bad gig, you get to play with paint, too fun."

"Sanitation?"

"Kid wouldn't last a day."

"Mistletoe Picker?"

"I'd kill for that job! Do you have any idea how much action those guys get? No way."

"Gift Wrapper?"

"Ahh Gift Wrapper."

"Yes, a nice soft giftwrapping job."

"For our nice soft boy!"

"Perfect." Hunchback gasps.

"Perfect!" Plumper agrees.

In a split second the Redcoats wipe their grins and snatch Willie, throwing his hands behind his back in one fluid move. They meet his initial resistance with even more force, dragging him away before slamming the front door shut behind him, leaving Ursus stuck inside. Willie finds humor in the injustice, laughing to himself about the madness of it all.

After a slog through the streets Willie is tossed into the oppressive Gift-Wrapping Factory. Unlike the creative and skilled work that occurs in the workshops, the basic but necessary unskilled labor takes place here in the factories. It's the factories which dominate the industrial zones of the North Pole and are manned by the vast majority of the population.

Willie dusts himself off and realizes this is his first experience inside a factory. It's massive, many times larger than the Maven Workshop, and filled with squeaky metallic tracts that grind against each other, perpetually circulating with a maddening, clattering jangle. The serpentine tracts are flanked by lines of workers that extend out for almost a mile, while each assembly line has its own extremely specific and horrendously repetitive function. Some assembly lines handle paper measuring, others paper cutting, then wrapping, taping, tying bows, taping bows, curling ribbons, wrapping ribbons, inspecting, re-inspecting and all the alike, down to the smallest detail. And they repeat their specific functions over and over, at what must be a rate of a million gifts a day.

The Redcoats leave Willie in possession of Jeanie, the gift taping manager.

Jeanie smirks, "Ready to wrap some Christmas presents, honey?" She says as she presents Willie with a hardhat and safety glasses before dragging him off to the taping line.

They arrive and Jeanie demonstrates the nature of the job: "Pull tape, rip tape, tape where paper overlaps, and repeat, and repeat, and repeat. Ad infinitum. Capeesh?"

"Capeesh."

Jeanie fakes a smile, "Good honey! And tape fast, really fast, as fast as those cute little fingers will let 'ya, okay?"

"Sure."

"Good, honey!" She giggles and makes off in a hurry.

Back at the Fortress the Germans try hard to keep themselves busy, dying of boredom and despair as they share prison cells, two in a cell. Klaus and Otto share a bench, trying to make sense of what's happening as they secretly try to tune Klaus' radio, searching for a signal but failing.

"Santa will kill us." Otto thinks out loud.

"What a Christmas tale that'd make." Klaus replies.

"Defeated Nazis fleeing to Argentina hit an iceberg, crash land in the North Pole and are axed off by Santa Claus? Yeah great Christmas story for the kids." Otto elaborates.

"You forgot the bit about the Maven elf and his very capable pet polar bear, before we all got slaughtered by Santa Claus. A tiny detail, but still important." Klaus half jokes.

"It doesn't exactly fit the Christmas genre. Very un-Santa like." Otto notes.

"He reminds me of Hitler." Klaus says, Otto agreeing with a nod as a long silence endures filled with painful memories.

"Remember all of those Christmas ornaments you used to make before the war? Maybe if you show off those well-hidden glass skills, he'll let us all off the hook?" Otto jokes.

"I miss glass making, and ornaments, and even Christmas for god sakes. I was great with glass. I'd kill to do that again." Klaus reminisces.

"The good 'ol days." Otto smiles gloomily.

"I think Santa is the only one here who knows about the war, he nearly said so in that crystal ball. Why else would those elves run out to the streets to help us if they thought we were a bunch of bloodsucking Nazis'?" Klaus poses.

"I don't know."

"If we knew Santa was such an egotistic pinhole would we be so excited to have him break into our homes every year?" Klaus laughs.

"He loves efficiency, and he loves power," Otto adds.

"Like Hitler." Klaus yelps, catching the attention of the Redcoats on guard as the two laugh hardily at their dire situation.

"He might just make us slaves." says Klaus.

"Or let us drift in the ocean."

"Or ship us off to the States, or England, or the goddamn Soviets." Klaus says.

"We'd be finished." Otto mutters.

"We need to figure out how this place works. If we can do that, then we might have a shot."

Their smallest sense of optimism gets them thinking as they head to the tiny barred up window, peering out and to observe the functioning of the society below.

Back at the Giftwrapping Factory, the water-tower sized whistle BLOWS at a deafeningly volume, signaling the end of the workday. The metallic tracts *screech* to a halt while the elves on the production lines nearly collapse from exhaustion. They're all thoroughly numb and depleted.

Willie's in pain, fingers bleeding, each digit with at least one excruciating paper-cut. He's tired and demoralized as he follows the quarter mile-long line of elves toward the exit. He returns his hard hat and safety glasses to Jeanie's underlings in exchange for a mere sugar cube of pay. Willie stares at the small cube then laughs out loud as if it were a prank—causing the other workers to look at him strangely. Like a lot of the elves in line without families, he takes a bite out of the cube and saves the remaining crumb for the eggnog vendor.

Willie has no intention of continuing this lifestyle, failing to comprehend how the masses of elves have learned how to cope with such horrendous circumstances. He figures there's no other way to cope than to be drunk, very drunk, at least. After punching the clock, he thinks just how cruelly their time is dictated to them down to the very minute. By the time he makes it outside it's dark, snowing and cold to the bone. The masses are headed straight for the eggnog and so is he.

As Willie makes a beeline to the nearest tavern Renee bumps into him.

"Oh, Willie, good to see you."

"Renee, hey, hi...what are you doing around here?"

"Actually, I've been looking for you," she says as she hands him a thick folder of documents. "These are the charges against the Germans, copied it off of my father's desk, it's something Santa himself provided. It looks serious. Thought you should know what you're up against."

Willie opens the folder, the cover page of the documents is titled "Declaration of Atrocities."

"That sounds grim. Is there proof?" He asks.

"Not that I see. Only this declaration of accusations. I'd say you have a case if you want to make one."

"That's kind, but why are you helping me?"

"Because I want to." She says. "Good luck." She blurts before making off into the crowded streets, leaving him with a smile.

Willie makes his way to the Fortress, escorted to Klaus and Otto's shared cell. He hands them the documents.

"This is what they're throwing at you, it doesn't look good." Willie tells them.

"Declaration of Atrocities." Klaus reads out loud.

Several particular lines jump at him, including; "Germans will be sent back to the countries where they had committed their most heinous crimes...judged on the spot by the peoples whom they have outraged...evidence of atrocities, massacres and cold-blooded mass executions which are being perpetrated by Hitlerite forces in many of the countries they have overrun and from which they are now being steadily expelled. Signed Franklin D. Roosevelt, Winston Churchill and Joseph Stalin."

Klaus and Otto share a chilling stare with one another. "And there's evidence?" Otto asks.

"Not that I'm aware of." Willie replies.

"War is complicated, Willie. I just want you to know there are two sides to every story. The victors always have the privilege of writing history and making accusations as they see fit."

"I'd like to believe you."

"You should." Otto states.

"Before the war you should know we were professionals. I was a scientist and artist. Otto was an...architect." Klaus says.

"A social scientist." Otto scoffs under his breath to Klaus.

Klaus steps on his toe, signaling him to shut up.

"What kind of science?" Willie asks.

"Mmm—Physics!" Klaus replies, "Ever hear of Albert Einstein?"

"No." Willie replies. "We only know about the North Pole, but even Santa keeps that stifled."

"Albert was an acquaintance of mine, before the war. He understands energy, and nature, and so much more. He was the most brilliant man, maybe ever. I was lucky to have known him." Klaus states.

"What about your art?" Willie asks.

"Ah—a simple glass blower. I loved it. I made a ton of handcrafted Christmas ornaments, whole collections of 'em. A real passion. I miss it."

"What about you, Otto?"

"Just designed a few buildings, nothing too fancy."

"Nonsense!" Klaus yells with a laugh. "Otto designed the blueprints for the Reichstag itself!"

Otto blushes, it's the opposite, but he enjoys the fallacy.

"The Reichstag?" Willie questions.

"Germany's capital building, not unlike Santa's Tower. It's most impressive in stature and style. The pride of Germany itself!" Klaus yelps with a hint of sarcasm that only Otto knows. Otto bites his lip trying to prevent a laugh, because it was Otto who designed the blueprints for destruction of the Reichstag. Figuring out how to make it go up in flames while framing the proper opponents takes careful consideration.

"Willie, you should know Otto and I are creative people, like elves. We love designing, building and expressing ourselves, that's all we ever wanted to do. To create a strong future." Klaus says.

"A strong, thousand-year future." Otto adds with a wink.

Willie thinks about Klaus' remarks on creativity, reminding him of his father's words, recalling the virtues of the workshop. Then he reflects dismally on his new life sentence of mind-numbing giftwrapping. In a sense he feels strangely aligned with the Germans and their predicament.

Klaus continues to bridge the gap, "There is no human society in the world that can do what you do here, and when humans are at our potential we're most like elves, building, gifting and providing for one another."

Otto joins in, "We can only hope for forgiveness and the opportunity to use our talents in the ways we once did - to make the world a better place."

"Willie, if you can help us get a second chance here in the North Pole, we will be forever in your debt." Klaus says.

It's a compelling speech but tall order. Willie deep down wants to help them, and he shakes their hands. "I'll do my best."

Suddenly the lights twitch on and off with the bulbs buzzing with electricity. It gets Klaus thinking just as Willie packs up to leave.

"How does the North Pole get its energy?" Klaus asks out of curiosity.

"Sugar." Willie responds to their surprise. "Everything in the

North Pole runs on sugar, from our factories and workshop to even us elves."

"How do you grow sugarcane in the North Pole?" Otto asks. "Or vegetation you could extract sugar from?"

"We can't, obviously. We import it. Santa collects all of those cookies and cakes and candies every year and brings them back to the North Pole, along with anything else the North Pole needs. Elves extract the sugar, collect and consume it. The sugar from Christmas provides for all elves. It's sugar that fuels society, provides for Kringle, and Kringle provides for all." Willie explains.

"Unbelievable." Klaus says, stunned with the revelation.

"Perhaps it is. I hope you can sleep on these prison mattresses." Willie says as a Redcoat escorts him out. "Good night," and the Redcoats close the cell door with a *clank*.

With Willie gone Otto turns to Klaus pulling out his hair. "We're done for." Otto says.

In a calm but forceful manner Klaus places his hands upon Otto's shoulders, stopping his frantic pacing.

"There's always a solution."

It's dark and foggy by the time Willie returns to his neighborhood. The Redcoat at the corner post notices him approaching. Once he realizes it's Willie, he stops him.

"You forgot your pet."

"He's just at home." Willie says.

"Get him."

Willie continues up the hill to his house. He turns into the yard and sees Ursus laying outside, chained to a metal stake in the ground. He fumes at the sight as Ursus growls in pain, limping around with the heavy metal chain and collar weighing him down. Willie notices a piece of the door frame missing, then finds it lodged in Ursus's paw like a massive splinter. There are claw marks on the door, it must've taken 15 Redcoats to have dragged him outside.

Willie is baffled but tends to the bloody paw and pulls out the splinter making Ursus *howl* in agony. He aids the bleeding using his scarf as a bandage, wrapping it tightly around the wound.

He walks up to the door and spots a note, "NOTICE TO VACATE under the authority of Santa Claus & Administration" nailed to it. He pulls on the door but it's locked, and rips the notice down to read the repressive language in fine print. The notice concludes with "Your relocation is ordered to Factory Neighborhood District 5D, Building D, Floor 4, Unit D, EFFECTIVE IMMEDIATELY."

Defeat further overcomes him as he sighs into the cold night's air. He walks over to his wounded polar bear to wiggle the iron stake that pins Ursus' chain into the frozen ground, further exhausting himself, yanking the stake back and forth until it finally wiggles free. There's no way of getting the metal collar and chain off right now so they journey with it on all the way to Factory Neighborhood District 5D.

Eventually they arrive and discover that Factory Neighborhood District 5D is an utter hellhole - crowded, cramped and noisy. The structures are prison like, symmetrically placed in specific patterns as if for the purpose of crowd control.

Finally, they find the decrepit Building D. Its rusty front door squeals in an uneven, rigid way as Willie uses all of his might to pull it open. They climb to the top floor as Ursus takes up the entire stairway, angering many of the neighbors and forcing them back into the hallway until they pass. They wonder what a posh pet like a polar bear is doing in their neighborhood, not to mention curious how the big bear would even fit in a room.

No key is needed to enter Unit D, as Willie nudges it open with a hard push from his shoulder. The entire space is about as big as his old closet. It's just a room with a bed, nightstand and lamp. He peeps into the hall finding a bathroom and kitchen space which the entire floor shares. Now the tricky part, getting Ursus to fit inside - he growls with annoyance as Willie pushes against his furry butt. By the third forceful shove the bear squeezes through the narrow door frame, but now there's zero room left, not even for an elf. Ursus lies on the bed. He doubles the size of it, but makes it work by awkwardly sleeping on his back. There's nowhere else for Willie to go except Ursus' chest, so he makes himself snug amid his fur in something of a comical sight. They're both fatigued as Willie leans over to turn off the light. Just as they're on the verge of passing out...

SWACK—the door flies open and slams into Ursus' shin.

A confused and irritated elf couple shuffles through the half-open door. They're factory elves through and through, both wearing hardhats and are beat from an extra-long workday. Enter ALABASTER, the beta-male, and BUSHY TINSEL, his wife and boss lady.

"That hurt him!" Willie complains.

"Sorry, who are you?" Bushy asks pointedly. "And what's that beast doing here?"

"I'm Willie, that's my pet polar bear, Ursus." He replies.

"Of course, right, pet polar bear, hmm..." Bushy sneers. "Would you look at that, Alabaster? Willie and his pet polar bear are taking a casual nap in our flat, like no big deal—ain't that great?"

"Don't get mad now, dear, I'm sure it's just a regular mix up." Alabaster responds.

"This isn't just regular mix up, *dear*, it's a giant bear and it's nearly stuck in our room. It's about to snap our bed in half!" She turns back to Willie, "Just what are you and a bloody polar bear doing here?"

"I'm sorry, they told me to report here." Willie replies. "Here's the paperwork." Willie hands her the notice which she inspects.

"Oh *jiggling gingerbread men*, another clerical error. The fat man's admin gone done it again."

"I told you honey, just a mix-up, a one-night thing, it will all be over with soon." Alabaster comforts.

"And where we gonna sleep, *honey*? Answer me that."

"I'm sorry, what's the problem?" Willie asks.

"Those file clerks always be mixin' up flats! This is me and my husband's flat."

"What do you mean?" Willie asks.

"You ain't ever had this happen?"

"No." Willie replies.

"Really? You're lucky then." She says, "They're always moving us around, tradin' one dump for another."

"Do you have somewhere else to go?" Alabaster asks.

Willie shakes his head no.

"Honey, he has nowhere else to go." He reiterates.

"I see that *dear*, but do you propose we sleep in the kitchen, or maybe the bathroom?"

"We'll leave...I can take the kitchen, or bathroom if necessary." Willie says.

"Absolutely not, just look how snug you both are. We'll make this work." Alabaster says.

"How?" Bushy bemoans.

Alabaster nods to Willie, gesturing him to scoot over on Ursus' belly, which he does as Alabaster climbs up and lays next to Willie with a chirpy grin. He softly rubs the space next to him, gesturing Bushy to join him there on Ursus.

"You're joking." Bushy says. "How do you know that thing won't eat us in our sleep?!"

"He's friendly." Willie adds.

"Oh, he's friendly!" Bushy mocks.

"Yes dear, he's friendly." Alabaster laughs, "Come on now."

"*Jiggling gingerbread men.*" She moans as she reluctantly climbs aboard, maneuvering around Ursus' bloodied paw and sharp claws that linger just overhead.

"You owe me a big vanilla pudding for this one, Alabaster." She says.

"That and so much more, dear." Alabaster replies before turning his head to Willie.

"You're new here, guy?" Alabaster asks.

"Brand new—um, to this district that is."

"I'm Alabaster Tinsel, that's my queen, Bushy, it's good to meet you." They shake hands.

"Willie."

"You look familiar, very Workshop Society looking."

"I'm a factory elf." He tries to say with a sense of pride, but it sounds especially phony to him when he says in out loud.

"So, you're assigned to a new factory?" Alabaster asks.

"Giftwrapping."

"Would you two *hush*! I'm trying to sleep, on top of a polar bear no less!" Bushy interrupts.

"Sorry love, we'll get right to that." Alabaster turns back to Willie, "Giftwrapping, oy, I've been there. It's pretty terrible. It won't get you any ladies, that's for sure. Very repetitive, oh and the paper cuts..."

Willie shows off the paper cuts that run up and down his hands.

"Ouch!" Alabaster shrieks.

"Dears, *please!*" Bushy yelps on her final nerve.

"We best get snoozin', if the queen doesn't get her beauty sleep then nobody will be happy tomorrow, trust me." Alabaster whispers.

Willie smiles back and they all close their eyes as the three subtly rise and descend on Ursus' chest in tune with his breathing, the soft rhythm of his powerful inhales and exhales rocking them asleep.

But their slumber only lasts a few hours, ending abruptly when the water-tower sized steam whistles from all over the factory districts simultaneously *blow*. It's a coordinated, thunderous steamy scream, meaning it's time for work, even if it's still dark out.

"Why so early?" Willie mumbles still in a deep slumber.

"What do you mean why?" Alabaster replies, awake and ready to go.

"Because the gifts need wrappin', that's why." Bushy answers.

"Right." Willie mutters.

"Good luck!" Bushy exclaims with a playful but sharp elbow to Willie's stomach, waking him for good.

6 - HIROSHIMA

Willie sits at the preliminary hearing of the German's pre-trial within the Great Room of Santa's Sphere. He's tired and uneasy, fidgeting at his desk after throwing back a Gingerbread Latte. The gruesome workday he's already put in at the factory has him searching for a second wind. Across him is Sir Louie Kendal-Crink along with his busy associates organizing case files while pouring Sir Louie his favorite licorice tea that he seems to *slurp*. Willie's animosity toward him is palpable as they await Santa, then Renee appears behind Willie.

"I hear they evicted you, where are you staying?" She whispers.

"I'm not sure, there was an administrative error with my assignment. I have a tiny room with Ursus and another couple."

"Terrible. I've got a little barn if you need a place to crash."

"A barn?" He laughs.

"Yeah."

"Ok, sounds good."

"You and Ursus would have plenty of space to stretch out and rest. I'll leave it open, it's just behind my family's tower, tucked underneath the evergreens. You'll find it. My helpers will get you in and out. They'll find you."

"I'll take you up on it."

She smiles back with reassurance and returns to her seat. Moments later, the militant trumpeters march in and play their glorious prelude as Santa descends on his floating platform, proudly posed as usual.

Kringle appears hungry, munching on whole stacks of chocolate chip cookies, non-stop devouring as he litters the floor with a trail of crumbs. It's such a mess that an old janitorial elf follows him around with a broom and bucket, cleaning.

"All rise!" A Redcoat announces.

Willie rolls his eyes and stands, as does the few hundred bureaucrats in the gallery.

"The preliminary hearing of the North Pole versus the Migrants of Germany is in session."

"All sit!"

Silence ensues as Santa's platform hovers to a stop. Like usual, Santa is impeccably dressed, this time in a dark red coat decorated with gold braid, gold buttons and gold-fringed epaulets hanging from his stern shoulders, presenting as if he were Napoleon. Santa stands straight up and stares down Willie, taking his time to observe his depleted state.

"What are the charges against the accused?" Santa asks, breaking between bites and chunky swallows of cookies.

Sir Louie rises, "The crimes committed outside of the North Pole are of incredible proportion and concern. We have documentation from the international community which *thee* Santa Claus has so prudently provided. With these descriptions the scale and scope of the crimes are as dark as they are epic. This slew of indictments fall within four main categories:

1. Participation in a common plan or conspiracy for the accomplishment of a crime against peace.
2. Planning, initiating and waging wars of aggression and other crimes against peace.
3. War crimes.
4. Crimes against humanity.

"These people are guilty of these treacheries. You should have no ill-conscious punishing them with the harshest penalties of your choice." Sir Louie states.

"And what would you have me do, Kendal-Crink, kill 'em? I'm the god damn Santa Claus for Christ' sake."

"No Sir, I'd recommend expulsion to the U.S., U.K. U.S.S.R., or any other nation where they committed their worst crimes. This procedure is already outlined in the international agreement set forth by the Declaration of Atrocities, that you've so graciously provided."

"It wasn't easy getting my hands on that." Santa irritably mumbles.

"Their infractions were against humanity and I believe it our duty to deliver them back to humanity for judgement."

"Thank you, Sir Kendal-Crink," Santa says, then turns to Willie, "and what do you have to say?"

"I look forward to the evidence of all these weighty claims." Willie replies. "Until then I will not turn on these people who've entrusted their lives to me. You owe the evidence not only for the sake of legitimacy, but you owe it to the tens of thousands of elves who've witnessed these poor people marched by club through our streets. If humans are so terrible and worthy of such harsh punishment why should we elves work so hard making presents for them? If convicted without evidence, you'd dilute the purpose and enthusiasm that is so necessary to the Christmas Mission. You would perpetuate the confusion that is dizzying the North Pole. You'd create a massive space for second guessing. Do you really want that?"

Santa fumes with rage, he's never been spoken to like this by an elf, ever.

"The Germans will be tried on all counts with or without evidence!" Santa yells.

"Yes Sir." Sir Louie replies, "the last thing the North Pole needs is a lingering distraction with Christmas so close."

"This hearing is adjourned!" Santa blurts.

"Santa, Sir!" Willie yells, shocking everyone in the great room. "If you won't give them justice then at least let them beg for their lives!"

"You keep up that tone and it's your life you'll be begging for, Maven." Santa spits.

"I am begging, Sir."

Santa leans forward steering his floating platform to Willie's desk, getting right up in his face.

"Beggars begging for beggars to beg. That's a lot of begging if you ask me. That's sad, elf. But I'll make you a deal. I'll give you back your name, your privileges, your family workshop and life - if you don't show up to trial. They get no say, just a shellacking, and you get your life back. What do you say?"

Santa lets the idea settle with Willie.

"The Germans have the right to plead so plead they must." Willie stubbornly answers.

Santa laughs hardily, generating a rumbling echo that reverberates through the chamber before floating to Sir Louie's desk, leaning into his ear.

"I want this quick and clean." Santa whispers. "Christmas is around the corner, and lower the damn Belief Meter, they need to be working at maximum capacity, Louie!"

Sir Louie nods with affirmation as Santa leans back into the rails of his hovering platform with a smirk.

"Tomorrow we shall hear a German plead!" Santa yells and laughs before floating up and away.

Later, Willie is still exhausted, returning to the Fortress to meet with an anxious Klaus and Otto.

"What we're looking at, more time in this prison?" Klaus asks.

"They're going to deport you to the U.S., U.K., U.S.S.R. or somewhere else, which I'm guessing are not places you're interested in going,".

"No." Otto remarks.

"The only thing I could negotiate is allowing one of you to plead your case. But Santa seems intent on sending you back out on those lifeboats you came in on. I'm sorry."

Klaus and Otto are used to bad news. "I'll do it, I'll plead." Klaus says. "But just to confirm, the whole North Pole runs on sugar, and they can't get it without Santa?"

"Yes, correct." Willie answers.

"What if I can show Santa another way, a better way to power this civilization? We can help him and maybe he can cut us a deal?" Klaus says.

"Maybe?" Willie says.

"It's a long shot." Otto says.

"It's our only shot." Klaus concludes.

Willie nods and turns on the radio, "Until tomorrow," he says with a sense of defeat before he heads off.

Otto erupts kicking the steel bars of their cell, injuring his foot. Klaus is equally frustrated, not to mention entirely burdened by their survival resting squarely on his shoulders. With angst he turns to his pocket-size radio, trying to see if he can pick up a signal if only to hear some music one last time. But it's more static as he searches and searches—until finally, melodic sounds from the device gently permeate the air waves. He turns it up ever so slightly as to not draw attention while the jovial music of the American doo-wop group, "The Ink Spots," play aloud. It's probably broadcast from a station in the Northern Territories of Canada, rebroadcasting an American station. Otto joins in to listen, both getting one last smile before it's too late. In the midst of the song the music turns to static before a man's voice comes on with a hasty tone.

"Pardon the interruption, we have a breaking news story, an address from American President Harry Truman."

More static follows as the station switches to the White House broadcast, followed by the voice of President Truman:

"Sixteen Hours ago, an American airplane dropped one bomb on Hiroshima, an important Japanese Army base. That bomb had more power than 20,000 tons of T.N.T. It had more than two thousand times the blast power of the British "Grand Slam" which is the largest bomb ever yet used in the history of warfare. *It is an atomic bomb.* It harnesses the basic power of the universe. The force from which the sun draws its power has been let loose against those who brought war to us..."

Klaus stares at Otto with shock. "The Americans did it, the war is really lost now, it's over." He lowers the volume contemplating the implications of what's happened. Moved by the news they pace around the cell leaving the radio exposed—it isn't long until the Redcoat guard spots the curious device, storms in and smashes to pieces with his club.

"No gizmos allowed!" The guard shouts.

"It was a harmless radio my friend." Klaus says.

"If I catch you hiding anything else, it's gonna be you that gets all smashed up." The guard yells as he slams the cell door closed and locks it.

"I have an idea." Klaus grins...

The next day back at Santa's Sphere the trumpeters play their welcome tune for Santa.

"All sit!" The Redcoat yells. Klaus sits next to Willie as Santa floats to the front and center of the court on his platform, still hungry and still getting cookie crumbs everywhere as his janitorial parasite-like elf cleans and cleans. Klaus is fascinated by the odd sight. He looks good for the hearing with Willie finding him a custom fit jacket with a fancy green and red stripped silk tie with some mistletoe and poinsettia leaves in his jacket pocket. Santa, always formidably dressed, appreciates the gesture of Klaus's formality, even though he knows the man and his people are doomed.

Klaus looks behind him spotting an elf nose deep in his newspaper. Above the fold is an article about the low and concerning state of the sugar supply and Belief Meter. Klaus skims it and senses how the North Pole's energy concern deepens.

Santa clears his throat. "Stand German, state your name."

"Klaus Mauser."

Santa coughs, nearly choking on his cookie. "Sounds an awful lot like Claus, why do you steal my name, German?"

"It wasn't up to me, Sir, very little in my life has been."

"I'm not amused, Mr. Mauser. I want to hurry this along so I suggest you get to pleading your case, your elf friend here has paid dearly for it. Or do you not fear death and so have nothing to say?"

"We all fear death, other people, and our own minds, Sir."

"*Cheeky.*" Santa quibbles.

Klaus turns to Willie, thanking him with an expression of sincerity before he turns back to Santa.

"I don't seek to plead to you, Sir. I don't seek your forgiveness and I don't even seek you finding us Germans innocent of the

68

accusations Sir Kendal-Crink is prepared to bring forward."

Santa laughs, entertained by this man. "Then what do you seek, name stealer?"

"A business relationship." Klaus answers as Santa sniffles. "I want to help you explore your energy options. I believe I have a solution that will revolutionize the North Pole."

Santa laughs louder, snorting, "Funny, however wisest not to test my humor, German."

"The real hilarity is the fact that the North Pole runs on sugar. It's inefficient, costly to you, and frankly it's a joke."

Santa turns deadly serious, "It's cleaner than coal and it works for the North Pole."

Klaus reaches for the newspaper behind him and holds it up, he reads "Struggling Belief Meter, Low Sugar Supply!" It hits a nerve and piques the interest of Santa and the crowd. "I imagine these things share a strong relationship, and the burden of the health of these things depends on you, every year, every day, hell, every moment."

Santa folds his arms allowing him to continue.

"Imagine a North Pole with some of Germany's strongest minds at work for you. Let us help you solve this endless energy crisis. No more meticulous management, no more anxiety, only *abundance*."

"Santa, Sir, this is no venue for cutting a deal." Sir Louie interjects.

But it captivates Santa, fueling society with enough sugar is his largest challenge.

"Easy Kendal-Crink, I'll allow the name stealer to pose a proposition."

Klaus tries to quickly wipe the sinister smile forming from his mouth. He proceeds...

"Santa, if you're as informed as I believe you are, you'd know that the United States has dropped a nuclear bomb on the Japanese city of Hiroshima. The Yanks beat us in the race to nuclear power. This power has and can be used for mass atrocity to the likes that the world has just witnessed, but it can also be used for the peaceful and efficient use of energy, many times more powerful than burning sugar. With nuclear power here in the North Pole your workshops and factories would not infringe upon the sugar stock that is also so necessary for your limited food supply. With this power you could circle the world twice on Christmas Eve. You could hit new territories, further expand Christmas and your name wider than you've ever dreamed. You could deliver Christmas spirit throughout the world without limit. And you could have every man, woman and child on Earth cheering your name, even restore a sense of morality back to the war-torn essence of humanity itself. I say let the entire world love Santa Claus and cheer your name. The world is yours, Santa, it always has been, and with new tech and a vast reservoir of energy, you can finally seize it, *all of it*. With nuclear energy and German engineering, it's all within your grasp."

The audience is moved by Klaus' passion, holding a sincere yet formidable gaze with Santa.

"Rousing speech, German. But how would the North Pole even make such an attempt?"

"It starts with research. If you can get us the soil samples from Hiroshima, as much as you can, then we can unlock the secrets of the atom. You'll never have to worry about powering your civilization ever again."

Santa is torn, thinking hard as silence permeates the excited crowd, everyone awaiting his word...

"You'll get your soil samples, German, but this trial isn't over. I'm coming back with that and plenty of evidence for the whole North Pole to see how terrible you really are."

Santa SWACKS his gavel as Klaus releases the subtlest of smirks.

Santa notices it before he floats up, up and away on his platform.

The trumpeters blow, signifying the conclusion of the session.

Klaus shakes Willie's hand with sincere gratitude. Klaus is in control and knows it, as long as Santa does what he says he'll do.

A week later Willie is escorted by Redcoats through the streets of Workshop Society. They're shuffling him along. His hands are bandaged from all the new paper cuts he's endured giftwrapping. He notices the hurried pace of the streets, there's an added sense of panic, more than usual with Christmas around the corner.

The Redcoats push Willie along the grounds of Santa's Hermitage and to the Fortress. He notices Sir Louie escorted by a small entourage back onto the grounds of the Hermitage too. Willie watches as Sir Louie accepts a handkerchief from a Redcoat and wipes his hands clean of grease. An interesting site considering Sir Louie isn't the type to work with his hands.

Willie is marched along but abruptly stops, spotting and pointing at Santa's sleigh high in the sky.

Santa flies awkwardly, almost uncontrollably, up and down and side to side as if he were drunk. Everyone stops to observe the peculiar sight as the reindeer wildly circle.

Everyone stares, watching as Santa is suddenly THROWN from the sleigh along with the sack full of Hiroshima soil and stacks of war crime evidence.

But the evidence, documents and photographs catch a cold

zephyr and are blown out of existence *as Santa tumbles through the air* until...*PLUNK*...His body hits the cobblestone and flattens out like an explosive pancake.

Santa's remaining corpse *spews blood* with his torn limbs and body parts littering the scene. The flailing bag of contaminated soil sprinkle upon the ground like rain as Sir Louie and the Redcoats sprint over.

The Redcoats turn Santa's torso revealing a disturbing sight. His face is deteriorated, his body cavity split apart while his suit is covered in dark green vomit. His skin is eerily discolored and covered in golf ball sized boils. He has blackened finger nails while the cartilage in the ears is deteriorated from the blood and puss that has collected there.

Willie and the Redcoats stare as the disoriented Reindeer suffer a botched landing on the cobble stone, skidding across it violently, breaking bones on impact. The Reindeer scowl at the body, even they can't believe Santa is dead and gone.

Willie looks up at the Fortress and spots Klaus and Otto staring back. Sir Louie recognizes their connection and immediately smells conspiracy.

Inside the prison cell Klaus grins to Otto.

"Radiation poisoning. Fat bastard never had a chance." Klaus says as Otto slaps his knees in laughter.

Otto catches his breath and turns back to Klaus, "Now what?"

Klaus just smiles and stares down at the scene of devastation, whispering...

"Out of order comes chaos, and out of chaos comes order."

7 – DEAD LINES

Sir Louie soaks in the catastrophe's gravity as he wipes Santa's splattered blood from his face.

"Close the gate for Christ' sake!" He orders the guards.

"Your Germans are done and so are you, Maven!" Sir Louie yells. "Take him!"

The guards drag Willie off to the prison tower while the other Redcoats scramble in every direction, frantically locking down the Hermitage.

Sir Louie's world spins as he stares into Santa's disfigured corpse. He's alone with Santa's body as a powerful despair consumes him. He tries hard to hold in the pain but can't, and he breaks into tears. He's given everything to Santa. His entire identity is tied to him, and now he's not so sure who he is without him.

Perhaps his own corpse should lay there next to his? He thinks as he wipes his tears before anyone appreciates just how devastated he really is. The hollow feeling eats at him to the point of incapacitation, but he shakes it and makes a dash for Santa's Sphere, on a mission to gather the high council, the senior most ranking members of Santa's Executive Cabinet.

Outside the Hermitage a crowd builds as a throng of elves are held back by Redcoats. It's becoming uncontrollable as the Redcoats plow back the mob so they can close the massive 200-foot iron gate doors. The panicked mob fills with rumor, they were all witness to Santa's plunge from the sky. Everyone gossips, describing what they saw, from how high they think he fell and if it's at all survivable? Confusion circulates as the last of the Redcoats get the iron doors shut, locking down the compound.

Back inside the prison the Redcoats toss Willie inside Klaus and Otto's cell. The three share an uncomfortable stare as their sense of trust deteriorates. Willie looks at Klaus point blank.

"Did you do something?"

"How could we, Willie? We're here, behind bars. That's what can happen when you venture out into the world of men, especially at the tail end of the most devastating war. I have no idea what happened."

Otto chimes in, "We grew up with Santa Claus, he's beloved by all of us. In fact, it's Germany that celebrates Christmas most enthusiastically, more than anywhere else in the world."

"How do we benefit from this?" Klaus poses.

"I'm not sure you do." Willie is almost happy to conclude.

"Me either." Klaus says as Willie breathes a deep sigh of relief.

Klaus walks to the narrow window in search of the Belief Meter. He can barely see it in the distance, but he can still make it out.

"The Belief Meter hasn't changed. That's interesting." Klaus says, trying to get a rouse out Willie.

"I'd say so." Otto snickers.

"When's Christmas? I've lost track of the days." Klaus asks.

"Two days away." Willie answers.

"Terrible timing." Otto says.

"How could the Belief Meter be this low so close to Christmas?" Klaus wonders.

"The meter's low this time of year, and strongest just after Christmas, naturally." Willie says.

"Seems like it should be the opposite, as if it's lower so elves work harder. Do you believe the reading is natural?" Klaus asks, forcing Willie to contemplate. The silence lingers until...

BAM—a pack of Redcoats burst through the doors and march over, pushing Willie aside and pulling Klaus from the cell.

"What's this?" Klaus demands as he's thrown into a choke hold.

"Shut it!" A Redcoat yells.

"Willie, help!" Klaus gasps.

"Where are they taking him?!" Willie shouts.

SNAP - Willie's knocked square between the eyes and falls flat on ground as Klaus turns blue, hauled off in a chokehold. The German prisoners are terrified as the barred door slams shut behind Klaus.

Meanwhile, Sir Louie is in his private chambers in Santa's Sphere. It's a closed-door meeting with the High Council. They're practically quivering as Sir Louie just delivered the devastating news.

"I don't have a solution, which is why I called you here." Sir Louie says.

Cabinet Member Nipper McJingles hits the table angrily with his fists.

"We're screwed!" McJingles yells.

"Obviously, Nipper. But I keep you around for solutions, not stating the obvious!" Sir Louie yells back.

"We need another magic Man-Elf!"

"God damn, what did I just say?"

"We need a miracle." McJingles blabs.

"Miracle men aren't created out of thin air. Kris Kringle was literally a Christmas miracle. One of a kind, and probably not even of this world. Let's not forget he protected us from men, first, then came Christmas. The elvish race would have been wiped out long ago without him, just like how the humans decimated the Neanderthals and even eradicate themselves. We face annihilation, ministers, unless we act decisively. Right now."

Cabinet Member Topper Trinket raises his wrinkly old hand, it's unnecessarily but he likes to be called on.

"Yes, Topper..." Sir Louie calls with annoyance.

"What if we create a secret sh-sh-sugar colony, in the Ca-Ca Caribbean, where sh-sh-sugarcane grows? We could be o-o-okay if we just have the sh-sh-sugar."

"Great idea, Topper!" Sir Louie shouts. Topper responding with a rare and soft smile.

"Now tell me which elvish Navy and Army regiments we ought to send in to take over Jamaica?!" Sir Louie screams, flipping over his chair.

The room is silent until the sole female cabinet member, Ginger Garland, stands. She's sexy, ice cold and all business. Not to mention sick of taking orders from these shriveled up old elves.

"We now require a reliable system of human intermediaries, and I think these Germans may solve the problem." Ginger says.

"A bad joke, Ginger?" Sir Louie says.

"It's our only option, I'm afraid." Ginger answers.

"I won't entertain it, not after the indictments I've seen against them." Sir Louie replies.

"You have no clue if those are authentic or something Santa whipped up out of thin air. He's done worse. I think that young elf, Maven, was right about demanding evidence. If you have any you should share that with us right now."

"It's a gut feeling. You'll have to take my word for it." Sir Louie drones.

"I'm sorry Lou, but we can't just take your word for it, or your gut, not now, we face dire times."

"You ought to. And don't call me Lou!"

"Sir Louie - without evidence we must consider a human/elf collaboration as our best option. If something better comes to stake our survival on, I'm more than open minded."

"But they're responsible for his death!" Sir Louie yells.

"And you know that for sure?" She asks.

But Sir Louie shrugs in silence.

"Then let's cut a deal with them and turn the tables later." Gingers suggests.

"You are devious."

"No worse than you, Lou."

"Sir Louie – "

"Of course, Sir Louie, but let's get on with it, shall we?" She says.

"It's risky, Ginger. I don't like it."

"If you don't deal with this, I'll be forced to. We only have two days until Christmas. We have to do something." Ginger stares him down, eyes piercing deep into his soul before she turns her to leave, slamming the door behind her.

Meanwhile, Klaus is locked up in solitary confinement. He's stuck within a dark murky dungeon, chained against a wet, moldy wall. It's pitch-black until a squad of Redcoats thrust open the door, escorting Sir Louie inside.

Sir Louie smiles as the dim light illuminates Klaus's bruised and bloodied face.

"Congratulations Klaus. Only superior criminals get to languish here. Top-level stuff. You should consider it an honor."

Klaus laughs. "I'm not a criminal. And who are you, exactly?"

"Sir Louie Kendal-Crink."

Klaus laughs even harder.

"You all have great such great names, I love it. So, what can I do for you, Sir Kendal-Crink?"

"Call me Sir Louie."

"Ahh - what can I do for you, Sir Louie?"

"I know you're responsible for this mess. You'll pay for it, probably with your life. But you just might survive, if you play your cards right."

"I don't know what you're talking about. I'm just a refugee awaiting judgement, or help preferably."

"Kringle never divulged the full extent of Nazism. All I know is you were a naughty boy. I even found your name on the naughty list."

"What do you want from me?" Klaus asks.

Sir Louie paces, "What do I want from you? Well, your plan to save Christmas, the North Pole, and yourself, of course. See, I know something other elves don't."

"What's that?"

"You're not as dumb as you look."

"I'm flattered, but there's no grand plan," Klaus replies, "you must really consider me capable."

"I do."

"Such a compliment coming from you. I'd be happy to offer

some suggestions, but what will you give me in return?"

"Your life." Sir Louie answers.

"That's hardly enough."

"This is your last chance." Sir Louie says. "Look at yourself, you have no leverage."

"Christmas is in two days and Santa is dead." Klaus replies. "If I lose my life, that's bad for me, but then your entire society suffers. I have *all* the leverage."

"Then what's your plan?" Sir Louie repeats.

"Get me out of these chains, treat me respectably, and I'll tell you."

Sir Louie stares at him blankly. "No."

"Fine, but Christmas as we know it, is canceled. There's no way around it. The sooner you can accept it the sooner we can move forward, together." Klaus says. "Don't be so difficult, it's not in your interest."

CRACK—Sir Louie punches Klaus, reopening a gash as blood seeps down his face.

"You're bluffing, you don't have a plan, you just want to make a run for it." Sir Louie states before he spits on him and departs with the Redcoats.

"There's a plan, there's always a plan." Klaus says. "I can make you an offer—*I can make you rich*, godly rich. But only if you work with me, only if you trust me. That or we'll all suffer."

But Sir Louie marches away as the dungeon doors shut.

Its pitch black again, bringing the roaches and rodents back into Klaus's space as he jumps to the cold wet corner, lingering in doubt.

Sir Louie returns to Santa's penthouse and sits behind Santa's desk as if claiming it. The penthouse balcony overlooks the Square below, which was the site of Santa's annual, famed Christmas Eve Address. It's already more packed than typical with the public eager for news. The High Council joins Sir Louie, contemplating their next move.

"And what of S-S-Sa-Santa's a-a-address?" Topper asks.

"I'll tell them that everything is fine." Sir Louie says.

"You're going to pretend to be Santa?" Ginger jokes.

"Perhaps."

Ginger bursts into a sardonic chuckle seeing he's serious. She doesn't talk him out of it. She could steam roll him politically once he makes a fool of himself.

"What will Santa tell them?" She asks.

"To get on with it!"

"Is that w-w-wise, Sir?" Topper poses.

"That's insane." McJingles drunkenly slurs, flinging scotch from his flask partially into his mouth but mostly on the rug. "They'll know you're lying, undoubtably."

"I think he should do it." Ginger prods. "Time is ticking. The North Pole is waiting."

The next morning sunlight breaks over the Artic Range. It's a strange Christmas Eve. The factories and workshops would typically be finishing orders as fast as possible, but today they don't even start. Everyone realizes there's something detrimentally wrong behind the walls of the Hermitage.

Sir Louie stares out of his tower window, gazing into the growing crowd of elves in the Square. He takes keen notice to their bubbling anger and confusion. He turns to look at his tailored Santa suit hanging behind him. The sight forces him to reconsider the idiocy and ridiculousness of trying to impersonate Santa and steal his identity. If, and when, he's found out about it'd be all over for him. He can't fly Santa's Sleigh, doesn't know how to coast along the floating platform or even endlessly eat cookies either, and those are just the easy things.

He finally accepts that it's time to take a chance on the Germans. It's time to strike a deal with Klaus before it's too late, so he struts back to the dungeon...

The Redcoats burst open the door, escorting Sir Louie face to face with Klaus.

"Back so soon." Klaus giggles.

"You still laugh, good for you. I'm glad we haven't depraved you of that, yet." Sir Louie says. "Oh, and Merry Christmas Eve."

"Merry Christmas Eve," Klaus pouts.

"I have little time, as you know, and I have a speech to give - but I still have no idea what to say, so what's this grand scheme of yours?" Sir Louie asks.

"Are you going to work with me or against me?" Klaus asks.

"I don't have much of a choice now." Sir Louie replies.

"I'm glad we're on the same page. Don't worry Sir Louie, you'll get to stay in power. Like I said, you'll be handsomely paid, as will I."

"I was never doubting that, German. Now how do we save Christmas?" Sir Louie asks.

"We can't. Not this year, at least."

"Then how does that help me?!"

"It helps a lot—so much so that Santa's absence becomes our inciting incident for a new path forward."

"I don't understand."

"If Santa is no longer around to deliver Christmas presents to the good boys and girls of the world, then their parents will have to *buy* Christmas for them. Toy stores will make a killing and we're going to make a killing supplying them. You see?" Klaus responds.

"What do you propose?" Sir Louie asks.

"I propose that you stay in power and that I get a company to run."

"A company? What do you mean?"

"A for profit venture, we'll call it *North Pole Inc*. It will be the greatest toy company ever assembled in the history of the world. It can become one of the strongest companies the world will ever know."

Sir Louie smirks at the proposition but plays hard ball. "It's not enough."

"Really?" Klaus laughs.

"What else is in it for me? How do I know I won't get left behind—how do I know that I WILL WIN?"

"Stock. Plenty of stock, you'll own a significant piece of the company. A minority stake, but still significant. We'll make your friends stockholders too, so much that you'll have seats on the Board of Directors, where the big decisions are made. You'll all become incredibly wealthy—which is so much more powerful than whatever title and office Santa ever gave you. It's more powerful because it can offer you true liberty, something I believe you've experienced very little of."

"Interesting." Sir Louie says. "But how would we begin?"

"For starters you're going to drop that stupid Belief Meter of yours all the way down to zero. I know it's fake—hell, you're probably the one controlling it."

"How do you know?"

"It doesn't take a rocket scientist..."

"Fair, but zero?" Sir Louie questions. "That'd cause a panic, it'd bring all activity to a stop."

"Once it hits rock bottom, the North Pole will cling to the only viable solution it's presented. We'll get to save the North Pole with a new Belief Meter and a new system." Klaus smiles.

"Yes, but *how*, German?" Sir Louie grunts, "I need the details."

"Instead of forced workers there will be paid employees. Instead of workshop heads and Workshop Society there will be executives and entrepreneurs. Instead of a self-appointed magical dictator there will be 'democratically elected' legislators, and a President—that's you. Instead of a sugar used for transactions a treasury will be created, and notes representing sugar, or value really, will be exchanged for goods and services. Instead of a North Pole production network and Santa Claus distribution mechanism, there will be one major company, North Pole Incorporated. The company will be serviced by numerous smaller companies and suppliers, or elvish workshops and factories that North Pole Incorporated will purchase its products from. North Pole Incorporated will be run by me, Otto and other Germans, in charge of sales, distribution, and financing the North Pole."

"Financing?"

"Yes, banking, loans and capital. A reserve will be created, the North Pole Reserve. It will provide the basis for the entire banking system. The bankers bank, and it will be interwoven directly into your government which will have a treasury that pays for its activities. The important thing to understand is *the relationship between the North Pole Reserve and the Treasury is circular*. The Treasury pays interest to the Reserve on the debt that the Reserve holds and, in return, the North Pole Reserve rebates that interest back to the

Treasury."

"Huh - sounds nonsensical, my friend."

"It's not, because the Reserve is a non-profit organization. All of its earnings, after expenses, are rebated to the Treasury."

"Well if it's the 'bankers bank' why bother calling it a 'Reserve' and not a bank?"

"Because if everyone realizes it's a really bank, well then we'd have real troubles. It needs to be confusing so it survives."

"I'll take your word, but anything anchoring a new system must be run by an elf." Sir Louie says.

Klaus hesitates, taking a prolonged moment of contemplation before he nods.

"Willie Maven." Klaus suggests.

"No way."

"Maven or the deal is off." Klaus says firmly.

Sir Louie thinks about it, huffing. "Fine, I can live with it."

Klaus smiles, continues; "The elves will become mighty entrepreneurs that service North Pole Inc. They'll also be the powerful officials underneath your command, not to mention the very backbone of the labor market."

"What's in it for your people...as these administrative, financial...beings?"

"Germans become middlemen, which we're fine with. That's what you need us for anyway, so it's a win-win for everyone. A beautiful system."

"What do you call this...system?" Sir Louie asks.

Klaus smiles back devilishly.

"Capitalism, my dear Sir. It's called *capitalism*."

"Funny name."

"I think you'll need my help explaining it in your speech. I can write that for you, that's if we have a deal?"

"Capitalism, huh?" Sir Louie puckers. "We must do what we must, to survive."

"We must." Klaus says with a smile, shaking his hand. "A pleasure to be in business with you, Sir Louie."

"The pleasure is all yours." Sir Louie utters "I assure you."

8 – WHERE CREDIT IS DUE

It's Christmas Eve. The panic of the crowd in the Square bubbles to a boil as day turns to dusk. Everyone stares up anxiously at Santa's Penthouse Balcony, still expecting Santa to deliver news, hoping for the rumors to be dispelled. Redcoats surround the square while the Belief Meter declines to zero.

Back inside, Sir Louie paces nervously amid Santa's office, eyeing the balcony with the empty podium that faces the crowd. He's dressed in his green and silver striped suede suit with gold epaulettes, grinding his teeth and quenching his fists.

He puts up with the stench of Klaus next to him, still in his filthy clothes but released from his handcuffs, having just written Sir Louie's speech. Klaus takes one last skim of the speech and snags Louie's pen to make several last-minute adjustments. At the very end of the speech he writes, "Give Credit Where Credit Is Due," with a smile. Sir Louie raises an eyebrow at the revision.

"Will it play?" Sir Louie asks.

"Yes."

"It better."

Ginger Garland joins the two in office lined with Redcoats. She's almost as surprised to see Klaus as she is to see Sir Louie in a green, not red, suit.

"It's time." Ginger says. "I hope you've got something."

"Yes Ginger, I do. No thanks to you."

She turns to Klaus with a nudge, whispering, "This will be interesting."

"You have no idea." Klaus replies.

The remark leaves her sour, because it's true.

With a final exhale Sir Louie struts out onto the balcony,

waving to the oceanic, flowing crowds of the North Pole. A spotlight shines on him, the warm light glimmering off his shiny stripes. The crowd quiets as he gestures for their attention. He takes a moment to let the gasps of confusion and surprise settle. With one last deep breath he points to the Belief Meter, directing their attention to it.

The Belief Meter hits rock bottom, *zero*, as he begins to speak...

"It is my duty to report that the delivery of Christmas Gifts will be delayed...

Kris Kringle is dead.

The gravity of this tragedy will change not only Christmas and the North Pole, but the entire world as we know it.

The great Santa Claus will be forever remembered, and a proper eulogy will be given, but this speech is not that eulogy. This speech is about survival, our survival.

Let me remind you all that Santa Claus is not Christmas, but a part of it. Christmas itself is a bold and beautiful concept which we all create, over and over through the many forces of the North Pole. Because of Christmas, elves and humanity have become entangled in an interdependent dance. A dance which has sustained the North Pole while enriching the rest of the world. Enriching it so brightly to where it is impossible for it fade. A day that burns so bright must be fought for and preserved for all time.

And so, without the delivery of our Christmas gifts the loving parents of humanity will now *purchase* toys for their children. The exchange of toys for money is the new paradigm if Christmas and the North Pole is to survive.

We stand at this crossroad with our hands forced. Only through embracing change is how we, as a civilization, will survive and thrive. How do we thrive?

We create.

We create the best toys, games, culture and technology we can, as efficiently as we can, just like the rest of the modern world. And like the rebuilding modern world the global marketplace shall determine our fate.

I'm pleased to say we're in a position to be competitive in this new landscape of the global economy, achievable through the forces of finance, entrepreneurship, labor and democracy. It is powered by the very nature of self-interest and profit motive which will put everything into motion and sustain that motion.

The sooner we embrace these ideas the sooner we will all start living new and exciting lives. In fact, we must continue as we have, through our ingenuity, unique skills and resourcefulness. Through our genius and artistry. Through our elvish know-how and work ethic.

No longer is there a Santa producing a list of good and bad kids to determine production and resource allocation. Instead that is based on the very demand of that thing.

To enhance the wealth of the North Pole, every elf, consistent with the law, will be free to pursue one's own interest, to bring both his or her industry and capital into competition with other elves. It's not the benevolence of the pastry chef, butcher, baker or eggnog maker that we expect our dinner. We expect it because of their rational self-interest. The elf is driven by private gain and led by an *invisible hand* of the market, which inherently promotes the public good, although that was no part of his intention.

An elf pursuing their own interest ought to align with their vision of happiness. Not coincidentally, private property is based on the natural desire and right to pursue one's vision of happiness. This vision is rooted in the property acquiring instinct, making the safeguarding of private property an essential pillar.

Therefore, a body of elvish lawmakers must be elected by all the citizens of the North Pole in order to protect not only life and liberty, but the virtue of ownership. No one elf possess Kris Kringle like magic or ability, so the responsibility of the general welfare must revert back to each elf. This is based on the common-sense idea that every rational elf knows their interests' best and should be permitted to pursue them.

In more than spirit, the right of private property becomes a moral and economic prerequisite for making the pursuit of elvish excellence possible. There can be no morality without self-responsibility and self-determination. But all of this depends on protecting private property rights.

And every elf already owns something - *their own labor.*

All elves are self-owners who have property in the free use of their time, abilities, and efforts. Each elf has the right to control his own labor power and to claim ownership of the fruits of that labor. All elves will soon possess the ability to claim ownership over their homes through generous but practical terms of credit, made available by each individual's ability to repay.

Thus, the North Pole must modernize and embrace the less tangible ideas of property as stocks, bonds, mortgages, paper money, options, futures and the alike. These symbols of ownership are real representations that we will employ and embrace.

Yet, the true understanding of these types of ownership require specialized knowledge which our German guests already possess. With that, the North Pole will integrate Germans into society as equals. They will be employed in the new roles of accountants, bankers, lawyers, brokers and managers, and they will aid the elf owner in determining the best uses of their newfound wealth and credit.

The legitimacy of our new credit, which will be materialized in a new physical form of currency called Sugar Dollars, will be derived from the world marketplace. The Sugar Dollar is backed by this vast basket of international currencies, our own government, and the fact that the government will accept it as payment for tax. But what authenticates the Sugar Dollar is our collective confidence in it, and in the North Pole itself.

Through the power of the North Pole Reserve, real credit will be created and transferred at interest into the banking system.

These German bankers will have the duty and privilege to lend credit, without bias, to the first generation of elvish entrepreneurs through loans made at a modest rate of interest as to allow for a modest profit, while balancing their risk and paying back the North Pole Reserve.

Most importantly, this credit will be the fuel of the future engine of our civilization - special individuals, called entrepreneurs.

The elvish entrepreneur is to reform or even revolutionize production by creating an invention or, more generally, an untried method for producing a new commodity or producing an old one in a new way, or by opening up a new source of supply of materials, creating a new outlet for products, or by reorganizing an industry through any other productive innovation.

The entrepreneur is a pioneer who is able to act with confidence beyond the range of familiar ways. Her characteristic task becomes breaking up the old and creating the new.

So, allow me to introduce the North Pole's first private company, *North Pole Inc.*, tasked with purchasing the best toys, games and goods from the best elvish entrepreneurs and selling them direct to humanity's best toy stores, retail outlets or even direct to Christmas celebrators themselves.

The company will play the important role of distributor. Most vitally, North Pole Incorporated will protect and conceal the North Pole from humanity just as Kris Kringle has done. The Germans will interface with the rest of the world for the sake of our peace and preservation.

Through doing so not only will the company provide for the legitimacy of the Sugar Dollar, but it will also provide the money needed to purchase massive reserves of sugar, providing for   the first time in North Pole history, an abundance of sugar, so that no elf will go to sleep hungry again.

Further, Sugar Dollars can be exchanged at banks in real sugar. The Sugar Dollar is not an abstract idea, but a real representation of sugar that can be used materially in daily life. But unlike real sugar, the Sugar Dollar can be put to work and can grow through investment. In short, it can be *capital*. And once North Pole Inc. becomes a publicly traded stock everyone shall have an opportunity to own a piece of the company. In a literal sense we will all have the ability to own the North Pole, together, as shareholders with a vested interested in welfare, peace, sustainability and growth.

And that dismal Belief Meter you now see at zero will be *reinvigorated* with life.

The belief meter of the future will not be some magical or arbitrary number, it will display the real value of a single share of North Pole Incorporated stock, and thus will become the true barometer of the health of the North Pole as determined by the market, or perhaps even god himself, through the divinity of the marketplace.

And so, it's with boundless excitement that I'm pleased to be running for office of the executive and I seek your vote in a free election!

My promise is the guarantee that life and property are protected so that social cooperation may emerge and a nation of traders and producers may evolve into a thriving capitalist economy.

I invite any elf of any background to run against me, attempt to challenge these visionary yet precise plans, or better yet—propose a system which could possibly be better.

But that would be a difficult task—as an economy where the wants and satisfactions vary greatly, where private property and free markets allow elves to choose different occupations, products and lifestyles without interfering with the freedom of others to do the same is truly an ideal system of life.

Finally, a vote for Kendal-Crink is a vote to abolish Workshop and Factory Society. No longer shall our civilization be divided by the antiquated notions of birthright, but we will be united by the opportunity for all to create their own destiny and *pull themselves up by their own bootstraps*!

One does not need to await the election to start on the path to prosperity. As of next week, it is my Christmas gift to you all that the North Pole will be opening banks across the city, which will grant you mortgages for home ownership and credit for spending, as a reward your continued efforts in the Christmas Mission. Although we have no means of bringing Christmas to humanity tonight, we can save the spirit of Christmas as we can save ourselves.

I encourage you all to head to your nearest bank, get your credit evaluations, get a mortgage and go vote! Become an active citizen in our dynamic new society and *do your duty* not only for yourself but for all of elf-kind!

Give credit *where credit is due*!

Vote for Kendal-Crink! Godspeed citizens!"

Sir Louie licks his lips, subtly shivering as he stares into the dead-silent mass. There's no reaction. Out desperation he steps back up and lets out;

"And Merryyyyyyy Christmas! HO HO HO! Long live the North Pole! Long live Christmas!"

The crowd erupts. Their passions overcoming their fears as the city lights up. The roars deafening as Sir Louie riles up the crowd like a rock star, or messiah even, and the North Pole comes under his spell.

Sir Louie marches inside feeling like a conquering Julius Caesar returning to Rome in glory. He blows past a shell-shocked Ginger and hugs Klaus. Funny given his size, but fueled with adrenaline Sir Louie seems to effortlessly lift Klaus into the air and parade him around.

"Get me Axel and Renee!" Sir Louie shouts. "And Willie

Maven, and Otto! And eggnog, all the eggnog!" He laughingly barks as Ginger takes off in fury.

"Great speech, Sir." Klaus says. "Spectacular ending."

"Credit Where Credit Is Due! Credit Where Credit Is Due!" Sir Louie cheers.

9 - MACHINATIONS

The next morning, Willie, Klaus, Otto, and Sir Louie sit behind a roundtable at the penthouse of Santa's Tower. They're cleaned up but hungover from last night's celebration.

Sir Louie's thumping headache has him pressing his hands against his head while Otto's sunglasses help him dim out the morning light that peers over the Artic Range. They gorge on the impressive spread of baked goodies, excited to be off prison food and enjoying the finer things again, for the first time in a long time. Willie sips his peppermint tea as Klaus stuffs in a blueberry muffin until Sir Louie *pounds his fists against the table.* He's promised a lot but doesn't understand the first thing he needs to do to realize any of it.

"Giving credit where credit is due? How the hell do we do that?" Sir Louie fusses.

"We're on it, Sir L." Klaus says.

"Can you explain? Because it's a damn catchy slogan, and the elves aren't gonna forget it anytime soon."

"It's as easy as it sounds, we're just going to provide the credit." Klaus says.

"But we can't just make credit out of thin air." Sir Louie says.

"We're not making it, it's already there. We just need to quantify it."

"There's nothing! No marketplace, no currency, no taxes, no nothing!"

Klaus huffs. "Do you really think you've freed the North Pole? Do you believe that Workshop and Factory Society will just become equal? No Sir, you've merely redefined it. *The system works because there is no equality,* Santa's made sure of that. It works because the monetary system we're creating will simply quantify it, in Sugar Dollars, quantifying the social relations that already exist.

"But how is a Sugar Dollar more than just a paper note?" Sir

94

Louie poses.

"The Sugar Dollar is *money, money is value, value is trust, trust is a contract, and the contract is debt*. If elves have *confidence* in the Sugar Dollar, it can weather any storm."

"I don't get it."

"Just substitute the word '*debt*' every time you hear the word '*money*' and you'll find that *it is a world in debt*."

"A world in debt doesn't sound very appealing." Sir Louie blurts.

"Debt isn't inherently positive or negative, in my opinion. Its utility is determined by what the borrower does with it. Debt levels aren't automatically too high or too low, what matters most to us creditors are the *trends toward sustainability*, so that we remain creditors."

"Well it seems as if we're in the privileged position to anoint ourselves creditors, but what about everyone else?"

"Those elves who have the most valid claims on a means of production will become creditors, those without, debtors. All exchange functions according to a logic of imbalance and power differential.

"But we don't exactly have credit to give." Sir Louie repeats.

"But they have debt to take, and in doing so they create our credit." Klaus says.

"Come again?"

Klaus walks up to Sir Louie, "We'll soon have authority and legitimacy. As long as we have that we'll have the foundation."

Willie jumps in, "So we're not granting credit, we're granting debt?"

"Yes and no. You must come to see how debt is credit and credit is debt." Klaus says. "Two sides of the same coin."

Sir Louie scratches his head, "I don't like that. Tell me what you mean by credit or debt, really?"

"It's a promise of payment. What is a financial asset? A share or bond? It is the promise of future value. 'Promise', 'value', and 'future' are the keywords here, gentlemen, and to make this work we must *measure* everyone. Consequently, our first task is to seek those elves capable of honoring their debts."

"Workshop Society." Sir Louie answers.

"Yes, precisely. They have social and political capital, so it's logical for them to access financial capital as well." Klaus says.

"Fine! Very Fine!" Sir Louie remarks.

Klaus continues, "Each elf is a particular case which must be carefully studied. Each elf's future plans, lifestyle and 'solvency' guarantees the reimbursement of the debt they owe. This is how our bank credit works - we'll grant credit based on a personal application, following review of the individual's life, behavior, social standing and so on. The main purpose of debt lies within the construction of it, of making an elf a subject, and making that subject utmost aware of its debt. An elf that believes in his or her individuality stands as guarantor of their actions. They take responsibility for their way of life and for their debt. Ultimately the task is mobilizing the innermost depths of the heart to guide behavior to ensure repayment."

"Elves will voluntarily honor their debts?" Willie asks.

"Well what are we beings, elf or Human? A bio-cosmic consciousness? An ever-expanding memory made of actions and words? Perhaps we are only as good as our words through which promises are made?" Klaus suggests.

"Perhaps." Sir Louie says.

"They must pledge allegiance to repayment." Otto says.

"A pledge, a promise, for certain!" Sir Louie spouts, "An allegiance to their government and their debt."

"That's not enough." Otto interrupts. "We'll need more...techniques, all a bit scarier than the next, so a pledge doesn't merely stay a pledge."

"That sounds scary." Willie points out.

"It is, Maven. But a thing must be burned into memory so it stays there. Only something that hurts is remembered, my tiny friend." Otto replies, as if speaking from experience.

"Blame, guilt, conscience, repression and sacred duty must be drilled into each debtor, so that debt becomes a form of self-torture." Klaus says.

Otto thinks about this, he has some experience with these matters. "It's a good state-security technique, by reducing the uncertain behaviors of the governed through training them to honor their debt."

"We'll maintain control of the future as long as our financial innovations have the purpose of possessing the future by objectivizing it." Klaus says. "Dishonoring debt will be punishable, even criminal."

"At least!" Sir Louie shouts with enthusiasm as Willie tries to stay open minded, but finds it increasingly difficult.

"The role of the government remains the same, construct memory, inscribe guilt, fear and bad conscious into the debtor." Klaus says.

"But what if everyone repays their debts? Surely everyone should have the opportunity to do so?" Willie wonders.

"Then the system dies."

"How?" Willie blips.

"An elf can honor some of his debts, but if he honors all debts then there's no longer any asymmetry, no more power differential, no stronger or weaker forces—no more capital. Credit and debt embody the differential. Debt and money must always be circulating for capitalism to function. And the engine for the circulation of money will come from new consumer goods—like Christmas presents. It's through the new methods of production or transportation, the new markets and forms of industry that capitalist enterprises create is also the very thing that incessantly revolutionizes the economy from within. It relentlessly destroys the old and relentlessly creates the new. It's this process of *creative destruction* that's the essential fact of capitalism, and it's what every capitalist concern has to consider." Klaus says.

"OKAY, OKAY economist!" Sir Louie complains. "But how are our banks to issue credit? How do we know how to pay the average elf? How do we measure their value?"

Klaus thinks about it. Actually, he's been thinking about the nature of value his entire life...

"The value of the working elf is the value of the necessary subsistence for the maintenance of that laborer."

"What?" Sir Louie spouts.

"It's the cost of the laborers survival. The base value of labor power becomes the value of the necessities required to produce, develop, maintain, and perpetuate the labor force. The laboring elf receives just as much, and only the bare minimum required to keep up the repetition of their same bargain, every day. The price of wage labor must be the minimum wage - the absolute bare-minimum needed to keep the laborer alive."

"But the capitalist must make a profit, how is that possible if the working elf is paid fairly?" Willie asks.

"The capitalist must make the laboring elf work more hours—render more actual services than the cost of sustaining those workers. They exact more actual hours of labor than they have paid for. There's a difference between the two values, *a surplus value*, and by virtue of the profit motive the *surplus value goes to the capitalist*."

"So, the capitalist exploits labor." Willie bluntly states. Klaus thinks about it while Otto and Sir Louie are perked up by Willie's spikey tone.

"Yes—they're exploited in this specific way, in that they

provide a larger profit to the capitalist than what they themselves are allotted to take, by a lot." Klaus says.

"Isn't there a better way?" Willie asks.

"I'm all ears." Klaus responds with a sting.

But the silence lingers as Willie is lost for words.

"OKAY OKAY I'm fine with it." Sir Louie yells. "Yes, the animal kingdom, state of nature, etcetera, all very well and good. But I still need to know how to grant credit to workshop and factory owners, or capitalists, or whatever you're calling them. How are we going to determine the credit a capitalist should have access to, and how the hell does that fit into a democracy?"

"Sir Louie." Klaus says solemnly as to calm him and earn his attention. "There's nothing democratic about it."

"Huh?"

"The state bank, the North Pole Reserve, must run completely independent from politics. You can regulate the private banks and create laws around it, but even that's ill-advised. The system works best when all actors operate freely in their own self-interest."

"But how will credit be granted?" Willie asks.

"For our large private banks and institutions like North Pole Inc., only the financial community is involved in this type of assessment. It will be done by something we'll call *ratings agencies*, which will be paid by the businesses, banks, or institutions they rate." Klaus explains.

"So those with more money can pay for a better rating?" Willie asks.

"Yes." Klaus answers.

"Isn't that a...*monumental* conflict of interest?" Willie points out.

"So what." Klaus responds. "They're not supposed to be independent assessment firms; their only job is to rate, through doing so the system further perpetuates and strengthens."

Willie doesn't like the answer, becoming flustered.

"OKAY, OKAY," Sir Louie shouts again. "But there's no reserve, no treasury full of money, as I keep saying. So how can we grant credit to the working elf?"

"As I keep saying, debt comes before credit, my good Sir." Klaus says becoming tenser.

"How?" Sir Louie demands.

"All social rights must be replaced by the right to access credit."

"You mean the right to contract debt." Willie interrupts.

"Again, same thing." Klaus says. "No right to pay raises, instead the right to consumer credit. No universal insurance, instead individual insurance. No right to education, but the right to student loans. And the ace in our sleeve that will kick-start the treasury; no right to housing, but the right to get home loans—just as you've already gloriously declared!"

"How delightfully devilish." Sir Louie stirs.

"They're going to line up at the banks because we're going to give them a mortgage with no down payment. Hell, we'll give mortgages to the poorest earners too, we'll call those subprime mortgages. That way even the poorest are still encouraged to own their homes. That means more money for the banking system. Meanwhile, we'll use the real estate as collateral in the event of default, so no matter what it's a win-win for us." Klaus smiles.

"How do we know they won't default on their mortgages?" Willie asks.

"They won't, not initially, at least. We can keep the payments low for the first few years, then bulk it up later. There will be some losers, the poorest that is, but they're supposed to lose—their default is practically built into the model."

"Is that so?" Willie says.

"If you want the majority to thrive there will always be a minority that has to lose, but until that day everyone will win and they'll love us for it. The achievements of society need to be built on the backs of someone. And yet, the average elf will finally own something substantial for the first time in their life, and through that we're creating something else very special..."

"Do tell." Sir Louie blurts.

"A market for debt." Klaus answers.

"What does that mean? You can't sell debt." Willie says.

"Of course you can, we'll take all that debt and sell it to the highest bidder."

"Why would anyone want to own debt?" Sir Louie wonders.

"The owner of the debt doesn't pay it. The owner of the debt collects the interest on it. As long as the debt is being repaid then that thing, that security, has value. It's called securitization. It's transforming debt into tradable securities in the financial marketplace."

"This is what you mean by finance?" Sir Louie asks.

"Yes, but I think it's more accurate to speak of it as debt and interest. Debt becomes a thing that capitalists can buy, sell and trade. It becomes an investment that must be managed, so the system of credit and debt further perpetuate. *It creates a process of infinite circulation and infinite debt.*" Klaus says.

Sir Louie takes this in. "The Infinite. A powerful thing. Infinite influence, infinite power, infinite victory! My god, it's beautiful. But if you'll excuse me, I need to piss out all that eggnog." Sir Louie excuses himself in an awkward dash.

"Can you securitize any kind of debt? Even state debt?" Willie asks.

"I'd say so. And now that we're alone, I'd also say that the capitalist class has a direct interest in the state's indebtedness."

"But if it's functioning properly, shouldn't everyone want a non-precarious state?" Willie asks.

"Think about it, the interest payments from that debt would become a chief source of capitalist enrichment. At the end of each year a new deficit and after the lapse of four or five years a new loan."

Willie considers this, still conflicted.

Klaus continues, "It's good for capitalists to artificially keep the government on the verge of bankruptcy, because it gives the bankers favorable conditions for renegotiation."

"You're explaining this as if I should be excited. Why is any of this good for me?" Willie asks.

Klaus stares out him with a smirk, realizing Willie doesn't realize he's a made-elf.

"Willie, why do you think you're here with us, right now? In what capacity?" Klaus asks.

"As your friend? I don't know. I'm here because you are, because you're going to save the North Pole."

"Willie, you're going to play an essential role. Do you really think it's just chance that we're gathered here today?" Klaus asks.

"No, I don't believe so." Willie says.

"Me either. I believe it's our destiny, that you were destined to save us, and that we are destined to save the North Pole, together." Klaus preaches with zest.

"What can I do?" Willie asks.

"What *can't* you do, Willie, ask yourself that! What can't you do?! Especially now you're the most powerful figure in the North Pole!"

"What do you mean?"

"You're not here only as my friend, but as the head of the North Pole Reserve itself. Which means you control the financial system, which means you control the North Pole!"

"Are you sure?" Willie asks.

"It's already done, congratulations." Klaus smiles, shaking his hand. "That bureaucratic parasite Sir Louie is too dim or too selfish to understand that now, but he will. It's you who wields the real power."

"How?" Willie wonders.

"Because I've made it so. You've saved my life now do me the honor of allowing me to save yours." Klaus professes.

Willie's confusion morphs into a pleasant surprise as he embraces Klaus back with a powerful hug. Klaus whispers into his ear, "Accept this, Willie, and together we'll rise to the greatest heights."

"Yes, together, for the best of the North Pole." Willie replies.

"You'll have their respect again. Immense respect." Klaus says. "I promise."

The words rattle Willie, and he pours his soul into their embrace, thanking him for redemption.

"I won't let you down." Willie says.

10 – PLEDGE ALLEGIANCE

Klaus watches a team of elves put the final touches on "Corporation Clock," a massive clock, Big Ben sized, now adorning the exterior of Santa's Tower.

Time will be more important than ever; every moment measured, every tick and tock dictating the very flow of all events and transactions. A perfect and infinite sequence of big and small arms spinning endlessly around and around, so logically and unrelenting. Klaus smiles and wonders if he's the only one in the whole North Pole who realizes that the substance of money as capital is *time* itself. The idea emboldens him, making him feel like a master of time, and through that, a master of the universe.

He takes a big breath of cool morning air, so cool it stings the back of his throat delightfully. He turns back inside to meet Otto. The room is full of documents and contracts piling high. Otto is all business as Klaus scribbles notes profusely. A pod of elf assistants encroach as Otto becomes infuriated with the swarming bunch.

"Leave us, minions!" Otto shouts as they scurry out.

"Willie Maven, head of the Reserve, huh. Is that wise?" Otto wonders.

Klaus sneers, "It's a big part of the negotiation. Besides, we must at least appear to give elves some form of power."

"What do you mean appear? That's real power!" Otto bursts.

Klaus paces, gesturing to Otto to calm, "No, not really."

"How? Why!?"

"Because public money appears powerful, but is always subordinate to profit, always secondary to the capitalist's use of money."

"How could that be?" Otto asks.

"Because private banks hold the monetary initiative. Public

money is secondary because it's only the capitalist's money that gets to function as actual capital. The sole mission of the North Pole Reserve is to meet the legitimate credit needs of private companies, banks and North Pole Inc. Its mission is to manage the overall harmony of those needs. Capital still needs the sovereignty of state money to make it all look legit, and in the North Pole that means an elf as the face of the institution. Better have a friendly and suggestible elf like Willie, than say Sir Louie as an appointee, yes?"

"Ok." Otto replies stubbornly.

There's a brief knocking at the door before Willie enters.

"Ah, good elf, we were just talking about you." Klaus says with a smile.

"All good things I hope."

"Nothing but." Otto grins as Klaus greets with a brotherly hug.

"Come on, I want to show you two something special." Klaus says spritely.

Willie and Otto follow Klaus into the comfortable quarters of Santa's reindeer drawn carriage. They're surrounded by a detail of Redcoats who trot along their own regally outfitted reindeer. They make their way through Downtown, watching as corner buildings are converted into private banks every five blocks. The construction sites are filled with busy elves working arduously in their remodeling, only a week away from opening.

"I was thinking elves could cast their ballot, open a bank accountant and get a mortgage all in the same hour, at the same bank." Willie suggests.

"Yes! Convenient, accessible, fast. Win them over in one fell swoop. I love it!" Klaus says.

"I'll get right on it." Otto steps in.

Willie interjects, "It's easy to see how an elf who calculates their real estate, including the current market value of it, will be urged to increase the value by increasing their debt. The debt positions should seem weak because the asset's value will grow faster than the additional debt they sink into it."

"True, so your Reserve should prepare credit to banks for all types loans." Klaus says.

"All of that is good and well as long as real estate values increase." Otto mentions.

"We're creating the real estate market, it's that flooded with demand, Otto. It will be on fire for a long time." Klaus accounts.

Their golden carriage passes various street venders, storefronts and small enterprises. They observe the daily transactions of elves exchanging their remaining sugar cubes for goods and services, watching how the small enterprises weigh and measure sugar prudently on the scales before haggling a bargain. The sight gets Willie thinking...

"I understand the big institutional needs, how they'll be rated by the credit agencies, and I get the workers making a predictable income based on their need to, how should I put it - survive and reproduce. I guess that should go without saying, but..."

"Survival is earned, my elf, as is reproduction, especially for Otto HAHA," Klaus jeers. "So, it shouldn't go without saying, nothing is given in this world."

"But what about these venders, freelancers and small operations? Are these the entrepreneurs you gloriously champion? Because, frankly, I don't see it." Willie says.

Klaus laughs. "Ah maybe I misspoke. Innovators are often entrepreneurs, but few entrepreneurs are actual innovators. I'm really talking about technology and how North Pole Inc. will invest a ton into that. Without Santa's magic we must make the North Pole the world's most tech advanced civilization. With that, it will be the most educated, creative and peaceful society on Earth—a great society. You'll see."

"Then what's the fate of these small businesses?" Willie asks.

Klaus thinks about it. "The independent worker's model is borrowed from salaried work, functioning like an individual enterprise, but with the owner constantly negotiating with themselves, because 'they're responsible for their own fate'. The system requires elves that take on the risks that North Pole Inc. would never tolerate."

"Besides we can always acquire the successful ones later." Otto interrupts.

Klaus continues, "It will be good to reward the minority who become wealthy, ingraining the population with the idea that success is possible if they're only willing to accept huge risks. Only two percent will make it, but it will serve as an endlessly chased carrot. It will be like a dream that feels attainable but is always just out of reach."

"What happens when they default?" Willie asks.

"They go into bankruptcy, end up in debt and will have to work to pay it off, like anyone else." Klaus answers.

"We can't accept endless cost and endless risk. Let the population endure that." Otto reiterates.

"So, the result is a majority of entrepreneurs who are more or less in debt, more or less poor, but always precarious?" Willie asks.

"Yes." Klaus answers. "It will keep them honest, on their toes. They'll debate with themselves, 'should I work or take a vacation? Should I relax or make myself available for the scantiest offer? What's worth more?"

"But they're free to make that decision, it's a free enterprise system after all." Otto tacks on.

"Ironic, being isolated by 'freedom'?" Willie asks.

"It's just the way it is." Otto replies.

Klaus interjects, "That elf is forced to compete not only with others like him but with themselves. Rendering them obedient, like everyone else. It's good for stability."

"Or domination." Otto laughs.

"Then the dream of individualism, self-control or self-made destiny remains a dream?" Willie asks.

"Don't say that out loud, those are the foundations of our mantra for god's sake." Otto sneers. "And it's not just a dream, even if a tiny percentage achieve it, that makes it real."

"You're in control because you're your own boss! Because you're your own manager!" Klaus laughs.

Willie still doesn't see an argument for anything better, and in a sardonic way he frees himself from his moral rigidity. He decides for once in his life that the path of least resistance might be worth trying. As if flipping a switch for a moment, he joins Klaus and Otto as kindred spirits while a devilish pleasure overcomes him. He smiles, contemplating the prospective power he'll soon possess through the simple act not resisting.

"To negotiate permanently with oneself, to obey oneself, is to fulfill the virtue of individualism!" Willie shouts as he kicks back and throws his arms around the guys.

"How the truth hurts my good philosophers! Oh, the tragedy!" Klaus laughs.

"Frustration, resentment, guilt and fear make up the passions of the self." Otto blips.

"Self-realization, freedom, and autonomy collide with a reality that systematically nullifies them! Klaus chuckles.

"Guilt, bad conscious, loneliness and resentment succeed!" Otto yells.

"The 'enemy' becomes indistinguishable from the self as complaints are turned against oneself instead of us!" Klaus hoots.

"It's kind of sad." Willie adds, then laughs to their pleasant surprise.

"The saddest!" Klaus blares irreverently.

"Hilariously sad! Terribly funny!" Otto giggles. "Don't make me cry!"

"I'd never, not on purpose!" Klaus jests. "Oh, how I hate to cry!"

"Crying's the worst!" Otto cracks up.

Willie catches his breath and takes in the conversation as his stomach goes queasy. "You're not joking, right?"

A brief silence resets the laughter to a somber atmosphere. Klaus places his hand on Willie's shoulder and leans in, "I laugh because that's how I live my life, but nature couldn't care less—and this capitalistic way of life has become our only means of survival now."

"The one and only?" Willie wonders.

"Yes, for better or worse, the one and only," Klaus answers as the carriage comes to a stop. "Don't worry, you'll love it."

"I hope so." Willie whispers.

"Good, because we're here, at the belly of the beast! Welcome to your new office, Willie." Klaus says as they disembark and walk out onto the cobblestone, arriving at the grand and beautiful state bank, The North Pole Reserve. The name is etched in stone and painted in gold-leaf, making for an intimidating entrance. The trio stare with awe as the work-elves dust it off.

"I mean I told 'em to make it nice, but this is something else!" Klaus smirks.

"This is my new office?" Willie asks.

"It most certainly is." Klaus smiles.

The Bank resembles a German castle, renaissance in style, a clear symbol of power with towering high ramparts. It's made of dark red brick, with a rounded out triangular stepped gable on the facade, appearing like a crown. Noble, powerful, daunting.

"May I give you a tour?" Klaus simpers.

"I'd love that." Willie replies, entranced by the sheer scale and beauty of it all.

"I was thinking this is the perfect place to sit with Sir Louie. We need to set some things straight, if you wouldn't mind hosting?"

"Of course not." Willie answers. "It'd be my privilege."

"Good, because he's a bit too comfortable at the Hermitage—he needs to feel the power of this bank." Klaus states. "Now let me show you in!" He guides Willie and Otto inside the palatial institution...

Several days later the trio are comfortably prepared for their meeting with Sir Louie, waiting within Willie's freshly furnished office. Sir Louie arrives, joined by Axel and his trusted sycophants Nipper McJingles and Topper Trinket, sitting opposite them, across a stately oak conference table.

The meeting starts as a stare down through the vintage dessert towers and porcelain tea cups and kettles. Sir Louie's stale expression suggests his discomfort. He doesn't really understand the nature of the Reserve but can tell how important it must be.

"Nice digs, Maven." Sir Louie says. "Twice the size of my office, you're trying to one up me?"

"Thank you, Sir." Willie replies. "But I'd take your office over this any day." He laughs, but Sir Louie barely cracks a smile.

"Location, location, location." Sir Louie mutters.

"No Ginger Garland, where'd she go?" Otto jabs.

"Who cares, she's not here and apparently not running against our elf." McJingles says.

"That's all I c-c-care about." Topper utters.

"Is anyone running against Sir Louie?" Willie asks.

"He is the only one on the ballot, no one has c-c-come f-f-forward." Topper answers.

"And how could they after that rousing speech!" McJingles yells with his blushed red face, swigging whiskey from his flask.

Topper stumbles, "A real c-c-c-crowd pleaser—inspiring speech S-s-sir L."

"You know I wrote the damn thing, right?" Klaus says.

"Just g-g-giving c-credit where c-c-credit is due." Topper laughs.

"Actually, you're not." Klaus replies.

Sir Louie interrupts, "So why do you call this session amid such a pressing time, gentlemen?"

Klaus bites into his scone and sips some tea before leaning back with bravado, "Because I need you to understand something before any of this begins..."

"I'm listening." Sir Louie utters.

"I need you to understand *the primacy of the shareholder above all things*. It's this very priority that's foundational to the functioning of the system."

"How do you mean?" Sir Louie asks.

"The principles of the government shall follow; the primacy of the shareholder over the director of the company; the subordination of company management to shareholder interests; and in the case of conflicts of interest, the primacy of the shareholder," Klaus says. "This is how things are done in the real world, and these are the international accounting standards that all companies operate by. I need you to respect and protect these standards."

"It means protecting shareholders over citizens, obviously." Axel flexes. "And why should he, really?"

"Because if you'd recall, you too are shareholders and board members, and once we have our operations in place we'll bring the company public. It will finance operations and endless growth. Those supporters who matter most to you, those former Workshop Society elves will be stock owners too, and they're going to get rich right along our side, making you forever electable." Klaus answers.

Sir Louie sips his eggnog. "Go on." He mutters, Klaus pleased with his lack of resistance.

"Company actors other than the shareholders, notably workers, are not owners of the wealth produced, even if they contribute directly to it. It's the shareholders who must decide, control, and prescribe how things are done. The shareholders dictate the procedures, the salary levels, organization of labor, pace and the productivity of the company." Klaus explains.

"Once North Pole Incorporated goes public the value of your shares will skyrocket, and everyone here will be rich reach beyond belief, even Topper." Otto adds.

"I like the s-s-sound of that." Topper sniffles.

"And what about normal elves?" Axel says.

"Any elf can pull themselves up by their *bootstraps!*" Otto snaps.

"Easy Otto," Klaus whispers. "We're prepared to train the next generation of the world's finest economists, right here, in the North Pole. All of society must be re-educated to understand economics, elves and Germans alike...because *economics is politics.* The nature of our professions will always be intertwined. It's the division of labor in the North Pole and abroad which represents the true constitution of power relations on the Earth today."

Axel looks to his father. "Do you believe that?"

But Sir Louie says nothing.

"The answers to the challenges of our future will be answered on measuring how a solution affects the growth of production and consumption."

Sir Louie smirks and nods at Klaus' passion.

"You'll have your glorious economy once I have my position as head of this North Pole City-State." Sir Louie says.

"You'll have it, entirely. So as long as we work together." Klaus replies.

Sir Louie smirks fiendishly, feeling power come into his grip. He abruptly jets up from his seat.

"I'm glad there's at least one elf on the other side of the table." Sir Louie says sharing a glance with Willie. He reaches for his glass of Eggnog, holds it up and toasts "to the North Pole!"

"To the North Pole!" They all salute and drink with cheer, in agreement.

The next several days are a whirlwind of chaos as Sir Louie and his entourage continue their politicking and backroom deals, meanwhile Willie and Klaus put the finishing touches on the financial system, offering Germans a slew of banking and white-collar positions. Even in their down time they select Sugar Dollar designs, work with elvish fashion designers on sleek new looks, trying on a variety of tight fitted suits, skinny black ties and colorful silk pocket squares. Klaus aiming to emulate the fashions of the "Madmen" advertising executives of New York, Paris and London.

Meanwhile Otto arrives in Iceland, setting up a discrete back office in downtown Reykjavik. It starts as a simple space, with a desk, telephone and Wall Street Journal. More uniquely the office is equipped with a live and ever buzzing machine that prints a long ticker tape of stock prices which come in through the telegraph lines and Transatlantic Cable.

Otto leans back and kicks his feet onto his desk, listening to the ticker tape stream in. He stares at a massive map of the world on his wall. He approaches it with a laugh and sticks red and green pins at the very top of Greenland, marking the North Pole. He marks Reykjavik with another set of green and red pins and stabs gold pins into New York, London, Paris, Hong Kong, Tokyo, Mexico City,

Moscow, São Paulo, Delhi, Istanbul, Tehran, Los Angeles, Toronto, and Johannesburg – all prime targets to start.

Otto steps back and exhales, absorbing the scale of the worldwide operation. There's a single directory on his desk, titled TOY RETAILERS INTERNATIONAL trade magazine. He turns open to page one and starts dialing. "Hi, this is Otto from North Pole Incorporated, President of Sales, it's good to meet you, I hear you're experiencing a shortage of toys with Santa Claus mysteriously gone...Which ones do you need, exactly? That many? No, not a problem for us at all." His grin widens as he frantically jots down a long list of orders...

Back at the North Pole, Willie and Klaus appoint a handful of Germans as heads of three new Credit Ratings Agencies. Klaus calls them "the big three" - Mistletoe Investors Services, Sugar & Poors and Frosty Ratings. Each company has swanky downtown offices with exposed bricks, glass walls and impressive war room style conference rooms. They're fully staffed and outfitted with highest end amenities.

Mistletoe Investor Services and Sugar & Poors specialize in credit ratings for the workshop and factory owners, basically those that control resources and production. The vast majority of these clients are of Workshop Society heritage. They're awarded credit based on their family legacy and relationships among the elite. However, very few grasp just how competitive the business environment will become. Like before, all workshops compete with one another, but this time instead of finishing last in Santa's eyes, they go bankrupt and disappear.

Last of the three, and perhaps most exceptional, is Frosty Ratings. Unlike other rating agencies these German rating officers are particularly dim and sought after by Klaus for exactly that. They drink heavily and have the most mindless task, which is to rubberstamp Triple-A ratings, the highest rating possible, for North Pole Inc., no matter what. For the simple gesture of the rubber stamping, Klaus and Sir Louie will provide these executives with a lifetime of luxury.

Before the banks are open the ratings agencies are booked with meeting after meeting, preemptively sorting their clients, calculating credit ratings, directing them to the proper banks who will then provide credit. One fact remains constant, the more clients pay the better they're rated. If they don't get what they want they'll just take their business to the next agency.

The ratings agencies are for-profit companies, just as Klaus described. The whole process is very gentlemanly, even communal. There's a real solidarity among these future rich and already influential as they're already the friends and family of what was Workshop Society. The sums of Sugar Dollars discussed are impressive, from the millions to hundreds of millions.

When there are deliberations, they are deeply philosophical. Ironic since the practice is supposed to be scientific. The long-winded conversations ultimately put a monetary value on intangible things, resulting in a number that feels fictional, or random even. Some of this money is designed simply to be thrown into circulation as capital without any material basis for productive activity. But the fiction is morphed into reality as soon as the handshake is made and the credit is allocated based upon what they've determined; *the net present value of future cash flows.*

Finally, the day comes for bank accounts to open and ballots to be cast. Corporation Clock rings aloud 10 times at the stroke of 10:00 AM and is heard across the North Pole. After the tenth strike Willie and Klaus ceremoniously reveal the tarp covering the sign of "Golden Bells Bank" along with its proud new owners, the Germans Ernst and Hanna von Wolf.

Ernest is rather ordinary looking, with stubbly dark facial hair and a bit fluffy, filling out his fine suit. But his sister Hanna is tall, blonde, blue eyed and slender, making one wonder how they could be related. She's ethereal. Almost too radiant and beautiful for this cold polar world. Willie can't stop staring as Klaus smirks, taking notice and nudging him to get a grip, but she thinks it's cute.

She's joined by Sir Louie. He smiles and hands her an outrageously large pair of scissors, which she uses to cut the massive ribbon wrapped around the bank doors. They all hold their hands high playing toward the cheering crowd, declaring both the bank and ballot booths open for business!

Not only Golden Bells Bank but all the (German owned) banks across the North Pole open simultaneously at the tenth strike of the clock. Other banks like Wreath Fargo, Scrooge Trust, Royal Bank of the North, Celebration Group, Snowman Sachs, Merry Stanley and the alike are birthed into existence. As the doors open the masses of elves rush inside to open their bank accounts, get their mortgages, access their newfound credit and cast their ballots (for the one and only Sir Louie).

Unlike the gentlemanly conversations between ratings agency, investment banker and captain of industry, there is no conversation or negotiation here. There is only measurement. The measurement of the individual elf based on what they're expected to earn through evaluating the likelihood of repayment. In this way the elf must be capable of standing guarantor for him or herself. Somehow the borrower is still considered a "free" elf, but their actions and behaviors are confined to the limits defined by the debt they've entered into. These elves shall be considered "free" insofar as they assume the proper way of life compatible with repayment.

Through measuring several key variables, like occupation, education, background, and lifestyle -the bankers go straight to their math formula and calculate the individual's credit score, turning each elf into a number, or risk assessment. The score corresponds to an approved amount the bank is willing to lend, and the loan is made as soon as the elf signs on the dotted line. The signature promising full repayment or facing consequence, using their property as collateral in the event of default.

The un-read contracts are written in another language, called legalese, and they're executed with excitement as the elves now own property that's growing in value. This leaves them with the option to refinance so they can draw even more money from the property going forward.

The lines at each bank stretch out the door and around the corner, shuffling elves in and out as fast as they can. After the first few hours the bank staffs have the drill down. Everything is going according to plan, and once the day is done most elves are voters, home owners with a mortgage and proprietors of checking, savings and investment accounts. The North Pole Reserve now has interest payments lined up from the private banks, and the private banks have interest payments lined up from their newly granted loans.

Meanwhile, the workshops and factories are all rated and supplied with vast amounts of Sugar Dollars. This is made available through their flexible and open-ended lines of bank credit which pays for wages, materials and operations. All of which is to be cycled back into the economy with money changing hands again and again, as fast as possible. The circulation goes from money to product to money again, with an increasing velocity sped by planned obsolescence, innovation and an ever-rotating cycle of fashion as dictated by the whims of high-brow culture. The cycle will continue ad infinitum so long as Otto calls in ever expanding orders from a world in demand of things, toys, games, presents and beyond.

High in Santa's Tower, Klaus enjoys an earnest moment with himself. Standing alone, he overlooks the city and contemplates all of the changes to come. He smiles, wanting to think he's doing the right thing, but he's too smart for that, and sees exactly what's going on. He knows *that the markets for labor, land, and money are essential to the functioning of capital and the production of value.* But even he cannot ignore the undeniable fact *that labor, land, and money are obviously not commodities*, and he's a bit shocked everyone's going along with it so easily.

First, what is labor but another name for elvish activity, which goes with life itself. That activity can't be detached from the rest of life, be stored or mobilized. Second, land is only another name for nature, which is not produced by man or elf. And Sugar Dollars, his blissful creation, is a mere token of purchasing power which is not produced at all but comes into being through state finance. None of these things are produced for sale, and so *the commodity description of labor, land and money is a complete fiction.*

But Klaus is determined to stay in control, and cannot allow others to realize this insight if the system is to perpetuate. He laughs, knowing that *labor, land and money must be totally objectified, minced, milled and broken down from their true nature and then sown back together under an umbrella of rights and laws founded on the principles of individual private property,* as guaranteed by the state.

With Sir Louie coming to power it shouldn't be hard. But what could be difficult is the overt oppression required to suppress any dissenter. They would have to be criminalized, or worse yet, labeled a terrorist. With that, the Redcoats, under the state, must have a virtual monopoly on violence.

Klaus snaps out of his trance as an eruption of fireworks composed of red and green explosions crackle off over the city sky. The display marking Sir Louie's election. Willie approaches with champagne flutes in hand and gives one to Klaus, joining him in watching the show, both loosening their own qualms as they drink.

"The North Pole is yours, Willie, are you ready for it?"

"I am." Willie smiles back.

They clink glasses, drink and gaze as the fireworks spectacularly burst amid the illuminated gas lanterns of the city, looking like an explosion of bright confetti amid a swarm of flickering fire flies spreading out as far as the eye can see.

Soon the whole party of Ernst and Hanna von Wolf, Renee, Axel, Topper, McJingles and Sir Louie join Klaus and Willie on the balcony of Santa's Tower, all armed with champagne.

Willie whispers to Renee, "Can you believe it? Your father is like the new Santa Claus."

"He is. But he can be bitter and belligerent, and he's never listened to a single suggestion of mine. I'm not sure how else to say this, but I don't trust him."

"Really?"

"Yes."

"Maybe we can change that?" Willie says. "But I think he'll

have to earn my trust first."

"I'd like that." She grins back.

"Me too."

Willie reaches for her hand but before he connects Hanna rubs against his shoulder. For a moment he's awkwardly straddled between the two females, but he gives into the path of least resistance as Hanna drags him back. She wraps her long arms around his waist, moving her hands onto his belt buckle, repelling Renee in an instant. Willie is frozen, wishing it was Renee's arms around him. With Renee gone Hanna droops over him.

But he escapes Hanna's possession, striding forward and raising his glass high.

"Ah, a toast!" Klaus shouts, pointing at Willie about to speak.

"No, a pledge!" Willie corrects. "As the borrowers have pledged to honor their debts, I pledge allegiance to you, Sir Louie, our leader, our President. May we always be in your good graces!" Willie shouts as everyone salutes, except Renee who escapes the room.

They drink and chant as Willie smiles sheepishly to Sir Louie, lifting an eyebrow toward Klaus.

"Ah, and may I make a pledge to my benefactors at North Pole Incorporated. May we always do our best to help each other! To good business!" Sir Louie laughingly exclaims, patting Klaus on the back.

Klaus steps forward. "And a pledge to you, Willie Maven. We are at the mercy of your good judgement, and may we always be in the good grace of your Sugar Dollars and interest rates!"

"Here, here!"

"Tomorrow we save Christmas." Willie cheers.

"Tomorrow we save the North Pole." Sir Louie jeers.

"Tomorrow we save ourselves." Klaus whispers to himself.

11 – CONCERNS OF PRIDE

Overnight the intimate victory party has morphed into an all-out extravaganza.

It isn't until the massive hands of Corporation Clock read 4:00 AM when the party inside the penthouse and surrounding luxury floors slow. Bottles and mistletoe are strewn about the grandiose halls and lounges, while Germans and high-society elves drink side by side, getting very drunk. The debauchery encourages couples of partygoers to run off, even several elves take off with Germans, after enough consumption.

Klaus pours Willie some scotch with a laugh, both inebriated as they *clink* tumblers.

"Credits for you." Klaus says.

"Credits of scotch, I see." Willie laughs.

"A credit, a funny thing." Klaus says, "A promise to pay."

"Funny things, these promises we're always making each other." Willie says.

"A promise to repay in a distant and unpredictable future. A promise exposed to the uncertainty of time." Klaus bumbles tipsily.

"How can anyone make these promises while starring into the abyss of the future?" Willie ponders in his drunkenness.

Klaus holds up his scotch and stares at it. "If they drink too much they'll forget. No one's allowed to forget, so no one's allowed to drink too much, except us."

Willie laughs.

"We'll remind them of all their promises, all the time." Klaus says.

"Laborious." Willie sputters, sipping.

"No doubt, elf, but control over the future is an artform." Klaus taps his watch, enjoying the slow but ever persistent spinning of the second hand. "The credit you grant will be locked into a never-ending wolfsled race against the uncertainty of time."

"How do you know it will work out for the creditor, given the uncertainty of time?" Willie asks.

"Debt neutralizes time and the risks inherent to it. The guilt and burden debtors face will be drilled into them, relentlessly. This bridges the so-called risk of the present with the promise of the future. In case you're wondering, that's good for you, assuming you want be to repaid, good elf."

"It feels funny." Willie admits.

"Cheer up, you're a creditor!" Klaus jostles. "You're free to create your destiny as you see fit. You get to create your future."

"I'm a creditor on behalf of the state, yes, but I'm a simple servant of it." Willie says.

"We're all servants, but you must also let others serve you." Klaus says as he hands Willie a fancy certificate with a grin. The decorated paper reads "North Pole Incorporated: One Million Shares." It's signed by Klaus and Otto with big flamboyant signatures. A stock certificate.

"Your compensation. For all you've done for us, and all you'll continue to do." Klaus says.

"What does this mean?" Willie asks.

"It means you own quite a bit of North Pole Inc. Otto and myself have the largest shares, controlling shares, but Sir Louie and those bureaucrats of his make up the rest of the board and major shareholders."

"Will the workers get any?"

"Once we go public, sure, we'll offer them a discounted price so they can buy a couple shares and feel good about it."

"So, we'd get rich and they wouldn't?"

"Stop worrying about everyone, I want you to worry about yourself. Now go get your workshop back!" Klaus encourages.

Willie is flabbergasted, realizing just how powerful this massive gift of shares is.

"I don't know what to say?" Willie admits.

"I want you to be proud again, truly proud." Klaus says. "The pride that's been stripped of you is exactly the thing you most deserve back."

Willie is stunned by his generosity, smiling ear to ear and hugs Klaus.

"I want it." Willie says.

"Good, now take it." Klaus smiles. "If you need quick cash just sell some shares privately, but not too many, they'll be far more valuable once we go public. They'll be paying dividends, which means paying ourselves out, tremendously. There's a windfall in store for us."

But the reality of the reclaiming the workshop under a new system hits Willie.

"I'd be liable for everything? From the workers to the profitability?" Willie wonders anxiously.

"Again, stop worrying. I've already spoken to Sir Louie and by a wonderful sleight of juridical reasoning mixed with some heavy drinking, it's transpired that ownership and responsibility are vested not only in individuals but *also in corporations*. Corporations under the law will be defined as legal persons, a masterstroke!"

Willie wonders, "So, I couldn't get in trouble for my corporation that represents my business interests? But my corporation could get in trouble? Jail trouble?"

Klaus bursts into laughter, so hard he almost squeals.

"Tell me just how a corporation is supposed to be jailed? Do we handcuff the paper it's written on? Or maybe toss the file folder behind bars?!"

Willie smiles back, loosening up.

"Once we go public you'll be incredibly RICH. You'll have a team of lawyers on staff ready to deal with any issue that comes across your desk."

"I get it." Willie smiles.

"I'd suggest you go get your workshop back before P Day!"

"P day?" Willie asks.

"Production Day!" Klaus says. "Day One of capital in the North Pole."

"The orders are in?" Willie asks.

"Yes, the orders are in from Otto, there're tons, and it's just the start! Now go get your workshop...and pickup something nice for yourself, before you do." Klaus says with a smirk, nodding toward Hanna who's laid out on a velvet lounge chair, smiling at them both. "We all have a weakness for beauty."

"It's true," Willie laughs, "thanks Klaus, I mean it, the workshop means everything."

"Stop it, I'll leave you to it, good elf, and good hunting!" Klaus cheers. "Oh, before you go, I have the most spectacular Steam Whistle being built, I want to show it off, it will be...so loud and shiny."

"A marvelous clock tower, a spectacular steam whistle, how about a Christmas Tree for Christ' sake? It's the North Pole, man." Willie smirks.

"Yes, like the one at Rockefeller Center. But bigger, more elaborate, more decorated!" Klaus stirs.

"I don't know that reference, but yes!" Willie barks.

"Yes, laborers deserve just enough cheer to get on with things, great idea!" Klaus says, skipping back to the bar.

Willie laughs to himself and takes another glance at the fancy stock certificate within his jacket pocket, just over his heart. He relishes at the sight of it and when he looks back up his eyes are locked with Hanna's. He makes his way to her as if she's been expecting him, and she delights with his arrival.

Hanna's several drinks in, evidenced by her flirtatious, boozy gaze. She makes a small space for him as she giggles drunkenly, almost with a snort. He scoots closer, awkward how his feet cannot touch the floor. She pulls him closer. "You've been looking for me, haven't you?" Hanna says as she brushes her arm over his shoulder.

"I've been looking for a banker, yes." He shoots back.

"Baha!" She spouts. "Are you sure that's all I can help with, Mr. Maven?"

He smiles back as coy as an elf can. "I need a line of credit, I have collateral."

"Collateral! Baha! Good, that's very good...Oh collateral, kind of a sexy word, don't you think?"

"Is it?"

"Collateral damage. Unintended destruction. It's kind of dangerous, and kind of sexy, is it not? I like both."

"Collateral and damage?"

"No, danger and sex, obviously."

"Oh." Willie blurts. "I suppose it is." He replies, flashing her the stock certificate. She's impressed by the sum. "But collateral is also a protection against danger."

"Bahaha! That it is, Mr. Maven." Her annoying goatish laugh would normally be a turnoff, but Willie finds it charming in how odd it is, not to mention how her perfectly angled face nullifies her most exasperating qualities.

"A damsel like me appreciates protection." She plays. "Golden Bells Bank takes a hands-on approach with our most valued clients." She says, messaging his back.

"Good, I'll need that." He grins.

But the massage ends and she crawls off the lounge chair and towers over him in a pose which flaunts her haute figure.

"See you soon, Mr. Maven." She says and kisses him goodbye on the lips for a steamy moment before she's gone.

The next morning the sun rises as Willie is joined by Otto. They enter the empty Maven Workshop together. Willie's hungover while Otto is fine, but bummed for missing the extravaganza while traveling back from Reykjavik. It's dead quiet inside, but the rare stillness of the workshop allows the duo to absorb how pristine it is.

Otto is entranced by all the elvish gadgets, machinery, tools and gear. The Maven Workshop has always been provoking and artful in their production, but now it also needs to be profitable, so Otto is here to consult. They need to figure out how to best run operations once Willie's able to officially reacquire it.

"How do we turn this into a money-making venture?" Willie asks.

Otto smiles, he likes to be needed by his friends. They pace around the workshop and visualize all the activities and process that take place.

"What an elegant workshop...it's so...cute." Otto chirps.

"What's beautiful is how elves gets to spend their afternoons on passion projects - like a distinct toy, or something unique and meaningful. They can express themselves through their work, and share that with the world. Those are the presents that make Christmas morning so special, those are the toys kids never forget."

Otto laughs in his face. "That won't fly."

"Why?"

"Because it's all about efficiency, good elf...and scale! You're familiar with these concepts, yes?" Otto asks half-jokingly while Willie maintains his silence. Otto continues, "Efficiency leads to profitability. To be competitive, you must make the production of your workshop highly efficient. You'll have to cut back, by a lot, especially on those so-called passion projects."

"That won't go over well." Willie says. "That's the main reason the workshop has always recruited top talent."

"I wouldn't worry about losing too much talent, soon they'll have nowhere else to turn. Every workshop will have to function productively and profitably, those that don't will go out of business, it's that simple."

"Sounds like you want to turn it into a factory." Willie replies.

"I know, right?" Otto laughs. "Look, when you're the boss you're responsible for profits. Essentially, you must disaggregate the complex activities of the workshop and transform them into specific and simple tasks that can be undertaken by different elves on something like an assembly line."

"But that's how factories operate." Willie says.

"Like I said, there's going to be little difference going forward for those who work with their hands," Otto explains. "There's no room for a middle ground when it comes to your profitability, and you'll be at war with labor, fighting it on two fronts."

"I just want to run my workshop, not fight a two-front war." Willie complains.

"Business and war are similar."

"I wouldn't know." Willie admits.

"I know, that's why they keep me around." Otto says. "First, capitalists like yourself will slowly snatch every profitable factory, workshop and boutique business. Once there's a monopoly over the means of production the workers have no other option but to take part within our system. Many different craft workers could then be brought together under your direction, into a process of collective labor to produce...anything."

"Because there's nowhere left for them to turn to?" Willie asks.

"Yes, and while this happens the factories and workshops that brought these different tasks together will reap huge gains in efficiency, and therefore profits."

"And the second plan of attack?" Willie asks.

"Deskilling." Otto says.

"But we need high skills."

"You actually have a vested interest in degrading them."

"But elves are proud of their skills." Willie says.

"I'm not concerned with their pride, Willie," Otto responds, "I'm only concerned with yours."

"So, we just let them become jaded and disempowered?" Willie stings.

"Which works to your benefit! All you need to remember is it all comes down to your profitability, dear friend."

"You're serious?" Willie asks sharply.

"There'll be bumps but there's a solution to every crisis, as Klaus likes to say." Otto states. "You ought to concern yourself with something I call scientific management. It simplifies the production processes to where a trained gorilla could undertake production tasks."

"Sounds like a zoo factory." Willie says with sarcasm.

"Maven, that's the point. The science I'm talking about is a science of process. Time and motion studies. It's all about the using the techniques of specialization to simplify all the needed tasks to maximize efficiency and minimize costs."

"But the products are complex, Otto. Kids want the best the North Pole has to offer, and this requires skill." Willie protests.

Otto paces, taking in the statement. "I'm not all for the eradication of skills per se but the abolition of monopolizable skills."

"What do you mean?" Willie asks.

"Let's say a new skill become important, like electrical work, then the issue is not necessarily the abolition of those electrical skills, since we need those skills..." Otto says.

"But..."

"But capital must undermine their potential monopoly character by opening up abundant avenues for training."

"Opening up more schools, like trade schools, etcetera?" Willie wonders.

"Yes, and when the labor force is equipped with electrical skills for instance, that grows from a relatively small group to a super-abundant bunch. Hence, their monopoly power is broken and brings down the cost of electrical laborers greatly. When electricians are ten-a-Sugar Dollar then we capitalists should be happy to identify them as skilled laborers. We can give them some fancy pins, pretty certificates, maybe a three to five percent raise, or something like that. Recognition comes cheap. Real reward is emotional, not fiscal."

"So, these skilled laborers can to become capitalists, per se?" Willie asks.

"Sure, cute tiny capitalists who feel important making big money for their bosses. Those dogs would love to be called capitalists, but they aren't capitalists like you or I!" Otto corrects. "Let's just call them the upper-middle class. They'll be in charge of 'expert' opinions, like lawyers practicing law, managerial level bankers, or manipulators of symbols and such. It gives the lower classes something to aspire to, another carrot for good behavior within the system."

Suddenly the front doors swing open, it's Sticky and the Ickles, and they're not thrilled at the sight of Otto.

"Willie? I didn't expect to see you here." Sticky says, surprised.

Willie grins and approaches him gently. "I'm buying you out, Sticky."

"I'd be happy to employ you Sir, but the workshop is simply not for sale." Sticky answers.

"It has and always will be the Maven Workshop, 'ol Stick. You'll still run the day to day with your boys."

"But you haven't even approached me and now telling me what to do again." Sticky yaps.

"I'm approaching you now, why else do you think I'm here?" Willie says as he pulls a fancy fountain pen from his jacket pocket and walks right up Sticky. "At least entertain my offer, ol' Stick."

"What offer?"

"Be a gentleman and I'll give you one."

"I'm an elf and so are you." Sticky replies sternly.

"Then be a gentle-elf, semantics, Sticky, jeez! Now stick out your palm."

Sticky isn't amused but he abides, "This better be good."

Willie takes his fountain pen and writes a large Sugar Dollar figure out on Sticky's hand, the tip of the pen sharply chiseling into his hardened skin with a pinch of pain.

"What's this?" Sticky asks.

"My offer." Willie replies.

Sticky looks back down at his hand, smiles and faints plummeting to the ground with a PLOP! Willie laughs and looks to the Ickles. "I think we have a deal, congratulations, your family is now very rich."

Willie looks to the Otto, "I need to make a trip to the bank to get a check for these boys."

Before departing Willie takes a glance at all the machinery, contemplating how it's all powered through the sugar power plants. "And let's calculate how much our energy costs will be. Significant, I'm sure." Willie says.

"It will be much cheaper for us to burn the coal instead." Otto replies. "Coal burns well and we'll be able to buy plenty once revenue comes in."

"We have tons of it here in the North Pole." Willie replies. "Hasn't Santa left you coal before? You strike me as a deviant child."

"Hah! I had my moments." Otto yelps. "If there're tons of it here then it should come cheap."

"But Santa didn't want to burn it, he called it dirty energy, bad for the environment."

"Dirty energy, hilarious." Otto mumbles.

"How is that funny?"

"The environment? Who cares! Coal is cheap and that's all that matters!" Otto yells. "Didn't I just teach you anything?"

"Still learning, I guess." Willie says as he throws on his new shades and fancy deep green peacoat. As Willie leaves through the front entrance he nearly bumps into Hanna who's rushing in.

"Hanna!"

"Willie, just the elf I've come to see." She says.

"Funny I was on my way to see you."

"At my bank or bedroom?"

"The bank?"

"Bahah. I'm just joking Willie, you sailor. But I offer a hands-on approach, remember?" She says as she playfully pulls on his lapel.

"Right." He blushes.

"Now about that line of credit, let's get you signed up." She flirts. "And where are you living these days?"

"Around...empty offices and whatnot." Willie says as Hanna snorts another goatish laugh.

"What's whatnot?"

"Um - sometimes my friend's barn." He admits.

"No woman wants to be taken back to a barn!" She blurts.

"Perhaps a lady centaur would."

"Bah! Funny! A centaur! Are those real too?" She asks.

"Yes."

"Are you serious?"

"No."

"Oh – they're not?"

"Are you serious?"

"Never mind, Willie! I'm still getting use to the fact that elves exist, my sense of reality has been majorly tampered."

"Centaurs exist!" Willie shouts.

"Really!?'"

"No!" He spits, laughing hysterically to himself.

"Just for that you're going to get a mortgage from me too. A big one for a big place downtown, maybe not too far from me." She says as she throws herself into his arms.

"Sounds extravagant."

"The best or nothing, Willie. Come on now."

Hanna leans up on him, pretending he's keeping her warm as they stride outside with her piercing blue eyes locking into his.

"Right." He says to Hanna's delight, becoming lost in the prettiness of her doll-face.

"I'll have your workshop's line of credit and personal mortgage ready before Production Day. Until then I think you should enjoy your barn, I'm no centaur, you see." She walks off.

"Thanks Hanna." He bumbles.

She turns back with some concern. "You want to be rich, right? Because I don't want to waste your time and I don't waste mine either."

"I do. You have no idea."

"Good!" She smiles back, blowing him a kiss on her departure

12 – THE STEAM WHISTLE
AND
THE CHRISTMAS TREE

Willie and Ursus are passed out in the barn until a loud knocking wakes them. Willie checks his pocket watch, Ursus growls, it's 5:00 AM, way too early.

"Wake up." Says Renee from outside.

Ursus offers a tired growl in response.

"I'm coming in." She announces and enters. She stands over Willie, playfully nudging him to wake.

"What'd I do to deserve such torture?" Willie smiles.

"Klaus wants you at the Steam Whistle ceremony, pronto." She says, before inspecting her secret library. It's composed of books she's snagged from her father's private library, it's mostly 19th Century literature and philosophical treatise. She considers which titles to revisit as she thumbs through the spines, paying particular attention to *Capital: A Critical Analysis of Capitalist Production*, *Moby Dick*, *A Tale of Two Cities*, and *The Napoleon of Notting Hill*.

After a moment, she slides Capital decisively off the shelf with a coy smile.

"That man's more obsessed with ceremonies than Santa." Willie says as Renee applies pressure into his ribs.

"Come on, let's go, you've got a big P-Day ahead!" She says layered in sarcasm, though it's true.

"Yes, happy P-Day?" He says, wondering if that's an actual expression.

"The happiest of Production Day's to you."

Willie gets up from the scratchy hay bed and splashes water across his face. By the time the water is out of his eyes Renee has "Capital" right up in his face.

"You should read this."

Willie raises an eyebrow, skeptical and intimidated just by how thick it is. He cracks open the book to skim some lines. "It's dense. What is it?"

"An analysis of capital. You know, the system that you and these Germans are implementing. It turns out it isn't all Rainbows."

"That's too bad." Willie says dismissively.

"I'm serious."

"I'm too busy to read a...million-page book. And I've got a ceremony to run to!" He says.

"If you understand the flaws of the system you can make a lot of money."

"Then maybe I should read it," he chuckles.

"You could make a lot of money - or try to change the world for the better. One is easy, and the other is unimaginably difficult."

"No need to make life more difficult than it already is, 'eh."

"How disappointing," she blurts. "If you read it don't do it for me, do it for yourself. Just know there's no un-reading it. Once you understand how it works there are moral decisions to be made. Either way you're guilty – it's what you do with that knowledge that counts."

"I don't love making so called moral decisions."

"Maybe some things you're better off not understanding after all." She says with a sting.

"Don't worry, I'll be out of your hair soon." He says defensively, brushing his teeth with a mouthful of spearmint toothpaste.

"Moving already?" She asks, hiding a sadness that permeates just beneath the surface. "You just got here."

"Yes, moving downtown, to a big ol' flat."

"Sad, to think I was getting use to you in my barn." She replies.

"A real bachelor pad for a real bachelor."

"Just when you me convinced you were a simple elf. I hate it when I'm so easily deceived."

"I love the barn, don't get me wrong." He says. "Would've been great if someone visited a little more often. But now you'll have to swing by the pad!"

"Swing by the pad?"

"Yeah, swing by the pad!" He cheers. "What are your P-Day plans?"

"A lunch date with Ginger, she's collaborating with the guilds and the working elves that make up 99% of the population."

"Does your Dad know?"

"What do you think? And don't tell him either."

"Maybe you'd like to work for me?" Willie suggests, but he's answered with an offended stare. "Maybe you'd like to work *with* me?" He reattempts.

"Doesn't something about this whole 'market experiment' feel off?" She asks.

"Sure, but what are our alternatives?"

"Now you sound like one of them."

Willie realizes it's true, but it doesn't bother him as much as he expected it might. He shrugs his shoulders to her dismay.

"Happy P-Day." She repeats before storming off.

Later that morning, Willie, Klaus, Otto, Sir Louie and many administrative staffers and sycophants are back on the penthouse balcony of Santa's Tower. It's just before dawn as the sky above the Arctic Range lightens. Everyone in the Square monitors Corporation Clock just below the penthouse.

Klaus taps Willie's shoulder, "Isn't she beautiful?" He whispers. Willie smiles and nods, before protecting his ears again as they stare up at the latest addition to Santa's Tower; the slender, pure silver, North Pole Steam Whistle, overhead and atop of the tower dome. It's only moments before 6:00 AM as Klaus double checks his pocket-watch and motions everyone to place their hands over their ears like he is.

As the sun rises the rays break past the mountains and reflect off the polished silver, making the whistle glisten brightly like a hopeful beacon. Klaus relishes in its shiny brilliance, his smile almost as radiant as the glorious whistle itself.

The second-hand of Corporation Clock steadily rounds and hits the twelve as the whistle *bursts aloud* with a surprisingly powerful SONIC FORCE, produced by concentrated steam rushing through its narrow mouth, ringing in Production Day with the power of a *BOOM*, as its forceful shockwaves knock several elvish staffers to the floor as Klaus laughs and laughs.

The shockwaves rattle the city like an earthquake, with a physical rippling echo visible as it disperses outward like the waves of a stone tossed into a pond. The force of the boom travels all the way to the Arctic Range, evidenced by the ferocious avalanche cascading down the mountains.

"Hahaha! Now that's how you ring in *Production Day!*" Klaus barks, clapping vigorously with everyone joining.

As the morning sunlight fills the sky they watch with amusement as the quiet cobblestone streets transform into rambunctious flowing arteries, as if the boom of the Steam Whistle were an electric shock reviving the very heart of the northern-most civilization. With it, all activity returns to life. It almost looks like how things were, but only this time it's guided by the invisible hand of the market and the motive of profit.

"Now isn't that something." Klaus says.

"Shouldn't you be off to your workshop?" Sir Louie asks Willie.

"I was thinking I'd stop by the Reserve first." Willie says.

"Why waste time on P-Day? The Reserve lends to the banks at 3%, the banks lend to the elves at 6%, and the bankers are out ice skating by 3:00PM. 3-6-3." Sir Louie states.

"3-6-3. I like that, Klaus says.

"Very simple." Sir Louie says.

"I suppose you're right, then I'm off to the workshop. Straight to the center of production!"

Klaus laughs to himself, "The center of production no longer resides within the walls of the workshop or factory, it has drifted outside its walls. *Society itself is now the workshop! Society itself is now the factory!* And we're all enterprise individuals with it."

"Right. Happy P-Day, gentlemen." Willie says.

"Oh, Willie." Klaus stops him before he gets too far. "Big tree lighting ceremony tonight, per your suggestion. It is the North Pole after all."

"Yes, great, more ceremonies." Willie says with sarcasm.

"Life is to be celebrated, my friend! We found the most magnificent evergreen. We'll light it in the traditional fashion, with candles, ornaments, the whole nine. A proper, traditional Christmas celebration to honor proper traditions!"

"Awesome."

Later, Willie is happy to see the streets and pace of the North Pole restored to its former magnificence. He's about to enter the Maven Workshop but spots his old factory friends Bushy and Alabaster wondering.

"Bushy, Alabaster! What are you doing? How are you doing!?" Willie yells.

"Willie, good to see you!" Alabaster shouts.

"Actually hun, we're lost, can you help?" Bushy asks.

"Where do you want to go?' Willie asks.

"Looking for a job, aren't you? Bushy asks as Willie laughs.

"Look no further my friends! This is my workshop, we're busy and need part-timers, so come aboard!"

"Wait, you're Willie...Maven?" Alabaster asks as Willie nods. "Thought you were just messin'.

"*Holy ham!*" Bushy blabs.

"Get in here you little rascals!" Willie demands.

Together they enter the boisterous Maven Workshop producing at full steam ahead. Sticky and the Ickles rush to properly greet the boss and his friends.

"Glad to see you back on your feet, 'ol Stick!" Willie smiles.

"As am I, Sir, very much so." Sticky says, helping them all change into their workshop apparel.

"Alabaster and Bushy are two new part-timers, please show them around and get them started on something pertinent." Willie says as the Ickles whisk them away.

"Sir, all is moving forward but not without the help of some minor miracles performed by yours truly." Sticky says.

"Naturally – goes without saying..."

"My miracle making to be reflected in my bonus?" Sticky poses.

"We'll talk about it."

"Good." Sticky hands a small handwritten manual to Willie, it's titled "Just In Time Production."

"Your German friend Otto wrote this for us, once you left for the bank the other day. I've been studying, it's very interesting, quite different from how we used to do things around here." Sticky says.

"Fascinating." Willie replies.

"Our production depends on orders streaming inward."

Sticky says as Willie flips through the manual, intrigued.

"Very well." Willie remarks as he reads a couple of lines aloud while skimming. "Productivity gains are tied to the production of small quantities of many products, reducing defective output to zero and immediately responding to market fluctuations." Willie hums, considering.

Sticky picks out a passage, reads; "The Maven Workshop must become 'minimalist' in that everything exceeding market demand should be eliminated. Implement 'zero-stock' strategies as soon as you see an increase in unsold merchandise. There should be a prompt intervention to eliminate the causes of overproduction, either by getting rid of workers or of machinery (but most likely workers). *What's important is the elimination of all redundancy.* You'd be wise to await my sales report, because effective sales directly command orders and therefore, production. With this strategy your workshop will remain highly competitive."

"Interesting." Willie says.

"You'll fire elves when there are no orders to fill?" Sticky inquires with concern.

"Fire is a strong word - layoff sounds better."

"Oy." Sticky replies with distaste.

"We have to remain competitive." Willie says. "Otherwise the whole workshop goes bust. The stakes have never been higher."

"Then how do laid-off workers pay their bills?" Sticky asks.

"For better or worse I don't believe that's our concern."

"I see." Sticky shoots.

"You'll always have a job, ol' Stick, you're my Chief Operations Officer for god' sake. I think we'll need more of these part-timers, like Alabaster and Bushy. They're very...precariously employed and know it. They're lucky to have a job and I'm happy to give them one when I can. We need more freelancers and independent contractors, or call them consultants, who cares."

"Why do we need that type of employee over salaried ones?"

Sticky asks.

"Because they're cheap, easy to fire, easy to hire and we don't have to pay for all of those expensive benefits and bonuses. Only top caliber elves like yourself and your boys are worthy." Willie says.

"So, when they're unemployed hopefully they have enough saved to sustain?" Sticky asks.

"It's their responsibility to save, and their responsibility to be responsible." Willie yelps.

"I see." Sticky replies.

A messenger elf rushes in, spots Willie, and presents him with a fancy envelope which he rips open revealing a note from Ernst von Wolf;

"It's a gold rush Willie, they're privatizing everything! Markets where markets didn't exist before! Education, Health Care, Unemployment Insurance, Coal, Land, Utilities, you name it - it's all for sale. Come quick! Get to my office and place your bids before they're all snatched!"

"Got to run, Sticky." Willie utters.

"But you just got here." Sticky protests.

"You're a good elf, 'ol Stick. Oh, and it looks like the unemployed can buy unemployment insurance. How great is that? Our scheme is really coming together, so stop worrying."

"But I'm a worrywart, Sir!"

"I know and that's why I love you – but get over it, like me!" Willie exclaims as he hurriedly redresses into his business suit. "Buy, buy, buy!" He smirks in his rush out.

"Bye bye bye, Sir?" Sticky asks.

"Never mind, goodbye!"

After racing Ursus through the streets Willie bursts into

Ernst's private office at Golden Bells Bank, huffing and puffing as Ernst perks up in delight.

"More excited to see me than my sister!" Ernst laughs as Willie blushes.

"At the moment."

"Relax, I've got no problem with an...interracial relationship, if you can call it that. I know you don't have the size of the equipment to satisfy, but..."

"Do you always talk about your sister like this?"

"She's a man eater, I'm trying to be a good friend and warn you!"

"Then good thing I'm an elf!" Willie says.

"I think that only makes you more digestible, and sweet." Ernst sniggers.

"I'm not sure she's even interested in me like that." Willie says.

"Oh, she is, at least right now. If you ask me, she's just going through an 'elf phase,' but you know how women are, getting it 'out of her system,' so on and so forth...You're in prime position to take advantage, you sailor!"

"I don't 'take advantage,' in fact, she's probably taking advantage of me."

"Bahah!" He laughs goatishly like his sister. "You'll need that sense of humor...not to mention the motion of the ocean to compensate...for your shortcomings!" Ernst chuckles.

"Good one."

"I try, I try!"

"So, what does my banker have for me?" Willie asks.

"Please consider Golden Bells Bank as your investment management team as well." Ernst says.

"Whatever you sell you'll be earning a fat commission on,

yes?"

"Of course, that's how it works! And with Klaus and Sir Louie agreeing to privatize everything it's become a massive government sell off, it's like a feast!"

"Why are they doing this?" Willie wonders.

"More money for the government, more money circulating through the financial system. More space for capital accumulation. *Our capital must accumulate – that's its only purpose.*" Ernst preaches.

"So that the likes of you and I grow even richer?" Willie says.

"No need to feel guilty about it, that's just the way it is. Profit to the entrepreneur! Profit to the risk taker! Besides, the legitimacy of the whole movement is already successfully underpinned with the selling off of housing to tenants. The universal dream of individual property ownerships is becoming satisfied, and it's only just begun. Look at them relishing at the liberation of entrepreneurial opportunities.

"I see." Willie utters.

"To get rich is glorious!"

"That has a nice ring." Willie smiles.

"It does, now, what would you like to buy today?" Ernst grins and slides him a list of options as if it were a menu.

Willie takes in his enthusiasm and becomes more enthusiastic himself. "How about steel?"

"Mostly bought up, shares are on the rise, give that a beat to cool," Ernst fires.

"I'm actually interested in unemployment insurance. A society that cares for their unemployed is vital."

"I haven't heard any buyers say anything like that, but yes, a great idea. Securitized unemployment insurance bonds can be made available, cheap and Triple-A rated! What else?"

"What do you recommend?" Willie asks.

"Real Estate is safe and exploding in value. There are entire apartment buildings available for pennies on the dollar, especially near the Tinsel Factory. Some need improvements but even a modest investment would multiply its value." Ernst says. "Want one?"

"Done! Buy me one!" Willie shouts.

"What else?!" Ernst laughs.

"Coal." Willie says with intrigue.

"Interesting." Ernst hesitates. "Haven't had a bid on the coal reserves yet. Who'd buy that for Christmas? There's no Santa dishing out coal and this whole place runs on sugar, seems irrelevant, risky." Ernst says.

"Irrelevant until it isn't. High risk high reward, right?" Willie says.

"Oh my, you're getting me excited now." Ernst says. He takes a beat and thinks about it. "Chipper!" Ernst shouts as his nimble elf assistant, Chipper, rushes in.

"Yes Mr. von Wolf?"

"Chipper, remind me to buy a slice of the coal reserves." Ernst smiles. "Mr. Maven is *turning me on*, to it."

"Yes, sir!" Chipper says before disappearing back to his desk.

"Gross."

"Is that all?" Ernst asks.

"Yes, for now." Willie says. "Please take strong positions, I don't need my money sitting in the bank earning pennies on interest when it can be in the market really working."

"Couldn't agree more, Maven. So, it's coal, real estate and unemployment insurance bonds. A healthy, diverse portfolio. Great start!"

"Amazing, thank you." Willie says.

"The transfer of assets from the public and popular to the private and privileged truly is." Ernst smiles back. "And for so cheap,

143

too!"

"To get rich is glorious." Willie replies as the two shake hands to seal the deal.

"To get rich is glorious." Ernst repeats with a wide smile. "Now go check out your new real estate investment, why don't you!" Ernst says.

"I think I will." Willie replies.

In a flash Willie and Ursus gallop through the streets as the geography of the townscape shifts noticeably, trotting from what was Workshop Society into what was Factory Society. The Tinsel Factory is near the border of the two. It's loud and busy, churning out tinsel at a rapid pace while pouring an exhaust that stinks of burned sugar.

They continue a few blocks east and further into what was Factory Society before coming upon Willie's new apartment building investment. It's in okay shape, but a far cry from the flats a few blocks west. A property on the up and up, Willie likes to think.

Ursus slides across the icy street as they arrive at the front entrance. They're greeted by a strange, fat elf with crooked teeth. He's dressed in suspenders, wears thick rubber boots and hides an old leather belt in the back pocket of his pants, as if he's ready to quick draw the belt and use it as a whip.

"Mr. Maven, Mr. Maven! A pleasure, a great pleasure!" He greets. "Name's Mr. Snowball, but you can just call me Snowball!"

A funny name considering how he resembles a snowball, Willie thinks.

"The pleasure is mine, all mine!" Snowball reiterates. "Thank you, Sir."

"What for, Snowball?" Willie asks, as he shakes his lumpy hand with caution.

"For making me a very rich elf is all!" Snowball chuckles, "and saving me from that ghastly tinsel factory."

"I didn't realize I purchased the building from you, Snowball." Willie says to his surprise.

"Well yes, I was the longtime manager at the Tinsel Factory and hence the longtime manager at what we like to call the dormitory. My boss, Mr. Billingsworth, the Tinsel Factory owner was kind enough to consider me the de facto owner of the dormitory." Snowball explains.

"I image that I somehow purchased the building from all the elves who lived there."

"Funny imagination you have, Sir. I guess in a sense you did. I mean, I bought out all the units from 'em first. Unfortunately, you just can't kick these *little buggers* out without payin' em...Purchased at cents on the dollar - HAHA. But it comes as a profit to them, just as you buying me out comes as a profit to me – and in good time you'll have a profit too. Anyway, all those lil' buggers were happy to have received their unexpected Sugar Nickels, then bugger off! HAHA." Snowball literally spits.

"Congratulations." Willie says wryly, wiping his face of spit.

"Thank you. Retirement here I come HAHA," Snowball shouts. "And lucky for you, Sir, a whole new batch of workers have moved in. They're calling it a sexy 'up-and-coming part of town' because of all those little art galleries dotted about. The rent will be too high for 'em soon, but until then they're here all right. The building is completely occupied and all you have to do is collect the rent!"

"Fantastic." Willie says.

"And if any of these lil' buggers give you a hard time 'bout paying you, just let me know." Snowball sneers as he pulls out his belt from his back pocket. "I'm like the stepfather they've never had, and boy I love dishin' a good beltin'!"

"I will...call you." Willie says, anything to get Snowball on his way.

"Gosh, I don't know what I'll do with myself if I don't have any lil' nuggets to belt. Call on me, Sir, seriously. I'll need it to keep sane."

"I, um...will, yes."

"You've come in at a great time. Speculators like you are just buying everything up, prices are risin' and risin'. Lucky for you I'm craving a new venture, otherwise I would've held onto the place!" Snowballs says. "So grateful we managers are to be de facto owners of something! There's much money to be made here for the likes of us lucky few." Snowball replies.

"Perhaps more to be made in real estate speculation than the whole of production." Willie thinks out loud.

"One can always make money on housin' by buyin' low and sell high." Snowball says.

"In a funny way, increasing house prices makes us all feel like we're all becoming wealthier – *but it also means that our future generations will have to pay more for the same property.*" Willie blurts.

"Yes, the banks prefer speculative lending, Sir." Snowball says. "If I were to gander, it's safer for them to put a loan on something they can foreclose on. Better than watching their money disappear into thin air if and when a small business fails."

"I see." Willie replies.

"You should see some of these ol' factory workers trying to open their own tiny tinsel operations – they're all bound to go bust and soon! Meanwhile real estate is special!" Snowball spits.

"I guess you're right Snowball, houses are both a necessity and a luxury – *an ideal vehicle for money and bubble creation*...Getting out now before the bubble pops? Well played."

"Don't know about all of that, Sir."

"You should. There's no net gain for the whole economy when real estate increases – because it's nonproductive. Some get to gain now, like you, while most others will suffer later, by having to pay more."

"I'll believe it when I see it, Sir." Snowball yaps.

"Is it not inevitable?" Willie asks, "When the increase of home values don't create new jobs or lead to productivity. It's just a redistribution of wealth to those who own homes. The same who already wealthy."

"That may be, Sir, but that's how the banks like it." Snowballs argues.

"If a lot of bank money goes into mortgages, which as we know, don't add to actual productivity, the increased speculation only leads to inflation. Inflation means everyone's money is worth less. It becomes a tax on everyone, which hurts some much more than others, mostly the poor."

"That may be so, Sir, but you and I are in the fortunate position to take advantage of the situation."

"Ah, of course." Willie says matter-of-fact.

"At least you know your investment is protected when the officials are buying in. They wouldn't allow themselves a volatile position. Smart to piggy back off that."

"Right again, Snowball." Willie says.

"I'm smart, that's why I was the *manager*."

"Smart's an understatement, genius is more like it. Don't sell yourself short my elf!" Willie says.

"Thank you, Sir! Genius status unlocked, HAHA!" Snowball chuckles.

Willie paces and looks at the structure, wondering about the elves who once lived there. "Where'd the old tenants go?" He asks.

"Out of the city center, that much is certain." Snowball says. "The speculation on real estate has made everything from restaurants to retail expensive. The cost of living here has gone up quite a lot. The merchants need to mark everything up just to cover their rent. The businesses that don't own their real estate are in real trouble."

"Most of the locals have already moved out?" Willie asks.

"Yes, whip-fast, HAHA. Get it?

"Yes, sadly."

"They're off to the periphery, where the tundra meets the city's edge. It's a long commute for 'em."

"What portion of their income is used on rent here?" Willie asks.

"At least a third, maybe half." Snowball states.

"Half? That's massive."

"Life's expensive." Snowball says. "But if they want to save money on rent, let 'em commute hours if they must, not our concern. The true value is the value in which the property can be exchanged! That's my genius, Mr. Maven, uses no long matter, *only exchange does.* And I so appreciate you recognizing my insight."

"Don't be so humble, Snowball. Go on, I'm intrigued by your theories of value."

"Well, you extract rent, so there's your value. The government wins from those ridiculously high property taxes, the developers of new real estate win on profits earned from housing construction, and the bank wins on both ends, profiting from interest on developers and speculators, and then again in the form of mortgage payments from the new homeowners paying up the wazoo!"

"Ok – assume they're prosperous enough to live in a neighborhood like this, how are the elves living in these buildings supposed to save money?" Willie asks.

"I don't think they can, Sir. Not if they want to live this...'high class lifestyle' - HAHA!" Snowballs belts, Willie clueless as to what Snowball is talking about since there's nothing high class about this whole crowded, polluted situation, minus the high rent, that is.

"Right." Willie says curiously as Snowball picks up on his confusion. "So, saving for this breed of elf is some kind of joke. Even what they win in terms of small pay raises is captured back by the likes of landlords, merchants, bankers, lawyers and commission agents."

"True."

"And like a cruel joke a large chunk of what's left goes to the taxman?" Willie ponders.

"Correct, Sir." Snowball states.

"Fascinating." Willie says sadly. "How do you know all of this?"

"Well, once you follow the logic of profit everything falls into place."

Willie doesn't know how to reply, transcending into a haze as he reministes on Klaus's concept that the bulk of workers are to be paid only what's needed for them to survive and reproduce. He snaps back to reality.

"This profit logic is concerning, Snowball, see I'm hiring part-timers, short term contractors. If workers can barely afford to sustain life with a job. I'm not sure how an elf will ever sustain without one."

"That's why I'm going to open up a payday loan business!" Snowball blurts. "After I take some time off for a little rest and relaxation, and beltin' that is."

"Belting?"

"Beltin' yes, beltin'. Guess I can't truly retire, I have an active mind, you see."

"Ok." Willie rabbles, he knows Snowball means it literally. "Why payday loans?"

"So those numskulls can get their money up front and I get to charge high interest. They'll need more loans and more credit to buy up all the things they think they need. Especially as the cost of living goes up and up."

"Hell, of a phrase, isn't it - 'cost of living?' The cost of life itself, what a burden." Willie scoffs. "Funny to already be in debt for merely existing, and the Germans say it's only the Christ of Christmas who can absorb those debts and free us from our inherent sin."

"I'm not inherently bad." Snowball scoffs back.

"Are you kidding, Snowball, yes, you are, just look at yourself. You're like...the worst!"

"I don't understand, Sir, how so?!" Snowball asks. "I'm just looking out for my own opportunity. Those who do so are said to be making the whole of the new system work. I'm doing God's work, they say!"

"God sacrificing himself for our sinful debt is nothing other than God paying himself back. The great creditor sacrificing himself for his debtor, out of love for his debtor." Willie replies.

"But I'm no Christ, Sir." Snowball admits. "And I'm intent on collecting the debt owed to me just as much as that German banker is. I appreciate the logic of their...religion, because embedded within it are concepts representative of Christmas; that we're indebted to our beginnings is logical. This new system rings of truth!"

"I don't know about all that, Snowball." Willie replies.

"Then perhaps you're a dirty atheist!" Snowball accuses.

"Hah - perhaps!" Willie shouts back. "But Snowball, what are you selling as a payday lender if not the time that elapses between the moment you lend the money and the moment you are repaid with interest? Time belongs solely to God, does it not?"

"Perhaps I'm awakening the sense of god that lives within me!"

"Or perhaps you're just a thief of time, a usurer who steals God's patrimony." Willie accuses.

"Maybe I am!" Snowball yells.

"Fine!" Willie yells.

"Fine!" Snowball yells.

Snowball casually tosses Willie the key after he catches his breath.

"Great meeting you, Sir. I enjoyed this...conversation."

"The pleasure was all mine, Snowball, all mine."

"No, no, all mine, Sir!"

"Right, fine."

"Perhaps our paths will cross again." Snowball says.

"God, I hope not, for their sake." Willie nods toward the passing tenants as Snowball makes a big belly laugh, holding onto his lardy jiggling gut, chuckling hard as if he were Santa himself.

Afternoon turns to evening as Willie, Alabaster and Bushy ride Ursus. The couple having the best time on their first bear ride en route to the tree lighting ceremony, until Willie is struck with concern.

"You know the workshop pays an unemployment insurance tax. If that old fart Sticky were to lay you off the state will send you a check. It'd be small, so you might want to buy unemployment insurance just in case." Willie tells them.

"We're a bit squeezed for funds." Alabaster says.

"It'd be worth it, trust me." Willie reaffirms.

"I've looked into it." Bushy says to their surprise. "Everything that Santa used to provide now comes at a cost. We can't afford it."

"Never realized how much we've taken for granted. How many things we had for free that's now prohibitively expensive." Alabaster says.

"I see your point, still fill out those forms and send me the bill." Willie says. "I mean it."

They arrive at the Square just before tree lighting ceremony. The Christmas Tree is as large and splendid as Klaus promised, standing many stories high and surrounded by a small army of elves placing the final decorations. The tree looks at home in the Square, amid all the things central to the North Pole, standing next to the Belief Meter, Santa's Tower, the North Pole Steam Whistle and Corporation Clock.

It's magic hour, just before sunset. The sky and mountains glow in a sherbet palette of yellow, orange, pink and purple. The golden, soft light illuminates the Christmas Tree creating a beaming halo around it, giving the scene a consuming, divine quality that magnetizes attention.

At the base of the tree are large canisters filled with a fire preventative substance. Nobody notices a *mysterious figure* swapping out the canisters with another set of identical looking ones. The elves spray down the tree, while the crowd is entertained by the North Pole Color Guard and orchestra playing "Winter Wonderland" in brilliant fashion, keeping the crowd distracted until the tree is ready.

Ursus zigzags through the Square and charges up a massive spiral staircase until they find Klaus's party balcony, arriving in style as Klaus flags them down and Ursus slides to a stop.

"Always making an entrance." Klaus smiles, looking dressy for the occasion with his hair slicked back. Willie hops off and introduces Alabaster and Bushy to Klaus and then Sir Louie. At first the two newcomers feel out of place among high society until Klaus welcomes them with chalices of eggnog.

Willie cozies up to Klaus, "No tip about the privatizations? Just when I thought we were friends. I had to hear from my accountant." He jokes.

"He's your investment banker." Klaus laughs. "I can't give you every tip. You'd have a monopoly over the North Pole within weeks."

"Don't worry, I've still done quite well."

"I'm sure you have." Klaus titters. "So have I."

Willie's laughter quiets as Renee approaches. She's striking, dressed in a beautiful draping purple gown. She too wears a traditional green elf hat. She's stunning, armed with an easy smile and wavy blonde hair that flows effortlessly behind her every stride, moving in sync with the soft bounce of her gown. Willie greets her with a hug, and Klaus kisses her hand.

Together the three take in the splendor of the scene below. With a gentle wave of the conductor's baton the orchestra plays "Silent Night" as elves connected to an intricate pulley system glide through the air and light every candle on their way up to the top of the tree. The tree illumines, revealing the exquisiteness of the twinkling decorations, shining magnificently for all to admire.

The pulley system and towers are quickly disassembled.

Within moments Klaus points with excitement as an elf goes

airborne, tied to a set of colorful balloons in his ascent. At the top of the tree he extends his torch to light the last candle set within the hands of an angel ornament. The lighting is complete as the orchestra hits its grand finale, creating an undeniably serene sight. The shimmering tree unifies the crowd with a sense of oneness and pride that moves them deeply. It touches Renee too, compelling her to inch closer to Willie. He feels her presence, and as he contemplates reaching for her hand...

While a dancing flame makes its way onto the pine needles...

And the *branch catches fire.*

In a *flash* branch after branch go up, spreading the *blaze* instantly as if the tree were lacquered with fuel, which it evidently is. In moments the entire tree BURSTS INTO FLAMES. Burning hellishly as the crowd stampedes over each other as they scurry to escape the fiery debris raining down upon them.

Willie grabs Renee's hand, but does so in haste, and rushes her to Ursus amid the state of confusion. He and Klaus dash off the balcony and into the city Square, pushing forward as the current of chaos rushes past. Together they absorb the violent, visceral destruction. Within moments the massive fireball of a tree is reduced to a heaping pile of ash while the jarring sounds of panic and dismay morph into the silence of nothingness.

Behind the mound of ash Willie and Klaus spot the *dark hooded figure* looking right at them. The being holds up a fist that grips an envelope and slides it underneath a heavy, cracked ornament, before slipping back into the darkness.

Willie and Klaus make their way to the envelope amid the storm of swirling ash. They rip it open, "Gifts to the unions or coal in your stockings? A coal that will ignite and burn your workshops as bright as this tree. The choice is yours."

The threat gives Willie an eerie chill but to his bewilderment Klaus only chuckles...

13 – INITIAL PUBLIC OFFERING

One-week later Willie and Klaus are back at the penthouse of Santa's Tower. It's calmer and more decadent than before, as if they're getting use to their power. Alabaster joins them as Willie's new personal butler.

It's the start of the day as Willie and Klaus drink their whiskey filled coffees, their new favorite beverage, and they sip while enjoying their new favorite hobby - listening to the *clicking* of Otto's toy orders printing on the long ribbons of tickertape. They adore how the tickertape curls up into a messy pile as it runs out of space to elongate.

Most noticeably, Willie and Klaus have upgraded their wardrobes, flaunting loud pinstripe shirts, stylish, colorful silk ties and sleek navy-blue three-piece suits. As their coffees run low Alabaster refills with more whiskey.

"Thank you..." Klaus says, trying to remember the elf's name as he squints into his eyes.

"Alabaster." Willie says, re-introducing him to Klaus. "My new butler during the day and worker at night."

"I admire your dedication, Alabaster," Klaus says. "It takes something special to put up with this one all day. What's your commitment, 50 hours a week?"

"Closer to 80 hours, Sir."

"Hard work, a real virtue of the North Pole." Klaus says.

"I'll do anything required to survive, Sir."

Klaus doesn't know how to respond except by providing a firm nod.

In the distance Klaus points out the improvements to the Belief Meter. "She's almost there," Klaus smiles. "We go public tomorrow, big party when we ring in NPI."

"Everybody knows how you love a big party." Willie says as he takes another swig of his Irish Coffee before sharing what's really on his mind.

"You don't think it was Ginger behind the blaze?"

"She's fiery, but only in the crotch." Klaus laughs, "The curtains must match the drapes, 'eh?"

"I wouldn't know." Willie replies.

"Shame, you should."

"You don't think it was her?"

"She's a politician, not a fanatic." Klaus says. "Too bad she isn't a woman of industry."

"Maybe it's an underling of hers?" Willie asks.

"You should bring her to the IPO, for a peppering of questions." Klaus suggests.

"A light interrogation?" Willie asks.

"Why not?" Klaus laughs dismissively, which strikes Willie as odd.

A new series of buzzing beeps out. Klaus jumps over to the freshly printed tickertape.

"Ah, these orders are perfect for the Maven Workshop."

Klaus studies the tape, then rips off a long ribbon and hands over the orders to Willie, placing the massive order literally in his hands.

"Infinite thanks." Willie smiles.

"Thank me infinitely tomorrow, after we go public on the stock exchange! Then you'll be infinitely rich! So rich you won't know what to do with all of your money." Klaus says.

"Hell of a problem to have." Willie laughs as he takes another swig.

"Once we're public, the stock price is the only thing that will matter. The price per share. If we must bleed to make it rise then so be it. We must push the value higher and higher at all costs."

"Then production isn't relevant?" Willie asks

"I didn't say that, but perception is the priority. Perception is reality."

"I see."

"We manage perception through the story we tell and the financial statements we generate. It's everything." Klaus states.

"If we can earn more money speculating than actually producing, we could increase the value of NPI tremendously." Willie states.

"Now you're speaking my language, elf!" Klaus cheers.

"But what's our narrative? To the world? Exactly?" Willie asks.

"That we're a world class European toy research, development, production and distribution company based in Iceland that sells the highest quality products at the most competitive prices while operating far more profitably than Santa ever has! HAHA." Klaus cackles.

"But won't investors need to know about the North Pole?"

"Oh, God no! The less they know the better. Hell, who knows what would happen if the world found out this place was real."

"They knew Santa was real." 'Willie points out.

"Yes, but there's so much myth surrounding him nobody knows what to believe. Best leave the North Pole out of it, just as Santa did."

"You think investors would still buy in without knowing how the toys are made? Willie asks.

"All they need to know is that their investment is strong and providing healthy dividends. NPI is a black box and we must keep it that way." Klaus answers.

The next day all the usual suspects are at the unveiling of the new Belief Meter. Willie, Klaus, Hanna and Ernst von Wolf, Sir Louie, Ginger and even Otto is in from Iceland for the event. The crowd is much smaller than the Christmas Tree fiasco and Redcoat security tight. It's an intimate affair filled with capitalists, Germans, workshop owners and the alike.

The Belief Meter, like every project of Klaus', is epic in scale, sitting just outside the city Square. "North Pole Incorporated Price Per Share" is etched in stone and painted in gold at the mount. The actual meter still resembles the shape of a thermometer, with the bright, cherry red substance filling the glass. The top of the substance is still level at the $0/Share mark, while the top of the meter resembles a clockface, with an arrow set at 0%, to move either left (negative) or right (positive) percentage change.

Alabaster accompanies Willie and Hanna as he pours them another Irish Coffee, Willie's enjoying a good buzz along with the caffeine high a bit too much, yet Hanna drinks even more than he does.

Willie offers Ginger a cup...

"I don't mix." Ginger says.

"You don't mix?" Hanna asks.

"You know, a breakfast drink, coffee, with a dessert digestive like whiskey." She says.

"A dessert digestive is like a cream sherry or Grand Marnier, not Irish Whiskey." Willie argues, "And coffee isn't just a breakfast beverage, trust me."

"I disagree." Ginger says.

"Vermouth, amontillado, or even champagne make for aperitifs, trust me on this." Klaus says.

"Maybe even a wine." Hanna adds.

Ginger's annoyance grows, "An apéritif stimulates the appetite while a digestive stimulates digestion. That's all!" Ginger yaps.

"So, under certain circumstances whiskey could be an apéritif, digestive, or just plain ol' whiskey." Willie replies.

"Is this why you've dragged me here, to debate digestives and aperitifs?!" Ginger spouts.

Willie takes a sip of his Irish Coffee as Klaus laughs and laughs.

"No, we just want to know why your people burned down a damn good Christmas Tree is all." Willie stings.

"Good god, you'd make for a horrible detective." She fires. "The board room is my battlefield, not the streets, besides I'm too well paid to direct such a heinous act."

"How much?" Willie asks.

"You're a nosy little elf aren't you."

But Willie stares back at her, egging her on.

"Half a Million Sugar Dollars." She answers. Willie spits out his coffee, narrowly missing the top hat of Mr. Billingsworth right in front of him.

"The head of the Toy Makers Union earns a half a million! But I thought you were a nonprofit!" Willie yells.

"And why should a nonprofit not pay its employees handsomely?" She asks.

"Because...you're nonprofit!"

"Just because I represent the 'ol Factory Society doesn't mean I have to live like them!" Ginger turns her nose up.

All eyes move to the North Pole Clock Tower, it's a minute away from the opening of the New York Stock Exchange, and as the clock strikes twelve the Steam Whistle unleashes another SONIC BOOM - sending shock waves rumbling through the city. In that moment the cherry red liquid within the belief meter SHOOTS UP and fluctuates between $20.00 and $30.00 per share, before it landing solidly around $25.00 per share. Willie becomes amused in how the cherry red substance is in constant motion up and down.

"We've done it, twenty-five dollars per share! A fantastic start to the worlds' preeminent toy company!" Klaus yells as he's applauded by all, appearing to be in a genuine state of glee.

"Congratulations Klaus...and infinite thanks." Willie says.

Klaus laughs, "Congratulations to you! How about some aperitifs to celebrate, or is it digestives?! HAHA."

A cocktail party ensues. Everyone is drinking and bantering as Hanna attempts to drag Willie into the social circle, however he successfully stays on the periphery, unable to stand the scene. He seeks Renee, who he misses sorely, and finds her by the Belief Meter with her hand pressed against it, staring in awe at the giant thing. She smiles as Willie approaches.

"What do you make of this supposed stock market, with these supposed stocks, worth a certain supposed value in supposed units of supposed Sugar Dollars?" She asks.

"It supposedly makes sense." Willie replies.

"But how can we even tell what's real and what isn't?" She asks.

"What do you mean? It's all real, we make our own reality every day."

"Just because you create a world filled with these symbols of Sugar Dollars, which I'll remind you didn't exist until recently, doesn't make your ideas universal truths."

"Then what's real and what's fictitious to you?" He asks.

She ponders while watching the dazzling cherry red liquid oscillate. "I believe that Sugar Dollars, or capital, when it's used as such, is only real when it's invested into a physical and productive means of production. *This money is real so as long as it's used in a real, non-speculative way. Otherwise the market value of these stocks and securities are a fiction in that their value varies according to the expected return of those assets in the future.* That's only indirectly related to the growth of real production, at best."

"Then what is a stock or a share of a company, to you, at least?" Willies asks laughingly.

"It's exactly what it claims to be - a claim, or accumulated claims and legal titles to future production, and the income generated by that production. It's the net present value of expected future cash flows, you might say." She says.

"You're calling it fictitious capital but the ownership is real and legally enforced, as are the profits made from it." Willie points out.

"But the capital involved is fictitious. It's money thrown into circulation as capital with no material basis or productive activity. This is little more than tradeable paper claims to wealth."

"Well, what about non-paper claims?" He asks.

"Yes, tangible assets may also vastly inflate in price, like a house, but just look at this stock price move, it inflates and deflates shamelessly without a corresponding reality."

"Next you'll tell me that bonds are fictional, too." Willie jokes.

"They're only as real as a claim of ownership can be," she answers. "A simple claim to property rights or income, or to a share in future surplus. These bond and stock markets are markets for fictitious capital. *It is only a market for the circulation of property rights.*"

"You're saying the value isn't real because it doesn't function in the way you've defined capital, because there is no material basis?"

"It's a fiction in that it only exists on paper as a claim to future surplus. If it's unproductive capital, then the value of the paper claim is an illusion. The paper is a title of ownership which represents this capital and that's it." She says.

"If all of that is fictitious than what do you consider real?" Willie poses.

"The railways, mines, toy workshops, and all the like. The capital invested and functioning in such enterprises, or the amount of money advanced by the stockholders for the purpose of being used as capital in these kinds of enterprises is real. But this capital does not exist twice, it only exists when it's put to use in reality, while someone holding onto their piece of stock paper and trading it endlessly *produces no value*. That's merely a title of ownership circulating around and around based on speculation. That 'value' only exists on paper."

Willie isn't sure what to say but he enjoys playing devil's advocate, he gazes with her at the fluctuating price per share of the meter.

Renee watches as the price per share moves from $26.00 SD back to $25.00 SD. "Did you see that? The company just depreciated by a whole Sugar Dollar per share, that's a lot of value lost to the ether. But if we're being honest, almost nothing changed from that moment to this one. The wealth of the company is just as great before as it is after its depreciation."

"It's real!" He pokes.

"It's fake, it's so fake!" She yells back playfully. "Depreciation is only real if there's an actual stoppage of production, a suspension of the enterprise or a squandering of investments in completely worthless venture. Otherwise the company did not grow one cent poorer!"

"But profitability exists even when something creates no value." Willie says.

"It does, you can make tons of money off something that has no utility. I'm debating the real nature of value. Haven't you overheard some of those Germans who bought state debt bickering about their failed war bonds? Look at them, they've lent to the state to get repaid with interest out of the state tax revenues, even though the state did nothing but kill and destroy. Destruction doesn't create any value at all." She says.

"But real profit can be made purely from trading in a variety of financial claims existing only on paper." Willie says.

"For sure." Renee says. "Profit can be made like that, it can be made by the war profiteer, or by using only borrowed capital to engage in speculative trades. I'm saying this lack of a corresponding reality makes it without true value and therefore fictitious."

"But I invest in real estate." Willie says, feeling he's on to a strong counter. "I mean it has the word 'real' in it. It's a real, physical building where elves live."

"Yes, but the only real value is the value of the shelter to the elves who live there. You're merely dealing with the gambling of exchange values...Isn't the 'Ponzi' element of your dealings evident?"

"I buy a house on borrowed money and prices go up. I make money. So what?" He says.

"Then more buyers are attracted to buying houses because of rising property values. You all borrow more money to buy into a good thing, so housing prices go up even more, and now even more elves, Germans and institutions get into the game. You all create a bubble that can do nothing but pop."

"At least I invest in social services." Willie retorts.

"You're taking something that was once a right and now you're charging for it, hardly angelic."

"Well, there are more options to service these rights as long as they can be purchased."

"There are no more rights except the right to become indebted." She replies with mounting agitation. "There are no more 'values,' there's now only 'value'!"

"Only value?" Willie asks.

"If capital's only purpose is to grow, which it is, that's the only value it possesses - to become bigger. It's like the more you drink, the thirstier you are. The more you produce, the more you want to produce. The more you consume the more you want to consume. The more you accumulate the more you want to accumulate. It's a pointless, endless, vicious satanic mill that spins on and on."

"And yet Christmas presents bring joy." Willie protests.

"Temporarily and materialistically, sure, but beyond that fleeting sense of gratification production, consumption and appropriation provide no possible satisfaction. *It only leads to a cycle of desires and frustrations that feed off each other.*"

"Perhaps you're right, if that's something you don't value. Value is a funny thing to determine."

"Let's say for a moment that value isn't determined by how much work has gone into making something, or by the materials it's composed of, or by its overall usefulness. The only method left to make the determination is through the pure appearance of it."

"So?" Willie blurts.

"So, then a thing is only valued as it exists as an image in relation to other things, that are also images. Value becomes determined in relation between things. In the end it becomes more important for a toy business to have a great brand than it is to make great toys."

Willie stares at her blankly.

"I don't know about you, but I don't accept that conclusion as beneficial for the North Pole or Christmas."

"That's a very different definition of value." Willie says.

"But these things and services absorb labor no matter how well they're marketed – like the labor that accumulates in the steel that's sharpened into the blade that's attached to the ice skate. It is the social value of all that activity, of all that laboring, that underpins what that money represents. 'Value' is a social relation between the laboring activities of elves all around the North Pole, or even people all over the world. Either way, money is as inseparable from value as the amount it's exchanged for is inseparable from money. The bonds between money, the exchange value it sells for and the practicality of its utility, are all welded together."

"But a social relation is immaterial and invisible." He replies. "How can that be ingrained into something?"

"Value speaks to why sleds cost more than skis, houses cost more than sleds and eggnog costs more than water. These differences between things have nothing to do with their character as use value and everything to do with the labor involved in their production. The labor value being immaterial and invisible requires money to represent that. Your Sugar Dollars represent the immateriality of social value."

"How?"

"When money is used in gambling and speculation the gap between money and the value it represents creates a contradiction." She explains. "Money that's supposed to represent the social value of labor becomes fictitious capital – it stops representing real, productive social value and only represents itself as a symbol. This fictitious capital circulates to eventually line the pockets of the financiers and bondholders through the extraction of wealth from all sorts of non-productive, non-value producing activities of finance."

"Money then deceives us of its nature?" Willie asks.

"For sure, but not on purpose. It's real in that in represents real social relations but it's so easily misinterpreted to the point where it falsifies that basic truth all the way to the extent where *the desire for money as a form of social power becomes an end in itself.*"

"But the desire to be endlessly rich is natural. Greed is innate." Willie says.

"I disagree." Renee says.

"Then what's our fundamental driver, if not greed?" Willie asks.

"Did any elf dream of being fabulously rich before these Germans showed up?"

"They've craved social power and respect, at least." He says. "And now I want to be fabulously rich, is it not natural to feel this way?"

"Acting selfishly is related to the very nature of capitalism." Renee proposes. "Just look at how the game of Monopoly forces its players to act horribly while bankrupting their opponents. Take those same players and make them play something cooperative and they'll totally change their behavior."

"What of it?"

"Selfishness is not an absolute elvish trait, it never has been."

"Selfishness is not the same as viciousness." He says.

"We don't have to go far back to remember that economic life ran on social currencies. Interactions were based on mutual expectations, responsibility and reciprocity." She says.

"We were far from perfect before these Germans show up, you'd remember." He says.

"Highly imperfect. Perhaps our ancestors' greatest error was not fully resisting Santa's construct of the hierarchy of Workshop and Factory Society. It institutionalized inequalities and created this whole caste system.

"Perhaps we're bound to repeat history, just in new forms. Look at us elves ceaselessly repeating our flaws in ever-new ways." Willie says.

"How metaphysical." She laughs. "As if elves, by destiny, are to return to existence by the forces of karma, with time itself acting as the ultimate cosmic illusion. The eternal return to our physical existence into an indefinite prolongation of suffering. A Christmas-y suffering through the means of non-ending toy production. An endlessness of our collective slavery through the burden of existence."

"You lost me." Willie admits.

"You started it." Renee smirks. "I'm just saying it's not all too different from before, actually it looks like it only has the potential to get much worse."

"I'm optimistic." Willie says.

"They made you the head of the North Pole Reserve, but have they even taught you anything about it? Have you stopped to think about the actual nature of banking?"

"I have, but it's complicated." He states.

"Klaus, or yourself have no idea how many Sugar Dollars are in circulation, especially as the banks keep generating credit. We know there's only a fraction of the sugar available if every Sugar Dollar were to be redeemed tomorrow. The Sugar Dollar has no correlation with the sugar it claims to represent, nor the value of the labor it's supposed to represent - it's already a pure abstraction. The purchasing of a bond with Sugar Dollars is the equivalent of investing into a symbol on top of a symbol of the immateriality of labor, and it's treated as if the economic potential is limitless."

"But a dream of limitless economic growth is a utopia." Willie states.

"It's a perilous illusion." She retorts.

"The limitless growth of capital is as natural as our naturally infinite desires." He retorts.

"Infinite growth of material consumption in a finite world is as unsustainable as it is impossible." She says. "The requirement of capital to grow in a compounding way will destroy us long before it can circulate for the rest of time."

"Maybe one day it will circulate exclusively in an immaterial world." He says.

"Then we're back where we started, asking what's real and what's not?"

"Funny how you're so cynical when everyone else is excited." Willie points out.

"Hah - I'm no cynic," she blurts, "but cynicism is an obvious feature of capital whose purpose is not production, wealth, or employment, but only accumulation."

"And yet it's money that makes the world go 'round." He says.

Hanna suddenly appears creeping up behind Willie. "There you are! What in god's name are you two talking about?" Hanna interrupts.

"Just talking about all the money in the world." Renee says bitingly.

"Ah yes, we should have all of it, shouldn't we Willie!" Hanna yaps. "Speaking of money, darling, the money boys are over there - talking about the tons of coal they want to buy from you with the funds they now have available from the IPO. So, why don't you get going..."

"What will you do with your newfound funds, Hanna?" Renee asks sarcastically.

"I've come up with a neat little invention that I'm going to invest in myself, I think all of you should join me." Hanna enthuses. "Don't worry, I'll only charge you the 'friends and family' percentage."

"Don't leave us hanging." Renee pokes.

"Well, I'm calling it a CDO, short for Collateralized Debt Obligation. It's this fabulous bundling of mortgages into one...hmm, thing...that can be marketed worldwide!" Hanna states.

"Mortgages. Okay, but investors want to know who owns these homes, how well mortgage holders keep up with their payments, how they make their money and everything else." Renee states.

"Wrong! First, it's 'as safe as houses', I mean, the marketing alone is just brilliant, BAHAH. Second, CDOs are anonymous. Investors don't know who's mortgages they own and guess what - they don't care. Their only concern is that the debt repayment is manageable. And with the Marshall Plan real estate is booming everywhere. So as long as that's the case these CDOs are as good as gold!" Hanna smiles.

"As a broker you get paid no matter what, right? You make a commission for each transaction, so you can make the most of your income by frequent trading on a variety of...how should I say - financial...'things', that you sell, whether the trades do good or bad?" Renee replies.

"Yes, but like I said, I'm putting my own money in, and proving a point. It's a great investment because the risk is slight as my figure." Hanna says.

"How do you even put together something as fabricated as a CDO, slender girl?" Renee asks.

"Oh, it's magical, we group together mortgages in accordance of subordination. So, like, the first lot, the lesser one, would have the highest risk. The intermediate one has reduced risk, and the best one, made up of oldest, best assets, is secure. The greater lot is protected by the lesser ones, making the lesser ones the most exposed – but if the lesser ones weren't linked up with the better ones nobody would touch 'em, so they all have to be linked together for it to work." Hanna says.

"You're making access to a good house available based on a mathematical model of risk where elvish lives don't count for anything." Renee replies. "Where the poor are 'played' against the less poor, and where the public right to housing is secondary to the private right to realize a profit, like everything else you're all doing. This is a fiction run wild on steroids!"

"A fiction?" Hanna asks.

"Yes, and I think you're all crazy." Renee admits.

Klaus roles up, "Ahh the colorful part of the party, what have I missed here?"

"All the money in the world." Hanna smirks.

"Shame, I wanted it all," Klaus laughs, trying to defuse the situation as they're attracting unwanted eyeballs.

"Don't worry, Klaus," Renee says, "you didn't miss anything. I'm leaving. Good luck to you all and your financial...things." She says dismissively. Before her exit she leans into Willie's ear, whispers, *"Rebellion creates awareness, become aware."* Then she struts away.

"What's up with her?" Klaus asks.

"She's just concerned is all." Willie says.

"Too bad, that's the type that will miss on this next wave of wealth that simple businessmen like myself will capture." Klaus says.

"Simple businessman? Sure." Willie laughs.

"That's on nobody but herself." Hanna says.

"Speaking of wealth, North Pole Inc. starts buying your coal today. The lawyers are drafting the agreement as we speak and I think you'll find the terms more than agreeable." Klaus says.

"I'm looking forward." Willie says. It gets him thinking, "What about all of that preaching for nuclear energy program you were so fond of not so long ago?"

"Hardly practical at the moment." Klaus laughs. "What a joke!"

"Then why would you direct Kris Kringle to Japan to collect soil?" Willie inquires as Klaus becomes uncomfortably on edge.

Klaus turns serious, "I mean, it's not that far away, my elf, with some research we'd be there in no time. One milestone at a time, 'eh?"

Willie's a bit confused by everything and everyone at the moment, not to mention how he's been steady drinking trying to keep up with the Germans. Hanna sees how he's a bit wobbly and distracts him, pouring him even more champagne as she presses against his body.

"My god, it's good to be rich," she cheers.

"Indeed!" Klaus smiles.

"Champagne, aperitifs!" Hanna yells raising her glass, looking for a refill as the party continues with a renewed spark. They all clank champagne flutes again, cheers-ing to their position and dominance, and unbeknownst to Willie or any other elf - *for getting away with it all.*

Hanna tipsily leads Willie away from the crowd and lifts him by the arms like a big baby onto a barstool. She's still a few inches taller than him but not by much now. She looks up into his eyes and rests her head against his chest before slowly moving in for a sloppy, slobbery kiss, pushing her slippery boozy tongue further and further down his little elf mouth. And by god, does he love it...

Early the next morning Willie rolls out of bed in his new sleek downtown flat that Hanna just sold him. He looks back at Hanna, she's naked and passed out in the sheets. Even as she sweats and farts in her sleep Willie is still enthralled by sleek long legs and voluptuous curves.

Bottles, pants, shirt, dress, shoes, bra and panties are sprawled all over. He soaks up this strange scene, wondering if it's all a dream - but his pounding headache reminds him it's not.

He turns to his giant floor to ceiling windows to absorb the view of the changing city. For the first time he watches as dense clouds of smoke drift over the North Pole while the factory and workshop chimneys pump a black exhaust into the atmosphere. He's mesmerized by the dark sight, watching the thick murky clouds shift shapes as the winds blows.

Hanna awakes and comes up behind him, kneeling to his level before sensually pressing her naked body against his. She tenderly throws her arms over his shoulders and joins him peering out the window. They're enthralled by the view, but unlike his confused state she smiles with a deep satisfaction.

"Look darling, each little plume of smoke is as good as another Sugar Dollar in your pocket. What a sight." She whispers, massaging his back. "Your war chest will be...so big. The only thing you shouldn't waste your money on is taxes."

"What if I pay my workers more?" He asks.

"You know their going rates. Besides, no one should overpay just because they're rich, that's like...discrimination." She babbles.

"Oh, the discrimination, oh the discrimination." Willie sings.

"Well you can't leave your new money just sitting." She hints to selling him a new investment.

"You're right my Saxon Queen. When a pile of money no longer increases in value it's nothing more than a means of payment. A means of payment doesn't control labor or society. It can no longer create new forms of domination."

"Some CDOs then, *darling?*" She smirks as she smacks his tiny ass.

"Why not." He says.

"Fantastic."

"But I have my own plan I'd like to try."

"And what's that, my little dear?"

"Student loans and education."

"Education? How...different."

"Investments into all types of schools. Trade schools, graduate schools, student loans and everything to do with it. I'll train and pick from the best of the best to ensure my workshop's advantage. We'll even teach the ideology of business. We'll invest so heavily that the Maven Workshop won't show a dime of profit and won't pay a dime of tax! How does that sound, darling?"

Hanna smiles back and takes him by the hand, leading him back to bed.

"It sounds good, darling. It sounds very, very good."

14 – EDUCATION PROCLAMATION

Willie coughs from the blackened air as he arrives at the Maven Workshop. Despite his gasping, he enters with a skip, refreshed by the spirit of his new education initiative. The Ickles help Willie change into his workshop attire while Sticky greets him with a strict demeanor, carrying a laundry list of employee complaints.

"You're chipper this morning." Willie says.

Sticky hands him the list. He glances at it with surprise.

"Impressive list, Stick, sure you're running everything according to the manual?"

"To the 't', Sir. But these new methods have everything to do with efficiency and nothing to do with, how should I say...employee satisfaction."

"Time is money, walk and talk, Stick."

Willie and Sticky cruise through the corridors of the workshop. It's palpable how the once charmingly disordered creative space has morphed into a quiet, neatly organized and very sterile place. The random sounds of etching and dings of passion projects in production are replaced by a steady and predictable beat of machinery, with each BING, BANG and BOP of production equally spaced out and repeated from dawn to dusk. Even chatter has stopped almost entirely. The workspaces are void of conversation, with each elf focused on repeating their same miniscule actions as fast and accurately as possible.

The coldness of this once welcoming place sours Willie's mood and reminds him of the Giftwrapping Factory. He begins to understand the new nature of production and administration. In his path he spots an old, loyal employee. Willie pauses in his tracks, about to say hello, but finds the elf unapproachable, stuck in a robotic, single-minded trance.

He takes Sticky into his office, closes the door and watches through the window, witnessing the entire elaborate mechanical ballet of the production in motion.

"What's going on here?" Willie asks.

"Like I said, Sir, following the manual to the t. These new operations aren't only for us, all the top shops function like this now." Sticky says.

"It's scary out there," Willie says.

"Permission to speak freely, Sir?" Sticky asks.

"Yes, but please stop asking."

"Their jobs have become, how should I say? Bullshit jobs."

"Bullshit jobs?"

"Now they must pretend that their work isn't pointless. But it is, and deep down they know it too. I believe it's this falseness that degrades their self-worth and becomes psychologically destructive." Sticky responds, leaving Willie without words.

"How do we do to fix it?" Willie wonders.

"I don't think we can if we're to follow that manual."

"Well why is it so psychologically destructive, as you say?"

"In my humble opinion, Sir, all this comes down to *alienation*. The astonishing gains in our productivity, output and profitability come at this cost. Alienation effects the mental, emotional and physical well-being of the workers. The worker has become a 'fragment of an elf' because they're placed within a fixed and highly specialized position. This is all set within an increasingly complex division of labor. They're isolated and individualized, alienated from each other but also from their own sense of self. They're alienated from their nature as passionate and sensuous beings. And the psychological alienation has become physically alienating too, here and all over the North Pole."

"What about this new process deprives them?" Willie asks.

"They're deprived of mental challenges or creative possibilities. They've become mere machine operators, appendages of the machine rather than masters of their own fate. There's a lost sense of wholeness, not to mention authorship, and an utter collapse of satisfaction. Sir, creativity and spontaneity have undoubtably left the workshop floor. Activity for the sake of your profit feels...*meaningless*, and elves can't live in a world devoid of meaning."

"Like the Giftwrapping Factory?"

"Yes."

"This *is* bad." Willie admits. "How can they possibly develop any sense of self if ignorance and stupidity develops here?"

"I don't know that they can, Sir." Sticky replies, "So as long as their service provides for the many distant, unknown and unknowable consumers they produce for."

"The high destiny of any individual is to serve rather than rule." Willie says.

"I believe I taught you that once, thank you very much." Sticky sneers.

"That's Albert Einstein, ol' Stick, Smartest being on Earth, according to the Germans. But you're a close second."

"Great minds think alike." Sticky replies to his laugh, "But you won't find any geniuses here, not anymore."

"I remember we use to." Willie answers.

"Personal development or self-realization isn't well-matched with our demands." Sticky says. "A flexible, adaptable and to some degree, educated labor force is what's needed."

"So, the robot-like elf we've created must be replaced by the elf who's prepared for the different kinds of labor required?" Willie asks.

"Exactly, Sir." Sticky says. "We need the fully developed elf, capable of creative solutions and prepared to tackle a multitude of challenges. To this end we must strive for the educated and adaptable rather than the specific worker."

"Great minds think alike, Sticky."

"How are you to make such sweeping changes, Sir?"

"There will be a market for student loans, and I'm going to

invest in education as if it were a bond." Willie says. "Sir Louie's administration will need to make it legal first. In fact, I'll draft the letter to Axel now. Sir Louie doesn't read his mail."

"Interesting idea Sir, good luck." Sticky says as he closes Willie's office door.

Sticky notices how alone, alienated and isolated Willie is from the rest of the workshop, just like anyone else. He thinks, even if Willie wanted to make something unique, interesting or different, the entire workshop would be disciplined by the marketplace to conform to its demands anyway. Willie's alienation and lack of choice coincides directly with his employee's alienation in that both have little power over their own freedom, especially regarding the toys they must produce. In a moment of clarity, Sticky sees how the concept of alienation is embedded into the whole system of capital itself, and that it's a pillar for its working.

Regardless, Willie is determined, gripping his ink pen as he stares down the blank page. He knows his letter must support business then recommend how these advancements in education can help the working elves. He takes a deep breath and precedes to write;

"Dear Axel Kendal-Crink,

"The legitimization of our market movement is incomplete. The challenges which we face are as diverse as they are numerous. Today we know antagonistic, powerful, ideological influences circulate through the North Pole, while our own market ideology is hardly reinforced through our institutions. To stand our ground, we should support the development and organization of think-tanks with corporate support. We must simultaneously capture certain segments of intellectuals, specifically those at our society's most prestigious universities. With these powerful influences we can adapt the ways of thinking to create a climate of support for a market society to truly flourish. With it, we all shall see the market as the exclusive guarantor of freedom.

However, an open project around the promotion of economic power to a small elite will not gain support, but an ongoing attempt to advance the cause of individual freedom can appeal to the masses and disguise the initiatives that drive business to power. Ultimately, we must begin to see market ideology become society's 'common-sense' understanding of the world. The desired effect must be to see our ideology as a necessary, or even wholly natural. Political movements that hold individual freedoms to be sacrosanct are the most vulnerable to incorporate into our movement. Yet my own astute workshop manager, who holds the freedom of expression high, is quick to recognize the deficits of the system.

Before this criticism worsens, we ought to take initiative through the ingenuity and resourcefulness of elvish businesses. A united business front can be marshaled against those who would destroy it, such as those who've terrorized our glorious Christmas Tree. Our true strength against these belligerents lay within our ability to organize and proceed with careful long-term planning and implementation.

With that, I would like to propose the creation of a National Chamber of Commerce tasked with leading the charge. The initiative will change how elves think about the corporation, the law and the individual. To support this organization businesses across the North Pole along with North Pole Inc. should amass an immense campaign chest to lobby the government as necessary. Think tanks with corporate backing will construct serious technical and empirical studies and form political-philosophical arguments broadly in support of our market policies.

In the spirit of adjusting how our society thinks we must re-educate our fellow elves. First, it is true that traditional artisanal skills are of diminishing importance. Therefore, our interest lies in the procurement of a modestly educated workforce. One that is literate, flexible, disciplined and complicitous enough to fulfill the variety of tasks demanded of them. Second, the growth of education shall ease the lot of the regularly employed elves, and improve their skills and social standing. Therefore, there ought to be no objection to a student loan initiative, provided it teaches the laboring elves their proper place in society – *at work*.

We are at the forefront of a great opportunity to make education a 'Big Business' unto itself. Yet we can only achieve it through the powerful inroads of privatization. Together we are at the precipitous of an opportunity to change the very nature of politics. Business, my friend, must learn to spend as a class, and politicians must create new markets for businesses to invest in.

Thank you for your consideration and support during these exciting yet vulnerable times.

Your old wolf racing rival,

Willie Maven."

Willie puts down his pen, exhales deeply and stares at the words. He's surprised with what he's produced and contemplates it. He turns to stare at the workers below, feeling the weight of their fate in his hands. There's no stopping now, he thinks, as he folds the letter and seals it with hot wax, imprinting the signature Maven Workshop crest onto the melted dollop.

The next week Willie is in his finest pinstripe suit complete with a colorful pocket square, gold cufflinks and red silk tie. He awaits to be received by Axel in a backroom of Santa's Sphere. The chamber is as regal as it is daunting, with high ceilings and gold leaf painted coffers creating a temple like setting.

Axel's entourage of security, staff and administrators burst through the door in an orderly fashion. They set up opposite Willie before Axel struts in. He carries his usual air of arrogance, but his coldness wares away as he offers Willie a welcoming handshake.

"Good day, Maven. Straight down to business, shall we?" Axel says.

"Yes, that's why I'm here, business." Willie replies.

"It'd be nice to work together on something for a change."

"A welcome change." Willie smiles.

"You'll be coming under fire and I'd like to address my reservations before you do."

"Shoot." Willie replies.

"Primarily, if we must educate the laboring elf who knows what this 'totally developed elf' might read? What political ideas they might get in their tiny heads?"

"You're correct. And for this reason, ideological controls upon the flow of knowledge and of information become essential." Willie answers. "Text books can always be edited."

"Wouldn't the educated only be faster to realize their lack of meaning in a life of production?"

"I agree again, but a small and regular dose of pop entertainment and a chalice of eggnog can quell a weeks' worth of toil and anguish." Willie responds. "Trust me."

"However, society will surely pose a major threat to the reproduction of capital and that your intention of educating the future workforce could inadvertently strengthen that threat?" Axel asks.

"I'm pleased how your concerns lay within the reproduction of capital."

"You haven't answered my question." Axel jolts.

"Again, there are risks but ultimately the 'educated laborer' is required for progress."

"And this is worth the risk? The increased volatility for reform, or even violent revolution?" Axel asks.

Willie isn't sure what to say.

"This may lead us to a stark choice between an impossible reform or an improbable revolution. Either way, the game favors our position. We must act on it while we still hold a massive advantage." Willie states.

Axel stares back at him poker faced, contemplating Willie's argument. He finally smiles back and offers his hand to Willie, which he shakes firmly. "Good to be in business with you, Maven." Axel says.

"The pleasure is mine." Willie responds.

Axel's entourage packs and leads Willie to the floor of the Santa's Sphere. The specially formed committee awaits as Willie enters. Several large rows of polished oak desks are filled by the slippery, hair slicked technocrats – mostly made of Santa's former administration – now absorbed into the various facets of Sir Louie's government. Their seating arrangement forms a crescent around the grand marble desk in the center, where Willie sits.

As Willie takes his position he stares up into a fierce portrait of Santa Claus. His commanding spirit still resides here, along with his powerfully painted gaze, which glares down upon him.

Ginger Garland fastidiously calls the hearing to order.

"Good Day, Mr. Maven." She opens. "You are called here to defend or even elaborate on your legislative propositions. Although you will find many supporters, I assure you I am not one of them, so let's ‑"

"Perhaps I can persuade you." Willie smiles.

"Don't interrupt me, Mr. Maven."

He silences and straightens up.

"I'm taken by the idea of the various loans, debts and fees you've described in the elvish pursuit for their right to education." Ginger sneers. "What's been public and free you'd see replaced with financial burdens on the citizenry. This inevitably leads to a heavily debt‑encumbered labor force. How do you justify making society indebted for something they're required to possess for their livelihood?"

"Thank you, Ms. Garland – I will point out that an educated, although indebted labor force, also creates a productive labor force. This gives rise to something I'd call 'Elvish Capital Theory'." Willie says.

"I'm not here for a lecture, Mr. Maven."

"It's just a fancy term for common sense, really." Willie says.

"Mr. Maven ‑ "

"If you'd allow me to clarify ‑ "

"Please allow our guest an opportunity to respond," Axel interjects to Ginger's frustration.

"The idea is that the acquisition of talents, knowledge or

skills by workers through their education, study or apprenticeship always costs a real expense. But the talent, knowledge and skills also create real profits for the individual, state and society. I'm not alone in my capitalist ways, because we're all capitalists, actually. We simply earn different rates of return on our capital. If labor is getting low wages, this is a reflection that these workers have not invested enough effort in building up their own capital."

"You're saying it's their fault if they're poor and low paid." Ginger accuses.

"Yes."

"Have you been drinking, Mr. Maven?" Ginger utters.

"We all must accept responsibility for ourselves." Willie counters, "To be sure, skilled and highly trained labor might reasonably expect a higher pay than unskilled labor."

"That's a far cry from the idea that higher wages are a form of profit on the worker's investment in their own skills and education." Ginger says.

"Is it?" Willie asks.

"It is, Mr. Maven, because if an elf actually acted like capital then they may *sit back and live off the interest without doing a single day's work!*" Ginger snaps. "When it's all said and done, it's capital that reaps the benefit of productive labor, much more so than the other way around!"

"I beg to differ." Willie says.

"How can you when productivity has exploded but the rewards and living standards of labor have stayed the same or declined?"

"Their education allows them the opportunity for more complex job positions with greater rewards and bonuses." Willie answers.

"That may be so but it still doesn't compare to the massive gains which businesses and capital stand to make. What's most ironic is your demand to make the citizenry and not the private sector pay for it." Ginger adds.

"But a welfare state is too expensive. If tax relief were provided to business, we could stimulate economic growth faster, which, when the benefits are spread around would make every elf better off."

"And how are the citizens supposed to trust you, or any other capitalist to not take all the savings or pass along the benefits?" Ginger asks.

"You might have to take my word for it." Willie answers.

"HAH," Ginger spouts. "Good one, Mr. Maven, but this is Santa's Sphere. This is big business, I'm sorry, but I cannot 'take your word for it. You must prove it!"

"Contrary to whatever you might think, it's my aim to empower the disempowered. I'd like to vest them through financing, teach them financial literacy, open up lines of microcredit and legal title for land and property ownership, like capitalists. Is that really so bad, Ms. Garland?"

Ginger takes this in. "It is bad, Mr. Maven." She answers. "Financial literacy classes for the average elf will only expose them to predatory practices as they seek to manage their own investment portfolios. They'd be like *seals* swimming about an iceberg *swarming with sharks and polar bears.* Providing microfinance and small loans encourage elves to take part in the economy but does so in a way which maximizes the energy required just to stay afloat. Providing legal title for land and property ownership to the lives of the marginalized in hopes of stability *will almost certainly lead to their long-term eviction from that space* that they already hold the rights to through customary use!" Ginger exclaims.

"And that is your time, Ms. Garland." Axel interrupts as Willie breathes a sigh of relief.

"I'd like to request more time. Who will lend me several minutes?" Ginger says.

"Anyone willing to donate their time to Ms. Garland?" Axel asks.

But no one volunteers as the silence lingers, and Ginger's blood boils to Axel's delight.

"All of those in favor of introducing legislation to the floor in favor of Education...um...Reform. Say Aye." Axel states.

"Aye!" Everyone yells aloud, minus Ginger.

"Congratulations Mr. Maven, we're excited to bring your proposals through the legislator under my sponsorship." Axel smiles.

SWACK SWACK SWACK – Axel knocks his gavel ending the session as Willie nods back happily.

Axel pulls Willie aside into the backroom chamber and pours a couple celebratory tumblers of scotch.

"You've handled that well." Axel says as they clink glasses. "This will fly through the ranks, I'll have my father is ready to sign. I foresee a fruitful relationship ahead." Axel states with a slick grin.

"As do I." Willie says.

"To be sure, are you serious about those campaign finance ideas in your letter?" Axel asks.

"Of course, as soon as you make it legal."

"That will be next on our agenda. How would you further describe that idea?" Axel asks.

"Nothing more than a legal corruption of politics!" Willie laughs as Axel chuckles back nervously.

"No really, Maven, tell me what you mean." Axel says.

"Oh - it's a simple idea, the right of a corporation to make boundless financial contributions to political parties and political action committees should be protected as free speech.

"Interesting." Axel says.

"Once that's ready we'll establish Political Action Committees who'd ensure the corporate domination over both political parties. Your politician friends will benefit with ripe opportunities for monied special-interest groups. Legions of corporate lobbyists will come in droves to dish out funds and favors in exchange for prescribing law.

"Sounds rich." Axel smiles.

"It gets better," Willie winks. "We'll create a 'revolving door' between state employment and the much more rewarding corporate space. The realm between our two worlds will overlap. If your valiant friends here in public service ever want to get rich, they can."

"Love what I'm hearing, Maven. Keep it coming." Axel says sipping his scotch which burns his tongue most delightfully.

"Even the likes of your opponent, Ginger, and her party would have to become dependent on big money contributions just to remain relevant. They'll be vulnerable to the influence from business too, and in no position to pursue an anti-corporate agenda without severing connections with the powerful financial interests they'll depended on."

"Haha! Don't stop Maven, then what?!"

"Impose a mandated cost-benefit analysis on all regulatory proposals. If it cannot be shown that the benefits of regulation clearly exceed the costs then the regulations ought to be scrapped."

"Yes, more!"

"Revise the tax code! Make it possible to depreciate our investments with hazy accounting methods. Corporations shouldn't pay taxes, considering we're the drivers of society. Reduce the tax rate on wealthy individuals. The amount Ginger wants the likes of you and I to pay should be criminal!"

"You're preaching to the choir my friend." Axel says. "A true Machiavellian, perhaps it's you who should be in politics."

"I'm just a simple businessman." Willie winks back.

15 – CANDY RED SPLATTERS AND CANDY CANES

The newly furnished North Pole Reserve is fresh, immense, and ornately decorated. More uniquely, gold sculptures of sugar cube pyramids are scattered throughout the building. Unlike other institutions, this one is particularly hollow, lightly populated by silent German administrators and their nimble elf secretaries. The Reserve is quiet but has a current of flowing activity, providing a museum-like quality.

Willie struts about his mint-blue penthouse office sipping on whiskey mixed with his bold coffee prepared in his French press. He feels out of place, and if he's being honest, he knows this is his least favorite office of all, but it's also his most powerful. He searches within himself trying to embrace it as he slurps and stares up at a massive 20-meter by 20-meter map of the world, absorbing the world as if preparing to conquer it.

Klaus walks up to the office and catches Willie in a trance. He's about to knock on the wall but takes a moment to watch Willie studying the map. An ambitious Reserve chairman is good for business, Klaus realizes as he smiles to himself.

"It's big, isn't it?" Klaus catches Willie by surprise. "Even bigger than this map makes it out to be."

"It is a grand ol' world." Willie responds, "I'd like to see more of it."

"Perhaps one day you will."

"That will be the day, to find out what these green blotches represent. What a map."

"It's a real collector's item, from Santa's private map collection. I believe it most appropriate to hang this one in your office. Thought you might take pride in seeing just how far and wide our toys reach. How many lives they touch, in all corners of the world."

"Fascinating, the green and beige continents, and the big blue oceans. The geography, terrain and shapes. It's beautiful." Willie confesses.

"Distance is the soul of beauty, my elf. Only through distance does reality undergo a cleansing. The drudgery of daily life disappears with a look backward, where we can reveal the tragedy of life to ourselves with spectacular clarity."

"Well said." Willie replies.

"Thanks."

"So, you're a map enthusiast yourself?"

"Yes, I had to be, especially when I flew planes in Germany."

"Planes?" Willie asks.

"Aircraft. It's something like Santa's sled."

"I see."

"Let me tell you, the world is much more attractive looking down upon it from the gates of heaven. Much more beautiful than being in the literal trenches of it. Life in a war trench is hell, but I'll tell you both heaven and hell exist in this world, and we should fight with everything we have to live as close to heaven that God will allow."

"I'd say we're getting closer." Willie smiles.

"We most certainly are."

Willie takes another sip of whiskey coffee as he counts the various frozen islands that trickle up towards the Arctic from Canada.

"I can finally grasp how amazing the Christmas miracle is, given the vast distances of the Earth."

"Now that miracles are replaced by practicality, you have a scope of the vastness of the mission ahead." Klaus replies.

"How do our gifts move across these oceans and continents?"

"Money, my dear elf, like everything else." Klaus states. "Money makes the world go around, and with enough money you can really conquer it."

"It's unconquerable with violence, but conquerable with

gifts." Willie smiles.

"HAH! Spoken like a true elf. Conquerable with gifts, and *capital!*" Klaus adds with a laugh. "If I only had you around to tell Hitler that..."

"Tell me more about...Hitler. You mention his name every so often."

"Some other time perhaps, but please pour me some coffee, I'm deprived." Klaus asks.

"Irish?" Willie smiles.

"You know me too well, elf." Klaus says as Willie adds a healthy pour of whiskey. They sip on the fine white porcelain cups and gaze up at the map of world together in silence.

"Sorry, I know you don't like talking about the war. I won't ask about it, but I'm ready to listen when you're ready to share." Willie says.

"We're all learning to fight a new war, a more important war, together."

"What war?"

"Money is our military now. Each Sugar Dollar is a soldier we send to battle, to conquer, take other currency hostage and bring back home to safety."

"In that case we'll build a great army together." Willie replies with a smirk.

Klaus smiles back, "I need you to think as big as the world itself." He points at the map.

"Teach me." Willie asks.

"What I need from you, what we all need are low interest rates and access to easy credit. It will keep money flowing fast through the economy while growing it. We're stabilizing but we need a stimulus."

Willie consults his one page of how his job is supposed to work. He finds that lowering the rates should do that, but not without consequence.

"That's fine, except for the correlating inflation." Willie says.

"A moderate inflation is all right, so as long as it encourages spending, borrowing and investment." Klaus says. "But what we can't handle is a mob of unemployed former factory workers who don't have the means to pay for their most basic needs."

Willie says takes a large sip of coffee and thinks about it. "You're right, of course. I'll lower the rates."

Klaus elates and clinks cups with Willie.

"May the good times roll," Klaus cheers.

Sticky knocks at the door to their surprise.

"Sticky!" Willie shouts.

"Sorry to bother, Sir. But it's urgent."

"Spill the beans." Willie instructs.

"There's not enough coal to keep with the production. The price of coal has exploded. It's throwing off your profits. I thought it pressing to report."

"Thanks Sticky, but I'd be more concerned if I didn't own all that coal, I make money there too."

"Sorry Sir, didn't know."

"What a manager!" Klaus yelps, "I salute you, Sticky. We need more elves like you at NPI!"

"Don't get him too excited." Willie says.

"I'm jealous how you get intel faster than me half the time, speaks to the talents of your staff." Klaus says. "It is a good thing you own the coal mine, with lower interest rates you can hire more miners, increase the supply of coal and make more money on both ends."

"Mining's a tough job, it requires a certain type of elf." Willie says.

"I know some tough elves, Sir." Sticky shares. "Cheap, but tough, and proud. They're difficult to manage, especially the former prisoner types. Those recently released ones, they get little work, they're desperate. Conceivably a fertile ground for hiring?"

"That's why I pay him the big bucks." Willie laughs.

"What are you waiting for?" Klaus asks.

"Sticky, to the tavern!" Willie exclaims.

Willie and Sticky make their way across town and descend into the Coal & Stocking Tavern. It's a dingy dive bar with a long tradition as a coal miner hangout. The miners are uniquely impacted with the passing of Santa, having took particular pride in providing the snobbish children of the world with their black lumpy rocks. They're disgruntled how it's used for such practical purposes now. However, most patrons don't grasp coal's importance as the new fuel of society, not yet at least.

It's difficult for Willie and Sticky to keep a low profile as they inevitably draw attention with their fine clothes and flushed healthy skin among this pale, rough and tumble group. They shuffle through the crowd and awkwardly plant themselves at the far end of the bar. They work to get comfortable in the cramped and dark space as Willie breaks into a cough and orders a round of eggnogs. He has time to observe the rugged charm of the setting, picking up on its warmth, and even community.

"Funny these elves prefer keeping drunk in this cave than being out and about. I admit, I'm jealous," Willie says.

"Very funny, Sir."

"You crack me up, old elf." Willie laughs.

"What's your plan now?" Sticky asks as the eggnogs arrive, taking a gulp.

"My plan? I thought this was your plan?"

"Oh my, have I misspoken, Sir?"

"Stay calm, drink your eggnog. Let's just have listen, like spies."

"Ah yes, spying, how fun!" Sticky announces far too loud as Willie rolls his eyes.

They sip their drinks and lean clumsily into the surrounding conversations, but nothing is of interest until Renee enters the tavern to their surprise. She's with a SHADOWY SOMEONE, but neither can make out the figure through the smoky, crowded room. The figure leans into her ear as she smiles, striking a visceral jealously within Willie. They hug and the figure disappears back into the busy streets above.

Renee approaches the bar as Willie and Sticky panic.

"Quick, act normal." Willie says.

Willie grabs a lump of coal laying on the ground and shoves it in Sticky's hands.

"Dirty yourself." Willie says as he rubs the coal on his hands and face.

"How unlike you, Sir." Sticky says.

"We must blend in!"

"Oh, I see." Sticky says, following suit.

It's a dirt-poor disguise, literally, but it's enough to keep them unnoticed from Renee, who sits among a small group of miners and recently released ex-cons. Willie and Sticky lean in to eavesdrop, wondering what she could be doing in a place like this?

Renee talks to a group of ex-con miners. "You're free now, boys, congratulations, but have you wondered what that means? What's freedom when all you're free to do is work in the Maven coalmine?"

"What other options do we have?" A miner asks.

"What other options than drunkenness, poverty, hunger and despair? Under this system of disposability, there seem to be very few options, I'm afraid." Renee says to their grumblings. "Which is why we need better wages, more time off, and more dynamic opportunities to progress as individuals. If we're free to imagine alternatives then why don't we?" She asks. "We should imagine how we can all thrive together!"

"Yeah!" The crowd shouts.

"But we're employees of the Maven Mine, or desperately trying to be." A miner reminds.

"If we want to thrive together how can we without abolishing the barriers of scarcity and material needs? We all crave freedom, but true freedom can only be achieved beyond these barriers!" Renee jeers. "Your self-interest is best accomplished through collaboration and association, because we are not talking about one elf, but all of you. The true flourishing of creativity can only happen when we all collaborate with each other. So, we can do more than just buy things."

"But what is freedom good for if not for buying things?" A miner asks.

"That is materialist freedom, my friend, not true freedom. The freedom to purchase the few things you can afford only keeps your lot stuck. Your liberties become embedded within the social relations of market exchange, which is based on private property and individual rights *alone*."

"Who's to blame? A miner asks.

Willie Maven? The likes of your father?" Another miner asks.

"It doesn't matter who you blame. Neither voters, owners, producers or consumers will find themselves responsible for the struggling, poorly employed, unemployed or destitute. They all must turn a blind eye if they're going to sleep at night. They believe your struggle results from nature and destiny, and no one else is responsible for that but yourself, or maybe even God."

"Nonsense!" A miner yells.

"Even worse, they deny the obligation to do anything about your conditions in the name of freedom." Renee states before slugging back her eggnog, showing the guys she can drink too. She consumes her eggnog in one impressive swig before slamming the glass down on the bar.

"A system based on scarcity, impoverishment, labor surpluses and unfulfilled needs can't allow us real freedom." She says before letting out a massive belch, earning an applause.

Willie turns to Sticky flushed with disbelief, scared what this means for him.

Renee continues, "My friends, your only option is to unionize, and once we do that WE STRIKE."

Sticky spits eggnog all over himself in horror – blowing their "cover" instantly.

"Sticky? Willie? What are you doing here?" Renee yells. "And why are you so dirty?"

"Just enjoying some eggnog, or spitting it out in Sticky's case." Willie says.

"We're just spying on you dear, nothing more." Sticky mentions as Willie eyes roll back into his brain.

"You two are as nimble as a pair of walruses in a china shop." Renee says.

"We came to hire some workers and then you show up – to organize a strike against me? Not nice."

"You're upset? I was just spied on!" Renee shouts.

Renee turns to the enthused mob of miners behind her. "We're all free elves, and we have the freedom to unionize or the freedom to be exploited by Mr. Maven for immense profits, the choice is yours."

Willie pulls himself close to Renee, whispers to her, "Do we have to do this here, like this?"

She doesn't respond, instead she stands to project her voice, "There are two kinds of freedom, one good and one bad. Mr. Maven here represents the bad freedoms."

"And what are those, Renee?"

Renee speaks louder, "The freedom to exploit, the freedom to profit massively without equivalent service to society. The freedom to keep inventions from being used for public benefit, or the freedom to profit from public resources which have been secretly seized for private advantage, just like your seizure of our coalmine by Maven here, himself!"

Willie steps up, "Fine, but the market produces freedoms we all prize. The freedom of conscious, freedom of speech, freedom of meeting, of association, and even the freedom to choose one's own job. How many of these freedoms have we enjoyed under Kris Kringle? Very Few! And believe it or not I support working with your new union leadership, be it the backstabbing Ms. Kendal-Crink or otherwise!"

"We here in ye' ol' Coal and Stocking Tavern see your tricks." She says to louder jeers. "We cherish these freedoms but they are the byproducts of the same economy responsible for the evil ones. Don't let planning and control be attacked as a denial of freedom, in fact it's our only means of protecting it!"

"Free enterprise and private ownership are essential to freedom, no society built on other foundations is free!" Willie exclaims.

"As bold a statement as it is ridiculous." Renee interrupts.

"The freedom that regulation produces is unfreedom; the justice, liberty and welfare it offers is merely another form of slavery." Willie says.

"Slavery, Willie? Your idea of freedom degenerates into a mere advocacy of free enterprise, which means the fullness of freedom for those whose income, leisure and security need *no* enhancing, leaving a mere pittance of liberty for the rest of us. We supposedly have democratic rights so let's use them to protect against this ignorance."

"The votes have been counted, Renee, it's a landslide victory for your father and it's a landslide victory for the market. The market is necessary for the North Pole to survive and that's all I care about."

"You only care about the survival of your investments and the fattening of your bank account." Renee replies.

"I care about these things, yes, but I care for my workers too! I trust the skills that you all possess can and will be met in the marketplace. Greater freedom and liberty of action in the labor markets are a virtue for capital and labor alike. That's real freedom." Willie says.

"An empty stomach isn't conducive to freedom no matter how specialized or flexible or educated one might be!" Renee argues as the elves of the tavern roar aloud, each with their own stomach half full.

"Sir, I think it's best we leave." Sticky tells Willie.

"Best listen to your slave, Master Maven."

"He's his own elf and a respected one at that!"

"Sadly, that doesn't appear to be true either." Renee attacks, enticing the crowd as her words cut Willie. His heart breaks with a sense of betrayal.

In his defeat Willie guides Sticky through the angry mob as they're pushed and smacked around in their escape. They gasp for air upon their arrival to the street. From outside they hear Renee...

"With your support I'm pleased to form the Coal Miners Labor Union with all of you! Together we will strike for better wages, better conditions and respect and dignity itself. May the workers of the North Pole *unite!*"

"Unionize! Unionize!" The crowd cheers.

Several weeks later the Coal Miners union is demonstrating full force within the city Square. They picket and chant slogans, all led by Renee. They demonstrate peacefully under the close watch of the Redcoats, who remain armed with dense candy cane clubs, standing alert on the walls and surrounding buildings.

Above the chaos, within Santa's Tower lurks Klaus, Willie, Sir Louie, Axel and Otto. They watch, smoke, drink and contemplate solutions of the last resort. The coal miners work stoppage has brought production and every aspect of North Pole Inc. to a halt. Renee and the miners have finally realized their leverage as everything now runs on coal. But the two parties have been at a dead standstill, and neither show signs of backing down.

The desperate group of executives and officials return inside to Klaus' office, which has transformed into a war room as the thunderous chants continue below.

"They've been unpaid for weeks. Shouldn't their landlords be kicking them out by now?" Otto remarks.

Klaus stares daggers at Otto. "This has gotten way out of hand, hasn't it?" Adding an elbow into Otto's ribs.

"It has, it has..." Otto repeats as if he's responsible for the event itself.

"Renee's just trying to get back at us for not supporting her...politics." Axel remarks.

"She thinks you've taken her spot." Sir Louie tells Axel. "She always wanted to be a politician, like her father."

"And like her father, she's stubborn as hell!" Klaus yells. "You're the only one who can bring her to the table."

"Me? Impossible!" Sir Louie shrieks. "She'd love that – I'd never give her the satisfaction. She needs discipline!"

Willie rolls his eyes. "You know, I can take a hit on the coal investment if it's better to go back on sugar. Paradoxically these miners would lose their jobs because of it. But I could just close it all down, you know? That'd be a shame."

"An honorable concession, but we can't." Klaus says.

"It's the principle of the matter!" Sir Louie shouts.

"That and the fact that the banking system has created much more money than available sugar in the bank reserves. Using the sugar for production would strain the supply. It's the bank's sugar reserve that's supposed to anchor the system. If there's a run on the banks for sugar and we can't redeem it, there'd be a devastating blow to the confidence of the banks. At the end of the day it's confidence that the entire system runs on, nothing more." Klaus explains.

"What do we do?" Willie asks again.

"Unfortunately, we're left with one option." Klaus states bluntly.

"One option?" Willie questions.

"Force." Klaus says plainly. "Besides, how do we know it wasn't Renee's people behind the Christmas Tree burning?"

"You're serious?" Willie asks. "She'd never– "

"I wouldn't be so sure, Maven."

"I am." Willie answers.

"An illicit march in Germany would've been shut down with bullets!" Otto yells.

"This isn't Germany, it's the North Pole." Willie replies. "And it's only illegal because you all deemed it so."

Klaus pulls away and escapes to the window alone, the new vantage point offers him some space to think. He stares down into the scene of protest and spots an evergreen that's caught on fire. It could've been on purpose, it could've been an accident, but to him it doesn't matter. He grins as the flames illuminate his pupils while he leans into his view with an inspired idea.

"Everyone, they're burning another tree! It *was* them. That's what they do. *Sickening*, how they torch to the most sacred symbol of Christmas."

They all rush to watch as the small, undecorated evergreen burns. Klaus sips his scotch and thinks, it's all becoming clear to him. The time for action is now.

"Gentleman, gentle-elves," Klaus begins, "The freedoms we enjoy may sometimes rest upon the unfreedom of others. But with this revelation we have a true justification on our side. Yet even without it, the reality is both parties have 'right' on their side. We seek to extract as much labor from the workforce as possible while they seek to protect their freedom to live without being worked to death. *Between equal rights force decides.* It's the only way, so let's get on with it."

"Funny you consider these rights equal." Willie says.

"They most certainly are." Klaus says sharply. "And to our good fortune we already have them trapped within the Square and surrounded. Our position doesn't much better than this, right here, right now."

"There must be another way." Willie protests.

"We would've come up with it by now, Maven, I assure you!" Klaus uncharacteristically yells, pounding his fists against the oak desk. He takes a moment to cool. "It's the only way, and if any of you care for your sister, daughter or whatever you call Willie's relationship, then I advise someone to get Renee to turn herself in, or at least warn her, before it's too late."

"I'll remind you I call the shots here, Klaus." Sir Kendal-Crink challenges.

"I'll remind you that I fund your Redcoats, government and everything in between. So, no, I call the shots. Warn her or don't, it's not my concern." Klaus retaliates.

Willie slams the door behind him journeying to Renee as fast as he can.

He arrives outside the protest. It's snowing and bitter cold. The Redcoats have many spotlights shinning and illuminating the protesters, tracking their moves as they chant in a sing-song melody. Willie spots Renee in the distance and rushes toward her, pushing past the picket-lines and dodging snowballs, sprinting to her as if traversing an obstacle course.

He arrives to Renee out of breath. Her body guards surround him, but she nods, giving her guards permission to let him near.

"You have to shut this down, right now," Willie exasperates.

"You're out of your mind." Renee fires back.

"You see those Redcoats, they'll club all of you down, every last one, I swear."

"It's the North Pole, Willie, we're not violent brutes. This is a peaceful protest and negotiation."

"This isn't the North Pole you or I grew up in, it's a whole new world, Klaus already gave the order and your Dad doesn't seem to mind."

"If they want this over they can negotiate."

"You're not listening, Renee! There's no negotiation, only evacuation. Save your workers if you care, or do something, anything before it's too late. I'm begging you, turn yourself in and they might go easy on you."

"We're not backing down!"

"You'd let them be trampled because of your stubbornness? That's exactly what's about to happen."

"I'm not giving in to these intimidation tactics. All of you in that corrupt ivy tower need to be stood up to."

"Renee, I'm begging you – "

In that moment hundreds of whistles blow aloud as the Redcoats raise their candy cane clubs and rush into the Square. Willie bursts with adrenaline as he *pounces* on Renee, wrestling her to a safe corner.

But he's quickly attacked by her union body guards…until they're too distracted in their own defense and must fend for themselves amid the bum-rush of Redcoats.

Willie holds Renee tight, still against her will, but they watch as the Redcoats relentlessly club away at every protester in a bloody, horrifying scene of mass violence. Their candy cane clubs bash away *cracking* skulls and bones.

Within minutes the beaten down miners produce a glistening pool of candy red blood which flows atop of the cobblestone like a syrupy red stream. Even so, the Redcoats' brutality grows fiercer, pounding and pummeling away as if releasing a volcanic force of their own resentment.

From their corner Renee releases herself from Willie's protective cover. Their faces sparkle with the glitter of elvish blood. They wheeze, finding it hard to breathe as they watch the scene unfold, realize the truth of their new reality unveiling before their very eyes. They know this is the power dynamic and social relation playing out in the physical form. This is the domination of capital against the individual, manifest. *All the relations which money so neatly conceals and distorts becoming absolutely unraveled and stripped bare before them.*

Among the screams and confusion one thing is clear, the utter domination of the Redcoats over the protesters – and *the utter domination of capital against labor.*

Renee breaks down in tears as Willie tries to console her but she's quick to push him away.

"I'm so sorry – "

"Stop it –"

"Who was that elf with you when you entered the Tavern? Did they put you up to this?"

"Stop it –"

"I need to know how this got started."

"You think I'm incapable of thinking for myself, don't you?!"

"Who was that?" Willie asks.

"We live in different worlds, Willie."

"We don't..."

"You don't understand." She stammers, letting out a stream of tears, but by the time she dries her eyes they're surrounded by Redcoats. They shove Willie aside and throw Renee in handcuffs.

"Stop!" He screams.

But Renee is swiftly carried off, leaving Willie devastated. He watches as the last protesters are clubbed into the ground. Once they're unconscious or immobile they're chained up and dragged through the bloody cobblestone to the barred-up, reindeer-drawn prisoner carriages. Willie realizes there are a number of elves on the ground that are no long breathing. His tears flow while his heart nearly beats out of his chest.

Klaus approaches him with an entourage of Redcoats, arrives

with a hug, holding Willie tight in his unsettled state.

"I'm sorry, my elf, I really am. But it was the only way."

Willie pushes Klaus off and labors to catch his breath.

Klaus, unable to bear the disgruntled sounds fills the air with words...

"It's not just the miners' power we've had to dismantle, but the bargaining power of all labor. They're just the unfortunate example that had to be made."

"No." Willie gabbles inaudibly.

"Not only have we restored our power, but in doing so we've created an industrial reserve army. A real win-win, not to mention the system requires this, Willie. I will not feel bad when we have no other option. We need them to not only feel entirely replaceable, but they must actually be so. In several years' time we'll have a wholly compliant labor force and this little incident will have been worth it many times over."

"If they're stripped of their unions they'll just turn to gangs, cartels, mafias or cults." Willie mumbles.

"All the more reason to strengthen the Redcoats." Klaus says.

"You've turned them into attack dogs."

"Funny how a few good attack dogs create a situation where the many are governed by the few. Surprising, because force is always on the side of the governed. If they realized that we could be out in no time. The government is founded on control of opinion and little more, my elf."

"You've underestimated the terror of brute force."

"Oh no, I understand that quite well." Klaus replies.

16 – SANTA-TRON

FIVE YEARS LATER – the North Pole is much hazier in appearance and spirit, with an ever-clotting layer of brownish-yellow smog that thickens the air. The smog dims the once vibrantly colored homes as their formerly glorious facades have gone faded, and it permeates entire districts with a heavy metallic scent so dense that it can be tasted on the tip of the tongue.

Meanwhile, most elves have transformed into indebted, compliant, zombie-like creatures who quietly slog through the streets. They have little if anything to say to each other between labored breaths of their hurried commute. Those who breathe well do so because of gas masks, a gloomy yet popular new fashion. Overall, the joyous, charming character of the North Pole has been replaced by a steampunk culture that praises technology and machinery, with the traditional red and green color schemes traded in for shades of black and gray.

The elvish pains of their deteriorated conditions show up in obvious ways like cancer, sickness and heart attack. Yet, increasingly their collective stress is expressed in more common and subtle signs, like heavy dark bags under the eyes, premature wrinkling and an overall unshakeable sluggishness. The lethargy leaves elves with just enough energy to get through the working day and little more.

Sometimes an overload of coffee or sugar can provide just enough energy to prevent collapse. However, these "fixes" come at the expense of obesity, diabetes (which requires a ridiculous amount of sugar for an elf to incur) and a massive spike in depression and substance abuse. Suicide, an unknown concept to elves until recently, is "combated" by the installation of suicide nets, a newly required feature at all major factories still employing an elvish workforce. Perhaps more concerning is the death of the elvish imagination itself, as words, images and symbols are deflated of their meaning while the population absent-mindedly registers their own condemnation.

Contrary to the elvish condition, the grace and brilliance of the North Pole's newfound technology has become society's most magnificent feature. For instance, the glistening black locomotives, so shiny they're reflective, have changed the nature of urban transport. They glide swiftly through a network of tunnels like clockwork, and earn the praise of all who ride them.

Power Looms, Assembly Line Robots and numerous other technologies have disrupted the fabric of society. Even more fantastical, the birth and use of analog computers, coal powered land-ships, the inception of powerful calculators and thinking machines all massively affect every aspect of life.

Willie is older and flashier, but also harsher and emotionally vacant. He's still a classy dresser but even more Euro in appearance, so much so he's easily confused as a German with dwarfism. Perhaps his most noticeable update is the replacement of his hook hand with a high-tech platinum prosthetic. The robotic piece is composed of an elaborate gearset and is made visible through its outer protective glass casing, allowing him to show off the inner workings that resemble a precisely tuned Swiss watch. He finely taps his metallic thumb against each robotic digit while awaiting his ride. The dexterity and nimbleness with which he masterfully controls it gives him some gratification.

As he exits his chic multistory brownstone, Willie's stern expression softens as the uniformed valet escorts Ursus, who's bigger and now fully mature. Ursus snorts with joy as Willie scratches his face. The valet fastens an elaborately decorated, hand stitched leather saddle to Ursus' back. The stitching is a collage of meaningful images from Willie's life: Wolf Sledding, the Maven Workshop, the towers of Santa's Hermitage, the Sugar Dollar Symbol, coordinates of the North Pole (a nod to his fascination with maps and geography), his parents, Ursus, and lastly the German symbol of the twisted cross which has proliferated across the North Pole. The symbol has become so prominent it's now on every government building, legal document, flag and banner.

Today is a special day for Willie, one he's been looking forward to for five years – the release of Renee from prison. It's a particularly nerve-wracking one as they haven't seen each other since that violent, fateful night. Not only has Willie been denied visitation, but the German Prison Warden has kept her cut off from everyone.

Willie's got a surprise but he's in a rush to complete it – KITTY-tron. A robotic cat capable of emotional intelligence. It's like a real cat in that it can sense basic expressions and emotions. It knows to purr when you're frazzled, cuddle when you're lonely, and widen its eyes in the most adorable way as to make you smile. Although it's a prototype, Klaus has provided a vast investment to the Maven Workshop for funding its research and development. KITTY-tron is Willie's baby, but knows it's only a small part of a much larger artificial intelligence initiative, one that Klaus has particular interest in.

And like every surviving business in the North Pole, the Maven Workshop has endured an endless process of "Creative Destruction." Through being a well-connected cutthroat Willie has endured capital's endless process of replacing the old with the new. Meanwhile most elvish and even German businesses, outside of financial speculation and legal entanglement, have failed during this same time.

The survival of any North Pole business venture has become a ruthless process that all comes down to making or losing money. The possibilities for prosperity and the threats of destitution that the system operates by raises some and crushes others, over and over. But in pursuing wealth most entrepreneurial elves lose everything. Family fortunes vanish and whole regions of the North Pole have been devastated.

The fact remains that many businesses have died, few have survived, and the weak companies are consumed by the large and powerful in a process of mergers and acquisitions, a process that the German investment banks have profited handsomely from. Through consolidation there is substantially less competition as the mid-sized companies are consumed by the monoliths, while the boutiques, which are all in extreme competition with one another, struggle to survive in niche businesses that the monoliths are not yet interested in annihilating.

The essential idea that Willie has mastered is adapting to the direction of the blowing wind. He knows the system can never can be stationary, and the fundamental impulse that keeps the engine in motion comes from the ever-growing demand for Christmas presents, and the shifting fashions and fads of human children. With that, there are new opportunities for methods of production, along with new markets, organization and forms of industry that relentlessly revolutionize the economy from within, nonstop destroying the old, nonstop creating the new. Along with his newfound respect, or fear even, Willie has mastered the game.

The valet helps Willie onto the saddle and presents him with his gasmask, but today he refuses. His newborn perversion towards the accumulation of fortune has him enjoying his breathes of smog and fumes. In a way he feels as if he's existentially inhaling his fortune, making it a part of his physical being and becoming one with it. With a good whiff of the cool winter air followed by a slight chemical burn he and Ursus are headed back to the Maven Workshop. But like everything else the nature of his commute has transformed dramatically...

As they make their way down the old cobblestone streets, it's not long before Willie is flanked by a mob of elves. With some irony, these aren't protesters, coal miners or blue-collar workers, but are college educated elves. They wildly wave their resumes, shout their credentials and GPA's, all desperate for a job. As they get a bit too close Ursus fiercely *roars*, showing off his 42 teeth and sharp canines, making the desperate grads jump for a moment until they continue to swarm like pesky fleas...all the way to the Maven Workshop.

Underneath his brutish gaze Willie feels sympathy for these elves. They're crushed by the weight of their student loans, their debt already claiming their future labor as they fight for the rare and modest job offer they'd kill to receive. In this way *their future is already foreclosed in that they have to pay off their debt before they can have a life of their own.* The debt creates anti-value in that these grads won't have a right to the value they're going to hopefully one day create – because the capitalist owns that. They still have to figure out how to create value for themselves in order to pay off the debt, or spend a lifetime attempting to pay it off in small increments. It's a bad situation, and for most their odds for a good life are heartbreakingly slim.

There's a part of Willie that feels guilty, profiting immensely from the bundle of student debt he owns. But like every good capitalist, he's learned how to justify his ways and the nature of things, besides capitalism must develop the intellectual power of the worker. A knowledge solution to modern problems is cheap and limitless.

But to him, this mob of educated unemployed elves is a simple mismatch between supply and demand. There are too few jobs which require actual creative thinking and ingenuity, and too many over-educated elves with MBA's, Law Degrees and the alike. The misbalance creates unsatisfactory work conditions, employing many in substandard work at wages below those of the better-paid blue-collar elves.

Meanwhile, those who studied the arts, philosophy or humanities rarely have a shot of real employment or use for their degree, so Willie spares few feelings for those foolish dissidents. Those creatives, caregivers, intellectuals and everyday teachers, have been forewarned that those privileged enough to make a positive contribution to society is the reward itself, therefore any significant financial rewards aren't justified. Simply put, *the more your work benefits others and the more social value you create - the less likely you'll be paid for it.* Those who have chosen this path often accept their fate as martyrs or idealists, struggling and suffering for their dedicated pursuit, be it art, literature, intellectual contribution or otherwise. And their struggle is often a painfully lonely one.

Those unemployed, unsatisfactorily employed or unemployable add to the swelling group of intellectuals, and together they enter the capitalist system with deep resentment. That or they become adults living with their parents, or go homeless, starve or live on the fringe of society. The inescapable discontent breeds resentment and hatred, which is why Ursus is trained to defend Willie with his claws and teeth if necessary.

So those struggling without work resent the employed, and the employed are encouraged to resent the poor and the unemployed, who are constantly told are freeloaders collecting welfare to survive. Those trapped in mind-numbing jobs resent workers who get to do real beneficial work, and those who do real beneficial work go underpaid, degraded and unappreciated. This group resents those who they see as monopolizing the few jobs where one can live well while doing something useful or high-minded.

Willie keenly knows that these groups are united in their

loathing for the likes of Sir Louie, Axel and the rest of the corrupt political class. But it's all too easy for the master manipulators, like Sir Louie, to identify these groups and wield these divisions of hatred extremely conveniently, diverting attention from themselves and placing it on others.

As Willie arrives at the workshop he's greeted by an entourage of assistants and security guards. He collects a few resumes from the swarming flock before security pushes them away. He skims a couple, most look identical, a good school, a good GPA, nothing that really stands out. They enter the workshop and Willie tosses the resumes into the trash almost instinctually. He struts fast while his assistants struggle to keep with his pace, each trying to earn his attention with an impressive stack of paperwork requiring his approval.

"Where's the 'tron? Today's the day, it must be ready!" Willie shouts with urgency as he struts down the corridors.

"Which tron, sir?" An assistant asks.

"Kitty-tron, damn it! Is Kitty, ready?" He shouts.

"Ready as she'll ever be."

"Say that again." Willie demands.

"Ready as she'll ever be."

"You're fired."

"But" –

"Somebody get me Kitty!" He yells, while a faction of assistant break from the march rushing to find it.

As he cruises the workshop the most obvious update is the army of robots "manning" the assembly-line. The only elves on the floor are the engineers repairing, reprogramming or re-engineering the robots. Every other elf has been assigned an 8 x 6-foot partial cubicle, middle management at the 12 x 10 executive workstations, and top brass in their own offices – with every employee salivating over the corner offices with 180-degree views of the city.

Along with the all the specializations, every department head now needs a senior vice-president and vice-president below them, and each of them needs a management team, secretaries, administrative staff, temp workers and unpaid interns for the ultimate mind-numbing tasks, all of which create strong partitions and layers upon layers of red tape between the various divisions.

Occasionally Willie thinks if he didn't bother showing up a majority of his staff wouldn't notice. Perhaps they'd even carry on more effectively. The shifting outlook depends if he's feeling particularly self-hating that day.

Regardless of his mood it's easy for him to spot a certain, common type of employee, one who exists primarily to make someone else look or feel important. After all, Workshop Society has always surrounded themselves with servants, sycophants, and minions of one sort or another. Many are expected to do at least some actual work, but even within his office of CEO there are gate keepers whose job it is to stand around and look impressive. Besides you cannot be magnificent without an entourage, and for the truly splendid, the very uselessness of the uniformed security and hovering assistants is the utmost testimony to their supposed greatness. In reality, the whole point is to employ some handsome young elves in flashy uniforms to make one look regal while holding court.

But Willie spots other cases where the secretaries and assistants end up doing the bosses' jobs for them entirely. While the secretary's job description outlines answering the phone, taking dictation, and checking the telegram, in fact, they often end up doing the vast majority of their bosses' jobs, or sometimes, all of it.

The paradox of these paper pushing jobs is that most elves' sense of dignity and self-worth are caught up in working for a living, even though most hate their jobs, finding them physically exhausting, boring or even humiliating and needless. But they want to work because they're aware at some level that work plays a crucial role to the contribution of their social standing, becoming more and more an end in itself, which is ultimately the most harmful fact of the matter.

Although Willie's grown a contempt for his bureaucracy of paper-pushers, there's a special paper-pusher which he increasingly appreciates – his *lawyers*. Those sharp minded legal experts who used to be the highly creative and imaginative game inventors of the past. Game makers who created complex and interesting sets of rules in which multifaceted, strategic and dynamic games were made. But these days their best function is in regards to keeping Willie out of trouble, as a considerable amount of their energy go into the nonproductive struggles at the intersection of business with the state.

Willie knows the real power and brains of the organization are his technologists, scientists and engineers. These are the gifted creators who were the most passionate toy producers of the past – but their focus now is the maintenance and advancement of robots which produce toys. Ironically, their next project is building robots which build robots, in essence replacing themselves. Willie knows their real purpose is figuring out how to maximize profits, which typically means finding new ways to replace jobs.

There are other techies who build tools for the organization's workers. But many end up questioning if their inventions even slightly lightened the toil of any elf. Many find that answer to be a resounding *"no"* – because the very purpose of their technology is to extract more profit from labor, the opposite of lightening their load.

Today the Maven Workshop has about half the staff than before, and Willie wants as few paper-pushers fumbling about as possible. The good news for him, and the bad news for his employees, is the techies have identified that most complex jobs are just a series of narrowly defined tasks set within a sequence of actions. Robots are good at narrowly defined tasks and smart robots are good at them in a sequence. Software excels at looped behavior, so in another twist of dark irony the looped specialized skills that most students have drowned themselves in debt for, trains them to do what software already does best. Software threatens to replace every elf with a repetitive work process. The elves only real remaining advantage are *outstanding acts of creation* – that can't be taught or replicated.

"WHERE'S KITTY?!" Willie yells again as his engineers put the final touches on KITTY's learning algorithm. KITTY, like other smart robots, learn through data analysis, and becomes better at something through the relationships they discover. KITTY, and the process of machine learning shows more potential because the institutions of the North Pole are gathering data about everything. Through this vast data library machines can learn how elves do the things they do, and then do them better. The resulting benefits to Willie are a reduction of payroll costs by 50% the first year and 25% the second year – across a spectrum of jobs. Irony endures as every other job that opens at the Maven Workshop does not require a college degree.

The other hurdle facing Willie and capitalists is that knowledge-driven capitalism cannot support a price mechanism where the value of something is dictated by the value of the inputs needed to produce it. It's impossible to correctly value inputs when they come in the form of social knowledge. Knowledge-driven production tends toward the unlimited creation of wealth, independent of the labor expanded. But the normal capitalist system is based on prices determined by input costs and assumes all inputs come in a limited supply.

If a machine that lasts forever can produce a good that can be made with no labor input, that item transfers a near-zero amount of labor value to the product, so the value of each product is reduced. The pursuit of ever-cheaper goods for the sustenance of the labor force makes lower wages more acceptable. But if social labor disappears, if everything were made purely by machines, then there is no actual value to be represented in pricing. The representation of value – the Sugar Dollar – becomes entirely free from its obligation to represent anything other than itself.

Willie and his entourage arrive at his office as the assistants pile their stacks of paper onto his desk. He pours himself an Irish Coffee, chases them out and slams the door. He takes a breath and a sip before turning to his chalkboard and spinning it over. It lists three CEO goals that are always on his mind;

(1) increase precision in the labor process, (2) increase productivity and (3) disempower the worker. And the answers to these three concerns are tech. Besides, robots don't complain, answer back, sue, get sick, go slow, lose concentration, go on strike, demand higher wages, worry about work conditions, want coffee breaks or

simply refuse to show up. Tech is Willie's answer, and as tech becomes an independent business it no longer responds to primary needs, instead it creates innovations that have to find new markets as it creates new wants, needs and desires. In this the way the business further thrives and promotes his inherently flawed belief that tech fixes all problems.

As he takes a sip and lets the whisky burn, he contemplates perhaps his largest existential threat - the collapse of elvish demand for goods and services, especially as jobs and incomes disappear. He knows this will have catastrophic effects upon the North Pole economy unless the state intervenes with welfare payments to those *large segments of the elvish population which have already become redundant*. In fact, these welfare payments will have to happen for the literal survival of the North Pole – and if it doesn't happen it'd be *nothing short of catastrophic*.

But Willie has a plan to come out unscathed – to continue to rely on the circulation of fictitious forms of capital within the credit system. This makes the reinvestment of profits into stocks, bonds, hedge funds, mortgage-backed securities, futures markets and the alike – strategically much more important. To him, this far outweighs the reinvestment of funds into employees (except for techies), it outweighs investment into education (because elves already pay for that themselves, through debt), and far outweighs investment into job creation (which he actively works against).

He takes another sip of his Irish Coffee – not enough whiskey he thinks, and pours some more, much more, filling the mug to the brim before throwing it back in one quick *swig*, enjoying the temporary burn a bit too much.

"Where's KITTY?!" He drunkenly yells out the door.

Moments later a team of assistants frantically pour into his office. With them is the functional prototype of KITTY. They present it to Willie in a hurry as the skittish metallic cat hops from their grip to the floor. It scurries around, wanting to frightfully escape, but Willie is enthralled, delighted with its delicate quick movements, robust meows and realistic responses.

"Out!" He orders his staff as he sits behind his desk and disarmingly smiles at KITTY, showing her she has nothing to be afraid of. KITTY takes notice, slows its motion and softly approaches before *hopping* on his desk, investigating him with a gentle curiosity. They stare down one another until Willie slowly sticks out his hand allowing KITTY to sniff it, she does, and in that instant they become quick friends. KITTY rolls over and even offers him to pet her metallic belly (with pressure sensors just beneath her alloy skin). He laughs and pets her belly as she PURS with a soothing coo.

"Don't let me down, KITTY-tron."

That night, Willie, Sir Louie and Axel stand outside the doors of the grungy prison. Each hold their own wrapped gift as Willie's box rattles with KITTY inside. Axel rolls his eyes as they uncomfortably stand in silence awaiting Renee's release. With the *clanking* of gears the prison doors open revealing a beaten down Renee held up by a guard. She steps forward and nearly falls, but regains balance with a series of awkward stumbles before shuffling forward. She doesn't smile or make a sound, in fact she doesn't react at all, not even batting an eye at the three who stand there in shock.

Axel is the first to approach, placing his gift at her feet before moving to hug her – but she lifts her arm preventing him.

Next, Sir Louie moves in.

"Darling, are you okay? You're free now, you've done your time. We're overwhelmed with joy!"

She doesn't answer and just hobbles past him, not looking his way.

"There was nothing I could do, darling, the prison is privatized. It was out of my hands, Renee!" He pitifully pleads. Still no reaction.

Willie leaves his gift behind and approaches her.

"I'm so sorry," he tells her.

"You're all cruel." She says before shuffling on as a sleek land-ship with tinted windows and a driver pulls up curbside. Ginger

Garland opens the door from inside and pats the leather seat next to her. Her gaze offers Renee a soft, sad dose of sympathy and the only warmth in a world of cold.

"Come lovely, let's go." Ginger says.

Just as Renee is about the enter the land-ship Willie's rattling box bursts open with KITTY pouncing out. KITTY spots Renee (it's programmed to identify her) and *meows* with excitement as she skips and expediently hops toward her – making Renee shriek in fear. Out of the pure reaction Renee *kicks* KITTY'S head clean off, recoils and cries in panic before hoping into the land-ship. She slams the door and they speed off, the tires running over KITTY, leaving it utterly destroyed in the street.

"So that's KITTY-tron?" Sir Louie utters.

"That was KITTY-tron." Willie corrects.

"I need a drink. Where's the other 'tron? Is it ready?" Sir Louie asks.

"Just about." Willie answers dismally.

"Can I see it?" Sir Louie asks as Axel leaves the scene in disgust.

It's after hours at the Maven Workshop as Willie guides Sir Louie through the shop floor. They sling back a liquorish liqueur, passing the flask before Willie spots several of his techies "crunching numbers" on their boxed shaped analog computers.

"Is the 'tron ready?" Willie slurs.

"KITTY?" A techie asks.

"KITTY's dead." Willie responds to their dismay.

"KITTY's dead?"

"That's what I said, KITTY is DEAD! If you're going to cry do so for my investment, not for a robot!" Willie blasts.

"But all of our work -"

"And all of my money! Now is the other tron ready!?"

"Uh..."

"It best be!"

"Putting on the finishing touches now, Sir."

"Show me him." Willie demands.

The techies press a button lifting the protective metal blinds from their observation deck. With a flash of steam, a husky android carrying a large sack and missing a face is exposed on the floor. The group stares out with their eyes glued at the coming together of their masterpiece.

A machine arm reaches out and places a face on the android, completing its form. As the robot arm retracts the rudimentary metallic face of Santa Claus is exposed.

Willie smiles as he hovers over a red switch. "And now the moment of truth," Willie says as he flicks a switch and the Santa android twitches to life.

"I am Santa-tron." It says robotically.

"Wow." Willie smiles.

"Your interest payment is due. Make your payment, draw a new loan, or *take your chances*." Santa-tron says in a menacing manner.

"It works!" Sir Louie bursts in joy.

"It certainly does." Willie says.

"The future payment of debt is secure!" Sir Louie cheers.

"For now..." Willie quips.

"How does draw a new loan work?"

"Well it doesn't come from thin air, Sir L. It's a loan against the increasing value of an elf's home, an apparent windfall. Only homeowners qualify for that option."

"Ah, and, 'take your chances' - very funny, what's that?"

212

"A funny one indeed...Techies, get in there with Santa-tron and show your leader *take your chances.*"

"Do we have to?" Squibbles, the nerdiest techie, asks in his high-pitched voice.

"No, only you do, Squibbles. Now go!" Willie orders.

Squibbles reluctantly hops the barrier and comes face to face with Santa-tron who towers over him. Santa-tron's stiff expression morphs into a sly grin as his eyes light up with a bright red neon glow, making poor Squibbles shake in his boots.

"Really?" Squibbles begs one last time.

"You're well paid and have health insurance, do you really want to risk that? You'll be fine Squibbles." Willie says nonchalantly.

Squibbles takes a deep breath and utters, "I'll take my chances," to Santa-tron.

From Santa-tron's fat metallic stomach emerges a lever while simultaneously unhinging his jaw as a *holographic slot machine projects from its mouth* and into the space in front of Squibbles. There are four options which spin slowly then quicken to a dizzying speed. The possibilities are: (1) "Report to Credit Agency, Lose Credit", (2) Seize Collateral, (3) Risk Free 30-Day Extension and (4) an image of a Candy Cane. Squibbles holds his breath and pulls down the lever making the spinning wheel slow all the way to a stop before landing on...*the Candy Cane.*

"Oh dear," Squibbles utters.

Santa-tron laughs manically, pulls a metal Candy Cane club from his sack and *BAM* - clubs poor Squibbles over the head with one forceful swing, leaving him bleeding from the skull and knocked out cold.

"Holy shit!" Sir Louie yelps with excitement, "That's awesome!"

Santa-tron mechanically steps into the spreading pool of blood and hovers over Squibbles' comatose body. It wraps his head with a bandage and prints a ticket from its mouth. Santa-tron leaves the ticket in Squibbles shirt collar, it reads: "Interest payment due in three days or Santa-tron will find you."

"Now that's technology!" Sir Louie laughs.

"You bet your ass it is." Willie slurs, finishing the flask.

"There's a cost to living the good life, isn't there?"

"Always." Willie answers.

17 – MUSICAL CHAIRS

Later, Willie knocks on Renee's door...

"Renee, please. Can't we talk?"

Willie knocks and knocks, but still no answer.

"Please? I'm sorry. I just want you to understand."

Still nothing.

"Maybe tomorrow." He says dejectedly and leaves.

It's about to blizzard by the time he arrives outside. Ursus smells his grief and rolls over in the snow showing off his circus tricks, but Willie hardly cracks a smile.

"Not now."

Ursus groans as Willie crawls onto the saddle on his back. They stand stationary, blank and dismal, as Willie is overcome with despair.

"We should pay 'em a visit, come on."

They take off in the snow, crisscrossing through sections of town amid hundreds of Santa-trons collecting debt. Willie's desensitized to the odd sight as the Santa-tron has become a feature of everyday life. But the Santa-trons are acting funny in the more precarious neighborhoods. For the first time Willie notices a huge uptick of elves getting violently whacked, imprisoned, or having their property seized on the spot. Sometimes rendering whole families homeless, which in the ice-cold winters of the North Pole, is a particularly severe fate.

Willie isn't sure what this means, but this new reality must be concerning for his vast holdings of mortgage-backed securities and collateral debt obligations.

Out of the Santa-trons' three initial options; (1) make your payment, (2) draw a new loan, or (3) take your chances, many elves, especially those homeowners who've been displaced at work, scavenging for work, or living paycheck to paycheck – choose the easiest option; drawing a new loan from the value of their home to pay the interest they owe. But Willie witnesses how the average working elf is consistently maxing out his or her credit and unable to make a payment or draw new loans, so they're "taking their chances" more often. This isn't good.

Next, Willie notices how few lights and fireplaces are on inside the spectacular flats of the affluent neighborhoods and glamorous towers. Many of these high-end, contemporary buildings are not even lived in. But Willie remembers these buildings are little more than investments, not only for the ultra-rich but for anyone with spare Sugar Dollars to invest. Evidentially, capital is building out the North Pole for the sake of investment, not to shelter elves in need of a roof over their head. Even more ironic, the effects of these sprouting, elaborate buildings lead to casting elves out of their homes and into the cold cobblestone streets.

But beyond those unfortunates' there are plenty living extravagantly. Willie peers inside some lavish homes and watches as they pop champagne for no reason other than it's Thursday. Others smile and wave from their hot tubs as he passes. Entire wings of homes are added while stacks of packages pile up on doorsteps from hurried couriers. Willie's perplexed as to how these modestly paid elves are living as well as he is - considering how poorly they're paid. But it's an obvious answer; leverage and debt.

Ursus steadily plows through the snow as the storm upgrades to an icy blizzard. They pass by the Belief Meter, which is at an all-time high, then past a loud burst of the Steam Whistle, closing out the workday with its incredible eruption of sound. Undeterred by the elements they arrive at the Maven Memorial, a modest tomb within a downtown park devoted to the memory of James and Lucy.

He picks some fresh mistletoe from the bushes, assembles a bouquet and places it gently in front of his mother and father's names etched in tomb stone. He stands there somber with Ursus, taking a moment to remember and let in the pain. The rush of emotions awakens him and makes him feel alive as it reminds him there's still a soft soul somewhere in his being.

Unbeknownst to Willie, Hanna von Wolf watches him from her office. She's never seen him so stripped down – the sight even disturbs her. Minutes later she joins his side at the tomb. They're no longer drunken lovers but share a professional relationship. Like Willie, she's grown jaded too. Her perky ways replaced with a seriousness, while her once high-pitched voice has gone coarse from years of daily smoking and drinking. She greets him with a firm, warm hug amid his meditation.

"It's blizzarding. Come inside, my new office is across the street. Let's warm up over some hot cocoa." She insists.

"That's your new office?" He asks with amusement as he turns to the new and immense headquarters of Golden Bells Bank. What was once a local bank is now an ultra-slick steel and glass structure reaching high into the clouds.

"Surely you've heard?" She asks.

"With all the building going on I can't keep up."

"Let me give you a tour."

They arrive inside as Hanna flaunts her new digs with steamy hot chocolates in hand. Although the Steam Whistle blew hours ago many analysts and executives are still at work, crunching numbers and endlessly circulating communication.

"Why's your staff and office about 10 times the size of mine?" He asks.

"Well, we're masters of the universe, Willie." She laughs with an undertone of seriousness.

"Very funny." He says.

"We're innovators."

"Of what? You don't make anything."

"Sure, we do – we make financial innovations. The best kind of innovations. We've got all the best brains and discovered so many creative ways to form and circulate interest-bearing capital." She smiles.

"You mean the circulation of debt?"

"I know it may seem strange, to think of financial centers that dominate our skyline as debt bottling plants..."

"Yes, very strange." He replies.

"But that's what we do. You manufacture toys, Santa-trons and many funny things – and we manufacture debt."

"But debt is a claim on future value. It's only redeemed through value production. How can you be so sure that the value will be redeemed?"

"That's a silly question."

"If future value production cannot redeem the debt, there's a crisis." He states.

"That's not exactly true." She responds. "Last year's debts are retired by borrowing even more money today."

"That's what they call a Ponzi Scheme, Hanna." He retaliates.

"Call it what you will, but that's how it works."

"Then rich grow richer through your financial 'innovations' while the poor become poorer through the necessity to repay their debt."

"Funny how you talk about the poor as if you're a saint."

"Saint Willie Maven has a nice ring," he smirks.

"There's always been 'the poor' but look at the average elf. The average elf has never been so wealthy. And just look at the Belief Meter!" She exclaims.

"I'm starting to feel like this is *all* built on a house of cards." Willie admits.

"Think of it rationally," she says, "if profit is highest in property markets or other forms of asset speculation then a rationalist capitalist places their money in property speculation rather than what you might call, productive activity."

"But is that rational when the working elves can barely get by?" He asks.

"I stand by my bank, Willie, and you should too. I'm proud of the credit we provide, particularly the subprime credit...innovation..."

"Why's that so special?"

"Because subprime credit incomes have been redistributed while leaving the likes of your profits untouched! Do you not see that as an incredible feat!? A grand redistribution of wealth while reducing taxes." She preaches. "It's the only solution if everyone is to get rich. That's what makes it *so special*."

"Look at you, preaching about wealth redistribution." He prods.

"But it's not through taking it from someone...like you. That's why no one fights it. You don't make money? Not a problem! Take out loans to buy a house, its value will increase and that will serve as collateral on new loans. You know how Santa-trons work, you've built the damn thing."

"So, you're saying the CDO functions on the expectation of infinite increases in prices of real estate?"

"Yes, there's a major connection, especially in our current economy. Look, you have to believe that banks like mine are necessary if everyone is going to be better off. You shouldn't be so worried."

"I'm more worried that you aren't worried in the least."

"If elves and Germans want their fancy landships and big McMansions that they can't afford - then I'm necessary. The only reason elves continue living like royalty is because we've got our fingers on the scales and we're tipping it in their favor. If I take my hand off, well then, the whole North Pole gets really fair, really quick, Willie. Nobody actually wants that, they say they do, but they really don't."

"You never feel like a hypocrite, even a little?"

She laughs. "Consumers want what we have to give, but they also want to play innocent and pretend like they have no idea where it came from. That's more hypocrisy than I'm willing to swallow, and just plain stupid if they've convinced themselves that Santa-tron is giving away credit for free."

Willie rolls his eyes and laughs, unsure what else to do amid the awkward tension.

"Speaking of Santa-trons, I've watched those robots bat elf after elf over the head for money. I've never seen that before, in those numbers at least."

"You're concerned about your investment..."

"I'm concerned about my fellow elf."

"Sure." She says dryly. "Don't worry, the adjustable rate mortgages are about to spike, we're all about to make a lot more money."

"How?"

"The interest rates on our adjustable rate mortgages have hovered around at 2-3% for the last five years, tomorrow the rates adjust, hiking up to 7-8%."

"That will do more harm than good, especially for you."

"If you forgot, banks make more money when the interest repaid on loans are higher – and you own much bank stock."

"But if elves are struggling with their current rates how are they supposed to make good on their payment with more than double the interest?"

"The value of their real estate is going to continue to increase." She bites back.

"Not if entire buildings are going vacant, which they are. This will be a massive acceleration to devaluation."

Several analysts outside of their conversation stop typing and lean in for a better listen, Hanna becoming acutely aware of the ease dropping.

"Christ, don't cause a scene, Willie."

"I've seen it with my own two eyes." He replies.

"You don't know what you see. You're so far out of touch with reality you have no idea what's going on out there or in here."

"Then explain to me what's going on with my mortgage-backed assets." Willie blurts.

"Do you really want me to explain the rocket science behind mortgage-backed securities? I will if I must..."

"No. But I want to know what kind of dividend it's yielding me."

"Jesus, Willie. Sit down."

He pulls up a chair and leans a bit too close, staring.

"It's not yielding a dividend."

"What?!"

"But its value is increasing and so we're able to resell it for profit." She yaps defensively.

"Do investors even know what they're buying when you sell these? Because, I don't get it."

"Just think of it as a bundle of mortgages, that's it."

"But if those bundles of mortgages are performing as they should then I should be getting my dividend. So, they're not performing?"

"That's not what's important. What's important is that you can resell it for a profit."

"That's where you're wrong, and if I'm the owner of tens of thousands of garbage mortgages I'd like to know."

Hanna takes a deep breath. "We don't use the term 'garbage' - we call them 'toxic' - and yes, you own plenty."

Willie is at a loss for words, shocked.

Hanna leans in, seeing Willie's having a tough time processing. "A lot of the debt is probably toxic, but it's covered by creating even more debt."

"As what happens in a Ponzi scheme!"

"Willie, calm down!"

"This is ridiculous." He quenches his fists.

"Drink your hot chocolate."

"I want to sell. Sell it all!"

"You can't! You'd cause a hysteria."

"The hysteria is already here, I'm just the first one to realize it." He erupts.

Hanna lights up a cigarette within her trembling grip.

"Ok then, Willie, who are we selling this to?" She asks.

"To the Germans, elves of Industry, international buyers who probably think these mortgages are in South Florida, or god knows where else. Just sell it to the same people who've been buying. Sell it to whoever else you can."

"If you do this, you'll kill the market. And you're selling something you know has no value. Do you consider that ethical, Saint Maven?"

"Debating ethics with *you* is hilarious to *me*."

She smiles grimly and takes a deep drag. "You know all of those pension funds and life savings will disappear into a black hole. Is that ethical? Fortunes erased...in a mere poof." She says, blowing a perfect smoke ring, then watches how it fades away into nothingness.

"You're going to sell this to willing buyers at the current market price. You're going to sell so that I MAY SURVIVE! And if you don't, I will sink this bank with me. You have my word on that."

"We might never sell anything to any of these buyers again. My reputation will be destroyed. Do you understand?"

"Do you?" He fires back.

She drags on her cigarette, disillusioned.

"This is it, Hanna! This is it! I'm telling you. I don't want a single share of mortgage-backed securities by noon tomorrow!"

"You don't care for me, you never have." She drones, puffing out another cloud of smoke.

"Don't you realize I'm saving your bank? Imagine if someone else acts first? You could easily be the last one standing without a chair once the music stops, and believe me, the music has stopped, darling. In fact, *I don't hear a thing.*"

She exhales another puff that fills the room, considering the consequences of what she must do.

"I can't believe a bank as large as yours fails to manage a situation having to do with mortgages." Willie mutters.

"That's manageable. I'm not worried about that."

"Then what are you worried about?"

"I fear for the astronomical amounts of derivatives created from these underlying mortgages. The interest on the bundled mortgages supports a universe of unregulated, opaque, and highly profitable derivatives."

"Why in the name of St. Nick would you do such a risky thing?"

"Oh, beyond the killer profits?" She snarks.

"Yes."

"Because we could buy insurance to hedge the bet!" She shrieks. "AIG made a fortune off us. It appears they lent their good name and credit to something that doesn't have any."

"Well they're about to be in serious trouble, aren't they?"

"We're all about to be in serious trouble. AIG holds insurance and assets with every major financial institution and institutional investor, if they go down, we all go down. There's no way they have enough cash to cover what they've guaranteed."

"You know where you faltered, don't you?"

"Do tell." She blows smoke at him.

He coughs, taking a moment to wave her smoke away. "When a complex system is doubled, the systemic risk doesn't double, it increases by a factor of ten, or more. You shouldn't be so surprised, but you are...because you didn't get this concept. As the scale of your operation increases by derivatives *systemic risk grows exponentially*."

"So be it, but I have news for you. All those student loans you've created and own will suffer the same fate. It's just *another government subsidized bubble about to burst*. Most loans are sound and will be repaid, but *many borrowers will default because students didn't acquire the needed skills or cannot find jobs in a listless economy*. Your student loans are being pumped out by the Treasury and directed to borrowers with a high propensity to spend and a limited ability to repay. *It is economically no different!*"

Hanna drops her cigarette on the carpet and stomps it out.

"Perhaps you're right." He somberly admits.

"You're an elf who grew up near the mountains of the North Pole, so I think you understand the idea of an avalanche."

"I do." Willie replies

"*An avalanche is a perfect metaphor for financial collapse*. It starts with a snowflake that perturbs other snowflakes, and as momentum builds the snow tumbles out of control. The snowflake is like a single bank failure, followed by a sequential panic, and it ends in fired financiers forced to vacate the premises of their destroyed firms."

"Yet it's you, with your derivatives, who built a village in the path of the avalanche. A poetic ending – being destroyed by the monsters you've created."

"Poetic, sure. But my home isn't in the village. You see, my home lays high above the ridgeline, protected and secluded, not far from yours."

"We're practically neighbors." He says.

"I'd tell you to warn your friends in the village, but I don't think you have any left."

18 – GRAVITY, ANTI-GRAVITY AND
GRAVITY AGAIN

The next day, Willie sits behind his massive desk at the North Pole Reserve, feet kicked up as he stares deeper into the map of the world. He's now familiar with all the physical and political geography which was once so foreign. The map is the only thing he likes about the entire office, so he stops in irregularly and only when necessary, but he knows this is where he needs to be today.

He takes another sip of his whiskey coffee until his telegraph buzzes; "It's sold." It reads from Hanna.

Willie smiles as he takes another sip, then waits. Only minutes later, his telegraph is abuzz with overflowing distress from all over the North Pole. He swigs back his whiskey coffee with a smirk.

Klaus, Otto, Sir Louie and Ernst von Wolf arrive with their entourages, bursting through Willie's office like storm troopers.

"What've you done?!" Klaus accuses.

"Protected my assets. The market is at work, gentlemen. I recommend you wake up and smell the roses."

"Elves can't make their payments if the Santa-tron's stop lending!" Ernst exclaims.

"I've got no control over Santa-tron lending. That's tied entirely to the real estate market. Which, contrary to popular belief, I don't control."

"But you do control the North Pole Reserve." Otto states.

"Listen, everyone, we're heading into the midst of a credit crisis. If you aren't scared, you should be." Willie proclaims.

"We've seen this before in Europe. We have to be very delicate, Willie." Klaus says.

"No, I bet you haven't seen it quite like this. At first glance the entire thing presents itself as a simple credit and monetary crisis,

225

when in fact all it involves is the issue of exchanging mortgages into money."

"Sounds like an easy fix." Sir Louie jabbers.

"It's not, because a tremendous number of these mortgages represent purely fraudulent deals as our friend Ernst can attest to."

The groups eyes down Ernst who shuns their glares.

"Now that they've come to light and exploded in our face, not only with our assets, but with borrowed capital, the real estate becomes either devalued or unsaleable." Willie explains.

"What do we do?" Ernst asks.

"As we sit here babbling the crisis is spreading through the mortgage finance companies and all the way to our major financial institutions," Willie says.

"Wreath Fargo, Scrooge Trust, Royal Bank of the North, Celebration Group, Merry Stanley and even Snowman Sachs are in jeopardy." Sir Louie realizes.

"The criminals at Snowman Sachs will be just fine, trust me." Ernst snarks.

Otto steps up, "Willie, I know you don't love these financial institutions."

"Although they've made you godly wealthy." Ernst adds.

"But perfectly good workshops, like yours, and factories, will suddenly be financially stuck because they can't roll over their debt. They won't even make payroll." Otto says. "They're trying to rescue themselves by laying off scores of workers and keeping wages repressed. If debt-fueled consumerism and effective demand stop then consumer confidence will fall off a cliff."

"Gentleman, that's exactly why we're here and must further prevent." Klaus says.

"But most of our banks are still holding these 'toxic' securitized mortgage debts that nobody will buy," Ernst warns. "It's spreading to other institutions that either invested in the debt or insured this stuff, like Advent Incarnate Group." Sir Louie adds.

"Just call them AIG like everyone else, Louie." Willie snickers.

"It's Sir Louie."

"Good god – "

"Gentlemen!" Klaus yells as he smacks Willie's desk. "A devaluation of credit money would *destroy* all existing relationships. *The banks must be rescued no matter what. The value of money is only guaranteed as long as money itself is guaranteed!*"

Klaus catches his breath as the room goes silent. "Many millions worth of commodities must be sacrificed to save a few million in money, no matter what the social need."

"What are you saying?" Willie asks.

"I'm saying *everything must go on as it has before!*" Klaus yells.

A petrified silence ensues. Nobody has ever seen Klaus so shaken.

"Fine, and the solution?" Willie breaks the silence.

"Lower the North Pole Reserve rates to 1%, hell, make it 0%. We need to get banks' lending so as long as we can avoid inflation." Otto says.

"What about the millions of disease-ridden bags of excrement on the banks' balance sheets?"

"Nationalize the banks." Klaus answers.

"That stands against every idea you've ever uttered about free markets and laissez-faire."

"A fully self-regulating market economy is a utopian project. It's something that cannot actually exist." Klaus says.

"But you've always said that the economy is self-regulating," Willie argues.

"It self-regulates until it can't. A real market society needs the state to play an active role in managing markets. Without swift and decisive action today, there won't be an economy tomorrow. Do you understand that? If you allow a bank to fail you allow a huge chunk of money to disappear with it!"

"I don't like the sound of this." Ernst says.

"Stop crying, we'll do this in the form of loans which Willie will happily write you from the North Pole Reserve." Klaus says.

"Oh really?" Willie says.

"Yes, and they'll pay it back with interest as the banks become stronger than ever before." Klaus preaches.

"I don't know." Ernst mumbles.

"Stop dragging your feet, Ernstie! It's your only option but it's also entirely desirable. *Toxic assets to society and the good assets to private citizens! Socialize the losses and privatize the gains!*" Klaus professes as the group becomes inspired by his enthusiasm, minus Willie.

"And how do I know that Ernst, or any other bank will make good on this?" Willie wonders.

"Because they're protected by the government, and because they're the most heavily subsidized business in all the North Pole."

"Just how are we subsidized?" Ernst asks.

"Through fractional reserve banking you have the license to create money - you make it out of nothing and loan it at interest, for god sakes!"

"Oh yes, that's right." Ernst smiles.

"Hate to rain on your tea party but the debt problem would still be very much with us." Willie says. "That will only shift private banking debt to sovereign state debt. These enormous sums must now be 'reimbursed' by the taxpayers and not by the shareholders and purchasers of stock."

"Yes, exactly. Your point?" Sir Louie asks.

"Then you're all okay with the highest costs being borne by wage-earners, beneficiaries of the few public programs that still exist, and the poorest of the population?"

"Yes." They all respond in unison to Willie.

"Let me get this straight - you'd have the costs of reestablishing this relation of exploitation and domination paid for by its victims. Or am I missing something?"

"Oh, boo-hoo," Sir Louie utters.

"Without credit the masses are designed to be cash strapped. Always." Klaus says.

"You are literally telling me it's my duty to fulfill an obligation for private debt and pass the bill onto social debt?" Willie asks.

"Yes." Klaus answers.

"That'd require dramatic drops in social spending and tax hikes." Willie points out.

"Wait - tax hikes on who?" Sir Louie nervously inquires. "I'm strapped, just bought my seventh Rolls Royce landship, those aren't cheap!"

"We'll tax the middle class." Otto says.

"That obvious?" Willie asks.

"Well, taxing the rich is against our mantra. Besides campaigns are expensive. We can't isolate our major donors," Sir Louie highlights.

"By taxing the middle class, you split them in half, you divide them and win many over. So, the likes of Ginger Garland are relevant but made less powerful." Otto enlightens.

"How?" Willie asks.

"They fracture into supporters of the poor and supporters of their own self-interest. You tell them how they're being ripped off by 'takers' and 'elves in need' and how they shouldn't pay the tax for elves who aren't qualified. You turn the middle vs the bottom and turn the upper middle into rageful elves."

"Rageful elves, huh, that's your answer?" Willie says plainly.

"Unfortunately, it's the only answer, good elf." Klaus says. "Nonetheless, all politicians need to leave the top 10% alone. There's no deviation possible."

"With these new plans we'll finally be in complete conformity with the markets," Otto says.

"Good brainstorming, gentlemen." Ernst says.

"Productive session." Sir Louie adds.

"But we're not changing anything. Not really." Willie says.

"That's right, we're doubling down. You'll thank me later, trust me. Now if you will, please prepare the rescue loans." Klaus says as he hands Willie a fountain pen.

Willie stares as a team of Klaus' lawyers and lobbyists move in, surrounding and presenting him with a stack of prepared papers. A lawyer flips over the stack exposing the final signature page.

"Sign." Klaus says. "Please."

Willie stares at the massive unread stack of legalese, sighs and reluctantly scribbles his name before the whole room politely claps.

Over the coming weeks Willie watches as scores of elves are foreclosed on, go homeless, have Santa-trons deny credit and outright seize property. Any savings salvaged from failing investments have been taken to pay back as much debt as possible. It's a ruthless process. As the situation worsens Willie grows more dismal, especially as Ginger and Renee lead protests through the streets and sometimes outside the Maven Workshop, where crowds hurl eggs at his office window.

Willie's uncontrolled nerves make him shake while watching the visceral anger of the mob play out. Yet deep down he'd like to join them. How funny that'd be, protesting himself. It's becoming a more appealing thought as the idea of a glorious act of self-destruction becomes more and more alluring. Yet it's his isolation that still hurts him the most. If he could just slip into someone else's skin, maybe he'd experience that special warm feeling that only comes with comradery. He'd give his entire fortune to feel that fraternity, especially if it meant another chance with Renee.

But Sugar Dollars can't buy such things and he knows it, so he spends his time locked up in his various offices, alone, sulking, drinking eggnog and scotch, wondering what could have been. The more he drinks the worse he gets, but he convinces himself that the bottle is his only escape. So, he doubles-down on his drinking, just like how he's forced to double down on the usurious financial system.

Back in his office at the Maven Workshop Willie sips eggnog and spins a globe with his robotic hand. A quick and powerful flick from his metallic digits keep the globe spinning for minutes. He becomes entranced in its motion as it swirls and swirls, becoming lost in drunken consideration, dwelling on all the places he's never been and will probably never go. His office is his prison and the only thing left to do is drink.

But he snaps out of it once he hears the boisterous, upbeat echoing of Klaus' voice from the engineering department. What could this man possibly be so damn happy about?

Willie waltzes over with a stumble as Klaus holds court with the engineers. He's gesturing, smiling and speaking like a prophet as a half dozen Redcoats accompanying him. From the corner of his eye Klaus spots Willie above.

"Ah, good elf, join us! Your geniuses are hungry for a new project so I've satiated them!" Klaus yells.

"Of course you have."

"Get down here! I've got a gift for you...for us. Come check this out!"

Willie makes his way down and spots a half dozen Santa-trons, even more fierce looking than the typical prototype, along with one jolly and dapper-looking Santa-tron with a creepy faux smile.

"Why are you so happy?" Willie asks. "It's not like it's Christmas morning."

"Ah, far, far better my elf!" Klaus shouts. "Look at these customized Sanat-trons!" Klaus shouts with glee. "They're even more capable than before, like ninjas, and I've had one commissioned to be our own specialized Real Estate Agent, his name is Steve, HAHA. Don't worry Steve doesn't actually charge a commission. Let's take 'em for a spin!"

"You'd trade your Redcoats for Santa-trons body guards?" Willie asks.

"Like I said, they aren't any 'ol Santa-trons. Just watch." Klaus turns to the custom Santa-tron. "Santa-tron activate, neutralize Redcoats."

"Sir – what's going on?" A Redcoat panics.

"Save yourselves, boys! There's six of you and one of it. Come on, fight!"

The Redcoats perk up with adrenaline as they slowly surround the bulky Santa-tron with their clubs. They're about to move in for the kill – but the Santa-tron spins its head, cracks his mechanic knuckles and...SMACKS, KICKS, PUNCHES, and KARATE CHOPS the Redcoats in a combination of lighting fast moves that leave the whole group bruised, battered and sprawled across the floor in pain.

"Target neutralized." Santa-tron says as the Redcoats nurse their shattered ribs and bloodied faces.

"HAHA. Thank you Santa-tron, thank you!" Klaus laughs as he claps stridently. He turns to Willie, "Yes, I'd take them over Redcoats. Now let's get going, times a wastin'!"

"Where to?"

"Everywhere! Just bring your checkbook!" Klaus cheers.

Klaus and Willie suit up in their warmest designer mittens, custom top-hats and sleek black peacoats. They hit the icy streets led by Steve, the Real Estate Agent-tron, and surround themselves with the dozen impenetrable Santa-tron body guards.

"Why are we parading around like open targets?" Willie asks.

"We're not parading, we're buying – we're going to buy up as much of it as we can! Now's the time to strike."

"Doesn't this feel...counter-intuitive? We've lost fortunes these last few weeks."

"Willie, in a crisis, *assets always return to their rightful owners.* Never forget that."

"We're the rightful owners?"

"Yes, good elf, of course! Who else would be? This crisis has left a mass of devalued utilities, homes and even businesses that can be picked up for a Christmas Carol! Oh, marvelous day!"

"But isn't the entire system still in jeopardy?"

"Don't let those chanting fools trick you. Crises don't spell the end of capitalism, *they only set the stage for its renewal.* They're never more than momentary, violent solutions for the existing contradictions. Violent eruptions that re-establish the disturbed balance for the time being, that's all." Klaus says, patting Willie on the back.

"You've seen something like this in Germany?"

"Close to it. It's all very natural. There are many undertakings where the first investment is sunk and lost, and those first owners go bankrupt. It often isn't until the second or third hand owners come along that those investments become fruitful. We're lucky enough to be holding piles of cash while other capitalists can't even get a loan." Klaus sniggers.

The duo march past the Belief Meter, seeing how the NPI stock price remains strangely high. In the background Willie takes notice to the normal - Santa-trons foreclosing and evicting defaulting elves en masse. Willie notices how some Santa-trons act differently, escorting the most heavily indebted elves down the streets as if taking them somewhere specific – to jail?

"I should have told you, we've updated their code." Klaus says.

"Oh – why?"

"To make them more...multi-purpose. They really are splendid machines."

"Where are the Santa-trons taking them?" Willie asks.

"I'll tell you when you're ready."

The remark disturbs Willie but he doesn't push it. Klaus continues, "These defaulting elves are problems for everyone. They'll be welfare leaches at best, sucking the efficiency straight out of the system. It's tolerable until it isn't."

Willie blankly nods, but doesn't like what he hears.

They continue through downtown and witness elves setting up a new and even bigger Christmas Tree in place of the one which burned down so spectacularly.

In fact, it's not a tree at all, but the future sight of the "TREE OF TREES" – thousands of individual trees bound together to create what will appear to be one massive tree, bigger than any structure ever built in the North Pole. The army of elves hard at work are supervised by a legion of Santa-trons, as if they're prisoners to their machine overlords.

Through a massively coordinated effort the Santa-trons order the elves to lift, push, pull and tie the trees together in accordance with the master blueprint. The operation resembles Egyptian slaves building the Great Pyramids, equipped with an elaborate pulley and crane system, but largely reliant on their muscle, nimbleness and know-how. Klaus smiles as the crew nearly completes the base layer of the structure.

"An awe inspiring 'Tree of Trees' to be mesmerized by all whom lay eyes upon it. An ode to the mastery we possess over our universe. Oh, and the decorations, they're going to be incredible, you'll see." Klaus says strangely, but Willie doesn't read into it, concerning himself with more practical matters.

"When are the banks going to lend again?"

"Soon, maybe? It's good they aren't now, otherwise we'd have a lot more competition today. They're using those new funds to wipe their slates clean."

"Shouldn't they be using that money to loan out?"

"Probably, but not our problem. One elf's loss is another man's gain!" Klaus smiles. "Those poor suckers, all of that land and property foreclosed on and ripe for the taking. Ah, the magic of the sub-prime mortgage, isn't it beautiful?"

Willie doesn't know what to say, soaking in the sight of mass foreclosures surrounding them.

Klaus listens intently as Steve robotically spits off prices, facts and figures about the surrounding real estate.

"Even better, Willie, look at these buildings, they're practically new. Devaluation and depreciation don't mean the destruction of a functioning house. Look at this huge stock that can be bought up for next to nothing and put back into profitable use. It's like a Christmas foreclosure miracle!"

Klaus' cheer rubs Willie the wrong way as scores of desperate elves shiver and beg for food as they stroll past. Willie absorbs the despairing scene while Klaus keeps an intent ear focused on Steve, listening for the best deals.

"The future itself is foreclosed on, Klaus."

"Ah, well said, elf."

"Instead of an accumulation of values and wealth, capital has produced an accumulation of debts that have to be redeemed." Willie says. "Hasn't it?"

"Hah! Perhaps, but it benefits us so long as we're the owners and not the redeemers – and that should never change! We will own more, build more, construct more."

"But it's clearer than ever, that every productive act of capital is also destructive."

"I think that's true and a part of what makes it all so elegant. Like the yin-yang. I accept that and advise you do too."

"Right." Willie says uncomfortably.

"So, what are you buying?" Klaus asks with excitement, changing the subject. Willie shrugs his shoulders, uncertain.

They continue walking until stumbling across the Jensen-Gin Silversmith Workshop. There's a giant foreclosed sign upfront as Rebecca Jensen-Gin, Willie's old Wolf Sledding rival, walks out of the front door. She's crying as she posts a "Closed for Business" sign and locks the door shut with a heavy padlock and chain.

The Jensen-Gin's, a once esteemed family of the North Pole, have lost it all. He's never seen Rebecca, such a fierce competitor, famed Silversmith and sharp business elf, so broken and hopeless. Her sadness moves Willie. She's one of the toughest elves he's ever known. If the toughest, most talented, and even privileged elves can break down, how can any other elf expect to thrive? Especially if they're not in tech, law, finance, government, or a corporate suit at a big five workshop?

Willie halts the caravan of Santa-trons and approaches Rebecca gently. He knows exactly what's happened, so he doesn't bother for details. He stares at her sadly and they share a hug, holding onto one another as if it were the last of days.

"I want to help you." Willie says. "You and your staff are the best damn Silversmith's the world over." He smiles. "You need to continue. The North Pole needs your workshop."

"I wish that were true." She cries.

"It is."

"I'll do anything." Rebecca replies.

"I need you to manage operations and oversee everything, just as you and your family have done since the dawn of Christmas."

"Yes, of course."

"What's your price?" Willie asks.

"Excuse me?"

"Name your price, I'd like to own the workshop so you can work for me."

In that moment Rebecca transforms from a broken elf into a rageful one, *slapping* him across the face before rushing off in tears.

Klaus laughs, "Women, huh? Classic. HAHA! It's foreclosed anyway, just buy it from the bank if you want it so bad."

Willie stands there shattered, taking a moment to compose himself. Once he sees straight he approaches Steve. "What's the discount on this enterprise, Steve?" Willie asks.

Steve ticks and beeps while his metal Santa Hat twists all the way around, gears softly clicking internally as he calculates.

"Purchase Discount, Jensen-Gin Silversmith Workshop...available for five cents on the Sugar Dollar," it says mechanically.

"I'll take it, Steve. Thank you." Willie announces as Steve breaks into a creepy robot dance while Klaus claps and laughs even louder.

"Another business acquisition by the Maven Workshop, 'eh. At this rate you'll own everything. A real Mr. Monopoly!" Klaus cheers as Willie grows even more dismal inside.

19 – AN ELF'S WORD

A rambunctious crowd of protesters are led by Renee, all chanting and marching outside the Maven Workshop – which is now one of the five major workshops of the North Pole, having acquired many smaller operations in pursuit of domination.

Willie gulps his Irish Coffee while nervously taping against the window with his metal fingers. He wonders if Renee somehow forgot the entire violent shutdown that landed her in prison? Regardless, it's clear her bitterness fuels her motivation. Fortunately for Willie, and the protesters own bodily health, they have little leverage – no work stoppages, no threat to the supply chain or system at large. They're a nuisance. Little more than an ongoing noise complaint, and perhaps that's why Klaus and Otto don't mind.

Although he was skeptical about the bailout, he hoped the action might help the average elf. However, low interest rates have only increased volatility and inequality. Money has been "printed" and the money supply has increased. When this happens, money is supposed to be worth less because of inflation, where more money chases after the same number of commodities, but that isn't happening.

With no middle class, the money only accumulates in the pockets of the rich. All the gains have gone to the top who play the stock market. The money goes from the North Pole Reserve to the banks to their richest clients who use the money to buy shares on margin. Meanwhile, businesses that produce things face a market of elves who can't afford much, and if they raise prices, they'd lose customers. Perhaps if Willie and his lot buy up a lot of stuff, there would be inflation, just as there's been with the inflation of luxury goods, but society wide inflation could devastate. Inflation in the world of luxury is trivial because the rich can easily afford the increases.

Willie studies the crowd as he sips and slips further into his morning drunkenness. He notices how the crowds are shrinking. There are fewer protesters than a week before, and the week before that. Is their movement losing steam? The protests used to jam the streets, densely packing the district with wildly mad elves screaming for better wages, yelling for a right to this or that. All things they used to have but now don't have the money to pay for.

He sympathizes with their injustice but doesn't feel responsible for it. Was he designed not to? Was the rioting designed to happen? Everything is happening as it should, he thinks, but are there stronger forces behind the scenes manipulating this reality? Maybe he's paranoid or maybe he's just really drunk again. With such powerful hatred pointed at him he just wants to disappear into oblivion, but all he has is his bottle of whiskey. Good enough, he thinks. It's his only escape from this unbearable feeling of rejection. He refills his mug, but only with whiskey, and slips further into his stupor. He becomes dizzy, stumbling around his office before returning to the window, leaning against it sloppily, barely holding his balance as he stares out.

With a squint he spots Rebecca Jensen-Gin among his part-time and freelance employees. He further scans until finding Renee with a megaphone. After a moment both realize they staring at one another. She puts down the megaphone and they share a sad gaze. It's clear this is her payback, but contrary to his belief she doesn't enjoy making Willie miserable.

In a moment of despair amid chants for a higher minimum wage of $15 Sugar Dollars per hour – Willie is overrun with a sudden burst of compassion. He runs to his desk, nearly tripping over himself, and whips out poster board and an ink-jar before hurriedly writing in large letters. He smiles from ear to ear with his message and returns to the window where he slams his poster against the glass.

It reads, "YES, $15 SD/HR!" as the crowd celebrates.

He raises his hands like a champion and stares in glee to the appeased crowd. They almost can't believe it, nor can he. Willie watches Renee as Rebecca nearly tackles her with a tremendous hug. Even Renee flashes a genuine smirk, making him melt inside just as the glaciers of the North Pole are starting to.

Willie relishes in this moment of victory while avoiding all the frantic incoming calls from furious Germans businessmen. He watches Rebecca leave Renee's side as she makes her way through the crowd to the Maven Workshop. She wants in and Willie grants her access. Alabaster prepares a whiskey coffee before she is escorted inside his office.

"Alabaster, slap me." Willie orders.

"Come again?"

"Slap me, I need to sober up."

"Oh." Alabaster smiles. "Sure." He winds up with some power, and – *slap* – five fingers to the face. It stings, but Willie feels more alert.

"Thanks." Willie pouts with a bright pink cheek as Rebecca enters.

"Hi Rebecca, care for an Irish Coffee?"

"Just coffee." She says. "Thank you, that was the right thing to do."

"You're not here to slap me again?"

"I'm sorry for that."

"No, I deserved it. I've been getting slapped a lot lately" He eyes Alabaster.

"Maybe you did, a little," she laughs, "but I know you're lonely. I know what it's like, running a workshop, alone. I mean, I knew. All I want to say is you don't have to be alone." She stands about to leave.

"Wait, at least finish your coffee."

She returns, sympathetic to the desperation in his voice.

"I need to understand what's happening out there, the only elves who talk to me these days are my most petrified employees."

"What would you like to know?" She asks.

"What's your path forward in this new world? I mean, you'll

be okay, right?"

"My business went bust but I have enough in my savings account, if that's what you're asking?"

"You'll start a new business?" He asks. "I don't see you becoming an employee at a Big Five-Workshop, you're not the type."

"I can barely think of any investment opportunity that's worth the risky pursuit. I don't have the faintest idea of what to do next, in business at least." She says.

"I think that's why I bought your workshop. There's just so few things worth investing in and I have more and more capital that needs to be making a return."

"Our challenges are very different." She scoffs.

"Sorry." He mumbles.

"I'm saying, there's little left for entrepreneurs to do. Everything is dominated by just a handful of giants. I thought one of the great success stories of capitalism was how it supposedly takes the natural proclivity of elves to compete, unleashes it from social constraints and harnesses it through the market to produce a dynamic system for the benefit of all. But there's no competition anymore, everyone's been bought up or gone under. And we treat the existence of the few remaining giants as abnormalities, as unfortunate departures from an ideal equilibrium. But this can't be an abnormality when it happens in every major sector of the economy. It's the norm. It's the very nature and tendency of the system itself."

"But you're in disagreement of the nature of markets, and supply and demand? I mean this is economics 101."

"Market failure is also econ 101." She replies.

"Can you really argue with how markets distribute goods in services, is it not wholly natural?"

"Markets distribute things, but in a particular way. Say there's a limited supply of cookies, and demand increases, driving the price up until elves who wanted the cookies can't afford the cookies.

The market allocates scarce goods and services to those with the most money. That isn't efficient, moral or ethical – especially for necessities or things that are lifesaving. Markets only serve those that are the richest within it, and they'll use the market to stay the richest. It isn't a neutral efficiency mechanism, not by a longshot."

"Maybe so. Maybe you can find an area of business that isn't dominated by the giants?"

"The giant companies have taken almost all possible, profitable initiatives." She says.

"Tech is an area left for innovation."

"Maybe the only one left."

"Why don't you learn that?" He asks.

"I'd spend my last dollar on that education and it still wouldn't be half done. Besides, innovation is being reduced to routine. Technological progress is the business of teams of trained specialists who turn out what's required. The romance of the commercial adventure is dead, at least to me it is."

"Romance is dead, isn't it?" He cackles.

"Specialized office work blurs out individual personality. Seemingly, except for you, the leading elf no longer flings herself into the fray. Even executives are becoming just like any other office worker, and one who isn't so difficult to replace." She says.

"You no longer have energy for business?"

"I think my energy and brains will be better spent elsewhere."

"Like silversmithing?" He asks.

"For my own art, yes, maybe."

"I'm surprised, but happy for you."

"Thanks." She replies.

"So, Renee and Ginger Garland's ideas resonate even with you?" He asks.

"Yes." She takes another long sip. "I once had a dream, maybe it's still your dream, I don't know, but my fantasy was the pursuit of an industrial dynasty. More than just a small-scale Silversmith operation. I felt unstoppable and more ambitious than my parents or probably any other Jensen-Gin that came before. But it all unraveled. The dynasty is dead, and even much more modest goals are so incredibly difficult to attain. Renee's critique is attractive these days."

"But you were rich. Won't you miss that?" He asks.

"I don't think so. I've become practical in spirit. A successful-enough elf can live a fine life with the mass-produced goods of the North Pole. Yes, far below the extravagant lifestyle of my ancestors, but that lifestyle isn't relevant anymore, except among the very few, like you." She says.

"I'm finding it hard to believe you don't want these things anymore."

"Well, elves are less traditional these days. There's less incentive for kids because they're so expensive – and raising them right without a built-in community is a massive undertaking. I'd feel strange not providing my potential elf-lings the same opportunities I've had, and I don't think they'd have anything close."

"This is the source of your newfound minimalism?" He asks.

"There's less incentive for the family home, with more comfortable living in condos and apartments. Maybe consciously or unconsciously our motives behind wanting to earn fortunes are shaped by the vision of the massive family home and the necessity to work and save primarily for spouse and children. Maybe I'm a different kind of elf, I don't know, but from the standpoint of utility, the behavior of that old type doesn't make much sense. The ethics of the capitalist no longer apply, but through not wanting fortune I feel liberated." She says with a soft smile.

Willie takes a slurp of his whiskey coffee, envious of Rebecca's newfound levity amid financial disaster.

"Without a family motive, the timeline of your funds shrinks roughly to your life expectancy?" He asks.

"I mean, what's the point, really, of earning, saving and

investing at this point? Especially if it would only swell my tax bills."

"You're not saving?"

"I'm ready and willing to spend my money on experiences before I'm dead and gone. Why have we all neglected our eventual fate? Seafaring is necessary, living is not." She says with a smirk.

Willie smiles back and clinks mugs.

"I like that." He says.

"I must get going."

"One last question, are those crowds getting smaller or are they losing momentum? What's happening out there?"

"The protests do feel smaller. We know the Santa-trons have been deporting the defaulted and credit-less further to the edges of the city. Once they're so far out by the tundra, it's a lot more effort to make it to a protest. It's hurting, for sure."

"I see."

"That's my theory, at least." She says uncertainly as she gets up to leave, but he's feeling refreshed and spontaneous.

"The Jensen-Gin Workshop is nothing without you. I need you back. You'll have equity and cheap stock options you can pickup as you go. We can be partners. We could have a very productive partnership." He says.

She smiles back at him, "I would've said yes, but I'm no longer interested in productivity. I've got other things in mind, more important things, for me and the North Pole."

"I understand."

She bites her lip, witnessing Willie revel in his confusion, doing well to hide his sadness but it most obviously lurks.

"Would you like to see Renee?" She asks.

"I've tried, but she won't have it."

"I think you'd be surprised. I have an idea." She smiles.

Weeks later - it's night, dark and cold as the flurry of snow creates halos around the gas lamps that line the streets. Willie rides with Ursus while a perimeter of the upgraded Santa-trons guard them. They proceed past the "Tree of Trees" superstructure, which is finally built, standing 50 stories tall. It's in mid decoration, as elves carefully hang *immense and brilliant blown-glass ornaments* from its branches, each ornament *sparkling magnificently* and uniquely. The brilliant shine makes him curious – he's never seen anything quite like it, but that's happening more and more these days.

Willie and his caravan proceed until they stop outside of Renee's apartment where Rebecca awaits him.

"Come on, ditch the Santa-trons. Do you want to freak her out?" Rebecca says.

Willie signals the Santa-trons away into the alley where they rest in sleep mode. They enter the building together and knock on Renee's door with Willie a few steps further back.

"Hey Renee, it's me, open up!" Rebecca says as the door swings open to meet a smiling Renee.

"Hi!" Renee blurts, but her smile turns into anxiety once she lays eyes on Willie.

"The ol' bait and switch, sorry." Rebecca says. "You two should talk, I'll leave you to it." Rebecca says before departing.

Willie approaches, "Can I come in?"

Renee reluctantly lets him inside, there's a fire going. He's happy she's kept her little library filled with literature. It's a cozy scene as Willie inhales the scent of cookies baking, the smell relaxes him. On the kitchen table are papers sprawled about with handwritten ideas and long flowing notes that read like a stream of conscious.

"What's this?" He asks, looking at the papers.

"Getting my thoughts down. I need to figure out the slogans here before we chant them out there."

"Of course."

"So, what do you want?"

"Cookies." He smirks.

"They're not for you." She replies.

"Oh, who are they for?"

"Not your business, Willie. Now please tell me why you're here?"

"I want you back in my life. Can that ever happen?"

"After all you put me through?"

"I could've done more. I see that now. And I'm sorry, really sorry, for all they put you through." He says desperately. "I've always been on your side, even now, I mean, I just raised the minimum wage at the workshop, for you."

"You didn't do it for me, I don't work for you."

"I mean, yes, for my employees, but for you too." He stumbles.

"Are you drunk?" She asks.

"Always, ever nicely buzzed."

"That's why you're trembling?"

"I'm trembling because I'm nervous. Because all I want is to be with you. That's it. I don't care what it costs."

"Well, unlike everything else in your life, I'm not for sale."

"I didn't mean it like that. I just – I don't know how to get you back?"

"There's no getting me – and we were never together! There is no 'us' or 'we' or anything like that, and there never will be."

"But there's *something*, I'm not making this up, and you know it much as I do."

She takes a deep breath, smells that the cookies are ready, pops them out and serves a couple to him anyway.

"There are lots of reforms, I have an agenda. If you can play along and help the North Pole become a more just society, then I'm open to having a business relationship for the sake of the greater cause."

Willie puts his cookie down. It wasn't the answer he was hoping for. He buttons his jacket preparing to leave.

"You're just going to go?" She asks. "Think about what we can do, together."

"It's not worth it if we can't be together." He says.

"That's where you're wrong, but if that's how you feel…"

Willie drags his feet, too sad to look back. When he returns outside the cold feels twice as bitter with the icy sleet blowing in his face. He makes his way to the dark alley where the Santa-trons rest, but instead of turning them on he stays hidden among the shadows, sulking. He removes his glove watching how his fleshy hand trembles.

Once he catches his breath he stares into Renee's window. He notices how she perks up with a grin at the sound of a knock on her door. He can't see who it is but it feels like that mysterious figure from the scene of the Great Christmas Tree lighting - or burning, and that same masculine form who was with her briefly at the Coal Miners Tavern. Willie watches as she becomes playful and warm, kissing this shadowy someone romantically. The mere thought of Renee in love with someone else is enough to transform Willie's despair into a burst of anger, but he tries to control his impulse.

Willie repositions, directing his Santa-trons to a dark corner, awaiting to attack once this figure steps foot outside. A few minutes later the lights from Renee's apartment turn off – it could be a long night but Willie stays put.

But only moments later the front door swings open as the figure steps out onto the street. Willie orders his Santa-tron's into attack mode - they pounce and shine their powerful spotlights from their eyes out onto...Otto.

The betrayal feels like a knife to the gut. It's enough to bring him to his knees, but he stands his ground before approaching Otto who's caught up like a deer in headlights.

Otto squints trying to see past the spotlights and recognizes Willie.

"Willie? Is that you? What's this?" Otto asks.

"You tell me."

"Come on, we're adults here, just calm down." Otto says, hands up, moving closer to the perimeter of Santa-trons.

"You'll want to stand back." Willie says, but Otto continues forward.

"Or else what?" Otto responds, stepping closer until SWACK, PUNCH, KICK – from the metal fists and boots of his Santa-trons. They leave Otto beaten and bloody on the cobblestone.

"Who the hell do you think you're dealing with? I'll have you stripped of everything, ELF!"

The Santa-trons move in sensing the threat to Willie as Otto backpedals, slipping in the snow. Willie orders their halt just before they're about to kick him while he's down.

"Tell me what you're really doing here."

"You jealous, pathetic, drunk little creature. You will pay for this."

"You speak to elves like inferiors."

"You are, obviously!"

Willie winks at a Santa-tron giving him the go-ahead to KICK him in ribs. He takes particular pleasure in watching Otto take the blow as he gasps for air. A shocked Renee storms out onto the scene.

"Stop this right now! What the hell are you doing, Willie?" Renee yells.

"We're going to find out what your boyfriend has been up to. He's supposed to be in Reykjavik, but he's sneaking around up here.

"He's been with me you idiot!"

"You're being played Renee, I don't know how, but I'm going to find out." Willie says.

"Are you delusional, paranoid, both? We started working together and now we're together, so get over it!" She shouts.

"How can you be with a man who hates elves?" Willie asks.

"We're working together to save elves, especially from the likes of you!"

"You're just a propped-up figurehead." Otto yells. "A lucky drunk at the right place at the right time, that's all, you parasite, you're nothing."

"You're a conman and a traitor, burning down the Christmas Tree. Terrorizing the North Pole. I want to know why."

"How could you even accuse him of that, you're acting insane!" Renee accuses.

"Because I saw him." He answers.

"*Did you?*" Renee says.

"I think so." Willie says.

"Your friend lost his mind, he needs help, Renee." Otto interrupts.

"There's something very slippery with this man, always has been and I will find out why." Willie says as his Santa-trons move in.

"If those machines lay another metallic finger on me, I'll take you for all you've got and have you thrown in prison!"

"Not if you're thrown into my prison first." Willie snaps his fingers as his Santa-trons descend on Otto.

Renee screams. She dashes back in her apartment, telegrams Ginger Garland the frantic news, but to her surprise she receives a message back that reads, "Let's see how this plays out." Leaving her dismayed. She remains inside with the door locked while Willie and his Santa-trons carry off Otto kicking and screaming.

A couple days later Otto is locked up in a makeshift prison cell, held back by iron bars amid the dark and dank basement of the Maven Workshop. His face is bruised and swollen from his capture. He passes the days by playing chess with himself, spinning the board every time he makes a move. He sips on cold peppermint tea and chews stale graham crackers, bored out of his mind, desperate for contact.

Suddenly he hears a noise and leans against the bars in anticipation. It's Willie, by himself. The two stare in a tense silence.

"Have you had enough?" Willie asks.

Otto thinks about it. "Are you willing to kill me?"

"Are you willing to die for whatever secret you're trying to keep?" Willie asks.

Otto doesn't answer.

"I know what you want." Willie says.

"What's that?"

"Money. You're a man and men want money."

"That simple?"

"Yes, for you at least. So, now we're both here why don't you get yourself out of this mess?"

"What do you want to know?" Otto asks.

"What's *really* going on."

"You'll set me free if I do?"

"Yes."

"You swear?"

"On all that's sacred in the North Pole." Willie says. Otto knows elves keep their word and expect the same in return. A fact he's used endlessly to his advantage. He offers Willie a nod of agreement.

"Why Renee? Do you love her?" Willie asks.

"Hah! Love? No – perhaps that's to your relief, besides she's an *elf!*" Otto blurts. "She fits the profile, and I had to exploit that. It's a job, but that doesn't mean she doesn't love me, I can't help that."

"She matches a profile? For what?" Willie asks.

"For a strategy, Willie. Actually, I'm upset with how long it's taken you to catch on, but in a way I'm happy to share it. It was a secret between Klaus and I.

"But here we are."

"Yes."

"What kind of strategy?" Willie asks.

"Something more sinister than the normal, because it plays on those who think they're in open rebellion, or progressive, or just standing up for themselves. They're not, but we need them to feel that way."

"What do you mean? Why are you doing this?"

"Why? For the survival of the system, like everything we're concerned with." Otto says.

"Give me the details, I didn't come for a tea party."

Otto shovels a couple of dry graham crackers into his mouth then slurps some cold tea helping him swallow. "It's an idea – something we call DOUBLE-MOVEMENT." He says mid-swallow.

"It doesn't sound sinister," Willie states.

"It doesn't have to," Otto says. "You see, market societies are made up of two opposing movements, the laissez-faire free market movement, to expand the market, and the protective counter-movement that emerges to resist it. The forces of the counter-movement need to be propped up by the likes of an ambitious elf bleeding for the cause."

"But you're one of the biggest free market Germans I know." Willies says, confused.

"Yes, and the counter-movement stabilizes capitalism, locking it in *stalemate*, which works to capital's benefit. The stalemate *ensures that the system survives.*"

"So, it was you who lit up the Christmas Tree and instigated the Coal Miners' Strike? And Klaus knew?"

"Yes, yes and yes!" Otto yaps. "We had to send a message since you all thought the labor movement didn't have teeth. We had to show that it does. Even better it brought terror to Christmas, it got everyone talking. And the strike worked – even if it cut more into our profits than expected, but the capitalists perked up. Like how you conceded to their minimum wage demands."

Willie is silenced by the revelation.

Otto continues, "The working class has always been a key part of the protective countermovement. Our sympathies are generally with the protective countermovement. They're good, hardworking elves trying to squeak out a living. But their interests are necessary to create the political-economic impasse. The system flourishes and we get rich so as long as the stalemate ensues. As long as they fight for their benefits *within the system*, like fighting for a raise. Instead of fighting outside of it, or revolting against capitalism itself. If they did that, then we'd be in real trouble."

"You've framed Renee." Willie states.

"She's nearly done it all herself, she just needed a little push in the right direction."

"But the crackdown in the Square, and tossing her in prison for years, that was all by design?"

"Now you're catching on." Otto replies as Willie seethes inside, but he hides it well.

"Smart," Willie says, "in a dismal, counter-intuitive kind of way. So, even the counter movement isn't natural? Everything about it is manipulated and – manmade."

"There's nothing natural about any of it. Even Laissez-faire isn't 'natural'. Free markets could never have come into being by just allowing things to take course. Free trade must be enforced by the state just as the protective countermovement must be assisted by it."

"I'm having a hard time believing you." Willie admits.

"Not my problem."

"Strange that you, of all Germans, have been touting all the arguments that every business-elf, German financier, capitalist, rentier, workshop or factory owner has ever despised."

"Most are too dumb or too selfish to realize these counter-ideas actually benefit them in the long run," Otto says. "Don't be one of them."

"Give me an example, like one of Renee and Ginger's protest points, say taxing the wealthy. How does it help the wealthy if they're high taxed? Or if money is redistributed to the poor?" Willie asks.

"Even the ancient Greeks dictators taxed the aristocrats because they knew the distribution of wealth is only a means of bringing money back to the rich. That heavy taxes are good for business. Money – or more importantly, *the circulation of money* – is the means for *rendering the debt infinite*. Debt becomes a debt of existence on the subjects themselves, and it keeps the rich, rich...But we need not do that just yet, we're loving these low taxes. Do you need more?"

"Even if you redistribute money to the poor, they'll still be poor?" Willie wonders.

"Poverty will always exist. It has to because the wealthy are creditors and the poor are debtors. If you've forgotten, interest from debt flows from debtors to creditors, so the financial system distributes money from the poor to the rich. Taxing the rich and redistributing it to the poor changes nothing – it only strengthens the cycle and the creditors end up with the money anyway, and more of it, as more debt and money is created."

"But how?"

"When one Sugar Dollar created equals one Sugar Dollar of debt, the poor and lower classes end up with debt – which they pay interest on, and it cycles back to the banking sector. More specifically it gets distributed to those working in finance, in the city center, and flows from the poorer regions to the wealthier ones. Flowing from small businesses to the financial sector, and again, from the poor to the rich. It always has and will, Willie."

"Still, it's a very funny idea, this *double movement*." Willie admits.

"There's only one takeaway – if the market economy is left to evolve according to its own nature it would lead to its own self-destruction."

"I'll think on that." Willie says as he stands and stretches.

"Good. Now let me out." Otto orders.

"One last question, where are the Santa-trons taking the poor elves?"

"That's not my department."

"Okay then, maybe I'll catch you next year?" Willie says as he walks away.

"Hey! Let me out! You told me you'd let me out!"

Willie glances back. "Answer me."

"I can't!"

"Then I'm gone and you'll be down here rotting for a very long time." Willie replies.

"You gave me your word. You swore on all that's sacred in the North Pole!" Otto shouts. "An elf's word is his bond!"

"There's nothing sacred left, only Sugar Dollars, but I don't consider that sacred in the least."

"I'm the good guy, I hope you'd see that!"

"But you're not." Willie says, walking away and turning the lights off, leaving Otto in his dark cold cage.

Willie emerges from the basement and hits stop on the recording device he's hid behind his back. He's got the whole conversation on tape. He pops the cassette out and hands it to his assistant.

"Make copies. Send one to Renee and another to Ginger, *as fast as you can.*"

20 – MELTING GLASS, MELTING GLACIERS

Willie stands outside Renee's door, softly knocking, but still no answer.

He leans against it and hears her crying. He tries the knob, the door's unlocked to his surprise. He nuzzles it forward as his eyes meet hers. She's there, weeping by the fireplace, spinning the cassette between her fingers.

"I'm sorry, but I thought you should know the truth." Willie says.

"I should." She says. "Where is he?"

"He's fine."

"That's not what I'm asking."

"He's in a cage in the basement of my workshop." He says, unsure if it was right to admit.

"Good." She replies to his relief.

"Can I come in?"

She nods as he gently approaches, joining her by the fire, warming.

"You've listened all the way through?"

"Yes."

"What do you think?"

"I've been played. I'm an idiot. Jesus, Willie, is that what you want to hear?"

"No."

He stares deep into the fire. "I'm the idiot. Maybe we've all been idiotic, letting these Germans build up our egos while they grab control from right up under us."

"We need to find out where those robots are taking all those elves."

"Seems Otto rather rot in a cage than tell me, so you know it's bad. But I'll find out."

"I want to help." She says.

"Are you sure?"

"Yes, absolutely."

He smiles and reaches to hold her hand. She squeezes his back and together they stare into the flames.

"Good," he says. "There's nothing more valuable than genuine friendship with an elf who loves the truth."

"We should start right now." She says.

Willie smiles. She smirks back and they take off!

The duo runs outside, hop onto Ursus and charge down the streets with vigor. The storefronts rattle as they sprint by. They rush by the Belief Meter which is soaring at all-time highs, and cruise by the Tree of Trees, still in mid-decoration with massive crews of elves placing more and more of those brilliant, shiny and sparkling glass balls and disks all over.

Ursus comes to a sliding stop at the North Pole Reserve with a plows' worth of snow flying in the valet's face, burying him.

They dash to Willie's office and lock the doors. He grabs his binoculars and scouts the city. Renee works to direct him to certain areas, like the old Factory Society neighborhoods and ghettos on the fringe of the city where they'd most likely find an indebted elf in mid-eviction.

But the vastness and chaos of the city make it impossible to spot isolated acts in the shadows. They switch on and off with binoculars, tag-teaming the scouting effort, slugging coffee back and forth.

Still no luck as Willie stares out and scans – until Renee notices a Santa-tron roughly escorting two raggedy elves on the street just in front of the North Pole Reserve.

"Look, down there!" She exclaims. Willie can hardly believe his eyes, it's –

"Bushy and Albaster," he says fearfully, "let's go!" They dash out and hop back onto Ursus, grabbing a tight hold on his elaborate leather saddle, the one with the North Pole coordinates and twisted crosses amid symbols of the North Pole.

They work to catch up but the Santa-tron pushes Bushy and Alabaster quickly and crudely through the streets, making it difficult to track. Once Willie and Renee have Bushy and Alabaster within their sights, they slow Ursus to a stalking mode, tailing their friends across long stretches of the city, doing their best to keep distance but not lose sight. As they get further from the city center there's less to hide behind, until the stalking becomes obvious. Bushy takes notice and makes Alabaster aware of their presence, becoming hopeful that help may be on the way.

The pursuit continues through the maze of city streets and all the way to the edge of the tundra. Willie can't believe how far the Santa-tron's have pushed them, and when it doesn't seem like there's anywhere else to go, the Santa-tron forces Alabaster and Bushy onto the snowy plains.

"Where on Earth can the Santa-tron be taking them?" Renee wonders aloud.

There's no way to follow them now without the machine noticing. Willie ponders if Ursus could take down the lethal robot on his own, but realizes it's wishful thinking – these upgraded models are powerful. They hesitate – but realize their only option is to follow them out on the snowy plains.

It doesn't take long for the Santa-tron to catch on once Ursus enters the tundra snow. Santa-tron stops in its tracks and extends its arms to grab Alabaster and Bushy by their collars, lifting them off their feet before sprinting to Ursus. In the processes Alabaster and Bushy are nearly choked to death before being tossed aside.

"Stop following Santa-tron, this is restricted area." It states in its mechanical, monotone voice.

"Have you forgotten your god, Santa-tron? I'm your creator!" Willie jokes.

"You are in violation of North Pole Inc. code 1175. No elves permitted on tundra. Disperse immediately."

"I'm your creator, Santa-tron, and you will listen to me." Willie blurts to Renee's surprise.

"You are an elf. You are in violation."

"Who do you think created you?"

"Disperse now. Disperse now."

"I'm Willie Maven, your ultimate creator and you will allow us on this tundra."

"This is your final warning."

"This is your final warning, Santa-tron, before I have you decommissioned! Now run my identity." Willie yells.

Santa-tron buzzes and clinks. "Thinking." His hat spins slowly then fast until it abruptly stops as a bright optic laser *shoots* from its mouth and scans their faces in detail. "Willie Maven, Renee Kendal-Crink. Identities confirmed. You are permitted on limited parts of the tundra - for investment purposes only. Are you here to invest?"

"Yes, Santa-tron." Willie replies.

"Calling you a real estate agent-tron ...to escort you...to potential investment... opportunities." It says as a small antenna pops out of its metal hat, buzzing as it spins.

"Damn it, Santa-tron, don't-"

"Steve will be here shortly. Good bye."

"No, not Steve!"

"Yes, Steve." It blurts then hurries off and picks Bushy and Alabaster up out of the snow.

As the Santa-tron pushes them through the tundra Bushy and Alabaster glance back at Willie and Renee, all sharing a dreadful sense of despair, but Willie holds his fist up in a sign on strength before they're lost in the white abyss of the drifting snow on the horizon.

"Greetings Mr. Maven, greetings Ms. Kendal-Crink!" The cheery and eloquent real estate agent-tron says behind them, catching them by surprise.

"My god, you scared us." Willie says.

"My name is Steve, don't you remember me?"

"Yes, Steve." Willie frowns. "How could I forget?"

"Steve?" Renee asks.

"Yes, Renee?"

"Oh god – ok."

"Ok, Renee." Steve buzzes.

She glances at Willie, "Creepy, ew."

"He's kind of funny." He whispers back.

"No, he's not." She replies.

"How is the Jensen-Gin Workshop doing for you, Mr. Maven? Paying off well, I suspect?"

"Very well, Steve."

"Good. Now, let's get you off of this restricted land and to some fabulous investment properties, shall we?"

"You bought Rebecca's family workshop??" Renee whispers with anger.

"It was foreclosed...it's a long story."

"Fine, but what the hell are we doing?"

"Just go with it," he whispers back.

"This way." Steve says, as Ursus follows close behind. "What kind of tundra investment property are you looking for? Commercial, Recreational, Residential? Perhaps a nice little tundra get-away? I get it."

"No, Steve, you don't get it. How could you?" Renee moans.

"You're right. I'm just a robot, yea, yeah ‑"

"I see where it gets its humor," Renee rolls her eyes.

"He's kind of funny." Willie whispers back.

"What brings you investing today?"

"Always the same issue, Steve. Sitting on a war chest of money with a limited amount of worthy investments."

"That's why Steve is here to help. Afterall, we are in a new era where the workshop and factory production are replaced by Stock Managerial Capitalism. Non‑financial companies have drastically increased their own investments in financial products instead of industrial plants or the workforce. More than ever, workshops are more dependent on income and profits from their financial investments. Much more than their productive activities. The Maven Workshop is no different."

"You see me as a mere manager of capital instead of a producer of toys and innovation?" Willie states.

"Yes, well, of course you make toys, Mr. Maven. But profits derived from those sales are dwindling, especially compared to what you earn on your investments. Good that you are adjusting, others are far behind. Too bad for them, especially as we're headed to a golden age!" Steve chants.

"How the hell are we headed to a golden age?" Renee asks.

"By reducing social spending and taxes simultaneously. Reductions benefit business and the wealthiest segments of the North Pole. The state has engaged in a transfer of revenue to business and the wealthiest while expanding government deficits. The deficits have become a source of revenue for creditors buying state debt. The virtuous cycle of the debt economy is near complete." Steve says, matter of fact.

"Sadly, it's not all that it's all cracked‑up to be, Steve." Willie mutters.

"That's too bad, Sir, I'm programmed to believe it a glorious day."

"And yet I need more investment opportunities because my capital compounds. You know, it's a tedious task searching for evermore profitable opportunities." Willie says.

"A zero-growth steady state of capitalism would be a welcome change." Renee riffs.

"HA-HA - I'm sorry to laugh, Ms. Kendall-Crink, that is how I am programmed. A steady state of capital is not possible. Capital is about profit seeking."

"I'm aware, Steve."

"Capitalists realizing a profit requires more value at the end of the day than there was at the beginning. Without constant expansion, colonization, imperialization there can be no capital."

"Steve - "

"If prolonged, zero growth would destroy capitalism."

"Steve, spare us, please!" Renee shouts. "Even your robots' man-splain." She nudges Willie.

"I didn't program him."

"I'm sorry Ms. Kendal-Crink, I'm programmed under the value system."

"Of moral justice?"

"The value system of...values. Economic value. Maybe both, I don't know? What is moral value, from the perspective of a robot? Economic value must be moral value." Steve concludes.

"It's often the opposite." Renee says.

"You're going to make me short circuit, Ms. Kendal-Crink, HA-HA. Let's find you some creative investments before I do. HA-HA...HA-HA."

Renee becomes is further agitated as Steve laughs at his own jokes and uses the term "creative" in a financial way.

"That must be why those snobs masquerading around as

creative professionals' are strong on the rise. Zipping through the streets in their sleek, stretch landships with ice buckets full of champagne, sucking the life out of the economy to support a class whose one aim is to compound its own already immense wealth." She says looking at Willie. "Downtown North Pole has a huge concentration of so-called creative talent."

"Creative accountants and tax lawyers," Willie chimes in.

"Creative financiers armed with creative investment vehicles."

"Creative manipulators of information. Creative hustlers of creative non-sense." She adds.

"Creative Steve's!" Willie shouts as they both laugh.

"I'm not programmed to detect sarcasm, but I think that's it." Steve says.

"Machine learning is incredible," Willie chuckles.

The group makes their way through the tundra over ice fields covered in black soot from the burning of coal. Even here the air quality is affected by climate change, as the North Pole has climbed ever steadily warmer, like most other places that shouldn't be. The warming makes for incredible, new, unnatural sights. Including the melting and collapsing of vast chunks of glaciers off the coast as masses of ice crash into the ocean with explosive power.

They travel closer to the Atlantic, where the intimidating mountains of the North Pole range meet the frozen coast. It's close to where Willie helped rescue the Germans. After an incline they arrive at a powerful and newly formed waterfall. The water rushes down from an impressive height, all derived from the melting glacier on the mountains above.

"We're here," Steve says as he mechanically smiles. They pause and gaze out at the powerful force of nature in the midst of the artic alcove. It's a naturally enclosed intimate space. Even Renee sheds her tough layer, becoming mesmerized by the loveliness of the sight.

"Isn't it wonderful?" Steve asks.

"It's beautiful." She says.

Steve surveys the land, relaying all the relevant information while Renee takes keen notice to the large chunks of ice falling amid the flowing waterfall. The sounds of crashing ice blends in seamlessly with the continuous crackling.

"You could make a lot of money with a high-end resort. The wealthy from all over the North Pole would pay dearly to experience this up close and personal, especially if you figure out how to heat the water – perhaps by tapping into geothermal." Steve says.

"How would I monetize it, in your professional opinion, Steve?" Willie asks.

"Each natural curiosity, be it a rock, grotto, waterfall, or glacier – everything, even the sound of an echo – can be owned. Enclose the site with decorative but strong iron gates, then hit the North Pole with a sexy yet emotionally gratifying ad campaign."

"You think that'd do the trick?"

"I do, Mr. Maven. Just think about it - how glorious it'd be to capture a Sugar Dollar for every shimmering photon of light bouncing about this smatter of falling droplets, ever forming and ever fading. How grand to profit from the zephyrs of wind that morph these heavenly sheets of mist. How transformative to allow that soothing sound of a cool breeze translate into the cool clinking of coins in your cash register. How wide you'll smile at the electronic zip of your bank machine as it deposits your dollars into your account. How can you say no?"

"Poetic, Steve, you really are programmed to sell." Willie smiles. "But beyond its beauty, why is this a superior financial investment?"

"It's a naturally scarce opportunity, and one which would allow you to charge high amounts in perpetuity for a relatively modest upfront cost."

"But nothing is being produced here, it's an unproductive investment at the expense of a productive one. If we keep investing in real estate, art and all other types of non-productive assets - then ultimately there will less capital for productivity."

"I'm not sure if I can fully process those semantics, Sir?"

"Semantics, Steve, really?"

"I'm sorry, Sir."

"If I invest more into unproductive assets there is less capital available for productive ones, all the way to the point where productive capital is suffocated."

"Processing. Processing." Steve says as his hat spins while dancing in a jiggling manner in circles.

"What the hell is he doing?" Renee asks.

"I don't know."

"Can we hit him?"

"Risky, try it." Willie replies. She picks up a stone and sneaks up behind Steve, but Steve suddenly stops jiggling as Renee tries to drop the stone discreetly, worried Steve may have overheard.

"I see your point, Mr. Maven. But long-term effects that may emerge are beyond my current programming. I can request more features in my next update."

"Very well, Steve, but your incompetence offends me. How will you make up for it?"

"Come again, Sir?"

"There's no way I'm going to buy property from you now. I'll buy something else from some other broker, and I'll have you reported. You'll be decommissioned. You wouldn't want that, would you?"

"No, Sir."

"Then I want you to get underneath that waterfall and sing and dance for me!"

"Huh?"

"You heard me, Steve!"

"Oh, by golly. What song?"

"Rudolph the Red Nosed Reindeer!"

"Really, Sir?"

"Yes, Steve, God damn!"

"Oh, ok - "

Steve clinks and clanks before moving into the cold glacial water, clearly unhappy about it. Renee laughs, realizing what Willie is trying to do – getting Steve positioned underneath the waterfall.

Steve gets a few meters in, "Rudolph the red nose reindeer, had a very shiny nose –"

"No, Steve, No! Closer to the waterfall!"

"But I'll get all wet!"

"You'll be fine, you're a robot! Remember!? Now do you want to make a sale or not?"

"Oh golly, ok..."

"Good, underneath you go!" Willie demands as Steve mopes to stand underneath the waterfall.

"Rudolph the red nose reindeer, had a very shiny nose, and if you ever saw him..."— *CRASH* – a chunk of ice as large as a landship collides into Steve, *crushing him like a can.* All that remains is scrap metal, with its face pushed inward toward the pelvis, head ripped open, and component parts floating about the lake as the hallow body cavity fills with water and sinks.

"Holy shit!" Renee cheers as she embraces Willie with a celebratory hug, much to his delight. "Now let's find your friends."

"Bushy, Alabaster, we're coming!" Willie shouts with glee as they hop back onto Ursus. "Where to?" He wonders.

"We'll need a better view." Renee responds.

Ursus howls with a renewed spirit as Willie directs them up the steep hill that twists and turns up narrow mountain passages until they reach the top of the waterfall.

But the sight is harrowing - *tundra as far as the eye can see.* They turn around, but there's the vast and jagged North Pole Range along the melting glacial cliffs. The scenery leaves them confused as they scan every part of the vista for clues as Ursus patrols a mile out, smelling and searching. But the bear returns up the mountain with nothing.

They're stumped - until Renee notices something far in the distance. It's a giant gray cloud emanating into the air. It hovers slowly, close to the horizon in a condensed cluster, then dissipates out to the ocean with the wind, in a constant way. She points out the unnatural sight to Willie, they can't see a smokestack but there must be something.

They must reposition to see the origin of the clouds, but they realize the Artic Range is impossible to penetrate, with its icy rock walls shooting up for thousands of feet. If there's something on the other side of the range it can only be accessed by a dangerous journey over the melting coastal glaciers. They turn to each other and know what must be done.

"To the cliffs." Willie directs.

Ursus tenses, sensing the peril before them, but relaxes once Willie and Renee give him a reassuring pet after climbing atop his back.

Soon they arrive on the slim, icy passage that outlines the coast. Ursus saunters, sensing the fragility of the glacial ice under his paws. With the right amount of weight and pressure they could trigger the ground to fallout from beneath them. The sun breaks past the holes in the thick clouds and the ice cracks under their weight as webs of cracked ice forms beneath Ursus, eerily expanding outward on contact.

As they cautiously proceed Renee spots a cargo ship in the ocean. After a closer look they realize the ship is full of Santa-trons. They're patrolling the deck as the ship steers to the origin of the dense gray clouds. It's a strange sight but they know they're onto something.

They get closer to the ever-flowing cloud until they spot its source - a MASSIVE SMOKESTACK - pumping gas into the atmosphere at an extraordinary rate. The colossal size and scale of the smokestack is impressive, standing taller than the highest tower of

Santa's Hermitage, and it has a giant twisted cross, a swastika, on its side that faces the ocean.

They're only a mile away from the smokestack, but the thin glacial path comes to a dead end at the foot of a fierce mountain just as the sun retreats. The incline is too steep for Ursus to climb, so Willie and Renee must leave him behind for now, to at least get a better look at what lies on the other side. Willie pets Ursus' face as he gently purrs in return, proud how his beloved bear has gotten them so far.

"Stay put boy, we'll be back soon." Willie says.

The duo leaves Ursus and begin their climb up the mountain. It's a steep, with several challenging vertical walls of rock which they must masterfully scale. They're without tools or even rope. The hiking is an endurance test but the real challenge are the sets of vertical climbs which has them searching for precise crevices and footings to reach for in their treacherous ascension. Renee is methodical and experienced enough to keep herself steady while Willie trembles with each move up. It'd be impossible if he didn't have such an advanced piece of technology for a hand – it grips firmly on the most challenging stretches.

They reach a small plateau after an exhausting journey up. Willie looks down on one end and checks on Ursus while Renee explores the plateau.

"Willie, come quick!" She shouts.

Ursus looks well enough, so Willie joins her in a hurry. He catches his breath but is transported into a state of awe as they stare upon an enormous FACTORY from which the smokestack protrudes. It's more immense than any factory they've ever laid eyes on. Bland and sterile, without decoration or color, and entirely industrial.

From their position they study the structure and layout of the various buildings, and the flow of elves from one building to another. The elves appear to be more like prisoners than factory workers. Perhaps it's an elaborate, insane debt repayment operation? Whatever it is, it's a new height of depravity.

If Willie didn't feel betrayed by the Germans before he certainly does now. There must be no end to their lust for profit.

Suddenly he becomes enlightened about the weight of crimes he's committed against his own kind. The emotions flood his heart, filling him with guilt and a fiery brand of self-hatred.

Renee pulls him close and they observe how the masses of elves are dragged off the old Icelandic naval vessels. Each vessel carries a pair of artillery cannons, but the Icelandic flag is painted over and covered by the swastika. These vessels turned cargo ships are operated by the Santa-trons and a handful of German sailors. The ships pull into the freshly built harbor, which is linked to the factory with smoothly paved roads outlined by high protective brick walls.

They're entranced by the scene playing before their eyes, paying little attention as the sun peers back from behind the clouds, warming their faces...and everything else. They count the buildings over and over, mesmerized by the dismal campus, and scan for Bushy and Alabaster. But they can't spot them amid the tens of thousands of elves being pushed around by the mechanical force.

Willie turns to the ships, watching how the Santa-trons clear the decks of elves then setup a system of conveyor belts, which load one thing and one thing only – *ornaments*. Those shining glass balls, spectacular glittering disks and artfully shaped colored glass that decorates the "Tree of Trees" so splendidly. *Elves in, ornaments out.*

The revelation sends a horrifying shiver down Willie's spine, giving him an uncontrollable tremble. All the while the sun shines stronger, raising the temperature until – SMASH – a piercing echo rips through the airwaves and *SHAKES* the mountain. Willie rushes to the ledge from which he's climbed and peers out.

The glacier just crumbled into the ocean, shattered into a billion pieces. Gone.

And Ursus is gone with it.

Willie's collapses to the ground, crying.

Renee rushes to him, and holds him with all of her love. Within her clench he regains strength and reaches back to hold her. Through their desperate embrace they feel an unbreakable bond forge between them.

They gaze into one another, without a clue what to do.

They're stuck atop of this cold plateau with only one way down, and it leads to the factory.

21 – THE ORNAMENT FACTORY

Willie and Renee wipe their tears and scan the vast oceanic horizon for Ursus.

Yet hope dwindles as the sun sets. Renee surrenders and holds Willie, knowing they won't survive the freezing night temperatures atop the high-altitude plateau. She locks eyes with him, acknowledging that Ursus is lost, tenderly trying to get him to realize the same.

"He's gone, Willie. I'm so sorry."

"He could still be out there."

"Even if he is, what can we do?"

He shrugs his shoulders, they're powerless from where they stand and he knows it too.

"We need to get off this mountain before the sun sets. There's only one way off now," she says, looking toward the dramatic slopes that lead to the factory.

Willie lets the pain set in, laboring awkwardly trying to stop his stream of tears.

"Let's get off this ledge in one piece first, then maybe we can still find your friends." Renee replies.

"Even if we make it into that dismal factory, I'm not sure we'll make it back out."

"At least we'd be among elves." She says. "Together."

"Until the bitter end." He replies.

Before she can face away, Willie grabs her hand and pulls her close, placing his forehead against hers, reciprocating the warmth she's given him. He moves in softly, inching closer, while she allows him to take control. The wind swirls sending streaks of glittering snowflakes dancing across the sky. The last sunrays shine upon them. Within that moment they shed all armor and bare their raw vulnerability, forgiveness and love. They're ready to die, and with zeal

271

Willie delivers the only honest kiss he's ever given – and Renee leans into him with everything she has to give back.

Eventually they untangle and move toward the ledge, hand in hand. They give each other one last deep-set smile before starting on the daring journey downward.

Renee discovers the best path down the mountain and makes the first move in the descent, Willie following close behind.

The darkness makes the descent even more chilling but also provides cover as they near the factory. Maintaining their stealth in the thick of the forest they're able to evade the patrols of Santa-trons and dodge the ever-searching spotlights from the guard towers. The moving lights come dangerously close as they duck and dive for cover.

They dust themselves off and search for a weakness in the fortified perimeter – it's heavily guarded, protected by layers of concrete walls, ditches and barbwire. They stay encamped, wracking their minds for an inspired idea.

Meanwhile, in the midst of the Atlantic the steady chop of frigid waves is interrupted by a desperate splashing from...

URSUS - gasping for air, paddling manically and holding onto life. He spends the last of his energy with a roar as he lifts his heavy body and climbs onto a raft size iceberg. After a few slips he makes it on. He tries to shake off the weighty wet leather saddle but can't, it's latched onto him like a tight belt. He shakes more freezing water from his fur and passes out from exhaustion.

Night turns to day before Ursus awakes in dire isolation, floating along, taking swings at the occasional passing fish. He's hungry and stranded but clinging to life. All appears hopeless...until he squints and perks up at the sight of a BATTLESHIP on the horizon.

It bears a high-flying American flag waving proudly about the prevailing winds. The sailors and marines amid the captain's deck spot Ursus with their naval binoculars and observe just how weak and desperate the poor bear is. They notice his peculiar looking leather saddle. Why would a Polar Bear, in the midst of the ocean nonetheless, be wearing one? With Christmas approaching and nothing but a boring training mission at hand they find it in their hearts to change course and make a beeline to Ursus. The entire crew cheers when the stoutly captain announces the fun-loving rescue.

The sailors dispatch a small fleet of nimble gunboats which surround a nervous and dizzy Ursus who *roars* in panic as they encroach. Even though the sailors and marines are smiling and friendly looking, Ursus can't handle the stress and faints again, passing out with a hard THUD against the ice as the sailors hop onto the life-raft of an iceberg. Most of the men are too confused or too afraid that Ursus may suddenly awake and attack - but a rugged marine, Joey McCarthy, approaches and reaches out to place his callused hands upon Ursus' fury face. Joey smiles feeling Ursus' subtle breathes from his wet snout, and calmly strokes his neck while the group watches in amazement. From his back-pocket, Joey takes a syringe and injects Ursus with a tranquilizer, making sure he's knocked out, just in case.

Joey touches the saddle, running his fingers along the intricate stitching - admiring and studying the enigmatic designs of elvish imagery. He investigates and discovers the strange Northern coordinates – the longitude and latitude of what can only be the North Pole. The mysterious coordinates make him smile. Once the other sailors realize Ursus is knocked out they move to investigate the strange artifact for themselves.

The team sneaks several ropes underneath Ursus and assembles a pulley to load him up and onto a gunboat. The pulley lifts Ursus from his side into the air. As he's hoisted a feeling of wonder and adulation takes a sudden turn to fear - *as the prominently displayed swastika on the other side of the saddle is revealed.* Joey and the sailors freeze and stare before continuing to load Ursus aboard.

Once he's secured on the gunboats Joey takes one last look around with his binoculars – from behind a distant iceberg emerges a cargo ship. Joey observes the large guns and Nazi flag on it. He's aghast at the sight, not to mention wildly confused with the presence of robots patrolling the deck.

The German sailors steering the ship recognize the American

battleship instantly. Almost out of instinct they load their guns and *fire* at the gunboats – narrowly missing them as huge blasts of fire and water burst against the ocean surface. Before the Germans can reload Joey and the sailors race back to the ship and report to battle stations.

Meanwhile, Willie and Renee are exhausted, hiding amid the dense forest on the foot of the mountain. Their minds race with hopeless ideas until they spot Bushy and Alabaster being pushed around the factory grounds by the same Santra-tron. Realizing the Santa-tron will surely recognize them Willie is hit with an epiphany. Suddenly Willie makes a dash to the barbed wire fence, startling Renee as he bum-rushes, trying his best to use his nerves to fuel his upcoming performance.

"You dumb piece of metal, stop where you are!" Willie shouts to the astonishment of all of a gleaming Bushy and Alabaster.

"Willie Maven." The Santa-tron says robotically.

"That Santa-tron you've called – Steve - is an absolute piece of scrap metal! He short circuited and we were left in the wilderness to die. What kind of investor service is that?!"

"Steve went offline 24 hours ago. Anomaly event. Suspicious. I can arrest you."

"Do it, I dare you. But once I get out, I swear I'll have you decommissioned!" Willie yells.

"I can arrest you - for trespassing – on non-investment - elf restricted - land."

"First, there are elves all over this godforsaken factory, so it is in fact not elf restricted!"

The Santra-tron stumbles, hat-spinning, "thinking", somewhat puzzled by the logic.

"Second," Willie continues, "this establishment blatantly violates North Pole liberalism. There is no market participation from this so-called FACTORY, which is against every rule in the book!"

"It produces ornaments." Santa-tron replies.

"But who are they selling them to?"

Santa-tron is stumped.

"Nobody!" Willie yells. "Because they're placing them on that 'TREE OF TREES' with no exchange taking place *whatsoever*. In fact, this entire factory is a fraud in that it's not for profit. Santa-tron, this factory *is the investment property*, now take me to your boss so I may purchase it and run it with efficiency!"

Santa-tron is baffled, hat spinning around faster. He jiggles and spins in circles before it breaks out stuttering "Thinking, Thinking..." in its monotone robot voice. Bushy and Alabaster chuckle at the sight as Renee rejoins Willie at his side with a smile.

Santa-tron stops, his face turning serious with his electronic eyebrows narrowing. It steps forward and places its arms within the barbed wire.

"Access granted." It says as its powerful metal arms spread the barbed wire thin with a sharp metal against metal shriek from the friction within its grip.

Willie and Renee move forward then share a recommitting glance. If they couldn't turn back before they definitely can't now, and they enter the point of no return crossing into the factory yard as they shimmy underneath the barbwire. They hug Bushy and Alabaster under the soulless, redeye gaze of the Santa-tron. It releases the wire behind them which snaps back like a slinky, but it tangles. Santa-tron works to undo the metal knot buying them a private moment.

"Thanks guys, for trying." Alabaster says.

"Still gonna get us outta this hell?" Bushy asks.

"Yeah, somehow." He replies.

"What is this place?" Renee asks.

"They move elves through these grounds like a toy down an assembly line." Alabaster replies.

"Off those ships, then under these thin tents. It's freezing."
Bushy says. "It's horrible."

"Today they had us polishing those glass ornaments,"
Alabaster adds, "tomorrow, god knows what."

"Every time a new ship of elves arrives, we move into the next
building," Bushy explains. "We're cut off from any other group that
came before or after us. We don't know where anyone goes."

"Terrifying." Renee says.

"Some think they're here to repay their debt. Thinkin' they get
to go home once they put in their time. But it's so unclear, and so
extreme. Doesn't feel right." Bushy says.

Nothing about any of this sits right with Willie. Everyone
quiets as the Santa-tron finishes untangling the barbed wire before
approaching.

"Take us to the boss, Santa-tron." Willie demands with faux-
authority.

"Now what?" Renee whispers.

Willie doesn't reply, not having the slightest idea.

They follow the Santa-tron. It looks back keeping watch of
their every step as it directs them through the numbing factory
grounds, passing by the main group of elves that Bushy and Alabaster
arrived with.

Willie is struck how their actual enslavement isn't very
different from the pseudo enslavement back in the city – in that
handcuffs and chains aren't necessary. Sadly, the whole group wreaks
of guilt and bad conscious for their debt. Debt they were designed,
encouraged and practically forced to incur. They all seem to bear the
weight of that debt and accept it, after all it's their signature on those
contracts. They feel as if they've given their word, making their self-
responsibility coincide with their complete alienation. An alienation
that transcends the mass of them into depression. An utter sadness
stemming from their bare powerlessness to act or take control of
their destiny.

He watches the group move about the grounds almost

automatically. Everything about the factory, and even the whole system of capital feels automatic. Is it not just one giant automation? A soulless machine process devouring society? Willie wonders if there is no alternative because the market and debt economy are governed by automatic operations, or even laws of nature?

But Willie snaps out of it. He was there in the drawing room and even helped create the blueprints of the system – nothing about it is automatic. *When things seem to function automatically, it's always because of political domination over the behaviors of elves.* Whether it be the structure of society under the patrimony of Santa Claus, or how life operates within the ever-devolving process of capital. Even here, walking these perverse factory grounds, Willie needs to remind himself that he's not the crazy one.

They arrive at a guarded gate of the main factory, standing at the bottom of a long winding staircase that leads to the entrance of a palatial office, presumably overlooking the factory floor. The massive smokestack shoots out of the facility, so it must be the site of ornament production.

Santa-tron nods to the other robotic guards as they open the gates with a prolonged unlocking processes of the safe-like doors. The staircase is steep and spirals around the base of the smokestack to the high up office. They climb higher and higher. Their collective anxiety nears a breaking point as they come up on the shiny, sliding gold office doors.

Santa-tron inputs an elaborate password into the security device. Willie still hasn't a clue what to do. Renee panics, mind racing, heart beating hard, adrenaline flowing. The gold doors slide open as Willie, Bushy and Alabaster step inside. Renee is about to follow, but out of sheer survival instinct she *kicks* the Santa-tron square on the shin – knocking it off balance before it goes flying, CRASHING, twisting and tumbling down the steep metal staircase until it's destroyed with a booming SMASH against the steel doors at the base.

"God Damn!" Willie shrieks as the gold doors slide open - he yanks Renee inside before it closes.

"That was amazing." Bushy says as the four of them share a moment of elated surprise.

They turn around and realize they're inside a fancy office that doubles as an elaborate control center. It's abuzz with computers, monitors, bells and whistles. A fascinating site and much more complex than what's necessary for ornament production. Fortunately, they find themselves alone. As they explore Bushy discovers an emergency tool kit with a welding torch - she uses it to weld the sliding gold doors together, locking themselves in.

Warning lights flash and spin with an echoing alarm sounding off.

"The factory is starting. The alarm sounds before the smokestack gets going." Alabaster says as the monitors come to life while a raucous grinding of gears and squeaky metal tracks turn just beyond the other side of the blacked-out glass.

Seemingly the control panel overlooks the production line below, but they're unsure how to bring down the covers. Soon the loud clinks and clanks smooth out to a steady hum until an *explosion* rings aloud. It's followed by a hellish grumble which blends into that constant grinding and buzzing.

Amid these sounds erupts a series of horrifying screams, distinctly elvish, growing closer as if coming down the factory floor. Willie and Renee desperately try to make sense of the control panel, searching for an emergency stop. But the whole process is locked into motion. They scramble for an answer as the Santa-trons SLAM against the welded gold doors, punching against them so hard they dent and cave inward like a crinkling can.

The petrifying, relentless pounding against the door interrupts Renee's focus until she discovers a unique looking switch and gives it a flick. The blinders covering the windows fold back to reveal their worst nightmare...

A long, single file row of doomed elves traveling atop a conveyor belt, cuffed down by their wrists and ankles, bound against the belt as it clinks toward a fiery furnace awaiting them on the other end.

The elves burst with primal, terror filled screams, realizing their final fate awaits them in the fire. The flames grow hotter with each passing inch. The hellish scene fills the four elves with absolute scare and sadness, especially in how mechanical and soulless the genocide is.

Willie, Renee, Bushy and Alabaster break into tears watching the elves being cooked alive as they're delivered into the mouth of the furnace. The victims screams heighten to a climax as their skin blackens, peels, then flakes off while their blood boils. An excruciating death. It isn't until they're well inside the furnace where they're engulfed by flames, then incinerated, reduced to a small pile of sparkling dust.

Renee slams buttons across the control panel trying to find an emergency stop, but nothing works. Bushy kicks the controls and takes the welding torch to it, but even that doesn't have an effect. The death factory is locked into motion.

Willie is glued to the ghastly scene, staring out with watering eyes. He picks up on other details, like how the sparkling dusty carbon is collected by slides on each side of the conveyor belt within the furnace. He notices how the slides are oriented in a certain direction and run to another section of the factory. Looking across the office he discovers another view exposed by the lifted blinders.

From this viewpoint they gaze into a glass blowing studio, watching how the sparkling dust travels down the slides and fills large drums on the floor. Santa-trons march over to the filling drums with long blowpipes that are equipped with bright yellow and orange globs of molten glass. They dip the globs into the drums of sparkling elf remains that evidently give the ornaments their signature glittery shine. Then they place the glob-end of the blowpipe into one of the numerous furnace small holes in the wall.

Suddenly a man in a protective suit enters the floor. His back is turned toward the four as he works – blowing glass, shifting and shaping each molten glob into its own unique and desired form. The master glassblower juggles many forming ornaments, concentrating immensely as he rotates and swings pipes while controlling the temperature as he blows and spins them.

The glassblower creates a great variety of forms and shapes, each with its own color palette. Watching the glassblower is mesmerizing, like getting lost in the movement of a dancer, with his hypnotic motions and skill on display. But the perverseness of it all makes Willie want to destroy every ornament he's ever seen, and remembers the thousands upon thousands of ornaments already "decorating" the "Tree of Trees."

The glassblower grabs another blowpipe and turns ever slightly. Willie recognizes his profile...

It's none other than *Klaus* himself.

And to Willie it's like a dagger through his heart. He nearly falls to his knees as Klaus fully turns and waves to them, greeting the four as if nothing is wrong.

"I'll be right up!" Klaus yells before turning back to finish more ornaments.

"He's gone mad." Willie utters.

"He's been mad." Renee replies.

Willie slouches and stumbles over to Bushy and Alabaster who cry in each other's clutch. He wraps his arms around them, joining in their remorse as the Santa-trons PUNCH and POUND down the door. Renee hesitates to admit defeat, but soon softens and falls into Willie's arms. Cornered and with no backup there's nothing else to do, and the four embrace each other in a tight hold as the Santa-trons kick down the gold door and push their way in.

Through the cleared path emerges Klaus and Otto at his side, along with a dozen Sanat-trons surrounding the quad.

"Now, where do we start?" Klaus asks.

"Why?" Willie replies, "Just tell me why?"

"Isn't it obvious, Willie?" Klaus says.

"I should've let you all drown, or freeze, or just rot in jail. I had the opportunity to do each but I did the opposite."

"I thought you might say that, always so shortsighted, never seeing the bigger picture. It's your biggest fault in business, a real weak spot my elf."

"Now look at you." Otto blurts.

"Shouldn't you be locked up in a basement?!" Renee jabs.

"It wasn't hard to find Otto, and besides the Santa-trons have been tracking your every move since you've step foot on the tundra." Klaus states.

"You didn't answer my question." Willie says.

"Why open this wonderful ornament factory?" Klaus clarifies.

"Why?" Willie repeats.

"Because, from the standpoint of capital, elves have become another disposable population, just like one of the many inferior, redundant, costly populations which needlessly take up space."

"That's what you're going with?" Willie says.

"Their prolonged suffering and inefficient path to extinction must be replaced by an efficient, final solution, to rid North Pole Inc. from their collective liability. It's all comes down to the standpoint of capital, the only perspective that matters."

"What the hell do you mean from the standpoint of capital??" Willie asks trying to control his fury.

"Capital has become so powerful relative to the elvish workforce to where elves themselves are the major risk to the economic and political stability of the North Pole."

"You're worried they'll demand welfare, and rebel if they don't get it?"

"Yes, welfare, government support, the canceling of debts, all of that. We can't do it."

"What's that even matter when it's a drop in the bucket?"

"It's the principle that matters, my elf! And what do you think would happen to our stock price once we have to support an entire disposable population?"

"Who cares – it doesn't compare!" Willie spouts.

"It does, now answer!" Klaus demands.

"I don't know."

"THE STOCK WOULD GO DOWN! There'd be less

dividends for shareholders as there'd be more expenses and less profit! You must face how the poor are already effectively dead, I'm merely speeding up the process and making the company more profitable, like a good CEO does!"

"You're literally achieving profitability by genocide." Willie states.

"I'm achieving it by the necessary means," Klaus says. "All that government spending that bleeds North Pole Inc. for tax revenue, and all burdensome welfare spending, for what? Especially when they can't even make their minimum payments on their own debt."

"But from the standpoint of capital you're losing the market for elvish goods and services." Willies points out.

"That never mattered. Even if it were more significant, I'm sure we could just have our *machines and artificial intelligence not only produce but also consume the goods and services to make up for it.*"

"And what's point of that?"

"Profitability! Profitability for god sakes, Willie! *That's all that matters!* The elvish race has become a heavy burden that must be sacrificed. *They're a burden at best and the single biggest threat to our system of capital at worst.*"

"But elves aren't just another line item in the budget!"

"That's where you're wrong, and it's time to take the trash." Otto says.

"Or recycling, in this case." Klaus says with a grin. "The glittering carbon of the elvish carcass makes for incredible glasswork. I turn them into something beautiful, into high art, and put them on display for the whole North Pole to admire. I take them from something with negative value and transform their very essence into an expression many consider priceless...All the while ending the inevitability of their prolonged suffering."

"You're a sick man," Renee utters. "If there's any pure form of destruction and so called 'negative value' you are surely the embodiment of it."

"How much are you worth, Renee?" Klaus asks.

"That means nothing." She replies.

"It means everything!" Klaus yells. "I'm worth billions and you're worth nothing. You see the difference?"

"Willie is still worth something." Otto says.

"For now, only because we let him. That's his repayment." Klaus says as he turns to Willie and leans into him with a heavy stare. "What will it be, Willie? Will you join them as another ornament on the tree, or rejoin us and live like a king?"

Willie takes a deep breath and steps forward inches from Klaus' overbearing stare, glaring straight up at him.

"You can turn me into a god damn glass star." Willie delivers.

Klaus and Otto laugh among themselves, somewhat in disbelief, until Klaus turns back to Willie with a deep sense of gravity.

"Then so be it." Klaus utters with disdain before stepping back, letting the Santa-trons descend upon them.

Moments later Willie, Renee, Alabaster and Bushy are thrown onto the conveyor belt, locked on their journey to the furnace. Klaus and Otto oversee. Willie is in front with Renee behind. Her skinny arms have a little room to slide further in the metal cuffs. She reaches for Willie's hand, holds it tight, and glances into his sad eyes.

"Until the bitter end." She tells him.

"Until the bitter end." He replies with tears.

The WAIL of the incinerator is crushing as they make their way down the clinking conveyor. Bushy and Alabaster lock hands. Alabaster reaches for Renee's hand, connecting the four in a chain as they approach the mouth of the furnace with the heat blasting against them.

They close their eyes and turn away - except for Willie who stares forward into the fire until the heat becomes too much to bear. He shuts his eyes. The end is inevitable...

Until sudden EXPLOSIONS blast all over! A flash tears through the factory roof and another explosion destroys the conveyor belt engine, stopping the elves on the track as the roof abruptly falls in. Falling debris crashes at the mouth of the furnace, clogging it and reducing the overwhelming heat. The elves can hardly believe they're alive while Klaus and Otto duck for cover as the factory crumples.

The powerful rolling thunder of explosions are like an unending series of blasting earthquakes. With a fresh hole burning open in the control-room, Klaus and Otto look through it and spot...

The AMERICAN BATTLESHIP STEAMING TOWARD THE FACTORY, firing round after round off the ship's massive guns. Joey McCarthy and his battalion of marines gear up for combat. Ursus rides upon the deck as the Captain strokes his neck and smiles while the artillery unyieldingly pounds into the swastika marked smokestack and factory. The gunners take careful aim, steering clear of the elvish holding camps, thinking those prisoners could be their own, old, allied POWs.

Soon, the once massive smokestack is reduced to a heap of rubble. Klaus and Otto share a stare of disbelief before making a desperate escape, running furiously through a maze of debris, dodging explosions left and right. Willie, Renee, Bushy and Alabaster are left behind, still locked to the conveyor belt, holding hands and praying, having failed to make sense of the surrounding apocalypse.

The booms of shelling are replaced by the *tic-tic-tic-tic* rattling of machine gun fire. The battleship enters the harbor and the marines storm the docks, shooting down every Santa-tron that rushes to challenge them. Their fire power is superior to the Santa-trons hand-to-hand combat, but danger grows as the fighting becomes short range.

The marines push forward, taking out position after position of Santa-tron, and for the first time they come across the raggedy elves in the encampments. They're shocked - not only by their existence, but by their horrendous condition. How could elves possibly be treated in such a way? The site disgusts them, but also fuels them to fight fiercer as they invade the grounds, fighting up all the way to the factory. The advance is steady but gives Klaus and Otto enough time to escape through a mountain tunnel to the tundra within their quick and capable land-ships.

With an aggressive charge the marines shoot down the last of the Santa-trons and capture the factory. Willie, Renee, Bushy and Alabaster shout for help, trying to be found amid the maze of wreckage. They yell at the top of their lungs until they're discovered by Joey and his squad. Joey is taken aback realizing they're trapped on this conveyor belt of doom. The furnace still burns, everyone is drenched in sweat as the marines' struggle to free the elves, but a pair of barbwire cutters does the trick, bringing tears of joy to the rescued four.

"Thank you." Willie cries as he gives Joey with a massive hug. Renee, Bushy and Alabaster all join in to Joey's bemusement and delight.

"You're incredible. You poor elves are so incredible, and you speak English!" Joey says with a smile.

"We do," Willie laughs, "and we can't thank you enough."

"It's our duty," Joey replies. "Unbelievable, all of this. Your existence. Nazi's and Killer Santa-machines..."

"Santa-trons." Willie says.

"Yes, unbelievable!" Joey yelps. "Let's get outta here before this whole place blows!"

The marines help the elves out and move to a safe spot below the mountains, securing the position as Joey bandages up Willie.

"How'd you find us?" Willie asks.

"We found a polar bear floating on a tiny iceberg in the middle of the ocean. He was wearing a saddle with these approximate coordinates...and a Swastika. Then we came under fire."

"Wait, you found a polar bear? A big white polar bear with a saddle?" Willie asks.

"Yes."

"Ursus!" Willie shouts, "You saved Ursus, my pet bear! I can't believe it! You've saved so much already." Willie cheers as Joey wears a smile from ear to ear.

"Have you saved the North Pole yet? Have you liberated the

city?" Renee asks.

"A city?" Joey replies.

"Yes, the North Pole. Our civilization, it's been taken over by Germans. They've enslaved us elves as wage laborers. We need help." Alabaster says.

"We thought the Nazi's were done running, guess not." Joey says.

"Will you help us save the North Pole?" Willie asks.

"It would be a privilege, but there's protocol. I need to call this in, put together a strategy..." Joey replies.

"I know these Germans, by the time you do all that us elves will be wiped out. We need your help now." Willie says.

Joey contemplates the tough scenario. He's never broken protocol or the chain of command before, but he sees the desperation in their eyes and knows Willie isn't lying.

"Ok." Joey answers.

"Amazing." Willie smiles.

"We need all the help we can get." Renee says.

"How did all of this happen, Nazi's coming to the North Pole and taking control?" Joey asks.

"It's a long story." Willie says.

"There're some Germans in Reykjavik, too. At the corporate office." Renee adds.

"Corporate office?" Joey asks.

"Like I said, long story." Willie says.

Joey turns to his men. "You heard the elf, there's more Nazi's out there. Let's resupply and roll!" He orders with utmost purpose.

"We have one more thing to do..." Willie says.

Willie, Renee and squad search the grounds and liberate masses of tortured elves from their flimsy camps and holding cells.

They find the last of the remaining survivors and lead them onto the battleship. As they board the ship Ursus nearly tramples Willie, giving him nonstop slobbery kisses as they reunite. The sight reminds the crowd of elves they're still capable of laughter. Once loaded, the massive propellers of the battleship start and they prepare for their final battle.

A nurse patches Willie up around a group of sailors talking about the strategy of the upcoming assault. They're describing it in terms of American Football, with defensive and offensive lines, running backs, quarter backs, and the alike. The references go over his head but he hears a funny term uttered over and over – the "Hail Mary Pass" – and learns the desperate nature of the play. "Hail Mary" Willie says, "Hope it doesn't come down to that." The sailors laugh in agreement, amused with an elf talking football.

Meanwhile, Joey prepares his marines as they gear up, readying a small fleet of Howitzer Motor Carriages, armored cars and even a Sherman "Jumbo" Tank. Meanwhile the captain introduces Willie to the ship's wheel, letting him steer as they pass the most intimidating heights of the North Pole Range parallel to them on the coast.

They search for the best landing spot while the captain helps him avoid a minefield of icebergs. After some searching, they find the perfect spot to park the ship, aligning it with a narrow icy peninsula that jets out into the ocean. From here the North Pole is mere miles away as the captain takes back the wheel and parks the battleship along the ledges.

Some elves stay onboard for now, either too sick or weak to journey and fight, but a determined group of elves with a burning desire for revenge seek Willie's permission to join. Willie knows they'll need as many fighters they can get if they're going to take back their home. The elves know just as well as the Americans can remember - Nazi's don't go down without a fight.

Soon Willie and Renee along with a motley crew of zesty elves arm themselves with machine guns and ammo, much to their satisfaction.

Willie and Renee are first off of the ship. Together they look as if they're claiming back the land upon which they stand, as the ragtag elvish forces behind them march to join. The duo assembles the company of elvish fighters into orderly rows, while Joey and his company of marines depart the battleship with the platoon of armored vehicles and rumbling Sherman Tank. Between the marines, elves and vehicles, it's small battalion of about 400 fighters in all. A force to be reckoned with, but given the scale of the task ahead it doesn't look like enough.

Joey rolls up in a quick moving armored Jeep equipped with tank tracks instead of tires. He hits the breaks hard and does a stylish skid across the snow before flashing a grin at Willie and Renee.

"Go time." Joey says, "Don't be shy, get in." He smiles says as they leap into the Jeep. Willie climbs half out of the roof, faces his army and punches the sky with a strong fist - his proud, fleshy elvish fist – and holds it high leading the army forward through the snow storm.

Soon they traverse their first steep incline, kicking vehicles into gear, desperate for traction while climbing the slippery hill. They reach the hilltop. Willie orders the army to a halt. From here the sight of the sprawling North Pole civilization fills the vista. The view of home still makes elves smile, giving them hope and reinvigorating courage. The Americans stare in wonder at the vastness of the magical sight. An otherworldly city so beautiful and sacred is absolutely worth fighting for.

As they merge their forces an opposing army of Germans and Santa-trons appear on the horizon, just outside the city. The dread of the steely, bleak army they oppose entrenches their position. Their bulky mechanic presence blackens the sky with a thick layer of exhaust, sending a shiver through the elves and Americans.

Willie's reconnaissance through the smog of exhaust is limited, but what's clear is that neither side is backing down.

He grabs Renee's hand. They've escaped a doomed fate before but he isn't so sure they have the karma to do it again...

22 – HAIL MARY

The elves and Americans advance through the tundra to the city.

Joey knows their advantage lays within the long-distance artillery of the tank and the marines' M1 81-millimeter caliber mortars. Meanwhile, the Santa-trons' hand to hand fighting style is haunting, knowing that when death comes, it will be up close and personal through their robotic grasp. So, Joey finds it odd how a whole company of 200 Santa-trons patrol the tundra like sitting ducks.

"It's an open shot. We should take it." Joey says.

"Do it." Willie agrees.

"With pleasure." Joey replies, ordering the massive tank into an attack position with the mortar cannons.

As they maneuver Klaus retreats personnel and war-machinery back into the city streets, oddly leaving those Santa-trons still out in the open.

With the tank, mortars and marines with their long-range riffles ready, Joey orders...

"Fire!"

Explosions rain across the tundra, obliterating squads of Santa-trons within the flashes of fire and a hail of bullets as they scurry around the wet fields of melted snow. It's like an open range. A total onslaught, but Willie knows it's all too easy. After a minute of devastating bombardment, Willie orders a cease-fire, catching Joey by surprise.

"Something isn't right." Willie says.

Renee snatches the binoculars from Willie and gazes at the devastated Santa-trons amid the crater laden tundra. Her jaw drops, hands trembling. Willie takes the binoculars back and looks for himself. The Santa-trons aren't Santa-trons at all, but elves forced into Santa-tron get-ups. It's a massacre.

As the smoke clears the gruesome sight of bloody body parts are revealed sprawled across the snow, staining the white landscape and coloring it in ten shades of red. Not a single one is left standing. Willie clears his teary eyes before pointing the binoculars back at the rooftops, watching as the Germans retreat and push further into the city where an army of Santa-trons await.

"Let's go." Renee says as Joey hits the gas, leading the tip of the spear.

Willie absorbs the scene. Where he once had pity for the obedient German pawns, he now has a burning vengeance. Yet he knows these German foot soldiers aren't fanatic sociopaths, like Klaus or Otto. They're rather banal and trite, most are mere conformists and careerists. Perhaps that's where true evil manifests – *through the deeply average person who relies on platitudes rather than thinking for oneself.* Evil stemming within people who are motivated by promotion, not ideology. Their actions dictated by a stupidity that's wholly unexceptional and falsely justified through the act of obediently following orders like dogs. What these Germans fail to admit, whether under the totalitarianism of a dictator or the totalitarianism of the Sugar Dollar is *there's always a moral decision to be made,* and that choice has consequences, even when the chooser feels powerless.

Willie looks back, watching the elvish army become sickened at the sight of their mutilated fellow elf. The fact they're responsible for it brings their spirit near a breaking point, just as Klaus designed. But before the army enters the eerily quiet city streets Willie tells Joey to stop driving. With a deep breath Willie jumps out of the Jeep, standing atop of it, addressing his army:

"Brave elves and men, today we fight to the bitter end, *together*. We'll fight our enemy on the ice or snow, on the cobblestone or city Square. We'll fight them in their glass palaces and skyscrapers, and we'll fight 'em in our factories and workshops. We will defend our home at any cost. Let's liberate the North Pole! Let elves be *free of all shackles for all time!*"

With a renewed morale they proceed forward into the city and down the streets. The soldiers search for movement. It's spooky, like the calm before the storm. Willie wonders what traps Klaus may have in store for them.

With persistence, the army rolls and marches through the wide-open streets undeterred for several miles until Joey orders their halt. They're at a fork in the road, but Willie knows it's only the start of a series of crossroads. They could march the army down a single path but the entire force would be vulnerable to an attack on the flanks. That could trap them within the narrow confines. Dividing the army up isn't appealing either, but if they can speed down these squeezed alleys they'll arrive in the Square by the "Tree of Trees."

Willie, Renee and Joey determine that the Germans won't be able to flank every route of the split roads. Getting the army to the Square will be best by taking all paths simultaneously. They split the army into platoons, with each platoon commander realizing they're on their own as they hurry down the winding, dividing streets and alleys.

Willie and Renee leave the Jeep to climb atop Ursus. The iconic sight of Willie and Renee strutting down the streets with Ursus provides a dignified flair to the fighting force, lifting the hearts of the terrified elves in hiding, giving them hope as they wave and smile while passing their boarded-up homes.

Gun shots break out several streets over. Their platoon speeds down the rolling cobblestone streets while the cacophony of automatic rounds burst on their flank. Willie fills with alarm thinking the Germans may have an ambush already on every route. The dissonance of the unseen machine gun fire feels like the army could be in the midst of a full-scale fight, but their only option is to dash to the rendezvous point. They spot the Square, filling them with adrenaline as they make an all-out dash.

Their platoon is the first to arrive, making them fret, wondering if everyone else has been cut down in the journey or in mid-fight. With eagerness they peer down the various streets but don't spot a single platoon approaching. Joey directs the soldiers to build defensive barriers – but there aren't enough materials, so he orders the soldiers to wire up and explode several empty buildings.

With the fragments they scurry to build a series of circular barriers, layered three rows deep with the "Tree of Trees" at the center.

Willie looks up at the towering Tree of Trees. The sparking disks and ornaments decorating it almost makes him sick. The sight of it stirs the emotions of many elvish soldiers, making them weep as they absorb the reality of how those beautiful disks were their loved ones, and could have easily been themselves. Though it's a horrific sight in one way, it's sacred in another.

Renee leaves Ursus' by a concealed area at the base of the monument and joins Willie's side. Together they stare up at the massive sight, taking in the scale and detail of it. The sight shakes them but reminds Willie that elves can achieve great things, and if they can build something so amazing under slave-like conditions, they can surely do so as free and liberated beings. That so much more can be achieved through a new way of life, provided they're endowed with an abundance of freedom. That's what's at stake; liberty, equality and fraternity for all elves.

Suddenly various platoons arrive. The jumbo tank makes an entrance too, powering through a tight space and destroying several buildings as it enters the Square. Soon distressed platoons come within sight, fighting fiercely. Many soldiers resort to their pistols or hunting knives as the Santa-trons jump from roof to roof before pouncing.

The robots are fast. They crack skulls against the cobblestone or twist their heads *clean off*. Necks are broken with one loud *crack* in a swift and lethal motion before jumping to their next victim. Most Santa-trons are soaked in blood, some sparkling red elvish blood, others covered in the thicker, syrupy human plasma, or splattered in a Jackson Pollock like combination of both.

Overwhelming gunfire pummels the Santa-trons back, either destroying or leaving them immobile on the streets. Some gunfire merely dents their metal, but a headshot to the eyes or mouth does the trick. Their metal joints are vulnerable, but unless it blows their limbs straight off the Santa-trons keep attacking like an ever-pressuring zombie army.

Joey realizes about a quarter of his army is lost, if they haven't made it to the Square they've likely died trying. Losses are high, considering they'll need every elf and man. Ammunition is low and further depleting while the handful of medics' scurry, patching up the wounded as best they can.

With the army reconvening Joey, Willie and Renee order the platoons into defensive positions behind the barriers. Although they're well entrenched, they're susceptible to attack from each street and alley leading to the Square, from all sides.

Willie and Renee climb the Tree of Trees for a better view, ascending about twenty stories, lifting themselves from tree to tree and branch to branch, pushing through the pine needles and ornaments, until finding a spot with a 180-degree view of the battle Renee holds that position while Willie makes his way to the other side, covering the other half.

"You seeing what I'm seeing?" Renee yells.

"Santa-trons? A ton of 'em?"

"Yup." Renee gulps.

The two watch as the robots advance from all directions.

They notice how the enemy army is layered so that the Santa-trons make up the front line, the militarized elvish Redcoats make up the second, while the third and last line is reserved for the regiments of German soldiers.

Willie stares into the largest and most guarded enemy brigade with his binoculars, spotting Klaus and Otto in the far back. The sight of them makes Willie snicker, he's glad they've arrived in person and relishes in the thought of fighting them face to face. Willie rejoins Renee, watching the enemy march to the edge of the square.

"Joey, they're coming from every direction. Get 'em ready, 360 degrees!" Willie yells.

Joey barks orders getting the army into a circular position with their barricades shifting around the Tree of Trees. From the ground the Santa-trons come into view as Joey hops onto the jumbo tank and readies his crew. As the first Santa-trons are about to step foot into the square...

"Fire!" Joey yells, with the tank unleashing its firepower blowing up a squad of Santa-trons in mid-charge, rushing to reload, finding their next target, kill and repeat.

But the Santa-trons pick up speed, closing in as Joey jumps from the tank to the troops. "Fire mortars!" He orders, as the shells bombard the Santa-trons with scattered accuracy.

The ever-rumbling tank and mortar volleys hold off the Santa-tron advance, but the killing machines are relentless as they enter the Square in full sprint, squeezing the elvish/American position tightly, putting them under immense stress.

"Give 'em hell, keep firing!" Joey yells as the tank and mortars kick into a rapid-fire pace, exploiting their advantage in distance until the soldiers' brace for hand-to-hand combat.

Renee snags Willie's binoculars and studies the faces of the Redcoats. They're confused and bitter, moving sluggishly and whispering secretly to one another while dodging the view of their German superiors. They've always been a recklessly obedient bunch, but even they themselves can't ignore the massive contradiction - that they're elves too.

Renee searches the Redcoat lines and spots Axel at the helm of a regiment. Her stomach knots as she watches his dismal face stare forward, awaiting orders, clearly sensing a deep guilt knowing his little sister is out there on the other side.

On the front lines, the brutality of the Santa-tron assault devastates, with the killing machines overwhelming defensive positions through the power of sheer numbers. As soon as one or two Santa-trons make their way over a barrier it's downhill from there. One piercing Santa-tron quickly leads to two, two to four, four to eight and so on, until a position is overrun, leaving behind a bloody trail of the decapitated bodies.

Joey maneuvers the tank and troop positions with resolve, directing soldiers on the falling front lines to withdraw to the secondary barriers. The smaller circumference of this defensive layer allows for more focused firepower, as the fight progresses it's clear they're out-numbered, but the liberators strangled position makes them fight harder as they dig in and spray down the constant stream of charging A.I. slaughterers.

With incredible effort an attack of Santa-trons are successfully held off. The fallen Santa-trons laid to waste by gunfire only mere meters from the barriers. The small victory bonds the elves and men, morphing them into a unified fighting force.

But Willie and Renee only see more Santa-tron reinforcements marching forward, readying to pour into battle. Willie looks into his binoculars, to his surprise he catches Klaus staring right back at him. Klaus puts down his binoculars, grins and waves to Willie, knowing that Willie's end via his own hands is near.

Klaus's unflinching confidence makes Willie wince. The inevitability of his situation seems to be approaching its natural conclusion. Teetering toward hopelessness, Willie scurries back into the center of the Tree of Trees with Renee. He wonders if a tooth and nail fight to the last elf is what he wants. He reflects on all they're fighting for and reaffirms that it's better to die with purpose than to live without it. That it'd be better for his brave comrades to fight and die than live under oppression, just as it'd be better for their whole civilization to have a memory of their bitter struggle, if only to remind elves of their dignity and pride inherent within them.

Renee *shakes* Willie, awakening him back to the dire moment. She shares his awareness of their ominous predicament, but knows the Maven Workshop practically invented the Santa-tron, and through that he must be able to do something.

"There's got to be another way," she says, "they're only computers. They do what they're told."

"They run on code." He replies.

"Right, and we can manipulate that code. Your techies must be able to do something!" She says.

"They're not 'my techies' anymore, I'm sure Klaus has turned them against me."

"Do you have a better idea?"

Willie thinks, shakes his head.

"Then it's our only hope."

There's a brief pause in fighting, allowing both armies to regroup. From their high up spot, they see the next wave of Santa-trons marching forward. They may have a minute until the Santa-trons arrive at the brink of the square.

Renee leads their escape down the skeleton of the monument with Willie close behind.

Klaus observes their movement through the thick pine needles. They reach the bottom and jump from the base onto Ursus' back, near Joey.

"Hold 'em off as long as you can!" Willie yells to Joey.

"What are you doing?" Joey yells, confused.

"A Hail-Mary!" Willie yells.

Joey smiles, impressed with Willie's reference, and agrees that's the only play left.

"Godspeed Maven, Kendal-Crink!" Joey nods.

Willie takes a deep breath and grasps Ursus' saddle as Renee locks her arms around him. On Willie's command Ursus unleashes all of his power with a strong thrust from his hind legs, leaping out and speeding to a full-on sprint, running faster than he ever has. Willie and Renee barely hold on as they dash through the killing fields, skidding across a puddle of blood into a narrow passage leading into a maze of alleys.

Klaus and Otto watch angrily as Renee and Willie escape. Klaus orders a platoon of Santa-trons to chase them, then commandeers an armored landship, throwing out the driver as Otto jumps in.

"Keep the Santa-trons attacking, no matter what!" He yells to Axel, who digests the order with a bitter but confirming nod.

Klaus and Otto take off in a zip, heading into the labyrinth of city streets.

"Where are they going?" Otto asks amid the thundering rumble of the engine.

"The Maven Workshop, where else!?" Klaus yells.

23 – THE TRUE MEANING OF CHRISTMAS

Willie, Renee and Ursus blaze through the tight alleys and corridors to the Maven Workshop.

The route seems open until a duo of patrolling Santa-trons spot them and instantly pursue.

Renee panics as the Santa-trons get behind her and start swinging, one *grazing* her shoulder.

"Hold on!" Willie yells as he leans into Ursus, getting him to run even faster as they jump over landships and food carts, pivoting then leaping over the empty gap of a half-built bridge.

But the Santa-trons keep pace and overcome each obstacle with their own crafty robot maneuvers, taking closer and closer *swings* at Renee, as she holds on for dear life with her arms wrapped tight around Willie.

Willie spots an incline ramp ahead, there's a sturdy pole on top. He points it out to Ursus – and with incredible conviction, Ursus dashes up the ramp, jumps and grasps the metal pole as they rotate through the air, around the pole in a 180-degree rotation – flying into the Santa-trons at full force. Just before contact Ursus uncoils his hind legs and *stomps* the robots into the ground.

All three share a sigh of relief arriving at the back passageway of the Maven Workshop. Willie hops off Ursus dizzy, taking a moment to regain balance. He inspects her back, it's marked up with jagged rips, fortunately only penetrating her tough jacket, not her skin.

Willie and Renee take inventory, feeling lucky to have survived before turning to Ursus, giving him the tightest loving hug. The three hold each other warmly, acknowledging this may be their last moment together. The heart-wrenching embrace centers them before Ursus offers a few big licks and a soft purr that morphs to a howl.

"It's time." Renee says, offering her hand to Willie.

He grabs it and together they make their way into the workshop, spotting the Ickles and flagging them down. Within moments, Sticky, fabulously surprised, arrives.

"Wasn't sure I'd see you again, Sir." Sticky excitedly blurts, guiding them inside.

"Me either, Stick...But you and your boys should get out of here before it gets ugly. They'll have your head if this doesn't work out."

"We're all in this together, Sir." Sticky replies.

"I can't convince you?"

"Never." Sticky says with a smile. "Where to?"

"Tech department." Renee utters.

Sticky guides them discretely to the Santa-tron production line. It's booming, turning out a new killer robot every minute. Willie and Renee spy on the operation, sneaking through the familiar corridors when the coast is clear. But Willie's done hiding inside his own workshop, he stands up straight, puffs out his chest and reminds himself he's still the head honcho.

"The boss is back, boys." Sticky announces as Willie rounds the corner and struts into the techie's den.

He surprises the crew, everyone shocked by his presence, and they pick up on his nervousness. Willie thought he knew what he wanted to say but it's lost on him, sharing an awkward silence until he finds Squibbles. The meek elf looks up at him with a blackeye.

"What are you doing here?" Squibbles asks angrily. "You're no longer the boss, orders of North Pole Inc."

"Squibbles, my poor elf, you look great. All considering," Willie says.

"I do not, nor does my bank account. Apparently, insurance doesn't cover what they call 'willful acts of self-mutilation,' even when your boss orders you to do it and tells you you're covered."

"Squibbles, from the bottom of my heart, I am sorry."

"That doesn't sound very sincere." Squibbles sniffles.

"I don't know how else to prove it to you." He says. "I'm sorry."

"Good, now that we know Mr. Maven is sorry, let's let him acknowledge how much of a jerk he's been." Renee says.

"Oh, I've been the biggest jerk. The worst. I was out of control." Willie admits.

"A grade-A jingle berry jerk!" Squibbles lets out with release.

Unbelievable how effective emotional intelligence can be, Renee thinks.

"What else Squibbles? He's not your boss anymore, just let it out." She encourages.

"A giant-eared reindeer lover!" Squibbles yells.

"Good one." Sticky says.

"What else?" Renee smiles.

"Dumb as a Yule Log!"

"I deserve that."

"You silver spoon-fed, scrooge-esque, money grubbing, condescending, know it all but knows nothing, value sucking, money squeezing, rat race designing, patronizing pompous profiteer, vampire-leech like, elf!" Squibbles exasperates.

"Whoa." Willie mutters, feeling a touch stung. "I can't believe that was the elf I've become. If you can't forgive me, I understand, but I'm afraid we'd all be done for unless we stand up to the Germans – right now."

Squibbles looks back to his co-workers. They all know it's true, just not to the extent that Willie and Renee do.

"I lied." Squibbles says, throwing Renee and Willie off. "Insurance covered it, but NPI even took that away once they fired you. Then they cut our benefits in half. This system is crap, even for the smartest and hardest working. So, we're in!" Squibbles announces and the techies cheer in agreement.

"Can you flip off the Santa-trons?" Willie asks.

"We don't have that kind of authority, only NPI controls can do that."

"What can you do?" Renee asks.

Squibbles thinks about it, unsure, until his eyes light up.

"We can redefine the debtor I.D. logic, then wildly turn up the collection amounts and actions," Squibbles says, "I've got an idea!"

Squibbles turns to his keyboard and codes furiously. His team scrambles to his monitor reading as he types his masterful code. Some breakout in laughter, amazed by the commands he fastidiously inputs. They get what he's doing and run back to their computers to follow his lead. Amid the fury of excited typing Willie and Renee don't understand what's going on, uncertain if they have anytime left.

BOOM, BOOM, BOOM – the unmistakable sound of Santa-trons barging through the workshop fills everyone with fear. They type faster, sweating, but the code isn't ready. The impending danger pushes them into a hyper-performance. In moments the Santa-trons arrive in full force, making way for Klaus and Otto as the last keystrokes are hit but still go incomplete.

A Santa-tron picks up Sticky by the neck and tosses him violently against the wall, knocking him out on impact.

"Sticky!" Renee yells, running to his side.

"Times up, nerds. Pencils down." Otto states.

A techie keeps typing as Klaus signals a Santa-tron to take care of him. The robot hovers over the geeky elf with its blood thirsty, blank red eyes, grimacing.

"You said pencils!" The techie yells as the Santa-tron lifts him.

In a flash the Santa-tron thrusts the elf down against its metal knee - *splitting the elf in half* before tossing his two ends to other sides of the room, his insides unraveling out.

Squibbles looks at the last bit of code he's written – it's missing a single, final line. He just needs to type that and hit "Enter" to run the update - but it could be suicide.

"The game is over you two," Klaus says. "Nice try."

"Any last words?" Otto tags on.

"Capitalism is broken. You know every flaw, but you don't fix it, you just exploit it, and that's wrong." Renee says.

"My dear, the virtue of selfishness ensures individuality, liberty and freedom." Klaus replies. "Greed motivates all societies on the most fundamental level, that's how it works."

"I don't believe that." Renee says.

"Of course you don't." Otto scoffs.

"I don't because those virtues are the aim of my politics," Renee replies. "It's accomplished through collaboration, in a shared drive to eliminate the barriers of scarcity and needs. When we can overcome that then we can experience true freedom."

"I already experience freedom." Klaus replies.

"Through your wealth." Renee points out.

"When the accumulation of wealth is no longer important there will be strong changes in morals." Willie says. *"The love of money will be recognized as a sickness, one of those semi-criminal, semi-pathological illnesses that'd be diagnosable as a mental disease.* Maybe we ought to check you in early, ol' Klaus."

"The accumulation of wealth isn't going anywhere, elf." Otto says. "Neither is capitalism."

"Every crisis that capital fights it learns from and readjusts.

It's like a virus, constantly evolving and overcoming." Klaus adds.

"Devastating, destructive and lethal like a virus, for sure." Renee jabs. "It will thrive like a virus until it's ripped wide open, or until it collapses upon its own contradictions, or until there's a cure."

"Funny you say that," Klaus utters, "is it not easier to imagine the end of the world than it is to imagine the end of capitalism?"

"Or easier to imagine the end of capitalism by imagining the end of the world?" Otto laughs.

"I'm not sure which?" Klaus smiles. "It's a fun discussion, but that's all the time we have, so let's get this show on the road, shall we?"

Squibbles twitches in the corner, hovering near Sticky's unconscious body. He knows what needs to be done but remains paralyzed in fear...

Klaus and Otto turn their back, not wanting to watch the violent end to their one time most cherished friend, as the Santa-trons close in on Willie.

Willie pulls Renee close, holding her tight in his arms. "I love you." He whispers as the Santa-trons loom over them, about to strike.

"I love you, too." She whispers back.

The Santa-trons move in but suddenly Squibbles JUMPS to his computer and starts typing, distracting the robots as he gets off that last line of code before hitting ENTER, running it. A Santa-tron turns to Squibbles to exterminate him. The update runs, it's only mere moments from completion as the Santa-tron places its cold metal hands around Squibbles neck, ready to decapitate...

Squibbles braces until the Santa-tron STOPS in its tracks. Its grip loosens around his neck as its bright red eyes fade into the darkness of its empty eye-sockets. It happens to all Santa-trons, including the one looming over Renee and Willie. *They're resetting.* Seconds later their eyes light back up with that menacing bright red light, but awakened with the new code. Klaus and Otto are startled as a roar of cheers erupts from the techies.

Klaus and Otto try to run but the Santa-trons block them in. The robots aren't interested in the elves this time around, as the Santa-trons stand over and scan the faces of Otto and Klaus, shaking in their boots.

"Let us out, Santa-trons!" Klaus yells.

But none of them abide.

"We own the North Pole, you listen to us!" Otto shouts.

"Santa-tron collects debt. The North Pole must pay its debt. You are responsible." Santa-tron plainly says to their terror. It unhinges its mouth and scans their faces underneath its harrowing red light. "Identifications confirmed." It says. "Pay or face termination." It tells Klaus and Otto.

"What?! Santa-tron, hold up! We're not the North Pole, per se, we're North Pole Inc., the company that owns the North Pole. We're too big to fail!" Otto shouts.

"Santa-tron collects debt. You own company, company owns North Pole, North Pole has debt. You owe Santa-tron, or Santa-tron will terminate you."

"We have legal protections!" Otto yells.

"Santa-tron is programmed for debt collection."

Klaus stands in shock as Otto continues to plead their case. "But the money needed to pay all the debt in the system *does not exist. In fact, it can never be repaid because the compounding interest on the debt will always exceed the total supply of money. All of society within the whole of capital must always be in debt.* It's uncollectable!"

"Must terminate." It utters.

"Santa-tron no!" Otto yells.

"Goodbye."

"Santa-tron, listen!!!"

It lifts its metal fists high and *BASHES* Otto's skull, killing him instantly as his brain and blood pour from his cracked open head.

The Santa-tron moves to Klaus.

"Wait!" Willie yells.

Willie and Renee couldn't stop the robot if they wanted to, but they don't want to, and the Santa-tron lifts its fists high...

"Good luck, Maven." Klaus utters one last time.

CRACK - Klaus' skull is mercilessly crushed. His corpse *flops*, joining Otto on the cold hard ground, covering the floor in a pool of pulpy blood.

Willie takes in the sight as his mind races, thinking how pitiful it is to die with no one caring to mourn. What good was their unquenching thirst for wealth? Or did any of it matter at all? Especially when you end up dead on the ground with your brain spilling out? How incredibly misguided to have spent one's life in the pursuit of profit or the accumulation of wealth. How they must've regretted everything in their final moments, and how entirely pathetic their ending.

The exuberance everyone else experiences isolates Willie. It's a bittersweet victory for him, finding himself lost in a hazy sadness. Renee whisks him away and brings him to Sticky, and together they help resuscitate him to consciousness, giving Willie a much-needed thrust of joy.

With Sticky saved they turn their attention to Squibbles. The sight of the tiny hero brings a sense of gratitude, and a reminder that the mission remains incomplete.

"Squibbles, you did it!" Willie smiles.

"Happy to play my part, Maven."

After a final salute to the elves, Willie and Renee rush out to Ursus and ride like hell back to the Square.

Soon Willie and Renee close in on the scene of the battle. Ursus comes up on an incline, high enough to see the battle playing out below. They reach the top and look down upon a miraculous event...

Santa-trons chasing down Germans and beating them into submission. Many Germans surrender and are placed under arrest. They're turned over to Axel and the Redcoats who now fight on behalf of the elves and Americans. It's the most glorious and fulfilling sight for Willie and Renee, providing them with catharsis of bliss.

"We did it." Renee whispers, smiling.

By the time they make it to the Square the fighting has ceased as the thunderous booms of battle are replaced by the howls of victory. Willie and Renee enter the Square as their army greets them joyously. Joey is the first to embrace them with a powerful hug as their soldiers unleash a cheer.

Willie and Renee climb the Tree of Trees and wave to the crowd, smiling but reserving a space for sorrow. They take in the devastation and loss of life, both on the cobblestone and in the form of those shinning ornaments. The cost of their struggle is everywhere, but their newfound freedom moves them to a spiritual place. They absorb the destruction and channel it into an inspiring vision for rebirth and renewal.

Willie and Renee climb down from the monument, but feelings complicate as Axel arrives. He smiles earnestly at his sister, which compels her to give a loving hug, letting in the warmth and forgiveness they both need.

Joey barges in with orders to Axel.

"The prisoners are coming back with us to the States, they'll stand trial for all of their crimes once we round up the last of 'em in Reykjavík." Joey states.

"We'll hold them until you're ready, Sir." Axel replies.

"We have a lot of work to do, don't we?" Renee says.

"We do." Willie agrees. "But first we celebrate, with a

celebration to rival Christmas itself!"

"A day to salute our victory, and a day to forgive – to forgive ourselves, one another, and debt." Renee says.

"Cheers to that!" Axel barks, throwing his arm around his sister.

The sun sets behind Willie and Renee as they lead a solemn ceremony, burying the dead and mourning their loss. Willie leads the eulogy, speaking to their bravery and valor, but acknowledging their common struggles in life. Struggles that connect all elves in their common suffering underneath this period of corporate domination. Yet the sorrow of loss morphs into the joys of victory as Willie announces that this day, every ten years, shall be forever known as the GREAT JUBILEE.

The crowd celebrates their unburdening debt. Through shedding this pain most feel like they can breathe again. With that, their prospects for a bright future enters their collective conscious. Even the idea of a new lifestyle fuels them with an optimism that was thought to be forever lost. Seemingly, any reasonable alternative would be better than the drudgery of repeating the endless rigors of daily life under capital. Many fantasize how beautiful it'd be to do something creative, meaningful or even fun. How refreshing to do something novel, to live fully, lovingly and with purpose. Anything but waste away trying to recompense a debt that is often impossible to repay.

The display of sheer affection for their fellow elf moves Willie, compelling him to grab cannisters of oil and a torch. He lights the torch and raises it high, stirring up the crowd as he and Renee lead the mass of elves to the Belief Meter. The meter continues to bubble up and down, still marking the price per share. Willie's surprised it's still moving at all, guess word hasn't gotten out about the destruction of North Pole Inc. - but that's about to change...

He *douses* the Belief Meter in gasoline. With a mischievous grin Willie presses his torch against it and watches with great pleasure as the Belief Meter goes up in a *fiery blaze*. After soaking up the beautifully hellish sight, he runs back before it EXPLODES. Everyone welcomes the destruction with a cheer, witnessing the fiery demise of not only North Pole Inc. but also the powerful symbol of capital.

Willie continues the march, leading the crowd to the North Pole Reserve. The idea of its destruction is poignant for him. He possessed real power and respect for the first time within the offices and halls of it. The landmark status of the building with its redefining architecture and glamorous adornment has him further second guessing. But he knows it's too strong of a symbol of capital, and so it must go. Such a shame, he thinks, that such exquisiteness and resources were wasted on this institution. Ironic something so attractive is also the source of such immense suffering.

With reassurance Willie douses gasoline throughout the Reserve, notably in the ledger department, which tracks all the issued debt and monies the Reserve expects society to repay (but never can). Willie touches his torch against the scroll of the master ledger, smiling as the digits of debt turn to ash. Finally, this feels like liberation.

The fire spreads as he dashes out and rejoins the crowd, watching the blaze from the street. In moments the flames burn the wooden beams of the building, lighting it up like a straw house amid a wildfire. The support beams collapse, the roof falls in and the entire Reserve crumbles to the ground with a cloud of dust filling the night sky. The burning heat presses upon their faces and reminds Willie of the incinerator, making him cry in realization of just how lucky they are to be alive.

"I've got one more idea." Renee tells Willie, wiping away his tears of joy.

"Lead the way." He smiles back.

They march to their final destination, Santa's Hermitage. The gates are closed with a battalion of Redcoats guarding their posts. Axel looks to Renee with uncertainty. "Are you sure?" Axel asks as Willie and Renee nod. After a moment of contemplation Axel pushes against the gate ordering the commanding officer to stand down. The gates open as Willie and Renee guide the crowd through the maze-like passageways before broaching Santa's Tower.

Renee leads the climb up the harrowing spiral staircase until they reach the penthouse office – it's locked. Axel kicks in the door – revealing Sir Louie sitting behind the executive desk in front of the iconic balcony. He kicks his feet off the desk and approaches his son, daughter and Willie as the crowd builds behind them.

"Come to burn this down too? Maybe burn your own father alive with it?" Sir Louie asks. "I wouldn't put it past you. Might as well destroy the whole North Pole while you're at it."

"Did you know about the ornament factory?" Renee asks.

"I've heard rumors, it's nonsense!" Sir Louie yells.

"I can take you there." Willie says. "There's proof."

"Even so, what good is it now? We must uphold all that's been created. I still have the right to my position! I still have the right to my power!" Sir Louie shouts.

"We've come to forgive you." Renee says. "So, you can let go with dignity."

"You forgive me? Hah! As if I need *your* forgiveness. What crimes did *I* commit?"

"More than you'll ever realize."

"You know, for being a couple of spoiled brats it's strange how you've lost the meaning of Christmas. You're so caught up in this thoughtless fervor to realize it."

"Enlighten us, *Dad.*"

"The one thing this system produces better than anything is presents! Christmas is about presents, consumer goods, luxuries and indulgences! Materialism brings joy, it always has!"

"That's never been the true meaning of Christmas."

"Then what is it, Renee?"

"Come on. Don't make me say it."

"Say it and try not to cringe." Sir Louie spouts.

"Love, compassion and a spirit of *giving* – giving to those who need the most."

"You are a fool." Sir Louie jabbers. "We'll never see eye to eye."

"That's too bad, Dad. Now if you'll excuse me." Renee says, pushing past Sir Louie to occupy the throne-like chair behind the executive desk.

"What are you doing?" Sir Louie panics.

"One last blow of the steam whistle, but this time it's for the victory of labor, not the discipling of it." Renee responds with the crowd jeering.

She smiles and hits the big red button behind the desk – sending *an incredible scream from the North Pole Steam Whistle*, generating one final *booming shock wave* – marking the end of one era and the ringing in of something new.

Renee and Willie head to the balcony and scale the tower to the Steam Whistle, which sits above Corporation Clock. Once they're above it, Willie soaks the shiny silver whistle with gasoline before they head even higher to the tip top of the tower. Renee and Willie hold up the torch together, smile, and release the torch – letting it fall upon the Steam Whistle. In moments it's engulfed in flames. The structure of it is strong, as is the silver it's made of, but it melts, morphing into a droopy, Salvador Dali like shape, until it becomes an oozing liquid metal blob that slides its way down the tower.

The slow dripping, lava-like silver devours Corporation Clock. The clock cracking underneath the weight and heat of the molten silver, morphing the shape of it into a twisting falling form. The clock slowly sags until it's destroyed, appearing as if the clock has been transported to a fiery dimension of hell while *time itself has been retaken* by their collective will and delivered back to the universe, with the elves hopeful it will be returned to them in abundance, with a slower pace of living that can be sustained and enjoyed.

The drips of silver fall amid the elves' tears of joy, as the sight awakens a dormant emotional piece of their psyche that most have numbed. With their awakening comes the realization that they can take back their destiny. Through this incredible release the elves become intertwined as if melded together through a religious experience, momentarily binding their consciousness in one interconnected force. The power of their feeling runs so strong that many burst into joyous Christmas carols that are sung throughout the night.

Willie and Renee rejoin the crowd on the balcony and sing carols. Joey McCarthy rejoins them to celebrate. For a moment there's a break between songs. Joey leans into Willie and Renee, "I'd like to stay with a few men, if you'll have us."

Willie smiles back, "Anything for Joey McCarthy."

"Thank you." Joey says back. "So, the North Pole is a company town?"

"Was a company town," Willie corrects. "Now that North Pole Inc. is dead and gone we're just the good ol' North Pole again." He smiles.

"What do you mean, North Pole Inc.?" Joey asks.

"You know, North Pole Inc., the publicly traded company? I thought it was well known in the human world?" Willie asks.

"Wait – so the actual North Pole became North Pole Inc.?"

"Yes, once we lost Santa Claus and these Germans...or, Nazi's came in -"

"I own stock in North Pole Inc." Joey admits, overcome with conflict.

"Not anymore, you don't," Willie smiles. "As of today it no longer exists. We couldn't have done it without you!"

Joey conceals his resentment amid the jolly scene, taking a moment to think.

"I'm sure I can help get secure loans from the United States, or the International Monetary Fund, to rebuild. We can connect the

North Pole with the rest of the world. Free trade and markets will flourish. We can make the North Pole great again!"

"No thanks, we're done with all that." Willie fires back.

"All of what?"

"Loans, debt, interest...capital."

"But how are you going to rebuild if not through capitalism?" Joey asks.

"Through a new system, one of collaboration, trust, compassion." Renee says. "True democracy is difficult to achieve. We have a long road ahead, but we can do it. It can only go uphill from where we were."

Joey's blood pressure rises.

"You ought to stay around and help," Willie adds. "Your perspective is valuable."

Joey can't believe his ears, sensing he's just been swindled, feeling like those he fought with have betrayed his strongest ideas. He wonders if he just aided socialists with the overthrow capitalism? But the capitalists were Nazi's, and the socialists, these cute elves in need of help. How do you say no to an elf in need? Has the world has gone mad? Has everything he's known to be virtuous and true actually evil and false? He becomes dizzy with conflict, growing pale, sick even.

"Are you ok?" Renee asks.

Joey snaps out of it. "Fine, thanks, just a stomachache. We have a long road ahead." He smiles, hiding his frustration.

"Thanks for everything." Willie says before hugging him. "A tsunami of change is coming."

"A tsunami is coming." Joey replies as Renee smiles, joining in the hug as the celebration bursts blissfully through the night, all over the North Pole.

24 – VISIONS WITHIN A CRYSTAL BALL

The elves are busy reconstructing, cleaning, and re-engineering the North Pole. The whole city is in mid-rebuild, reverting the steely and dull industrial wasteland to its former glory. Masses of volunteers clean the streets, repair houses and repaint everything with vibrant color sets, often with rich reds and deep evergreens. The fresh text on signs and buildings are outlined in shinning silver and gold, while the comradery of the soulful effort rivals the spirit of Christmas itself.

Artists lead the effort as muralists paint on incredible scales, their work occupying vast walls and depicting elvish stories of life, death and the struggle under the capitalist regime. On the other side of the tracks are the soulless skyscrapers of the financial district. But that space once reserved for traders and debt-bottlers is overtaken by the craft-oriented co-ops.

Meanwhile, the reawakening of old elvish traditions refreshes even the most scrooge-like citizens, while it turns other traditions on its head, like how the grand gates of the Hermitage stay open to the public for the first time. Any citizen may enter, observe and interact with the temporary and newly formed General Assembly, the body tasked with forming a framework for the future democratic government.

Having relocated from the confines of the Santa's Tower, Willie and Renee chair the General Assembly within Santa's Sphere. The massive, pristine, crystal sphere with its elegant space is best suited for speech and debate - and with the General Assembly, it's finally used as a public forum.

Willie and Renee sit in the middle of a semi-circle of desks filled by familiar faces. Sticky and Axel take part, as well as everyday citizens like Bushy and Alabaster. Representatives of whole contingences, like Ginger Garland leading the miners' union, and Squibbles sitting in for tech workers, all sit together, eager for discussion. The seats for public observation fill as excitement permeates.

Willie spots Joey McCarthy sticking out like a sore thumb in the back. He doesn't make much of Joey's critical expression, then stands to call the assembly into session. Just as he's about to speak Sir Louie and his stiff old cronies, Topper and Nipper, enter alongside. They march through the sphere as if going to war, kicking off Squibbles from his desk before planting themselves sternly. Willie is about to cause a scene but Renee eyes him to play it cool. With a deep breath and a nervous smile, he addresses the assembly...

"Welcome elves, to the very first General Assembly of the North Pole!" He announces. "Today, and until we have a final resolution, we must work together, to provide the framework for how our future democracy is to be organized. This momentous task ahead will be difficult, but we shall achieve what no elf and very few people on this Earth have ever dared to. And, at last, *we are free to dismantle capitalism.* With that, I am pleased to call to order the first General Assembly of the North Pole!"

His announcement is greeted with a thunderous applause, but as it dies down Nipper McJingles stands up to Willie.

"Mr. Maven!" McJingles shouts. "Before we speak of high-minded propositions, I shall like to address our most urgent and pragmatic concern which weighs on the minds of all elves – our supply and concerns having to do with sugar. How do you intend to save us from shortages of our most basic need?!"

Willie stands to reply. "First, Mr. McJingles, with our current technology all energy used by North Pole industry ought to be sustainable, no more burning of sugar or coal. So, the only need for sugar will be the elvish diet – not energy for production or the basis of a crooked fractional reserve banking system."

"And how do you propose we even get our hands on that mere amount?" McJingles prods.

"Toys and Christmas. You might recall we're elves, that's what we do, and we ought to produce meaningful, quality things in exchange for sugar. So as long as sugar is traded for toys, which humanity has always accepted, we'll be fine. So, I propose the continuation of the system of logistics we've inherited from North Pole Inc."

McJingles huffs and puffs and plops down with his arms

crossed. Topper finds the strength to stand then points accusingly.

"But on the issue of Sh-Sh-Sugar Dollars..." Topper stutters. "The b-b-banking system worked well in m-many ways. We ought to use a v-v-version of it. The S-S-Sugar Dollars we have a-a-accumulated ought to have v-v-value in a new s-s-system of b-banking."

"Banks do more than hoard colossal amounts of capital, Topper." Renee says.

"Yes, they're very v-v-versatile."

"They also centralize data and knowledge. Making that unavailable to even individual capitalists. Only a select handful of monopolists are truly enabled, via their banking connections. First, they recognize the financial position of other capitalists, then move in like sharks to control them, and finally ascribe their fate. A new system must emerge."

"B-but everyone is richer b-b-because of it." Topper replies.

"We are two times richer but money is short everywhere. Well, everywhere except the stock market, tax havens, and the bottom lines of multinational companies and the bank accounts of the smallest segment of citizens."

"B-b-but the beauty of the market – s-s-supply and demand. Equilib-r-r-rium!" Topper shouts with all his breath.

"We've only seen evidence for the opposite, the laws of supply and demand continually amplify disequilibrium." Willie says.

"B-but c-co-com-competition!"

"The transition from competition to monopoly is embedded in the very nature of capital just as we've seen play out!"

"W-Wh-what of production!?" Topper yells.

"We've produced hugely before capitalism. Capital's goal was never production but profit."

Sir Louie jumps from his seat, "And how do you know elves don't want banking, Maven? Do you claim to represent them?!"

"I only represent myself and we'll vote on it, but the faux-democracy of the past should be replaced with a real one."

"It was a true one. How can you deny it?" Sir Louie poses.

"We gamed it. All the while your regime only produced corruption, not representation. It doesn't even produce growth, just wealth for the likes of you, me and your entourage."

"The profit is the growth, you ninny! And I spend it...and sometimes it...trickles down, I think." Sir Louie retorts. "Elves ought to pull themselves up by their bootstraps, *like me!*"

"Yes, just like you." Renee quips, "while dropping their expectations of what constitutes a decent life to a rock bottom."

"But...*bootstraps!*" Sir Louie exclaims.

"They can't afford boots without getting further into debt." Renee says.

"That's why debt is good, so elves can buy things!"

"The fight against the debt economy must be absolute," Willie retorts, "starting with the elimination of the morality of guilt, which is a morality of fear. We are held hostage by debt morality. *Leaving debt morality behind is the only thing that will set us free.*"

"But you, Mr. Maven, have eliminated debts, or in my case, interest due to me, without any authority!"

"I will possess that authority very soon." Willie says.

"Not if I have anything to do with it." Sir Louie jabs.

"This is not about you anymore, Dad. *We've lost too much precious time trying to clear our debts. In doing so we are already guilty – it must end! We must all rid ourselves of guilt, of everything owed, of all bad conscious and not repay a cent!*" Renee yells in a burst of passion that earns her an ovation from the crowd.

The echoing cheers within the chamber leave Sir Louie with no option but to take his seat in concession. After the wave of applause, the crowd calms. Willie's embolden by the victory, but tries to stay level as the indomitable Ginger Garland rises to offer a sting of her own...

"Willie. Renee. My brave elves, your proposition is intriguing but leaves out the miners and so many other workers who have been most loyal to our cause. If they're to be displaced because we're moving off coal energy and because leaving coal in the Christmas stalking's of bad children has gone out of fashion, they'll be out of work."

"I guess that's true." Willie admits.

"Then so be it." Ginger says to Willie's surprise. "So as long as you don't punish them for their inactivity, as both systems before have done so."

"What are you proposing, Ms. Garland?" Willie asks.

"I'm not entirely sure, but the intersection of labor, production and producers have always been the strength and weakness of North Pole tradition. Is your solution supposed to be emancipation from work or through work?" She asks rhetorically. "I'm of the strong opinion that we must not take labor, whatever it may be, as our starting point, but always the refusal of work." Ginger states.

"A bold proposition." Renee compliments.

"Given today's technology, isn't it shameful we're still obliged to work simply to survive? Obliged to work just to exist? It's a disgrace!" Ginger yells, earning an applause. "So, I'm proposing what artists alone have followed through on – *the right to be lazy*," she smiles. "Any system that allows the North Pole to follow a single laborious path so that no inactive person remains is exactly the thing which leads to true laziness. *If we start with labor we always end up with labor –* and we shouldn't accept this giant waste of time in our era given the technology that's already available to us."

"You're calling for laziness?" Sir Louie yaps with confusion.

"Lazy is one word, free-time is another. The citizens of a dignified society ought to have plenty of free-time. *Real freedom is a world in which we have free time to do what we want,* so yes, elves must do what they would like with their valuable and limited time on this Earth. Lazy action is the opposite of the purpose-driven action of capitalist production, for which the end, money, is everything, and the process of how profit is achieved, is nothing. The latter would not exist if it did not produce money. Once we free ourselves from this purpose driven profiteering our society can unleash its vast potential."

"Thank you, Ms. Garland, for your passion." Willie says.

"I'm looking forward to further discussing." Renee adds with a smile.

Sir Louie jets out of his seat in fury. "Outrageous! A right to laziness?! This has never been and will never be the nature of elves!" He yells. "And freedom is a useful fantasy, the idea can ignite a fervor in the mass of elves, but individual freedom does not exist!"

"It can, at least in other forms of living, with lifestyle that don't tout *money* – the true thing which restricts freedom. *The need of money is the excuse elves give themselves when they shut down exploring unconventional life choices. Capitalism is the machine that traps elves in a cycle of working in jobs they don't like so they can buy things they don't need.* The necessity of these material things beyond our basic needs don't exist in reality, it's only an artificial construct leading elves to deny themselves of their freedoms. Join us, Sir Louie, and free yourself." Willie implores.

"Hah! And join you poor elves, I'd never."

Ginger stands, "There are only two types of poor elves, those who are poor together and those who are poor alone. The first are the true poor, the others are rich elves out of luck."

"I don't buy it!" Sir Louie spits.

"Then you live in bad faith, in that you think you must exist in one specific way." Ginger says. "You are so convinced that your present job is all you can do, or rather all you're *meant* to do, that you never consider doing anything else. We alone are responsible for everything we are. By not exploring the myriad of possibilities life presents we alone restrict our freedom, and are left without an excuse."

"What in the hell are you talking about?! Let's get back to reality and not your existential ramblings, Ginger! Speaking of my job, and my work, there is dignity in it, and work keeps at bay three great evils: boredom, vice and need!"

"Yes, there's dignity in dignified work, but the opportunities to be paid for such work hardly exist." Ginger replies. "There must be equal opportunity for the many who want to contribute in this way and not starve for it."

"Hah! And what is this contemptible notion of equality? That elves are created equal? It isn't true. We must uphold the natural *inequality* of elves!" We capitalists have worked our way to the top through our capacity. Through our strength, intelligence and know-how, through a process of natural selection that proves the worthiness of our higher status again and again, and with it comes our right to lead!" Sir Louie yells, fuming, even shaking.

Willie can tell Sir Louie is truly committed to these ideas. But he also recognizes their origin...

"You're quoting, Sir Louie, almost directly if I'm not mistaken."

"Is that so Mr. Maven? With all of your worldly wisdom, please tell me who I'm copying?"

"Adolf Hitler." Wille says, "But you knew that."

"And how would you know?" Sir Louie asks.

"Because his apparent henchmen were my only friends for a long time!" Willie yells. "I've learned their way of thinking even better than you and it's entirely backwards."

"And what's your evidence for the contrary?!"

"Every bit of destruction they brought! Those Nazi ideas of superiority that you echo were their most obvious flaw."

"You mistake me for a German," Sir Louie retorts. "But you also mistake me for a common elf. The claims of my family on this kingdom have existed for millennia."

"You mistake superior income for superior worth." Willie says. "You mistake economic success as evidence of superior knowledge, rather than your inherited advantages and command over accounting tricks and legal loopholes. You don't know how to listen to the plight of the North Pole because you can't acknowledge your responsibility for the depravity and destruction of it. You don't see your own contradictions. But I beg you open your eyes and see the light."

"And what light do you see? By removing economic care from the shoulders of the individual you think you can magically release immeasurable energy that's gone wasted in the struggle for daily bread? Or do you believe public authorities are up to discovering and harboring talent either in the arts, science or industry?"

"I do." Willie answers.

"There's no sound reason to believe that future institutions will appreciate Beethoven any sooner or more efficiently than a capitalist society does."

Willie leans in, "Even if you're right, the fact remains that *the new world will not suffer the social losses from the wildly unproductive activity of our society's best brains.* Capital left intelligence and talent to waste away in law, finance and even engineering. Just like those technologists forced to sink their effort into the design of debt collecting Santa-trons. All of this comes at the cost of real productivity, potential for true innovation, expression and genius. There's so much more to aspire to than profit, and considering how awfully infrequent good brains are, their shifting to other activities will yield a much more advanced and righteous North Pole."

"But you offer no vision, none of you do! What is this great glowing light at the end of the tunnel, show that to me and just maybe I'll shut up!" Sir Louie yells.

"The aim of life should be to create as much happiness and as little misery as possible. Ideally, we'd find a system that balances freedom with altruism. Only activities motivated by a concern for others' well-being can be constructive."

"Hardly pragmatic, Renee!" He shrieks. "You don't even know how you'd start to change things."

"Do you want a list?" Willie asks. "It will take time but I can read but if that's what you're looking for..."

Sir Louie reacts with a blank expression as Willie continues, "Okay – first, a means of exchange is to be created. One that facilitates the circulation of goods and services but limits or excludes the capacity of private elves to amass money as social power. Second – "

"*Can-it, Maven!* I've had enough of your utopian fantasies!" Sir Louie roars. "You're all too young and naïve! Don't you see, once a revolution establishes itself it doesn't recognize new problems, it only becomes institutionalized and calls anyone who dares to question it a traitor! If you don't want to be a hypocrite do you truly seek *perpetual revolt*? Because I do not!"

"That's exactly what I seek." Willie says.

"Just...*unbelievable*. There is no compromising with any of you." Sir Louie says. He realizes he's completely outnumbered and overwhelmed. His labored breathing continues as he feels the weight of his world collapsing upon him, losing grip on the power he's always known and wielded with an iron fist. But Sir Louie's never given up, there's always a way to win, so he's taught himself. With a furious pounding of his fists against the desk he storms off before making his way through the boisterous crowd cheering his defeat, their provocations further fueling his anger.

Renee cracks a smile, but she knows this isn't over. It's only a matter of how far her father will go, and that much has always been unpredictable. He is capable of anything when he becomes an opponent.

Sir Louie escapes the Sphere and finds Joey pacing awkwardly outside. Sir Louie notices his sweating and clenching fists. He shuffles around with as much anguish and confusion as himself. He motions to Joey to approach.

"Good man, you don't approve of this?" Sir Louie asks.

"No, not at all." Joey replies, crouching down on his level.

"Me either."

"What do we do?" Joey asks.

"Well, you have the guns, the only question is if you're ready to use them again?" Sir Louie asks.

"Depends. What's our justification besides the fact that we disagree with them?"

"If you ask me that's enough, but we should have more." Sir Louie admits as he paces around, wracking his brain looking for an answer.

From their elevated position atop of the grand staircase he searches the city scape for inspiration. It doesn't take long for his eyes to be drawn to the bubbling neon remnants of what was the substance of the Belief Meter. He stares deep into the slow flowing puddle of shinning fluid, the light reflecting bright off of the amorphous liquid form.

"I have an idea," Sir Louie deviously smiles. "We don't have a moment to waste."

Sir Louie takes off running, with Joey following.

"What idea?" Joey yaps.

"The stock's still trading. Just because you blow up a meter doesn't mean the company dies. NPI hasn't missed any investor calls, quarterly earnings reports or anything – until today." Sir Louie answers as they sprint through maze after maze within the Hermitage. Sir Louie proving he's quick on his feet, surprising given his portly build.

"Nobody knew how North Pole Inc. worked." Joey says. "Investors just saw it as a highly profitable toy company that took off when Santa stopped coming. I've learned that isn't a mere coincidence."

"Not at all." Sir Louie adds, keeping up his fast pace, powering through the poinsettia gardens. Joey barely catches up. "We do it all without Kringle." Sir Louie says with pride.

"All good, I guess." Joey mumbles. "So as long as the stock keeps going up. Would've never imagined the black box of North Pole Inc. would be..."

"The actual North Pole." Sir Louie says.

"Exactly."

"That was the point, but all that will change, and it will make you and I a lot richer."

The duo stops at the foot of a dark and secluded evergreen forest within the Hermitage walls. Sir Louie leads the way, cautiously entering the creepy woods as they make their way through the thicket before pushing through a dense series of vines and sticky spider webs. They keep pushing until they're at the mouth of a mysterious subterranean cave.

"May I borrow your lighter?" Sir Louie smiles.

Joey hands it over, confused. "The stock's about to tank with today's missed earnings report, so I'm going to snatch it up on the cheap." He says as he enters the cave and flicks on the lighter, the tiny fire guiding them through the complete darkness. "When the majority of shares are mine I will control the company, and then I can do anything I please with it. That's our justification."

"How are you going to buy it?" Joey asks.

Sir Louie doesn't answer, continuing forward until stopping, having found the torch he was searching for. He lights it, illuminating his menacing grin. He laughs as he turns to Joey and reveals...

A massive cavern full of treasure. The dunes of shining jewels, stacks of glistening gold bars and piles upon piles of good ol' American Greenbacks fill the damp cave. Joey can't believe his eyes, getting lost in the smirk of Benjamin Franklin, one of the many tens of thousands that surround them.

"This was Klaus and Otto's treasure, and now you'll recognize it as mine." Sir Louie states.

"What's in it for me?" Joey asks.

"A percentage. If your men take this treasure to New York and buy up all the North Pole Inc. stock on my behalf, I'll make you the sole broker to the North Pole once we open it up to the world. Every major deal from every major company must pass through you, and you'll deal with me. You'll be the middle man between humanity and North Pole Inc. You'll take a percentage on everything. How does that sound?"

Joey says nothing. He just smiles and shakes Sir Louie's hand with vigor.

"Congratulations, Mr. McCarthy. You'll be one of the richest men in history."

"We must depose of those communists first." Joey replies.

"Right you are."

25 – HOSTILE TAKEOVER

The General Assembly is vibrant, with a sense of electricity in the air. The session is in full swing with Willie and Renee at the helm. The assembly advances several proposals, not without debate, but all seems to be moving forward positively. The optimism of the assembly matches the Sphere's bright atmosphere that's filled with just enough sunlight, providing a heavenly quality. Amid their challenges, there's a miraculous sense that they will band together so long as everyone remains respectful and diligent.

But the energy turns sour as Sir Louie, Topper and McJingles come barging in. Their intense and determined rush startle the attendance. The elves perk up to the edge of their seats while Joey McCarthy quietly lurks in the back. Joey watches and waits, while Sir Louie *plunks* his oversized briefcase upon Willie and Renee's desk.

"Well, aren't you going to open it?" Sir Louie blurts.

"Why don't you tell us what it is, Dad?"

"No, no, open it. It will be fun, like a Christmas surprise!"

"I'm not touching it."

"This is ridiculous, give it to me." Willie scoffs, opening the briefcase, revealing a pile of North Pole Inc. paper stock certificates.

"Great, fancy notes, nobody cares." Willie says.

"Ah, I care a great deal. So do millions around the world." Sir Louie replies.

"Sir Louie, please sit down and wait your turn to speak."

"I don't think you're appreciating the gravity of your new predicament, Mr. Maven."

"Do us all a big favor by excusing yourself." Willie thrashes.

"You've always had a gift, Mr. Maven, for loss. Perhaps that's what makes you so likeable? Likeable because you're cursed. Or perhaps this is how it was always meant to be? In this reality or in an endless variety of alternatives, you always seem destined to lose."

"How metaphysical. Impressive coming from a bean counting company man." Willies interrupts.

"You know Maven, I've never seen a way for you to win. That's why I pity you."

"I don't need your pity, but even you have a right to participate here, just as much as any other elf. If you'd only cooperate."

"HAH!" Sir Louie taunts. "Reducing my rights to a common elf with the roll of your tongue. My rights and my position are worth a thousand-fold, Maven, no thank you!"

"Stop fighting and join us, Dad." Renee replies.

"My poor Renee, I'm sorry you've been dragged into all of this. But perhaps it was only destined to happen as well."

"Hate to break it to you Louie, but we've won. Consider yourself lucky to be welcome at our assembly, an assembly for elves, by elves." Willie spouts.

"And yet you two have self-appointed yourselves head of this makeshift commission." Sir Louie cackles.

"What's this all about? What do you want?" Willie asks in agitation.

Sir Louie turns to face the crowd, "It's about *you being wrong*, yet again, cursed elf. These aren't mere pieces of paper, they're REAL LIFE STOCK CERTIFICATES. In fact, they're stock certificates of North Pole Incorporated, which I've purchased a majority ownership of. It's called a hostile takeover. Pity you've never attended business school, you would've learned something!"

"Hate to break it to you, but North Pole Inc. ceases to exist. It's been eviscerated, just as our fellow elves have been in those furnaces. So, you see, these pieces of paper mean nothing, to no one, nowhere."

"Ah, wrong yet again, Mr. Maven!" He yells. It's the MARKETPLACE which spans this globe that recognizes my liberty. It's the MARKETPLACE that has validated my right to ownership, and it's the MARKETPLACE which has corroborated in the sale. By virtue of the MARKETPLACE, which is supported by all the governments of the world, North Pole Inc. is recognized as a living, breathing thing. Regardless of your delusions!"

"But elves don't recognize it, and because of that it does not exist."

"I'm sorry you're cursed, Maven, I really am, but I'm afraid to inform everyone that the BOARD doesn't recognize ANY of you. It doesn't recognize your weak claims to a false authority or anything else that this phony assembly of factory commoners may have to say. In fact, you're all TRESPASSING on company property and INFRACTING upon many company codes at this very moment! If you don't vacate, you'll either find yourself perpetually unemployed or LOCKED UP. So, everyone, please pack it and get out - NOW! Thank you."

You can hear a pin drop everyone is so shocked, until many elves who've been ordered around their whole life comply. Renee watches as they frantically shuffle their papers together as if afraid for their survival. She jets out of her seat and signals to Axel who's now firmly on her side. He nods back and readies his squad of Redcoats for action against their father.

"Everybody stop!" She shouts. "This is our assembly. This is our future! Never again will we hand it over to some dictator or cabal of exploiters, even when it's my own confused father and his crusty cronies!"

But in these defining moments the crowd continues to pack and shuffle out. Renee's heart breaks at the sight of their obedience.

Sir Louie laughs, "Sadly, you're the confused one, Renee. What are you going to do about it?"

"I think it's time you get a taste of what you've served me. Maybe five years in prison? How about ten? We're civilized enough to give you an actual trial first. Maybe one of your friends can represent you, like Topper. It will be fun, like a Christmas surprise."

Sir Louie laughs, impressed with his daughter's gall.

"Why are you laughing?" She asks.

"Because, even you, my brightest child, still can't grasp the undeniable truth."

"Which is?"

"That I WIN. *I AWLAYS WIN*. Haven't you learned anything? Haven't you learned at least that?!"

"You wretched elf. This isn't a hostile takeover, it's theater. A confidence game, and I call bullshit. Axel, Redcoats, arrest him." Willie orders, as Axel nods and approaches with his squad.

Sir Louie nods to Joey signaling his countermove.

"You see it's a hostile takeover, literally and figuratively. I own the STOCK, I've got THE MEN and they carry THE GUNS, many, many GUNS. I'm sorry guys, YOU LOSE. Now stand down before you turn this hall into a shooting range."

Joey storms his battalion of US Marines armed to the teeth into the Sphere. Within moments they have their rifles aimed at every elf behind a desk like a firing squad readying for mass execution.

"You're are capable of anything, aren't you Dad?" Renee says with her hands up. "You're a loyal servant of the status-quo."

"I'll take that as a compliment."

"You're a monster."

"How long behind bars for the two of you? Five years, ten? Or maybe I should have you shot where you stand?"

"Do it." Willie says.

Sir Louie laughs, "You'd like that wouldn't you, Maven? You know what, I'll go easy, we're family after all. Your sentence is five years. Congratulations."

"Go to hell." Willie spits.

"I hope you can find employment afterwards. Now everybody, GET OUT - *THE BOARD HAS RULED!*"

The last of the disillusioned crowd stumbles out at gun point as an enraged Willie vigorously walks up to Joey McCarthy's pointed rifle, pressing his head hard against the barrel.

"Kill me." Willie says with the barrel pressed strong against his forehead. "Do me a favor. Pull the trigger."

Joey considers it. Willie's politics are the antithesis of everything he's ever believed, so why not?

"Do it!"

Willie leans harder into the barrel, cutting his forehead on it.

"*DO IT!*" He screams again as Renee breaks into tears.

"And make a martyr out of him? I don't think so. Listen to your CEO and arrest him." Sir Louie orders.

"That's what I thought. Cowards. All of you." Willie steams.

"Have a great five years." Sir Louie says.

"This isn't over." Renee states.

Joey flashes a smirk before slashing Willie across his face with the butt of his rifle. It knocks him out cold as blood spills from his head.

Sir Louie stands over Willie's body as his sparkling blood spreads.

"I win. I always win." Sir Louie declares.

Willie awakens in Renee's arms. She smiles and lets him know they're both okay while maintaining a loving gaze. To be tenderly wrapped back in her arms feels like a dream, but soon the pain of his laceration pulses through his body with every heartbeat.

His eyes widen, finding themselves imprisoned within the same cell that Klaus and Otto were held in all those years ago. At least they have each other, he thinks, and a tiny barred up window to gaze out of. From high in the Fortress of Santa's Keep, the view below never grows old. Everything is always changing.

Renee helps him stand and together they stare out the window with a heavy sadness. They look out and see more of the same – construction cranes, steel and concrete, skeletons of vast towers, bulldozers and pollution, all amid the constant white noise of industrial activity. But this time the development is on steroids, not only in the sheer number of projects but the expeditious speed with which the construction crews work. They lean in for a closer look and watch the armies of men, not elves, working day and night around the clock.

They notice how the construction is concentrated downtown, as if building a tourist hub or main strip. They bulldoze whole neighborhoods and once charming storefronts which stood for hundreds of years, replacing them with towers, each one more extravagant than the next, even copying famous North Pole structures like the grand spiraling towers within Santa's Hermitage. But these building are several times bigger and utterly massive. Everything is wildly overdone, gaudy and disgustingly extravagant by design.

And the Belief Meter is back and bigger than ever, as is the ever-increasing value of North Pole Inc. stock. The massive twenty-story meter entrances its viewers with its multicolor lava-lamp-like elixir that bubbles almost always upward. The fluidity of the substance reminds Willie of how fluid money has become, as the addictive sight of the liquid color hypnotizes its onlookers, just like money. The meter has become more than symbolically important, as now its measured value is the main stimulating force for all economic activity.

Meanwhile, everything else is constructed in a very un-elf way, with shoddy workmanship paired with the use of plastics and cheap construction materials that allow buildings to sprout up overnight. The decadent facades of gold and platinum plates with bright neon lights hide the hollowness of the structures. The whole process feels like the physical manifestation of smoke and mirrors, with the skeletons of the buildings covered by a thin layer of kitschy architecture that wreaks of inauthenticity and falseness to the point of being offensive. It's as if the shameless architects enjoy the strange spectacle of their Frankenstein creations, while somehow being oblivious to the ugliness of it all. With the first few mega-resorts completed human tourists from all over the globe flock to the North Pole.

One night, Willie reaches for Renee's hand and together they stare at the Tree of Trees, which is available to their eyeline through the demolition of a historic building. Not only does it remain intact but the construction crews have built up the surrounding area, making it another tourist attraction. Renee smiles back knowing that they saved the North Pole, even if they could only do it once.

Holding each other lovingly they pass out on the floor. Throughout the night they cough, twist and turn as the frosty air freezes them while the dust of the construction blows into their cell, filling their lungs and making them break into coughing-fits, keeping them awake all night.

Watching the destruction of their civilization demoralizes and exhausts them, but their eyes are glued to it day in and out until they don't have an ounce of energy left. They critique the madness of the world below, making as much fun of it as they can. Sometimes it infuriates them and sometimes they don't have enough energy to care much more. They watch, and talk, make up silly games and try to reimagine things, like the battle of the North Pole. And they reminisce, cry, forgive, regret, debate, argue and do just about anything they can to maintain some semblance of sanity.

Poor Renee has spent nearly a quarter of her life like this, but it isn't easier the second time, even with a partner. It kills their romance, suffocating the life out of it drip by drip. And the world goes on without them, making them doubt if their existence ever mattered at all.

FIVE YEARS LATER – Willie's grown a long dirty red beard, looking more like a leprechaun who's been lost at sea than an elf. He's hunched over and disheveled, with his rusted-out prosthetic irritably squeaking as he scratches his dusty beard. But he hasn't forgotten that feeling of pride and self-respect, and even in the darkest of times he's found just enough strength to hold onto that. His moral compass remains strong despite the suffering and guilt that the guards have tried so hard to instill.

Meanwhile Renee's once fine silky hair has morphed into a shaggy tangle that extends all the way past her hips. Unlike her first stint in prison, which ignited a blazing fire in her soul, this term has only extinguished that once hot flame. At least she can take comfort knowing she gave it her all, and like Willie, she at least has her dignity.

While in prison they're informed how it became illegal to utter their very names "Willie Maven" and "Renee Kendal-Crink," and they're given new identities as the very bland "Jack Baker" and "Candace Cream," Renee particularly hating hers. They've been ordered to address each other by their new names but always do so sarcastically. They learn the entire episode of the German Era combined with the brief elvish revolution has been termed "The Struggles." Once the phrase is uttered conversation is supposed to change topics or come to an abrupt stop. In time this has eroded memories, stripped elves of their history and dissolved their collective identity.

On the last day of their sentence the bulky American prison guard escorts them from their cell and tosses them out to the cold street behind the Hermitage. Before doing so the brute informs them how even the Maven Workshop has been demolished and replaced by tourist attractions. He mutters on about the new and fully automated factories and workshops built within the even newer industrial districts on the outskirts of the city, amid most of the relocated elvish neighborhoods which remain openly exposed to pollution and industrial waste.

Willie and Renee gaze out on the street for the first time, feeling the stark contrast between the high-tech city and their deprived selves. They can see how everything has gone digital. In fact, the rest of the world still works to catchup. Paying in cash is still an option, but when the tourists land they're bombarded with credit card promotions and a healthy credit limit that most are eager to use. Therefore, most transactions are made with credit cards, unless it comes to gambling – the new "economic" driving force of the North Pole. Tourists and elves alike use the new credit cards however elves only qualify for the cards with low borrowing limits and loan-shark like interest rates of 30% or more.

Since the rest of the world is still behind in tech, all the debt data is tracked on the North Pole's very own FINANCIAL SERVER FARM, which has become the most heavily guarded location in all the North Pole, located just below Sir Louie's penthouse, still at the top of Santa's Tower.

Willie and Renee, shivering and hungry, begin a journey into the streets and discover that not only is their culture and architecture demolished, but elvish history has ceased to be taught. The only elvish education programs are the for-profit casino-gaming curriculums and hospitality schools. The only remaining authentic thing about the North Pole are the elves themselves, and they aren't allowed to unionize nor do they share in any profits from any of the big-money ventures. They never found the leverage to even think about making such demands.

Realizing they're lost and homeless, Willie and Renee wonder aimlessly amid the masses of clueless tourists. While journeying they can't believe how incredibly commercial, bright and distracting everything has become. The powerful glowing lights induce migraines while the hordes of tourists produce an inescapable stench of body odor. The bombardment of advertising dizzies them, all the while dodging the unending stampede of overweight humans who push and jostle past them on the jam-packed sidewalks. Most tourists don't even realize they're there because most can't see past their own hanging stomachs.

The duo arrives at the Tree of Trees, which is stunning when lit up in full luminescent splendor. But there's no memory paid to the elves who have lost their lives under the brutality of the German profiteers, whatsoever. No reference to the fact that the elves themselves make up a majority of the ornaments which still adorn it, as if it's a flat-out denial of the genocide. It saddens them as they stare up at the glistening ornaments, knowing the real story.

Meanwhile the masses of tourists take selfies in front of the Tree of Trees without the slightest clue. Willie thinks the American business partners don't want to expose the birth of the company was at the hands of Nazi's. But then again BMW, Mercedes, Volkswagen, Deutsche Bank and many others all seem to be doing just fine, evidenced by their flickering billboards that line the avenue.

They make their way through the city arteries to the dizzying main drag, now referred to as "The Strip," scuffling down the overbearing and overstimulated district. On their expedition they peer inside the massive structures and learn these are vast casinos where anyone can bet on just about anything. That's if you have the money to spare, which the elves do not.

Elves are in there too, just not getting piss drunk or donating their monies to the corporate overlords who own these establishments. The elves are the dealers, slot supervisors, bar tenders and cocktail waitresses. They're also the cooks and servers, the occasional pit boss, floor manager or even prostitute. In this new, glib society factories and workshops hardly carry any significance. With the near eradication of blue-collar jobs and the massive increases in things like fast food employment, it's clear to Renee that restaurant workers and the alike are the new working class.

Many casinos have an oversized and overdone North Pole theme. They often showcase Santa Claus video slots, indoor wolf racing, and even more gruesome - wolf fighting - where only one wolf is left hobbling after a fight to the death. This death sport drives high rollers from all over the world, as it's far more intense than dog fighting and unique to the North Pole gambling scene. Then there are the standard games of craps, blackjack, poker and all the rest, all playing out within the smoke-filled gambling pits, day in and out.

Willie and Renee are drawn to the grotesque yet mesmerizing establishments like moths to a light, like everyone else. Except security doesn't let them in over ten yards before they're turned around. Everything about it is so strange. They're left wondering what has happened to their home and what options might exist for them outside of that slim list of common casino jobs? Could Willie become a dignified bartender and Renee the most eloquent of hostesses? Is that the pinnacle of their potential given the opportunities available to homeless elves?

Willie charges into another casino but security comes down on him like wolves on a T-Bone steak. Before he's booted out he catches a glimpse of all the gambling. It reminds him of the Stock Market, but worse, in that the smallest percentage, if any, of the money is cycled back into any productive use whatsoever. Instead he knows it's headed to a reservoir of capital that a corporation is sitting on, bloodthirsty for evermore profit and power.

Tossed head first on the concrete, Willie lays battered at the feet of Renee on the sidewalk. Although in pain, he contemplates what he witnessed, considering the nature of property as represented by all the chips in the casino. But the chips aren't linked to a means of production, as it were in prior eras. Today, *property doesn't express any specific relation to production. It becomes unconnected with any other activity than speculation.*

At least that's how it appears for the gamblers, meanwhile elves' wages are as low as possible. If the casinos could pay them less, they would.

Renee tries to help Willie up, but he refuses, opting to stay sprawled out on the concrete, taking in the atrocities which have overrun their world. He notices ATMs sprinkled about "The Strip," with lines of people withdrawing cash – and once that runs out, he watches the masses head to the more desperate and seedy pawnshops sitting between the casinos and strip malls that occupy the dark crevices and alleyways of the city. He even recognizes Snowball, the hideous elf he once purchased real estate from, exiting his very own SNOWBALL'S PAWN SHOP, in fact it's a chain.

Snowball, as fat and laughable as ever, has replaced his cheap outfit and suspenders with a full three-piece suit. He loves the pawn game as it's a great foot in the door for his new and thriving loan-shark venture. Not only does he continue to belt elves, his favorite pastime, but he can even do it to the most desperate human debtors too.

Willie can't stand the sight of Snowball and turns to gaze at the many ATMs dotting the boulevard. It has him thinking how banking must be more expansionary than ever. He reminisces about a bit Klaus once told him, quoting his old American correspondent and Nazi sympathizer, Henry Ford. How Henry said, "It is a good thing that most Americans don't know how banking works, because if they did there'd be a revolution before tomorrow morning." Willie laughs, realizing this kind of artificial explosion in growth is only possible through *banks creating their own deposits instead of responsibly loaning out the deposits that households save.*

Because of this, the real limit to the amount of money circulating the North Pole comes down to how much the government, casino overlords, corporations and gamblers are *willing to borrow.* He wonders what would happen if the average mortgage holding tourist realized that the money their bank lent them is not the savings of some prudent depositor, but actually a mere electronic figure living on a computer monitor which the bank blew into existence, as if it were an act of magic from Santa Claus. Would they not be enraged? Who gave the banks this right when so many workers are required to give their blood, sweat and tears to survive? What about those who gave their lives?

Renee pulls Willie up and they continue their trek past the countless security cameras of the police state. The cameras are all equipped with the latest facial recognition systems. They're on high alert tracking their every movement as they proceed down the strip. Soon they come across the massive IGLOO CASINO AND RESORT, famous for being the largest dome structure in the world. Near the grand entrance of the casino is an excessive Artic Zoo exhibit. It's complete with plastic, faux floating icebergs, loads of fish and snowy shores filled with Ringed Seals, Reindeer, Walrus's, Artic Foxes and Polar Bears.

Willie is glued to the thick glass of the exhibit, searching keenly, and he finds him – *Ursus* – perched up on a little plastic iceberg, thin and lonely. Willie jumps and shouts trying to earn Ursus' attention, but it's clear the old bear can hardly see as he awkwardly bumps into things and comes up empty handed, repeatedly, trying to scoop even the slowest unsuspecting fish.

Renee's heart breaks watching Willie desperately trying to be recognized by his oldest, furriest friend. She calms him, helping him realize he won't be known by his old pet, at least not today, especially amid the madness of the other distractions which surround them. But Willie wants a job at the IGLOO, if only to have the chance to spend more time within the same vicinity as his bear.

They continue on, since there's nothing else to do or place for them to go. They go searching for anything left standing from the past, looking for anything authentic that might still be standing. As they journey, they can practically count the ancient relics on one hand but score a sentimental win when stumbling across the old Coal & Stalking Tavern, somehow miraculously left existing. Sadly, the number of bars not filled to the brim with tourists or video poker can be counted on one hand. The casinos own everything in sight. It's just a matter of time before the Coal & Stalking is gobbled up by a cheesy TGI Fridays or some F-list celebrity trying to play bar owner.

Pushing along, they discover they're far from alone in their homelessness with entire tent cities sprung up on the streets. The police and their latest edition Santa-trons drive vagrant elves to these places while keeping them contained. Fortunately, Willie and Renee hide in the nick of time before being spotted by a brutal military man.

While hiding, Renee sees a notice for a pending application of a fancy indoor/outdoor mall. Why build a homeless shelter when you can help fund commerce, or support gambling? Building and operating a sustainable shelter is hard - building a slapdash version of Downtown Disney is much easier. They laugh at the ridiculousness of it all and are thankful to have at least their sense of humor intact, and they slip back onto the streets...

As night becomes morning, they're surprised by the sheer mass of tourists still wondering about. They find a small alley to rest in. From here they can peak into the doors of one of the biggest casinos on the strip, watching the broke, miserable and addicted people make their way between the slot machines and poker tables. The constant sight of the depressed gamblers only further depresses them, so they move on but realize that the Strip simply connects you to other super casinos, hotels and shopping malls, each as ludicrous as the next.

Eventually they find themselves among the aimless people. Caught between tourists from Florida and Indiana, who urgently search of the nearest all you can eat meat buffet. Then they're hovered over by the lost-looking couple from China and bewildered British family who've come to get a "real sense" of the North Pole. They all walk pointlessly down "The Strip," pointing and giggling at the spectacles, somehow finding it all so amusing and fantastic while being oblivious to the fact that they're just a bunch of dollar signs to the casino-overlords, like Sir Louie. The amount of spending or gambling a person is encouraged to do is endless. Fortunately for the obese, electric wheelchairs and 3-wheel scooters are available. They're so popular that sometimes it appears as if a deranged electric go-cart derby is in progress.

What's really impressive to Willie is how completely hammered the tourists get. Sure, most have already blown their retirement to get here and buy a seat at the craps table, so why not ease the pain with a few over-priced eggnogs and Christmas themed cocktails? But the drunks can be entertaining, and Willie and Renee catch glimpses of how they molest the disgruntled lady elves dressed up as the non-existent Mrs. Claus. Sometimes they act out pretending they're Santa Claus, dishing out all sorts of drunk orders to elves, even spanking and tossing them about with a hardy laugh.

Several days later Willie and Renee clean up and apply to hundreds of jobs. They're turned down time after time, but their persistence pays off as Willie lands a job as a short-order cook at the (Hot Dog) Heart Attack Café, set within THE IGLOO Hotel and Casino. With some convincing, Willie's able to get the cafe to hire Renee as a server, as well as negotiating (pleading) for an extra fifteen minutes (on top of the normal fifteen-minute lunch break) to visit Ursus at the exhibit.

The (Hot Dog) Heart Attack Café is a sight on its own, with a distinctly distasteful hospital theme where the waitresses are dressed as "nurses" and take orders known as "prescriptions" from the customers known as "patients." Each patient dons a hospital gown and wrist band. Those who don't finish their meal receive a paddling from their "nurse" with the option to buy the paddle afterwards.

The menu is exceptionally high in calories with some exquisite hotdog concoctions weighing in at 8,000 calories. Beyond elaborate stacks of hotdogs, there's the all-you-can-eat "Flatliner Fries" (cooked in pure lard),"butterfat peppermint milkshakes," and soft drinks such as "North Pole Sweetened" Coca-Cola (made with pure cane sugar). It even offers fun perks for customers weighing over 350 pounds. These lucky winners get to eat for free. One of the most fun promotions is a reward for customers who finish a Triple or Quadruple Bypass Dog, after which they're placed on a wheelchair and wheeled out to their electric scooter by their "personal nurse."

Willie tries hard not to let the depressing circumstances get him down, so he throws himself into his work and becomes a beast on the grill, cooking up hundreds of dogs every hour as Renee slings them out to hungry "patients" as fast as she can. She pretends to be in some kind of fantasy world as to help ward off the feelings of futility. In a deranged way the dynamic duo is back, just under the worst of circumstances. They try their best to get by, but it will never be enough to fill their lives with any sense of meaning or purpose. At least they get to spend some quality time together at lunch, trying to rebuild the spark they once had, while watching Ursus from a secluded little ledge they found away from the crowds.

Yet the boredom and crushing inescapability stifles them. Willie hides in a quiet office within the vast basement of the Igloo, spending his nights writing the contemporary history of the North Pole, detailing every unique memory about the Germans, how North Pole Inc. worked, why society failed, and how they got to where they are today. He struggles with the title but names it "North Pole Inc." And he writes with a great sense of purpose, as if trying to save the world from itself, though he suspects it's entirely possible no one will read it.

Renee visits him at the office from time to time, which she learns isn't far from the fireworks storage. Those pretty explosives are prepped daily for the nightly show above the Igloo and "The Strip." She slips her way into the prep room every night before the show and steals a handful of fireworks, then hides them within Willie's commandeered office. He's disturbed by her dangerous, curious habit, but does nothing to stop her. He doesn't understand it, but she doesn't either. She's going off the feeling that the explosives will come in handy one day, and perhaps sooner than later.

Day after day they grill and serve, grill and serve, grill and serve, dying a death by a thousand cuts. Soon they take notice to a fit young elf, maybe 18. He's a wolf trainer, and he frequents the restaurant buying up pounds of hot dogs as training treats for his champion killer-wolf. Sometimes he even brings his wolf with him to the restaurant (wearing a muzzle and elaborate leash). The trainer has some edge and carries a bit of a chip on his shoulder. He's strong, confident and tall for an elf. Most impressively he's somehow achieved mastery over the killer wolves. As time passes, he realizes he recognizes Willie and Renee from long ago, and on one particular day he excitedly says;

"You're Renee Kendal-Crink, aren't you? That's Willie Maven back behind the grill, isn't it?"

Renee's impressed, even flattered to be recognized.

"Yes," she replies softly, "and you are?"

"Gabriel Star, good to finally meet you." He says delivering a handshake. "This is my wolf, Koko. Don't let the name fool 'ya. He's a sweetie but he's a stone cold killa. Ain't that right, Koko?" He laughs with a strange mix of wholesomeness and gallows humor. "I saw Willie Wolf-Sledding when I was a kid, a tragic day, I even tried to pull him up over the cliff. I doubt he remembers me amid all that happened. It was Willie who's inspired me to work with wolves – even though I'm forced into it."

"You're young for blood sport, where are your parents?" She asks.

"They've passed, in The Struggles."

"I'm sorry." She stalls, wanting to know more but it isn't the time or place. With resentment and in compliance with the law she searches for a new topic. "Do you like what you do, Gabriel?"

"Oh, God no. But I love Koko, and I'll do my damnedest to make sure he survives."

She nods back with understanding while the rumble of the nightly fireworks sounds off outside.

"Do you consider yourself a show-elf?" She asks.

"I guess I am." Gabriel replies.

"I'm secretly a show-elf, too," she winks, "and I'm gonna give the North Pole the greatest show they've *ever* seen."

26 – FIREWORKS

The morning feels like just another day at the Heart Attack Café, but it isn't. Today is special because it's the *Fourth of July*.

Yes, it's still hot dog after hot dog, grilled and served, grilled and served, grilled and served to the never-ending appetite of human consumption. And the tourists gobble and smile, gobble and smile, gobble and smile (except on the rare occasion when someone suffers an actual heart attack). It's a mind-numbing, soul sucking process that repeats and repeats in a routine that offers no escape.

Sometimes the pace is fast, sometimes it's slow, but it doesn't matter, Willie and Renee will make scraps anyway. The colorlessness of their lives leaves them dull and uninspired, while the very idea of an alternative way of life becomes incomprehensible. They're cornered into acknowledging it's this lifestyle or vagrancy. The day-to-day grind for survival leaves them exhausted and without savings. Meanwhile, their joint credit card debt compounds while they're unable to make their minimum interest payments.

The hopelessness of it all feels unavoidable. But Willie reminds himself that hopelessness isn't natural, it's produced. It's something that is created and upheld by a vast apparatus of prisons, police, private security, and propaganda, most of which don't attack alternative ideas so much as they create a pervasive climate of fear.

Their ever-growing resentment builds drip by drip, though any authentic emotion can be hard to detect amid their zombie state. Even with their backgrounds of privilege, their tolerance for the slave-like conditions has expanded to accepting the ever-permeating scent of sitting hot dog water which smells vaguely of shit. It's taken a while for them to accept things like the smell, among the many other degradations they experience daily, but now they've come to expect it.

If their sense of sanity were like a concrete dam, the little cracks of leaking water are like the drips of resentment forcing their way through the concrete under the immense force and weight of the river behind it. It can only hold the pressure for so long until the dam gives way and comes collapsing down. For them, it's only a matter of time before someone or something destructs, and that day is today.

With so many American tourists as their "best patients" the restaurant celebrates the American Day of Independence with their own bootleg version of the outrageous *Coney Island Hot Dog Eating Contest.*

The contest draws a massive crowd, making it the restaurant's busiest day. It's Renee and Willie's first year working the contest, and like everyone else they're expected to work the entire 24-hour shift to the bone.

The nature of the holiday, that it's supposedly a celebration of freedom, seriously bothers Willie. He finds it ironic but mostly sad, how a population of debt enslaved people whole heartedly celebrate all the things they mistake freedom for. Willie ponders how their collective, spiraling debt is only the imaginary money whose value must be realized in the future, through the profits and proceeds of exploited beings who, in essence, *aren't even born yet.*

Willie takes his eyes off the grill and stares into the casino. All the bustling action reminds him how finance is nothing more than the buying and selling of imaginary future profits; and once one assumes capitalism will be around for all eternity, the only economic democracy left to imagine is one where everyone is equally free to invest in the market — to grab their own piece in this game of buying and selling of imaginary future profits, even when these profits are to be extracted from themselves. Willie sighs with his natural conclusion, that the height of freedom in this perverse world has become the right to share in the proceeds of one's permanent enslavement. But for most, like him, they'll just be enslaved without a right to proceeds, so long as these barriers to alternatives persist.

The manager *snaps* at him for daydreaming, just as Bobby Walnut enters the cafe. Bobby Walnut, Joey Chestnut's young cousin (Joey is famous for holding the world record, eating 74 hot dogs in 10 minutes), has got a lot to prove if he wants to be taken seriously on the pro-eating circuit. The tourists crowd around him, pretending like the big spectacle carries the slightest amount of actual significance. With the masses growing the pre-contest countdown already busies the cafe.

Renee works vigilantly trying to keep pace with the madness of the action. In the process she realizes just how many credit cards she swipes all day. Amid her daydreaming a "patient" with oversized glasses hands over his credit card as the sharp edge of it slices her fingertip.

"Oh – sorry, paper-cuts are the worst." He says awkwardly.

"This case it's plastic." She replies in agony.

"If I could tip you I would, really."

Renee sucks her fingertip, the pulsating pain continues, but the sight of her blood on the credit card reminds her of earlier times, making her grin.

"It was an accident, it's okay." She says to his relief. Yet the simple action of wiping her blood from the credit card has her contemplating the electronic transaction.

"You look like a smart guy," she says to his delight. "Do you know how these things work?" She asks holding his credit card.

"That's why I come to the North Pole. To learn from the best in fin-tech." He says.

"What's fin-tech?"

"Oh – the space where finance meets tech, it's advanced here, the rest of us are just trying to catch up."

"So, you're some kind of credit card guru?"

He smiles back, "Yeah, well, more like a student really. I just took a 'high security' tour of the financial server farm they've got here. Some exciting tech if you ask me."

"What are server farms?"

"These credit card transactions need to be processed somewhere, so it goes up to the servers that record and operate the whole system in real time."

"Fascinating. So where is it?"

He gets out of his seat and points through the glass ceiling of the café straight at Santa's Tower just in the distance. "Up in that big ol' tower, near the top." He says. "It's guarded like a fortress."

"You're saying the server farm is like a digital bank vault?" She prods.

"Yeah, I guess you could say that. They need more server farms just like it across the world, so their data is safer – right now that's the only location, which is a risk."

"Interesting." Renee replies.

"It could be a real business opportunity for me. I'm going to raise some money and build a couple server farms when I get home. Hope to have my first one up by next year." He says with a smile.

"Exciting," she performs, then thinks how great it'd be to destroy the server farm before her papercutting friend can build a backup center. She becomes mesmerized in a fantastic daydream of blowing it up and erasing the debt. But she reawakens as several tables yell "Nurse! Nurse!"

"Good luck with your server farms." She smiles.

"Good luck to you," he says. "And like I said, I'd tip ya' if the resort allowed me."

"You've tipped me more than you know," she replies with a wink.

The pre-hot dog eating contest countdown wraps as the competitive eaters take to the stage. The crowd goes wild for Bobby Walnut before the 'Uncle-Sam' dressed official explains the rules – the contest is a race to consume the most hot dogs in 10 minutes. The stakes are high as the winner will qualify for the hot dog eating contest at Coney Island – the crème de la crème' event of the eating world. Amid Walnut there's a host of ridiculous contestants, including some semi-pros trying to make it on the "pro eating circuit," while others are just drunk tourists making a last-ditch effort to win prize money to afford a flight home.

BANG - the contest starts as the eaters shovel hot dog after Coca-Cola drenched hot dog into their stuffed mouths. The crowd cheers, the eaters struggle. It's an amusing, unnatural sight that's incredible to witness, especially as a fifth of the planet's population goes to sleep starving every night. And like a good contest it comes down the wire. Burdened with the pressure of living up to Joey Chestnut's great name, Bobby kicks his jaws into high gear and wins the contest with a glorious mad dash of hot dogs just before time expires.

Renee is tasked with placing the coveted gold medal around his neck. She does so cautiously, but as Walnut pumps his fists in victory he *PROJECTILE VOMITS* the 42 regurgitated hot dogs all over her. The vomit covers Renee, making it impossible to see her tears amid the dense, gelatinous flow of bile. She dashes to the kitchen sobbing. When Willie spots her she collapses to the ground and faints with an overbearing sense of worthlessness.

After a few minutes she's roughly poked awake by the Food and Beverage Manager of the Resort himself. He's a rather stout Middle-America type, but he knows all the elves at the café have been contracted for the entire 24-hour shift, and they've already been paid their pennies upfront. With a more than slight kick from the tip of his shoe Renee *gasps* back to life, seeing Willie behind the manager, powerless as he watches her wipe the bile from her face.

"Wake up, elfie, come on, back to work." The manager yelps.

She stares up at him, still in a haze but moving and breathing.

"There you go. Wash up and get back on the floor. It's the Fourth of July for cryin' out loud, *let's go*." He orders.

Renee, stinking and barely able to breathe, or even see, boils in rage and grabs the nearest blunt object - a rolling pin – and SLAMS it into the manager's crotch, knocking the wind out of him as he falls to his knees.

And with primal SWACK of the rolling pin against the back of his skull he's knocked out cold, collapsing to the ground with a *smack* against the tile.

She drops the rolling pin and laughs as Willie stares in horror. It's only mere moments before casino security pounces on her. They're disgusted at first, but they put on their gloves, snatch her and toss her out onto the streets for good. It's her turn lying there on the concrete, hysterically laughing and crying at the same time.

Willie rushes to her side with a bottle of water, she sucks it down as the surrounding tourists point and laugh at the sad sight. Renee doesn't want to get up, especially with the tremendous Fourth of July Firework show erupting. Willie joins her lying on the sidewalk, crying and holding hands. Together they stare up into the sky as the red, white and blue fireworks explode throughout the atmosphere in a show many times more powerful than the average nightly spectacle.

With a brief pause in the firework show, Renee stares into the night sky enjoying how the stars shimmer. She beams and escapes the dread of her physical form, finding solace in the stars, knowing that *a lingering sweetness will always return to the North Pole, even long after she is gone*. With this truth she can open her heart and be at peace with the idea of her own end, realizing her death may be necessary to transform elves from mere objects back to conscious, expressive beings again.

The fireworks resume as she returns to the present and notices how they're launched from the roof of Santa's Tower, instead of the roof of the Igloo Resort, as is standard. It's a special occasion after all. It gets her thinking about the server farm, and how close it is to that massive stock of explosives on the roof launchpad. The next time they'll launch from the tower must be Christmas Eve.

"Can you finish your book by Christmas Eve?" She asks.

"Why?" Willie wonders.

"Because we'll have one last shot to take back our home, and Christmas Eve is the only opening. If you're going to join me, well, you'll want to have your book done by then. But if not, I'll understand."

"You're motivated by your misanthropy," he says, "that's dangerous."

"I'm motivated to challenge those who either disguise or manipulate the fragility of elves for their own benefit. If I die trying then so be it, some things are worth dying for."

"But we've lost."

"My mind is made up. I'm doing this."

Willie thinks about it. He knows that a life at the Heart Attack Café would hardly be worth living alone. And like her, deep down, he wants retribution for all of those excruciatingly painful injustices made in the name of profit. That and he loves her too much to let her do it alone. The final stroke of convincing comes as he absorbs Renee's agony, paired with her newfound unflappable determination, which draws out his hidden resentment.

With a deep breath Willie sheds his sedated zombie state and lets the anger of his hidden fury flow through him, experiencing all the pain and trauma that's been trapped in him like a poison. Letting go of all the things he's lost reinvigorates his spirit, and allows him to break through his alienation to sincerely reconnect with Renee.

"To hell with this plastic casino world." He says to her smile before turning back to watch the finale of the fireworks light it up the night sky as if it were daytime, if only for only a moment.

"Cheer up," she says, "we might even make it out alive."

"That'd be something." He laughs as Gabriel Star and Koko arrive on the scene, about to enter the Igloo until he spots them on the ground.

"Renee, Willie? Is that you?" Gabriel asks, taken aback by their state on the concrete.

"Gabriel?" Renee replies, as he helps both up off the ground.

"Let's get you two cleaned up." Gabriel answers.

"Thanks Gabriel." Willie says, with Renee between them, holding her up, helping her walk. "I will have a book for you, soon. I'd like you to read it."

"I'd be honored, Mr. Maven."

"No, I would be."

Later, it's Christmas Eve in the North Pole, the most electrifying night here and for much of the world. It's also Wolf Fight Night at the Igloo. The Christmas Eve fight has become the biggest and most lucrative one-night event in all professional sports, with the snowy caged ring representing the epicenter of the entertainment and gambling universe. The crowds are abuzz wagering, drinking, smoking and waiting in anticipation for the deathmatch.

Gabriel goes about his pre-match ritual, stopping by the Heart Attack Café and ordering one hot dog for himself and one for Koko. It's their big night, but unbeknownst to him it's an even bigger one for Willie and Renee.

Renee approaches, disguised as a tourist, and Willie arrives with the hot dogs and the final copy of his book in hand. They sit together and share a meditative moment, each about to put everything back on the line, once again. With a smirk Willie hands Gabriel his book.

"It's the history of The Struggles," Willie says.

Gabriel reads the cover. "North Pole Inc."

"Guard it with your life," Renee adds, "and share it with whoever you can."

"I will." Gabriel answers. "But where will you be?"

"Working the firework show, and we're not sure if we'll be back for presents tomorrow." She answers.

Gabriel is humbled and nods, accepting the book, and the responsibility to protect it and spread the word.

"Good luck, Gabriel." Renee says, kissing his cheek before Willie hugs him.

"Good luck." Gabrielle replies, holding the book next to his heart, protecting it within his arms, before walking off to the ring with Koko.

The fight is minutes away. Koko is on one end of the ring *howling* within his cage. He's faced off against an even bigger wolf with sharper teeth. The opponent is filled with a manic, bloodthirsty rage as it bounces off the sides of its cage. Gabriel is used to the sight of intimidating opponents but this one feels particularly fearsome, as if it doesn't care if it lives or dies, its only aim is to kill.

Behind the opposing wolf just outside of the ring is his gruesome trainer, a beefy New Yorker who looks like a finely dressed butcher in his black on black designer suit, standing sternly and puffing away on a thousand-dollar Cuban cigar. There's something about his demeanor that suggests he's killed at least a thousand living things. His swagger emanating through his smirk, and how he puffs out the cigar smoke in perfect little smoke rings from each end of his mouth. His scarred bald head adds to his rough character, along with his wide chin and fat face that seems to connect with his shoulders as if he didn't have a neck.

The gamblers size up the Butcher against Gabriel's controlled poise, making him appear strong. He stands tall as he stares down the butcher without a flinch. His confidence is channeled to Koko and then back to him, like a feedback loop. In this extra-dimensional way, it's as if they're telepathically aligned, similar to Willie and Ursus or Santa and his Reindeer. But inside, Gabriel knows this victory will require a near flawless performance by Koko.

Meanwhile, Willie and Renee sneak out of the Heart Attack Café, traversing the tunnels of the underground back to their stolen basement office. There's a small TV displaying a fuzzy image of Gabriel, Koko, and the book within Gabriel's grasp. As the camera zooms in on Gabriel, Willie and Renee smile with a sense of pride, but move quick into their technician disguises and load their immense collection of stolen fireworks into a landship.

As the stadium lights dim the announcer comes on while a rare shiver runs through Gabriel. The lights brighten to illuminate the ring while the rumble of the crowd turns into a roar. The clock counts down from ten, as the entire human population of the North Pole is transfixed on the fight, making it a good distraction. The atmosphere is spellbinding as the gamblers await the wolves to swoop into action.

SNAP - the cage doors drop as the wolves come dashing out.

Willie kisses his fingers and places them on the image of Koko and Gabriel before turning off the television. With one last deep breath Willie and Renee spring into action, hightailing it through the underground tunnels which connect The Strip with Downtown and the Hermitage.

Willie and Renee speed through the narrow tunnels, gunning it to catch up with the fireworks crew. With the wolf fight happening the guards at the various check points don't seem to catch on to their counterfeit badges, allowing them to get where they need to go - the basement of Santa's Tower.

The tower is one of the few historic buildings with its original structure intact. Renee still knows all the vents, nooks and crannies like the back of her hand. Their nimbleness and slight stature are helpful in evading the high-tech security system.

Most effectively they make use of the forgotten executive elevator, a favorite of Klaus and Otto. But the secret shaft only takes them so far until they break into the dusty interconnected maze of vents, climbing and crawling all the way to the level just below the Server Farm.

Their timing is succinct. They unload the cargo as the building empties in anticipation for the fireworks. Between the wolf fight and the upcoming fireworks extravaganza, Santa's Tower is vacated. With the top floors emptied a platoon of fifty Santa-trons replace the American guards who move outside to work on crowd control.

Willie and Renee study the Santa-trons and pick up on their repeating, predictable patrol patterns. Their advance turns into a tense game of timing, stopping and starting on a dime - all the while lugging the bags of fireworks over their backs. They make it to the same floor as the cooling vent - which connects with the Server Farm, but the entrance to the cooling vent is on the other side of the floor.

They sweat amid the ducking and diving en route to the vent, often just dodging the sights and senses of the robots in the nick of time. They make it to the cooling vent undetected. Their hands go numb and tremble as they push forward, but with persistence they make their way up and eye the Server Farm.

With wide grins they're about to break in as Renee cuts through the vent with her power blowtorch, but during their journey one bag has unzipped ever so slightly, and as Willie lugs it around the corner - the momentum of the motion makes a *single firework pop out of the bag.*

He cringes watching the firework drop until landing hard against the floor of the aluminum vent. It nosily rolls down until it falls from where they entered, the impact causing the metal grate to fling open, as the firework falls and hits a Santa-tron on the head with a loud and distinct *ding.*

The killing machine scans the vent and adjusts its metallic body proportions becoming taller and slenderer before JUMPING into the vent and climbing the shaft.

"We've got company!" Willie yells.

"Handle it!" She shouts, almost done with breaking through to the servers.

Willie lights the tail of the firework and aims it down-shaft. He hears the Santa-tron just around the corner – it turns and rapidly charges just as the firework *launches* from Willie's hands, burning him, before it *zips* through the narrow vent and COLORFULLY EXPLODES against the 'tron with a direct hit, knocking it offline.

Renee kisses his burned hands before finishing the job, cutting all the way through the steel grate as it falls onto the floor of the Server Farm.

In a frenzy they take out the security cameras, stick ten fireworks to each of the numerous servers, and booby-trap the vent before connecting all the explosives to a remote detonator. They're safe for now within the vault-like Server Farm, so as long as it remains locked.

Only Sir Louie has the authority to override the security protocol. They know the security cameras caught their image before destroying them, so Sir Louie will know it's them - and they laugh thinking about the look on his face.

With the fireworks rigged and ready to blow they make their escape back into the vent. But the ALARM rings while the Santa-trons pound away at the door. Their powerful and erratic punching intermixed with the bursts of the erupting fireworks creates a cacophony of chaos as they hurry to escape.

They climb through the vent now lined with armed fireworks and stumble over the torn-up Santa-tron in their path. They gaze at one another and in synchronicity, move to peer over the ledge of the vertical drop – *locking gazes with the harrowing red eyes of several 'trons staring straight back at them.*

Willie and Renee instantly roll back and make a beeline to the Server Farm as the squad leaps into the vent. The robots are hot on their tail but Willie buys a moment by kicking the defeated 'tron carcass down the drop, its heavy metal frame *crashing* upon several robots in pursuit, knocking them back to the floor as Willie and Renee dive into the Server Farm. It's bad, with the mass of Santa-trons just outside the door while the other squad regrouping and making their way back into the vent.

"We have to blow the vent!" She yells.

"It's our only escape."

"We have no choice." She says.

"There's got to be another way."

"This time there isn't, I'm sorry, Willie." She says.

He fumbles with the detonator before getting a good grip on it – and lets it rip with an EXPLOSION that shakes the tower.

Willie breathes a sign of relief with the silence following the destruction. He thinks it might be difficult for the bulky Santa-trons to climb through a torn-up vent. It may even work to their advantage if they can slip into other tiny crawl spaces that may have been exposed.

Back outside at the VIP section of the fireworks spectacle, Joey approaches Sir Louie with a portable monitor.

"Sir, we have a situation inside the tower." Joey says, displaying the video of Willie and Renee destroying cameras within the server room.

"What are they up to now?" Sir Louie blips.

"We're under attack. We believe they rigged the Server Farm with fireworks, Sir."

"Fireworks?" Sir Louie blips.

"Tons of fireworks." Joey clarifies. "We need your authority to override the system and open the doors before it's too late."

"That'd be incredibly, incredibly bad for me. Which is incredibly bad for you - you realize?"

"Tens of Millions would be lost in an instant -"

"Yes! God damn it, you have my authority, now go!" Sir Louie yells. "Arrest those brats! They're gonna wish they never got out of prison! They're gonna wish they've never been born!"

Back inside the tower Willie peers into the vent with his flashlight. It looks dangerous, filled with sharp debris and no clear path, but he keeps scanning, looking for an open crawl space to get anywhere else. An open crack connecting to the elevator shaft would be a god send - but it's all just jagged dead ends, and their sense of hope dwindles with every passing moment.

But soon it becomes clear, there's nothing else to do but accept the inevitability of their circumstance, and she softly wraps her arms around him, bringing Willie back to the floor of the Server Farm. Within in her loving grasp he comes to accept their fate as well. Amid the Santa-trons bashing evermore violently against the door it feels like a déjà vu. But this time it's different. This time they know it's the end.

And they hold each other, delicately rocking one another back and forth as Renee picks up the detonator and carries it gently.

They share one last smile, holding their teary gaze until the last possible moment.

The electronic lock comes undone as they share one last kiss before the robots surround them.

And as the robots close in, Willie and Renee slowly interlock their fingers upon the detonator and within the warmth of their embrace, together, they press it down...

BRILLIANTLY and UTTERLY BLOWING UP Santa's Tower.

Providing a visceral experience of destruction delivered in the most beautiful form of ongoing red and green explosions...

The masses of entranced tourists cheer and spur on the sight, assuming it's all a part of the extravagant show. Everyone celebrates, except Sir Louie, who's sickened as the colorful explosions erupt, filling the night sky with splendor, as if it were the most spectacular finale ever conceived.

27 – STAR ATOP A TREE

Inside the wolf fighting stadium an earthquake-like rumble shakes the building as the lights flicker filling everyone with a worried sense of bewilderment, just as the marathon wolf fight nears its end.

The lights return on as the tremors quells. At this point Koko can barely stand, hobbling meekly, blood gushing from multiple deep bite wounds, covering the snow of the fighting ground in dark red. Gabriel must see it to the end, which comes when the enemy wolf takes a clean bite into Koko's throat before violently ripping him back and forth until he can no longer move. With his body limp and comatose, the enemy drops Koko, leaving him to bleed out.

After circling Koko, the enemy wolf is about to deliver the death blow, but cruelly the Butcher calls off the move, ordering his wolf to circle his prey. Everyone watches and waits for Koko to take his final breath, which takes several prolonged minutes of suffering before it finally arrives. When he lets go, Koko is officially pronounced dead as the victory bell *rings*.

Gabriel sheds a tear while the winning gamblers in the crowd cheer gloriously, as does the Butcher who raises his fists high while chomping on a freshly lit cigar. The Butcher is awarded a medal and a briefcase full of cash. After delivering many congratulatory handshakes he hoists up high the stacks of prize money, showing off his winnings with bravado. His favorite part of wolf fighting is how you don't have to share the profits with the fighter.

Meanwhile, confusion ensues as the masses of drinkers empty onto the promenade with every credit card being declined at the bar. They boo at the most unfortunate malfunction but soon realize their cards don't work anywhere.

With the stadium emptying Gabriel remains at his ring side post, heartbroken as Koko's bloodied and mangled body lay before him.

The stadium clears and the cleanup crew arrives. They unceremoniously toss Koko's body into a plastic bin before the league commissioner, a rugged Wild West type, marches forward. In the commissioner's hands are a litter of wolf pups, nine to be exact – eight healthy ones and one runt of the litter with a unique pinkish-red nose. Any champion wolf kills eight or so wolves during their training while the trainer determines which one is fittest for the pros. But Gabriel declines, unwilling to accept the litter.

"There's no choice for you, boy, now take 'em." The commissioner orders.

"I'm done with this madness." Gabriel states.

"And what, become a cook!?"

"Maybe."

"Well ya' can't, you make too much damn money." The commissioner says while brandishing his shiny silver revolver strapped to his waist. "You're too good to do anything else, ya see?"

"I'm going home." Gabriel spats.

"Not before you take these here pups, now."

"Or else what, you'll shoot me?"

The commissioner shifts the pups into one hand, quick draws his revolver and BLASTS a bullet into the air before pointing the gun at Gabriel's head.

"Ya' damn right, ya' dirty elf."

"Jesus, commissioner, take it easy."

"Take 'em, or they'll each get a bullet and you'll get the last. Ya' understand?"

Gabriel obliges and accepts the pups in his hands as the commissioner storms off.

He stands alone in the empty stadium demoralized. It takes minutes before he looks down at the cute wolf pups watching them play and tumble around the floor. He holds up his book and looks back at the pups, knowing he'll bring none of them to a wolf fight, ever. In fact, they'll become his new family, and once he understands the true nature of the North Pole, he'll set out to change it.

With a newfound rebellion he gathers his wolf pups and exits the stadium with a fiery ambition that burns within his gut. As Gabriel departs, he notices the angry crowds upset with the all the vendors declining their credit cards. He continues out, catching word of the epic firework display which destroyed Santa's Tower. Gabriel turns to stare at the book once more and considers how Willie and Renee delivered it to him in such a sentimental manner – realizing the destructive display was all a part of their plan. He smiles and laughs even, watching all the tourists and spenders getting turned away time and again. But then he recognizes the incredible danger Willie and Renee may be in. With an urgency he sprints with the wolf pups to what remains of the tower.

Gabriel and the pups arrive at the taped off scene filled with debris. He slides underneath the tape trying to blend in with the elvish cleanup crew working double time. He races them, searching and scanning the debris frantically. He notices two elves within the cleanup crew doing the same – Bushy and Alabaster.

"What are you looking for?" Gabriel asks them.

"Not what, it's who." Bushy replies.

"Willie and Renee?" Gabriel asks.

"How'd you know?"

"I was their friend."

"Us too. We've got a sense they had something to do with this..." Alabaster says as he shovels through the piles of wreckage and rubble. He turns over a metal sheet and discovers many shredded up data servers and exploded firework shells. He feels close to something, but still can't hear any cries for help as they search urgently.

Gabriel stumbles upon a glittery patch of dirt, dismissing it as exploded firework sparkle. But when Bushy and Alabaster arrive, they realize the true nature of the glitter and cry as they search for more clues. Gabriel stumbles across something in the wreckage. He picks it up and dusts it off.

It's Willie's prosthetic hand.

The three hold each other, comforting one another in their sadness knowing they're gone for good.

Bushy digs the glittery ash of their eviscerated bodies and shovels it quickly into her knapsack. She nearly fills it before adding Willie's platinum prosthetic, then zips it shut. Alabaster wraps his arms around Gabriel and Bushy, and the three take off with heavy hearts.

"Your parents pass in The Struggles, Gabriel?" Bushy asks.

"Yes, how'd you know?"

"Sorry, had a sense. Just know they passed as heroes."

"I'd like to believe that." Gabriel says as he takes out his copy of North Pole Inc. and shows it to Bushy and Alabaster. "Willie gave me this, he said it was about The Struggles."

Bushy ekes out a smile. "Good."

Gabriel musters a grin back as Alabaster and Bushy lead him to the "Unique Ornaments Shoppe," which Sticky, who's now rather old and rickety, currently manages.

The trio greet Sticky with a warm welcome. But the mood shifts when they deliver him the news of the contents of their bag. With tears Sticky accepts the bag and delivers it to his youngest Ickle son, who is a rare master glassblower. At the furnace in the back of the shop they watch as he fashions the most beautiful blown glass ornament – a grand, sparkling *crystal star*. It's champagne colored and filled with tiny reflective bubbles, while the platinum of Willie's melted prosthetic rounds the tips, providing the star with a strong outline, giving the ornament a sense of outer strength amid the delicacy of the fragile glass within.

The elves jointly smile, moved by the beauty of the forming ornament. Not only do Willie and Renee deserve to be atop of the epic tree, their beings deserve to be infused, united within a symbol of love and hope, for all elves.

Once the ornament cools Sticky wraps the impressive star into a blanket and ropes it around Gabriel's back before the group maneuvers to the Tree of Trees.

Using all of his strength, Gabriel climbs the height of the structure with the heavy glass star. He scales undetected and reaches the very tip top of the Tree of Trees where he removes the large generic glowing bulb. He tosses it aside, laughing as the cheap plastic bounces up off the ground on impact. With the bulb gone, the large spotlight underneath is exposed, radiating light high into the sky.

Gabriel undoes the rope and places the awe-inspiring ornament upon the spotlight – setting it in tight as the luminous star shines for the whole North Pole to admire.

The elves are deeply moved at the sight, many uncertain why it has such a powerful hold on them, but it does, and they share a deep sense of connection. The sight feeds their spirit and inspires them not only to survive, but to resist, so they may one day experience a North Pole full of love, freedom and liberty. It reminds them that elves can create beauty, and that they are beautiful all on their own.

Slowly, elves from all over notice the radiant shining star. They're mesmerized, gazing at it in contemplative silence, absorbing its exquisiteness. Many onlookers experience a flood of rushing emotions, joyful their elvish monument is adorned with a proper crown.

Gabriel descends the monument and rejoins the group in a tight embrace before Alabaster hands him his book and pack of pups. He's had enough of it all and wants to find himself in the wilderness, as far away from the confines of capital that he can get. He wants to discover his true purpose and desires to look to Willie's words for veracity. He gives the group one last hug, and with his wolves he heads for the heights of the Arctic Range.

As daybreaks Sir Louie is briefed with a damage report. It detais the monetary mutilation of lost revenue, uncollectable debts and the resulting tumble of the North Pole Inc. stock price. It's a disaster. He can only rebuild and re-consolidate from here.

Sir Louie chugs a fat glass of eggnog then *shatters* it against the floor as his terrified accountants tremble. They try to get through the details of the report as Topper and McJingles quiver alongside their assistants.

"We need new servers, more servers, spread out all over the world!" Sir Louie yells.

"Y-y-yes, Sir." Topper stutters.

"We need every operation back up and running. We need every gambler gambling away every dollar. *We need everything to go on as it did before!*"

"B-b-but, h-h-how, Sir?"

"Until operations are back online, we'll go the old fashion route. Cash only." Sir Louie says.

"And w-wha-what if they don't have cash, Sir?"

"Then LOAN IT TO THOSE DEGENERATE FOOLS, for god sakes...with *INTEREST!*" Sir Louie explodes, his face going from red to purple as his company of lackey's, yes-men, and corporate sock puppets scurry away with their orders.

...And far in the distance Gabriel Star ascends the Artic Range with his young wolfpack. He stops to take in one last vista of the city, paying respect to the star atop of the Tree of Trees. He absorbs the vast scale of the North Pole, and the enormity of his obstacles to come. And they continue their journey up into the mountains and to the very top of the world, on this most special Christmas Day.

-THE END-

NOTES

Preface Quote, Winston Churhill (*New Statesman* interview, 7 January 1939) "Criticism may not be agreeable, but it is necessary. It fulfils the same function as pain in the human body; it calls attention to the development of an unhealthy state of things. If it is heeded in time, danger may be averted; if it is suppressed, a fatal distemper may develop."

Chp.1 Pg. 9, Mark Epstein ("Thoughts without a Thinker" - Meditation pg.110-111, Basic Books 2013) *"Bare attention. "It's the clear and single-minded awareness of what actually happens to us, and in us, at the successive moments of perception. Take your unexamined mind and open it up, not by trying to change anything but by observing your mind, emotions, and body the way they are. Take in the bare facts."*

Chp.1 Pg. 10, Jiro Ono (Starring), David Gelb (Director), Kevin Iwashina, Tom Pellegrini (Producers) ("Jiro Dreams of Sushi" 2011 Documentary) Jiro Ono - *"An apprentice must not only master a technical skill but through doing so learns about social consciousness. Through that virtue every person has an obligation to create to the best of their ability as they expand their own mind. The obligation is spiritual and material, and it is their responsibility to fulfill the requirement."*

Chp. 3 Pg. 30, Albert Camus, Albert Camus Review of *Nausea* by Jean-Paul Sartre, published in the newspaper *Alger Républicain* (20 October 1938), p. 5; also quoted in *Albert Camus and the Philosophy of the* Absurd (2002) by Avi Sagi, pg. 43 *"Life can be magnificent and overwhelming – and that is the whole of tragedy. Without beauty, love, or danger, it would almost be easy to live...the realization that life is absurd is not an end point, instead it is a beginning."*

Chp. 5, Pg.53, Declaration of Atrocities, (signed by Franklin D. Roosevelt, British Prime Minister Winston Churchill and Soviet Premier Joseph Stalin, *Statement on Atrocities* was largely drafted by Winston Churchill) *"Germans will be sent back to the countries where they had committed their most heinous crimes...judged on the spot by the peoples whom they have outraged...evidence of atrocities, massacres and cold-blooded mass executions which are being perpetrated by Hitlerite forces in many of the countries they have overrun and from which they are now being steadily expelled."*

Chp. 6, Pg. 64, Declaration of Atrocities, *"Participation in a common plan or conspiracy for the accomplishment of a crime against peace. Planning, initiating and waging wars of aggression and other crimes against peace. War crimes. Crimes against humanity."*

Chp. 6, Pg. 67, President Harry Truman Public Radio Address, August 6, 1945 The White House Washington, D.C., United States, Department of State, Publication No. 2702, The International Control of Atomic Energy. Growth of a Policy (Government Printing Office, Washington, n.d. [1947]), pp. 95-

97. Words of Peace-Words of War.) *"Sixteen Hours ago, an American airplane dropped one bomb on Hiroshima, an important Japanese Army base. That bomb had more power than 20,000 tons of T.N.T. It had more than two thousand times the blast power of the British "Grand Slam"* ...

Chp. 6, Pg. 72, Friedrich Nietzsche. *"Out of order comes chaos, out of chaos comes order."*

Chp. 7, Pg. 83, Roger Arnold, ("The Treasury and The Fed; The Relationship Between the Two Organizations is Circular" Real Money, 2012, https://realmoney.thestreet.com/articles/09/27/2012/treasury-and-fed)

Chp. 7, Pg. 84, James Rickards ("The Death of Money" - Debt, Deficits, and the Dollar, pg. 198, Portfolio/Penguin 2014) *"The Federal Reserve status as a central bank has long been obvious, but...supporters went to great lengths to disguise the fact that the proposed institution was a central bank. The most conspicuous part of the exercise is the name itself, the Federal Reserve...the obfuscation was much by design...A key difference between a central bank and ordinary banks is that a central bank performs for public customers such as individuals and corporations."*

Chp. 8, Pg.88, Adam Smith ("The Wealth of Nations" pg.10), *"It is not from the benevolence of the butcher, the brewer, or the baker that we expect our dinner, but from their regard to their own self-interest."*

Chp. 8, Pg. 89, John Locke (Labor Theory of Property), *"Each person has the right to control his own labor power and to claim ownership of the fruits of that labor."*

Chp. 8, Pg. 90, Joseph Schumpeter ("Capitalism, Socialism and Democracy" pg. 132, originally published in 1942 by Harper & Brothers, Harper Perennial Modern Thought edition published 2008) *"The function of entrepreneurs is to reform or revolutionize the pattern of production by exploiting an invention or, more generally, an untried technological possibility for producing a new commodity or producing an old one in a new way, by opening up a new source of supply of materials or a new outlet for products, by reorganizing an industry and so on."*

Chp. 9, Pg.95, James Rickards (on the Contract Theory of Money, "The Death of Money" – Debt, Deficits, and the Dollar, pg. 167) *"The dollar is money, money is value, value is trust, trust is a contract, and the contract is debt... substitute the word 'debt' every time you one sees the word 'money'. Then the world looks like a different place; it is a world in debt."*

Chp. 9, Pg.95, James Rickards ("The Death of Money" - Debt, Deficits, and the Dollar, pg. 173) *"Debt isn't inherently positive nor negative... Its utility is determined by what the borrower does with the money. Debt levels aren't automatically too high or too low, what matters most to creditors is the trend toward sustainability."*

Chp. 9, Pg.95, Paul Volcker, Chairman of the Federal Reserve 1979-1987, *"If people have confidence in it, the dollar can weather any storm. If people lose confidence in the dollar, no army of PhDs can save it."*

Chp. 9, Pg.96, Maurizio Lazzarato ("The Making of the Indebted Man" pg.39, Semiotext(e) 2011) *"What is credit/debt in the most elementary sense? A promise of payment. What is a financial asset, a share, or bond? The promise of future value. "Promise", "value", and "future" are also key words in Nietzche's Second Essay. For Nietzche, the "oldest and most personal relationship this is" is that between creditor and debtor, a relationship wherein "person met person for the first time, and measured himself person against person. Consequently, the task of a community or society has first of all been to engender a person capable of promising, someone able to stand guarantor for himself, in the creditor-debtor relationship, that is, capable of honoring his debt."*

Chp. 9, Pg.96, Maurizio Lazzarato ("The Making of the Indebted Man" pg.131, 134) *"Each individual is a particular case which must be studied carefully, because, as with a loan application, it is the debtor's future plans, his style of life, his "solvency" that guarantees reimbursement of the social debt he owes. As with bank credit, rights are granted on the basis of a personal application, following review, after information on the individual's life, behavior, and modes of existence has been obtained...As Nietzsche says, the main purpose of debt lies in its construction of a subject and a conscience, a self that believes in its specific individuality and that stands as guarantor of its actions. It's way of life and takes responsibility for them."*

Chp. 9, Pg.97 and Chp. 11, Pg.120, Maurizio Lazzarato ("The Making of the Indebted Man" pg.45) *"What is credit? A promise to pay a debt, a promise to repay in a more or less distant and unpredictable future, since it is subject to the radical uncertainty of time. For Nietzsche, making a memory for a man means being able "to have...control over the future. Granting credit requires one to estimate that which is inestimable – future behavior and events-and to expose oneself to the uncertainty of time. The system of debt must therefore neutralize time, that is, the risk inherent to it. It must anticipate and ward off every potential "deviation" in the behavior of the debtor the future might hold...Debt is not only an economic mechanism, it is also a security-state technique of government aimed at reducing the uncertainty of the behavior of the governed. By training the governed to "promise" (to honor their debt), capitalism exercises "control over the future", since debt obligations allow one to foresee, calculate, measure, and establish equivalences between current and future behavior. The effects of the power of debt on subjectivity (guilt and responsibility) allow capitalism to bridge the gap between present and future.*

Chp. 9, Pg. 97 Maurizio Lazzarato ("Governing by Debt" pg.88) *"In finance capitalism, it is impossible to pay off one's debt, since capital, like money, in other words, credit, is by definition debt...reimbursement can never be achieved without destroying the capitalist relation. The creditor-debtor relation can never be settled because it assures both political domination and economic exploitation. To honor one's debts means escaping the creditor/debtor relation and this would mean exiting capitalism altogether. One can honor one's debts, but if one honors all of one's debts there is no longer any asymmetry, any power differential, no stronger or weaker forces – no more capital. Definitive repayment is, logically, the death of capitalism, for credit/debt embodies the class differential...Because credit is the engine of social production, it must be systematically repaid and yet immediately and necessarily renewed, ad infinitum. Capitalism does not free us from debt, it chains us to it."*

Chp. 9, Pg. 98, Joseph Schumpeter ("Capitalism, Socialism and Democracy" Introduction by Thomas K. McCraw XXIII) *"Creative Destruction" – two words he chooses to capitalize. He (Schumpeter) means the endless process of replacing old products and services with new ones, which he presents as 'the essential fact about capitalism.' From this essential fact flows a series of profound consequences – personal, economic, social and political...Creative destruction under capitalism is an often brutal process..."Prizes and penalties are measured in pecuniary terms. Going up and going down means making and losing money...The promises of wealth and the threats of destitution that (this system) holds out, it redeems with ruthless promptitude...Ceaseless innovation in the form of creative destruction bring heavy social costs. Family fortunes are destroyed, whole communities are damaged, and an intellectual class becomes alienated from the very materialism that brought it the leisure to think deep thoughts."*

Chp. 9, Pg. 98 & Chp. 16, Pg.202, Joseph Schumpeter ("Capitalism, Socialism and Democracy" pg. 82) *"The essential point to grasp is that in dealing with capitalism we are dealing with an evolutionary process (long ago emphasized by Karl Marx). Capitalism, then, it by nature a form or method of economic change and not only never is but never can be stationary...The fundamental impulse that sets and keeps the capitalist engine in motion comes from the new consumers' goods, the new methods of production or transportation, the new markets, the new forms of industrial organization that capitalist enterprise creates...if I may use that biological term – that incessantly revolutionizes the economic structure from within, incessantly destroying the old one, incessantly creating a new one. This process of Creative Destruction is the essential fact about capitalism. It is what capitalism consists in and what every capitalist concern has got to live in."*

Chp. 9, Pg. 98, Joseph Schumpeter ("Capitalism, Socialism and Democracy" pg. 26, "Marx the Economist" – Summarizing Marx's Labor Theory of Value) *"What he (Marx) wanted to prove was that exploitation did not arise from intellectual situations occasionally and accidentally; but that it resulted from the very logic of the capitalism system, unavoidable and quite independently of any individual intention. This is how he did it...The brains, muscles, and nerves of the laborer constitute, as it were, a fund or stock of potential labor. Now since labor in that sense is a commodity the law of value must apply to it. That is to say, it must in equilibrium and perfect competition fetch a wage proportional to the number of labor hours that entered into its production. But what number of labor hours enters into the production if the stock of potential labor that is stored up within a workman's skin? Well, the number of labor hours it took and takes to rear, feed, clothe and house the laborer...But once the "capitalists" have acquired that stock of potential services they are in a position to make the laborer work more hours – render more actual services – than it takes to produce that stock or potential stock. They can exact, in this sense, more actual hours of labor than they have paid for. Since the resulting products also sell at a price proportional to the man-hours that enter into their production, there is a difference between the two values – arising from nothing by the 'modus operandi' of Marxian law of values…and by virtue of the mechanism of capitalist markets goes to the capitalist. This is the Surplus Value. By appropriating it the capitalist 'exploits' labor."*

Chp.9, Pg.99, Maurizio Lazzarato ("The Making of the Indebted Man" pg. 139) *"Ratings Agencies: there is nothing democratic about it, since only the financial community is involved. Assessment is done solely by ratings agencies, which are paid by the businesses, banks, or institutions they rate. This entails a huge conflict of interest which no one seems the least troubled by. Ratings agencies are not independent assessment firms but are rather integral to the 'credit power' bloc."*

Chp.9, Pg.100, Maurizio Lazzarato ("The Making of the Indebted Man" pg. 66) *"Student indebtedness exemplifies neoliberalism's strategy since the 1970's: the substitution of social rights (the right to education, health care, retirement, etc.) for access to credit, in other words, for the right to contract debt. No more pooling of pensions, instead individual investment in pension funds; no pay raises, instead consumer credit; no universal insurance, individual insurance; no right to housing, home loans."*

Chp.9, Pg.100, Inspired by Margaret Thatcher's "Right to Buy" passed in the "Housing Act of 1980". (Further Reading: "The right to buy: the housing crisis that Thatcher built" by Andy Beckett, The Guardian, Wed 26, August 2015: https://www.theguardian.com/society/2015/aug/26/right-to-buy-margaret-thatcher-david-cameron-housing-crisis)

Chp. 9, Pg.101, Maurizio Lazzarato ("Governing by Debt" pg. 143 – the infinite in production) *"In capitalism there are no longer "values," there is only 'value'…Capitalism is also the first society to introduce the 'infinite' into the economy and production. The infinite repetition of production, the infinite repetition of consumption, the infinite repetition of appropriation…The law of capital states that the more you drink, the thirstier you are, the more you produce, the more you want to produce, the more you consume the more you want to consume, the more you accumulate the more you want to accumulate. Production, consumption and appropriation provide no possible satisfaction."*

Chp. 9, Pg. 102, Maurizio Lazzarato ("The Making of the Indebted Man" pg. 167, Karl Marx, "The Class Struggles in France") - *"The faction of the bourgeoisie that ruled and legislated through the chambers had a direct interest in the indebtedness of the state. The state deficit was really the main object of its speculation and the chief source of its enrichment. At the end of each year a new deficit. After the lapse of four or five years a new loan. And every new loan offered new opportunities to the finance aristocracy for defrauding the state, which was kept artificially on the verge of bankruptcy – it had to negotiate with the bankers under the most unfavorable conditions. Each new loan gave a further opportunity, that of plundering the public which invested its capital in state bonds."*

Chp. 10, Pg.104, Maurizio Lazzarato ("Governing by Debt" pg. 126, Semiotext(e) 2013) – (French Regulatory Theorist) Andre *"Orlean himself recognizes the subordination of 'public' money to the logic of capitalist valorization. The power of monetary*

sovereignty is contained is 'contained within strict limits. It is difficult if not to say impossible, for it not to validate private monetary creation.' The situation could not be otherwise, since private banks 'hold the monetary initiative,' that is, it is their money that functions as capital. ...Capital still needs the 'sovereignty of state money in order to assure the recognition and validation or non-recognition and non-validation of debts such as those currently overwhelming our societies."

Chp. 10, Pg.107, Maurizio Lazzarato ("Governing by Debt" pg. 185) – *"The independent worker, whose model has been imported from salaried work, functions like an individual enterprise and must ceaselessly negotiate between his economic 'ego' and 'superego' precisely because he is responsible for his own fate ("Should I work or should I take a vacation? Should I turn on my phone and make myself available to even the most meager offer of work or should I turn it off an and make myself unavailable? Etc.) Isolated by 'freedom' itself, the individual is forced to compete not only with others but also with himself. The permanent negotiation with oneself is the form of subjectivation and control specific to neoliberal societies...The order and command must appear to issue from the subject, because 'you're in control!'...Frustration, resentment, guilt, and fear make up the 'passions' of the neoliberal relation to the self, because the promises of self-realization, freedom, and autonomy collide with a reality that systematically nullifies them."*

Chp. 10, Pg.107, Maurizio Lazzarato ("Governing by Debt" pg. 93) – *"Even though neoliberalism equally involves the economy and subjectivity, 'work' and 'work on the self,' it reduces the latter to an injunction to become one's own boss, in the sense of 'taking upon oneself' the costs and risks that business and the state externalize onto society. The promise of what "work on the self" was supposed to being to 'labor' in terms of emancipation (pleasure, self-fulfillment, recognition, experimentation with different forms of life, mobility, etc.) has been rendered void, transformed into the imperative to take on the risks and costs that neither business nor the State are willing to undertake."*

Chp. 10, Pg. 111, Maurizio Lazzarato ("The Making of the Indebted Man" pg. 100) – *"New accounting is supposed to allow for comparisons between companies' financial performance at any point in time and for any business sector...The accounting standards consider the company to be a financial asset whose value is determined by the market...only the joint stock company has a legal existence. On the other hand, the law does not recognize the economic company, in the sense of an entity that produces goods and services. Company actors other than the shareholders, notably, the workers, are not considered owners of the wealth produced, even if they contribute to it directly....Shareholders and financial institutions decide, control, and prescribe the forms of valorization, the accounting procedures, the salary levels, the organization of labor, the pace, and the productivity of the company."*

Chp. 10, Pg. 112, Maurizio Lazzarato ("Governing by Debt" pg. 46) *"To (Carl) Schmitt 'economics is politics'...Schmitt's critiques liberal thinking and its claim to neutralize the political nature of the economy by transforming it into 'economics'. From the lofty perspective of its scientific knowledge, economics asserts that the political solution to the 'social question' depends on the growth of production and consumption, which can be understood and function only according to the laws of the market. Conversely, Schmitt argues that the economy is the contemporary form of the political such that the international division of labor represents the 'true constitution of the earth today."*

Chp. 10, Pg. 117, Karl Polyani ("The Great Transformation": The Political and Economic Origins of Our Time" pg. 72, first Beacon Paperback edition published in 1957, second edition published in 2001) *"The crucial point is this: labor, land, and money are essential elements of industry; they also must be organized in markets; in fact, these markets from an absolutely vital part of the economic system. But labor, land, and money are obviously not commodities; the postulate that anything that is bought and sold must have been produced for sale is emphatically untrue in regard to them...Labor is only another name for human activity which goes with life itself, which in its turn is not produced for sale but for entirely different reasons, nor can that activity be detached from the rest of life, be stored or mobilized; land is only another name for nature, which is not produced by man; actual money, finally, is merely a token of purchasing power which, as a rule, is not produced at all, but comes into being through the mechanism of banking of state finance. None of them is produced for sale. The commodity description of labor, land, and money is entirely fictitious."*

Chp. 10, Pg. 118, David Harvey ("The Seventeen Contradiction and the End of Capitalism" - Private Appropriation and Common Wealth, Oxford University Press 2015, pg. 59) *"It (the commoditization of everything) puts in place of all of this variety of being and living in the world a doctrine of the universal, self-evident and individualised 'rights of man', dedicated to the production of value, that effectively masks in universalistic and naturalised legal doctrine the lurid trail of violence that accompanied the dispossession of indigenous populations. To this day, however, opponents and dissenters to all of this – increasingly viewed as terrorists – are more likely to inhabit the prisons than live in the mini-utopia of the bourgeois suburb."*

Chp. 11, Pg. 122, David Harvey ("The Seventeen Contradiction and the End of Capitalism" - Private Property and the Capital State, pg. 39-40) *"Private property rights presuppose a social bond between that which is owned and a person, defined as a juridical individual, who is the owner and who has the rights of disposition over that which is owned. By a marvelous sleight of juridical reasoning, it has transpired that ownership is vested not only in individuals like you and me but also in corporations and other institutions which, under the law, are defined as legal persons (even though, as many like to point out, corporations cannot be jailed when they do wrong in the same way that living persons can)."*

Chp. 11, Pg. 126, David Harvey ("The Seventeen Contradiction and the End of Capitalism" – Divisions of Labour, pg. 117) *"Capital plainly had to do battle with this monopoly power of labour over its conditions of production and its labour process...First, it gradually asserted its own monopoly power with private property over the means of production, so depriving labourers of the means to reproduce themselves outside of the supervision and control of capital. Many different craft workers could then be brought together under the direction of the capitalist into a process of collective labour to produce anything from nails to steam engines and locomotives. While the narrow technical basis and associated skills of the individual tasks did not change that much, the organisation of production through cooperation and the division of labour brought these different tasks together to reap remarkable gains in efficiency and productivity. The costs of commodities in the marketplace fell rapidly to outcompete the traditional craft and artisanal forms of production."*

Chp. 11, Pg. 127, Frederick Taylor ("The Principles of Scientific Management" - Harper & Brothers 1911) On the term *"Trained Gorilla"* - *"Scientific management is to disaggregate production processes to the point where a 'trained gorilla' would be able to undertake production tasks."*

Chp. 11, Pg. 128, Harry Braverman ("Labor and Monopoly Capital" - Monthly Review Press, 1974, pg. 47) *"Capital, particularly in its monopoly form, has a vested interest in degrading skills and so destroying any sense of pride that might attach to working for capital, while disempowering labor particularly at the point of production."*

Chp. 11, Pg. 128, David Harvey ("The Seventeen Contradiction and the End of Capitalism" – Divisions of Labour, pg. 120) *"What is on capital's agenda is not the eradication of skills per se but the abolition of monopolisable skills. When new skills become important, such as computer programming, then the issue for capital is not necessarily the abolition of those skills (which it may ultimately achieve through artificial intelligence) but the undermining of their potential monopoly character by opening up abundant avenues for training in them. When the labour force equipped with programming skills grows from relatively small to super-abundant, then this breaks monopoly power and brings down the cost of that labour to a much lower level than was formerly the case. When computer programmers are ten-a-penny, then capital is perfectly happy to identify this as one form of skilled labour in its employ, even to the point of conceding a higher rate of remuneration and more respect in the workplace than the social average."*

Chp. 11, Pg. 128, David Harvey ("The Seventeen Contradiction and the End of Capitalism" – Social Reproduction, pg. 188) *"Robert Reich pointed out an emergent division between knowledge-based 'symbolic-analytic' services, routine production, and 'in-person' services. The 'symbolic analysts' included engineers, legal experts, researchers, scientists, professors, executives, journalists, consultants and other 'mind workers', who were primarily engaged in collecting, processing, analysing and manipulating information and symbols for a living. This group of workers, which Reich estimated made up roughly 20 per cent of the labour force in the USA, occupied a privileged position in part because they could practise their trade almost anywhere in the world. They needed, however, to be well educated in analytic and symbolic skills and much of this begins in the home, where, loaded down with electronic gadgets, children learn at an early age how to use and manipulate data and information adequate for an emergent 'knowledge-based' economy. This group forms the core of a relatively affluent though highly mobile upper middle class within capitalism and one that increasingly tends to segregate itself (and to enclose its processes of social reproduction) in privileged enclaves away from the rest of society. By way of contrast, traditional production workers (for example, in steel and car production) and ordinary service workers have very little future, in part because those are the jobs most likely to disappear and in part because even those jobs that remain are likely to be low-wage with very scant benefits simply because of the massive labour surpluses now available."*

Chp. 12, Pg. 137, Michael Hardt, Antonio Negri ("Declaration" - Argo-Navis, 2012, pg.16): *"The center of gravity of capitalist production no longer resides in the factory but has drifted outside its walls. Society has become a factory...With this shift the primary engagement between capitalist and worker also changes...Exploitation today is based primarily not on (equal or unequal) exchange but on debt."*

Chp. 12, Pg. 142, Deng Xiaoping "To Get Rich is Glorious" (Chinese Leader 1980s – however it is not proven he actually made this famous quote; "Great Idea but Don't Quote Him" LA Times, 2003, https://www.latimes.com/archives/la-xpm-2004-sep-09-fi-deng9-story.html_)

Chp. 12, Pg. 146, Mike Horwath, Michael Oswald (Documentary, "97% Owned" available on Real Truth Documentaries and Independent POV) https://www.youtube.com/watch?v=XcGhlDex4Yo (May 1, 2012): *"Increasing house prices makes us all feel like we're all becoming wealthier, but it also means that our future generations will have to pay more for that same property."*

Chp. 12, Pg. 148, David Harvey ("The Seventeen Contradiction and the End of Capitalism" – Capital and Labour, pg. 67): *"What labour wins in the domain of production is stolen back by the landlords, the merchants (for example, the telephone companies), the bankers (for example, credit card charges), the lawyers and commission agents, while a large chunk of what is left also goes to the taxman. as with the case of housing, the privatisation and commodity provision of medical care, education, water and sewage, and other basic services, diminish the discretionary income available to labour and recapture value for capital."*

Chp. 12, Pg. 149, David Harvey ("Marx, Capital and the Madness of Economic Reason" – Capital, Oxford University Press, 2018, pg. 47) *"Increasing the minimum wage or creating a basic income will amount to naught if hedge funds buy up foreclosed houses and pharmaceutical patents and raise prices (in some cases astronomically) to line their own pockets out of the increased effective demand exercised by the population. increasing college tuitions, usurious interest rates on credit cards, all sorts of hidden charges on telephone bills and medical insurance could steal away all the benefits. A population might be better served by strict regulatory intervention to control these living expenses, to limit the vast amount of wealth appropriation occurring at the point of realization."*

Chp. 13, Maurizio Lazzarato ("Governing by Debt" – The Infinite in Production, pg.143) *"The law of capital states that the more you drink, the thirstier you are, the more you produce, the more you want to produce, the more you consume the more you want to consume, the more you accumulate the more you want to accumulate. Production, consumption and appropriation provide no possible satisfaction. The cycle of capital can be described as a series of desires/frustrations that feed off each other forever."*

Chp. 13, Pg. 163, David Harvey ("The Seventeen Contradiction and the End of Capitalism" – The Social Value of Labour and Its Representation by Money, pg. 26, expanding on Karl Marx) *"In the case of social labour, 'value' speaks to why shoes cost more than shirts, houses cost more than cars and wine costs more than water. These differences in value between commodities have nothing to do with their character as use values (apart from the simple fact that they must all be useful to someone somewhere) and everything to do with the social labour involved in their production."*

Chp. 13, Pg. 164, David Harvey ("The Seventeen Contradiction and the End of Capitalism" – The Social Value of Labour and Its Representation by Money, pg. 33) *"The fact that money permits social power to be appropriated and exclusively utilised by private persons places money at the centre of a wide range of noxious human behaviours – lust and greed for money power inevitably become central features in the body politic of capitalism. All sorts of fetishistic behaviours and beliefs centre on this. The desire for money as a form of social power becomes an end in itself which distorts the neat demand–supply relation of the money that would be required simply to facilitate exchange. This throws a monkey wrench into the supposed rationality of capitalist markets."*

Chp. 13, Pg. 167, Christian Marazzi ("The Violence of Financial Capitalism" Semiotext(e), 2011, pg.40) *"The expansion of subprime loans shows that, in order to raise and make profits, finance needs to involve the poor, in addition to the middle class. In order to function, this capitalism must invest in the bare life of people who cannot provide any guarantee, who offer nothing apart from themselves. It is capitalism that turns bare life into a direct source of profit...the greater lot is thus protected by the lesser ones, in the sense that the latter will be the most exposed part of the securitized assets that will be the first to explode. The access to a good house is created on the basis of mathematical models of risk where people's life means absolutely nothing, where the poor are "played" against the less poor, where the social right to housing is artificially subordinated to the private right to realize a profit."*

Chp. 13, Pg. 168, Albert Camus ("The Estranged God: Modern Man's Search for Belief" 1966, by Anthony T. Padovano, p. 109) *"With rebellion, awareness is born."*

Chp. 14, Pg. 172, David Harvey ("The Seventeen Contradiction and the End of Capitalism" – Divisions of Labour, pg.125-126) *"The undoubted and astonishing gains in productivity, output and profitability that capital achieves by virtue of its organisation of both the detail and the social division of labour come at the cost of the mental, emotional and physical well-being of the workers in its employ. The worker, Marx for one suggests, is typically reduced to a 'fragment of a man' by virtue of his or her attachment to a fixed position within an increasingly complex division of labour. Workers are isolated and individualised, alienated from each other by competition, alienated from a sensual relation to nature (from both their own nature as passionate and sensuous human beings and that of the external world)...All creativity, spontaneity and charm go out of the work. The activity of working for capital becomes, in short, empty and meaningless, and human beings cannot live in a world devoid of all meaning."*

Chp. 14, Pg. 174, Albert Einstein ("Out of My Later Years: The Scientist, Philosopher, and Man Portrayed Through His Own Words" - p.20, Open Road Media) *"The high destiny of the individual is to serve rather than to rule."*

Chp. 14, Pg. 175, re: Capitalist Alienation, and Alienation embedded within Capital, David Harvey ("Anti-Capitalist Chronicles: Alienation – Part 1", Democracy At Work) https://www.youtube.com/watch?v=01A0prJud-A

Chp. 14, Pg. 176, David Harvey ("The Seventeen Contradiction and the End of Capitalism" – Social Reproduction, pg.183-184) *"Faced with the persistent pursuit of self-education on the part of at least an influential segment of the working classes, capital had to come up with something to put in its place. as Mr. Dombey put it in Charles Dickens's Dombey and Son, he had no objection to public education provided it taught the worker his proper place in society. Marx, for his part, while critical of much of the socialist utopian literature, learned mightily from it and likewise sought to create a whole anti-capitalist knowledge field that would provide a fount of ideas for anti-capitalist agitation. Heaven forbid the workers read such stuff."*

Chp. 14, Pg.176, Adam Smith (founder) on "Human Capital Theory" (*"An Inquiry into the Nature and Causes of the Wealth of Nations Book 2 – Of the Nature, Accumulation, and Employment of Stock"*; Published 1776.) *"The acquired and useful abilities of all the inhabitants or members of the society. The acquisition of such talents, by the maintenance of the acquirer during his education, study, or apprenticeship, always costs a real expense, which is a capital fixed and realized, as it were, in his person. Those talents, as they make a part of his fortune, so do they likewise that of the society to which he belongs. The improved dexterity of a workman may be considered in the same light as a machine or instrument of trade which facilitates and abridges labor, and which, though it costs a certain expense, repays that expense with a profit."*

Chp. 14, Pg. 176, David Harvey ("The Seventeen Contradiction and the End of Capitalism" – Social Reproduction, pg.184-185) *"As so often happens within the history of capital, education ultimately became a 'big business' unto itself. The stunning inroads of privatisation and fee paying into what had traditionally been public and free education have placed financial burdens on the populace such that those desirous of education have to pay for this key aspect of social reproduction themselves. The consequences of creating a heavily debt-encumbered educated labour force may take a considerable time to work out. But if the street battles between students and authorities in Santiago Chile that began in 2006 and have continued to this day over the expensive privatisation of both high school and advanced education are anything to go by, then this too will likely be a simmering source of discontent wherever it has been implemented."*

Chp. 14, Pg. 181, David Harvey ("The Seventeen Contradiction and the End of Capitalism" – Social Reproduction, pg.185-186) *"In recent times, for example, worker productivity has surged but the share of output going to labour has declined, not increased. in any case, if what the worker truly possessed in bodily form was capital, Marx pointed out, then he or she would be entitled to sit back and just live off the interest of his or her capital without doing a single day's work (capital as a property relation always has that option at hand). As far as I can tell, the main point of the revival of human capital theory, at the hands of Gary Becker in the 1960s, for example, was to bury the significance of the class relation between capital and labour and make it seem as if we are all just capitalists earning different rates of return on our capital (human or otherwise). If labour was getting very low wages, it could then be argued that this was simply a reflection of the fact that workers had not invested enough effort in building up their human capital! It was, in short, their fault if they were low-paid. Hardly surprisingly, all the major institutions of capital, from economics departments to the World Bank and the IMF, wholeheartedly embraced this theoretical fiction for ideological and certainly not for sound intellectual reasons."*

Chp. 14, Pg. 182, In reference to "Citizens United" - Citizens United v. Federal Election Commission, 558 U.S. 310 (2010), is a landmark United States Supreme Court case concerning campaign finance.

Chp. 15, Overall influenced from David Harvey ("The Seventeen Contradiction and the End of Capitalism" – Freedom vs. Domination, Chp. 14)

Chp. 15, Pg. 185, Simone Weil ("The Notebooks of Simone Weil" p.615, Grace and Gravity, Routledge) *"Distance is the Soul of Beauty."*

Chp. 15, Pg. 186, Kevin O'Leary (Shark Tank, ABC) *"Here's how I think of my money, as soldiers. I send them out to war every day. I want them to take prisoners and come home, so there's more of them."*

Chp. 15, Pg. 189, Karl Polanyi ("The Great Transformation: The Political and Economic Origins of Our Time" pg. 256) *"The passing of market economy can become the beginning of an era of unprecedented freedom. Juridical and actual freedom can be made much wider and more general than ever before; regulation and control can achieve freedom not only for the few, but for all. Freedom, not as an appurtenance of privilege, tainted at the source, but as a prescriptive right extending far beyond the narrow confines of the political sphere into the intimate organization of society itself. Thus will old freedoms and civil rights be added to the fund of new freedom generated by the leisure and security that industrial society offers to all. Such a society can afford to be just and free."*

Chp. 15, Pg. 195, Karl Marx ("Capital" pg. 235) *"Between equal rights force decides."*

Chp. 15, Pg. 199, Noam Chomsky ("Profit Over People: Neoliberalism and Global Order" Seven Stories Press, 1999, pg. 43) *"Hume was intrigued by 'the easiness with which the many are governed by the few', the implicit submission with which men resign their fate to their rulers. This he found surprising, because 'force is always on the side of the governed.' If people would realize that, they would rise up and overthrow the masters. He concluded that government is founded on control of opinion, a principle that extends to most depotic military governments, as well as to the most free and most popular. Hume surely underestimated the effectiveness of brute force."*

Chp. 16, Pg. 203, David Harvey ("Marx, Capital, and the Madness of Economic Reason" pg. 204) *"The disciplining effect of debt encumbrance is vital to the reproduction of the contemporary form of capital. Debt means we are no longer 'free to choose', as Milton Friedman in his paean to capitalism supposes. Capital does not forgive us our debts, as the Bible asks, but insists we redeem them through future value production. The future is already foretold and foreclosed (ask any student who has $100,000 in student loans to pay). Debt imprisons within certain structures of future value production. Debt peonage is capital's favoured means to impose its particular form of slavery. This becomes doubly dangerous when the power of the bondholders subverts and seeks to imprison the sovereignty of the state. It is for this reason that the only mode of capital's survival is through the coherence and fusion achieved through the state–finance nexus. With this, the alienation of whole populations from any real influence and power is complete."*

Chp. 16, Pg. 204, Paul Mason ("Post Capitalism" Penguin Random House, 2015, pg. 136) *"In the 'Fragment on Machines' (Karl Marx), had the idea – that the driving force of production is knowledge, and that knowledge stored in machines is social – led Marx to the following conclusions....First, in a heavily mechanized capitalism, boosting productivity through better knowledge is a much more attractive source of profit than extending the working day, or speeding up labor: longer days consume more energy, speed-ups hit the limits of human dexterity and stamina. But a knowledge solution is cheap and limitless.*

Chp. 16, Pg. 204, Joseph Schumpeter ("Capitalism, Socialism and Democracy" pg. 152-153) *"One of the most important features of the later stages of capitalist civilization is the vigorous expansion of the educational apparatus and particularly of the facilities for higher education. This development was and is no less inevitable than the development of the largest-scale industrial unit, but, unlike the latter, it has been and is being fostered by public opinion and public authority so as to go much further than it would have done under its own steam....There are several consequences that bear upon the size and attitude of the intellectual group....as higher education thus increases the supply of services in professional and semi-professional and in the end all "white collar" lines beyond the point determined by cost-return considerations, it may create a particularly important case of sectional unemployment. Second, along with or in place of such unemployment, it creates unsatisfactory conditions of employment – employment in substandard work or at wages below those of the better-paid manual workers...All those who are unemployed or unsatisfactorily employed or unemployable drift into vocations in which standards are least definite or in which aptitudes and acquirements of a different order count. They swell the host of intellectuals in the strict sense of the term whose numbers hence increase disproportionately. They enter society in a thoroughly discontented frame of mind. Discontent breeds resentment."*

Chp. 16, Pg. 206, Overall influenced by David Graeber ("Bullshit Jobs, A Theory" Simon & Schuster, 2018)

Chp. 16, Pg. 207, Kurzgesagt – In a Nutshell ("The Rise of the Machines – Why Automation is Different this Time" https://www.youtube.com/watch?v=WSKi8HfcxEk)

Chp. 16, Pg. 208, Paul Mason ("Post Capitalism" pg. 167) *"Machines where parts of value are input for free by social knowledge and public science are not alien concepts for the labour-theroy. They are central to it. But Marx thought that is they existed in large numbers they would explode the system based on values – "blow it sky high"....The worked exp. Marx uses in the Grundisse makes it clear: a machine that lasts forever, or can be made with no labour, cannot add any labour hours to the value of the products it makes. If a machine lasts forever it transfers a near-zero amount of labour value to the product, from here to eternity, and the value of each product is thus reduced."*

Chp. 16, Pg. 209, David Harvey "(Marx, Capital, and the Madness of Economic Reason" pg. 120) *"The fetish belief in technological fixes and innovations as the answer to all problems takes deeper root as does the false idea that this must be the prime mover. This fetish belief is nurtured by that segment of capital that transforms innovation and technology into a big business with consultants on organisational form peddling recipes for better management, pharmaceutical companies creating remedies for diseases that do not exist, and computer experts insisting on automation systems that no one except a few experts can understand. Capitalist entrepreneurs and corporations adopt innovations not because they want to but because they are persuaded to or have to in order to acquire or retain their market share and thereby ensure their reproduction as capitalists."*

Chp. 17, Pg. 216, David Harvey ("Marx, Capital, and the Madness of Economic Reason" pg. 188-189) *"Step back a moment and think about what is happening...The investment in high-end condos for the rich and the ultra-rich in New York City where there is a crisis of affordable housing and 60,000 homeless people on the streets. The seething slums of Mumbai are punctuated by palatial buildings for the newly minted billionaires. Many of these high-end buildings are not lived in. Walk the streets of New york and see how many lights are on at night in those spectacular condos for the affluent soaring high into the night sky. The buildings are simply investment vehicles not only for the ultra-rich but for anyone who has some spare cash to save...It's not only the billionaires who are doing it. Upper-middle-class people are pursuing a property and land grab wherever they can. Workers' pension funds invest in predatory real estate equity schemes because that is where the rate of return is highest. It can happen that these funds connive at the eviction of tenants who have investments in the pension funds that provide the financing. Capital is building cities for people and institutions to invest in, not cities for the common people to live in. How sane is this?"*

Chp. 17, Pg. 217, David Harvey ("Marx, Capital, and the Madness of Economic Reason" pg. 83) *"The formation and circulation of interest-bearing capital is in effect the circulation of anti-value. It may seem strange to think of the main financial centres of today's global capitalism, such as the City of London, Wall Street, Frankfurt, Shanghai and the like as centres of anti-value formation but that is what all those debt bottling plants that dominate the skylines in these global cities truly signify. The danger, which Marx hinted at in his writings on banking, finance and fictitious capital formation, is that capital will degenerate into one vast Ponzi scheme in which last year's debts are retired by borrowing even more money today. The central banks are currently creating sufficient new money to prop up stock exchange and asset values for the benefit of the oligarchy in the here and now. This then leaves the central bank with the problem of how to retire the debts they have accumulated on their balance sheets... The rich grow richer through financial manipulations while the poor become poorer through the necessity to redeem their debts (both individual and collective as in state borrowings)."*

Chp. 17, Pg. 219,222-3, "Margin Call" (Written and Direct by J.C. Chandor, 2011, Produced by Before the Door Pictures, Benaroya Pictures, Washington Square Films).

Will Emerson (Paul Bettany) to Seth (Penn Badgley):

"If you really want to do this with your life you have to believe that you're necessary, and you are. People want to live like this with their cars and their big fucking houses they can't even pay for - then you're necessary. The only reason people get to continue living like kings is because we've got our fingers on the scales and we're tipping in their favor. I take my hand off, well then the whole world gets really fucking fair really fucking quick and nobody actually wants that. They say they do, but they really don't. They want what we have to give but they also want to play innocent and pretend they have no idea where it actually came from; and that's more hypocrisy than I'm willing to swallow, so fuck 'em."

Sam Rogers (Kevin Spacey) with John Tuld (Jeremy Irons):

Sam Rogers: The real question is: who are we selling this to?
John Tuld: The same people we've been selling it to for the last two years, and whoever else would buy it.
Sam Rogers: But John, if you do this, you will kill the market for years. It's over. And you're selling something that you know has no value.
John Tuld: We are selling to willing buyers at the current fair market price. So that we may survive.
Sam Rogers: You would never sell anything to any of those people ever again.
John Tuld: I understand.
Sam Rogers: Do you?
John Tuld: Do you? This is it! I'm telling you this is it!

Chp. 17, Pg. 224, James Rickards ("The Death of Money" - Debt, Deficits, and the Dollar)

(pg. 247) – "Student loans are the new subprime mortgages: another government subsidized bubble about to burst...Most of the loans are sound and will be repaid as agreed, but many borrowers will default because the students did not acquire needed skills and cannot find jobs in a listless economy. Those defaults will make federal budget deficits worse, a development not fully reflected in official budget projections. In effect, student loans are being pumped out by the US Treasury and directed to borrowers with a high propensity to spend and a limited ability to repay...It is economically no different than the Chinese building ghost cities with money that cannot be repaid. Chinese ghost cities and US diplomas are real, but productivity increases and the ability to repay the borrowings are not...the long term effects of excessive debt combined with the absence of jobs are another encumbrance on the economy."

(pg. 290) – "The crux of the problem in the global financial system today is not money but debt. Money creation is being used as a means to deal with defaulted debt. By 2005 the US led by bankers whose self-interest blinded them to any danger, poisoned the world with excessive debt in mortgages and lines of credit to borrowers who could not repay. By itself, the mortgage problem was large but manageable. Unmanageable were the trillions of dollars in derivatives created from the underlying mortgages and trillions more in repurchase agreements, and commercial paper used to finance the mortgage backed securities inventories supporting the derivatives. When the inevitable crash came, the losses were not apportioned to those responsible – the banks and bondholders – but were passed on to the public through federal finance."

(pg. 265) – "An avalanche is an apt metaphor of financial collapse. Indeed, it is more than a metaphor, because the systems analysis of an avalanche is identical to the analysis of how one bank collapse cascades into another. An avalanche starts with a snowflake that perturbs other snowflakes, which, as momentum builds, tumble out of control. The snowflake is like a single bank failure, followed by sequential panic, ending in fired financiers forced to vacate the premises of ruined Wall Street firms. Both the avalanche and the bank panic are examples of what physicists call a phase transition: a rapid, unforeseen transformation from a steady state to disintegration, finally coming to rest in a new state completely unlike the starting place.

(pg. 267) – "In capital markets, regulators too often do not stay safe; rather, they increase the danger. Permitting banks to build up derivatives books is like ignoring snow accumulation. Allowing JP Morgan Chase to grow larger is like building a village directly beneath an avalanche path...Financial avalanches are goaded by greed, but greed is not a complete explanation. Bankers' parasitic behavior, the result of a cultural phase transition, is entirely characteristic of a society nearing collapse. Wealth is no longer created, it is taken from others. Parasitic behavior is not confined to bankers; it also infects high government officials, corporate executives, and the elite societal stratum.

(pg. 270) – "When a complex system is doubled, the systemic risk does not double, it may

increase by a factor of ten or more. This is why each financial collapse comes as a "surprise" to bankers and regulators. As systemic scale is increased by derivatives, systemic risk grows exponentially."

Chp. 18, Pg. 226, David Harvey ("Marx, Capital, and the Madness of Economic Reason" pg. 202) *"In a system of production where the entire interconnection of the reproduction process rests on credit, a crisis must evidently break out if credit is suddenly withdrawn and only cash payment is accepted ... at first glance, therefore, the entire crisis presents itself as simply a credit and monetary crisis, and in fact all it does involve is simply the convertibility of bills of exchange [mortgages] into money. The majority of these bills [mortgages] represent actual purchases and sales, the ultimate basis of the entire crisis being the expansion of these far beyond the social need. On top of this, however, a tremendous number of these bills [mortgages] represent purely fraudulent deals, which now come to light and explode, as well as unsuccessful speculations conducted with the borrowed capital, and finally commodity capitals [houses] that are either devalued or unsaleable."*

(pg. 207) *"Marx wrote, that 'a devaluation of credit money ... would destroy all the existing relationships'. The banks, as we now all too well know, must be rescued no matter what. 'The value of commodities is thus sacrificed in order to ensure the fantastic and autonomous existence of this value in money. in any event, a money value is only guaranteed as long as money itself is guaranteed.' Inflation, as we also know, must be kept under control at all costs. 'This is why many millions' worth of commodities have to be sacrificed for a few millions in money. This is unavoidable in capitalist production and forms one of its particular charms.' Use values are sacrificed and destroyed no matter what the social need."*

Chp. 18, Pg. 227-8, Christian Marazzi ("The Violence of Financial Capitalism" pg.48) *"The nationalization of banks in the insolvency crisis is seen as inescapable and/or desirable...Toxic assets to the State i.e., to the collectivity, the good banks to the private citizens! This is the usual song: socialize the losses and privative the benefits."*

Chp. 18, Pg. 228, on Government Subsidies to Banking; Mike Horwath, Michael Oswald ("97% Owned Economic Truth Documentary, how is Money Created" 2012) Independent POV https://www.youtube.com/watch?v=XcGh1Dex4Yo

Chp. 18, Pg. 229, Maurizio Lazzarato ("The Making of the Indebted Man", pg.115 - The Sovereign Debt Crisis): *"The debt problem is still very much with us. It has only shifted from private debt to sovereign State debt. The enormous sums that States have handed over to banks, insurance companies, and institutional investors must now be "reimbursed" by the taxpayers (and not by the shareholders and purchasers of stock). The highest costs will be borne by wage-earners, beneficiaries of public programs, and the poorest of the population...States have not rescued a functional structure of real economy financing, but rather a mechanism for domination and exploitation specific to modern-day capitalism. And, in a cynical turn, the costs of reestablishing this relation of exploitation and domination will have to be paid for by its victims."*

Chp. 18, Pg. 229, as influenced by Dr. Richard Wolff, re: middle class taxes and politics

Chp. 18, Pg. 233, Andrew Mellon (American Banker, Industrialist, Politician, 49th U.S. Secretary of the Treasury, 1855-1937) *"In a crisis, assets return to their return owners."* (i.e. him)

Chp. 18, Pg. 233, Karl Marx (Theory of Crisis) *"Crises do not necessarily spell out the end of capitalism but set the stage for its renewal."*

Chp. 18, Pg. 235, David Harvey ("Marx, Capital, and the Madness of Economic Reason" pg. 86-87) *"The depreciation of housing values in the crisis of 2007–8 in the United States left behind a huge stock of housing use values that could be bought up by private equity companies and hedge funds for a song and put back into profitable use. Marx was fully aware of such possibilities. He notes how capital 'undertakes investments which do not pay and which pay only as soon as they have become in a certain degree devalued ... (and) the many undertakings where the first investment is sunk and lost, the first entrepreneurs go bankrupt – and begin to realize themselves only at second or third hand, where the investment capital has become smaller owing to devaluation."*

Chp. 18 Overall, influenced by "Too Big to Fail" American biographical drama television film first broadcast on HBO on May 23, 2011 based on Andrew Ross Sorkin's non-fiction book Too Big to Fail: The Inside Story of How Wall Street and Washington Fought to Save the Financial System—and Themselves (2009).

Chp. 19, Pg. 238, Dr. Richard Wolff (on the Thom Hartmann Program, April 4, 2019) Can Interest Rates Hold Off Recession? - https://www.youtube.com/watch?v=RJCXnqR6wU8

Chp. 19, Pg. 239, David Harvey ("The Seventeen Contradiction and the End of Capitalism" – Monopoly and Competition: Centralisation and Decentralisation, pg.131) *"Read any economics text or popular defence of capitalism and the word 'competition' will almost certainly very soon crop up. in popular defences as well as in more serious theoretical works, one of the great success stories of capitalism is that it supposedly takes the natural proclivity of human beings to compete, unleashes it from social constraints and harnesses it through the market to produce a dynamic and progressive social system that can function for the benefit of all. Monopoly power (of the sort that Google, Microsoft and amazon wield these days) and its cognates like oligopoly (of the sort that the 'Seven Sisters' major global oil companies possess) and monopsony (the power that Walmart and apple exert over their suppliers) all tend to be presented (if they are mentioned at all) as aberrations, as unfortunate departures from a state of happy equilibrium that should be achieved in a purely competitive market. This biased view – for such I maintain it is – is supported by the existence of anti-trust and anti-monopoly legislation and commissions which proclaim how bad monopolies are and from time to time set out to break them up in order to protect the public from their negative effects."*

Chp. 19, Pg. 241, re: How Markets Distribute Things, as influenced by Dr. Richard Wolff (Economic Update: Democracy at Work – For Economic Justice)

Chp. 19, Pg. 242, Joseph Schumpeter ("Capitalism, Socialism and Democracy" pg.131-132) *"Technological progress is increasingly becoming the business of teams of trained specialists who turn out what is required and make it work in predictable ways. The romance of earlier commercial adventure is rapidly wearing away, because so many more things can be strictly calculated that had of old to be visualized in a flash of genius... Thus, economic progress tends to become depersonalized and automatized. Bureau and committee work tends to replace individual action...The leading man no longer has the opportunity to fling himself into the fray. He is becoming just another office worker—and one who is not always difficult to replace."*

Chp. 19, Pg. 243, Joseph Schumpeter ("Capitalism, Socialism and Democracy" pg.158-159) *"The arrangements summarized by the term Home were accordingly accepted as a matter of course by the average man and woman of bourgeois standing, exactly as they looked upon marriage and children—the "founding of a family"—as a matter of course. Now, on the one hand, the amenities of the bourgeois home are becoming less obvious than are its burdens. To the critical eye of a critical age it is likely to appear primarily as a source of trouble and expense which frequently fail to justify themselves. This would be so even independently of modern taxation and wages and of the attitude of modern household personnel, all of which are typical results of the capitalist process and of course greatly strengthen the case against what in the near future will be almost universally recognized as an outmoded and uneconomical way of life."*

Chp. 19, Pg.244, *"Seafaring is necessary, living is not necessary."* Inscription on an old house in Bremen, Germany

Chp. 19, Pg. 252-4, Karl Polyani ("The Great Transformation: The Political and Economic Origins of Our Time") *"Social history in the 19th century was thus the result of a double movement: the extension of the market organization in respect to genuine commodities was accompanied by its restriction in respect to fictitious ones. While on the one hand markets spread all over the face of the globe and the amount of goods involved grew to unbelievable proportions, on the other hand a network of measures and policies was integrated into powerful institutions designed to check the action of the market relative to labor, land, and money. (pg. 76) Double movement can be personified as the action of two organizing principles in society, each of them setting itself specific institutional aims, having the support of definite social forces and using its own distinctive methods. The one was the principle of economic liberalism, aiming at the establishment of a self-regulating market, relying on the support of the trading classes, and using largely laissez faire and free trade as its methods; the other was the principle of social protection aiming at the conservation of man and nature as well as productive organization, relying on the varying support of those most immediately affected by the deleterious action of the market - primarily, but not exclusively, the working and the landed classes – and using protective legislation, restrictive associations, and other instruments of intervention as its methods.*

Chp. 19, Pg. 253, Gilles Deleuze and Felix Guattar ("Anti-Oedipus – Capitalism and Schizophrenia" pg.197) *"Michel Foucault shows how, in certain Greek tyrannies, the tax on aristocrats and the distribution of money to the poor are a means of bringing the money back to the rich and a means of remarkably widening the regime of debts, making it even stronger, by anticipating and repressing any reterritorialization that might be produced by the economic givens of the agrarian problem.48 (As if the Greeks had discovered in their own way what the Americans rediscovered after the New Deal: that heavy taxes are good for business.) In a word, money—the circulation of money—is the means for rendering the debt infinite."*

Chp. 19, Pg. 254, re: Geography of money flows from poor regions to rich ones. Michael Oswald (Writer, Director, Producer) The Spider's Web: Britain's Second Empire (Documentary, Sept. 14, 2018) https://www.youtube.com/watch?v=np_ylvc8Zj8

Chp. 19, Pg. 254, Karl Polyani ("The Great Transformation: The Political and Economic Origins of Our Time" pg.76) *"Human society would have been annihilated but for protective countermoves which blunted the action of this self-destructive mechanism."*

Chp. 20, Pg.257, Baruch Spinoza (The Letters, pg. 146, xix) *"Of all the things that are beyond my power, I value nothing more highly than to be allowed the honor of entering into bonds of friendship with people who sincerely love truth. For, of things beyond our power, I believe there is nothing in the world which we can love with tranquility except such men."*

Chp. 20, Pg.261, Christian Marazzi ("The Violence of Financial Capitalism" pg.31) *"The transition from the Fordist mode of production to "stock managerial capitalism," which is at the basis of today's financial capitalism, is, in fact, explained by the drops in profits...the drop due to the exhaustion of the technological and economic foundations of Fordism, particularly by the saturation of markets by mass consumption goods, the rigidity of productive process, of constant capital, and of the politically "downwardly rigid" working wage. At the height of its development...Fordist capitalism was no longer able to "suck" surplus-value from living working labor...we know how it went: reduction in the cost of labor, attacks on syndicates, automatization and robotization of entire labor processes, delocalization in countries with low wages, precarization of work, and diversification of consumption models..Non-financial companies would drastically increase their own investments in financial products with respect to industrial plants and machinery and became ever more dependent on the quota of income and profits derived from their own financial investments with respect to the one derived from their productive activity. (pg.103) "By simultaneously reducing social spending and taxes (reductions that above all benefit business and the wealthiest segments of the population), neoliberal State policies have engaged a twofold process: a massive transfer of revenue to business and the wealthiest and an expansion of deficits due to fiscal policies, deficits which have in turn become a source of revenue for creditors buying state debt. The "virtuous circle" of the debt economy is thus complete."*

Chp. 20, Pg.263, David Harvey ("The Seventeen Contradiction and the End of Capitalism" – Endless Compound Growth pg.245) *"The parasitic forms of capital are now in the ascendant. We see their representatives gliding through the streets in limousines and populating all the upmarket restaurants and penthouses in all the major global cities of the world – New york, London, Frankfurt, Tokyo, São Paulo, Sydney ... These are the so-called creative cities, where creativity is measured by how successfully the 'masters of the universe' can suck the living life out of the global economy to support a class whose one aim is to compound its own already immense wealth and power. New york City has a huge concentration of creative talent – creative accountants and tax lawyers, creative financiers armed with glitteringly new financial instruments, creative manipulators of information, creative hustlers and sellers of snake oil, creative media consultants, all of which makes it a wondrous place to study every single fetish that capital can construct."*

Chp. 20, Pg.264, Elisee Reclus, ("Anarchy, Geography, Modernity" edited by John P. Clark and Camille Martin, Oxford, Lexington Books, 2004, pg. 124) *"At the seashore, many of the most picturesque cliffs and charming beaches are snatched up either by covetous landlords or by speculators who appreciate the beauties of nature in the spirit of a money changer appraising a gold ingot ... Each natural curiosity, be it rock, grotto, waterfall, or the fissure of a glacier – everything, even the sound of an echo – can become individual property. The entrepreneurs lease waterfalls and enclose them with wooden fences to prevent non-paying travelers from gazing at the turbulent waters. Then, through a deluge of advertising, the light that plays about the scattering droplets and the puffs of wind unfurling curtains of mist are transformed into the resounding jingle of silver."*

Chp. 20, Pg. 264-5, David Harvey ("Marx, Capital, and the Madness of Economic Reason" – Prices without Values, pg. 94) *"The qualitative incongruity between value and price is troubling and may be more significant than Marx allowed. The contradiction between them may have sharpened over time. If investors seek speculative gains in price-fixing markets for assets which have no value (such as art objects or currency and carbon futures) instead of investing in value and surplus value creation, then this indicates a pathway by which value can be leached out of the general circulation of capital to circulate as money in fictitious markets where no direct value production (as opposed to appropriation) occurs. When price signals betray the values they are supposed to represent then investors are bound to make erroneous decisions."*

Chp. 21, pg. 277, Maurizio Lazzarato ("Governing by Debt" pg.165) *"Capitalism would have us believe that it functions like an automation, that there is no alternative precisely because the market, the stock market and the debt economy are governed by automatic operations...In reality, when automatic mechanisms function, it is always the result of a political victory over conducts."*

Chp. 21, pg. 283, as influenced by the events of the Holocaust. The character holding hands en route to the incinerator as influenced by Toy Story 3 (directed by Lee Unkrich, written by Michael Arndt, story by John Lasseter, Andrew Stanton, Lee Unkrich)

Chp. 21, pg. 282-3, Martin Ford on "redundant populations" from the perspective of capital ("The Lights in the Tunnel: Automation, Accelerating Technology and the Economy of the Future" USA, acculant TM Publishing, 2009, p. 62) *"As the cutting edge of technological dynamism shifts from mechanical and biological systems to artificial intelligence, so we will see a huge impact upon job availability not only in manufacturing and agriculture but also in services and even in the professions. aggregate demand for goods and services will consequently collapse as jobs and incomes disappear. This will have catastrophic effects upon the economy unless some way is found for the state to intervene with targeted redistributive stimulus payments to those large segments of the population that have become redundant and disposable...Who is going to step forward and purchase all this increased output? ... Automation stands poised to fall across the board – on nearly every industry, on a wide range of occupations, and on workers with graduate degrees as well as on those without high school diplomas. automation will come to the developed nations and to the developing ones. The consumers that drive our markets are virtually all people who either have a job or depend on someone who has a job. When a substantial fraction of these people are no longer employed, where will market demand come from?"*

Chp. 21, pg. 282-3, David Harvey on "redundant populations" from the perspective of capital, and Martin Ford ("The Seventeen Contradiction and the End of Capitalism" pg.111) *"Martin Ford correctly poses the question: how will the resultant disposable and redundant population live (let alone provide a market) under such conditions? A viable long-term and imaginative answer to this question has to be devised by any anti-capitalist movement."*

(pg.249) *"It may be perfectly possible for capital to continue to circulate and accumulate in the midst of environmental catastrophes. Environmental disasters create abundant opportunities for a 'disaster capitalism' to profit handsomely. Deaths from starvation of exposed and vulnerable populations and massive habitat destruction will not necessarily trouble capital (unless it provokes rebellion and revolution) precisely because much of the world's population has become redundant and disposable anyway. And capital has never shrunk from destroying people in pursuit of profit."*

Chp. 21, overall influenced by Polish author Stanislaw Lem, ("Memoirs of a Space Traveler: The Further Reminiscences of Ijon Tichy", Evanston,IL: Northwestern University Press,1981[1971]19–20). *"Finally, realizing a system where both production and consumption were being done by machines was rather pointless, they concluded the best solution would be for the entire population to render itself—entirely voluntarily—to the factories to be converted into beautiful shiny disks and arranged in pleasant patterns across the landscape."*

Chp. 22, pg. 290, re: ethics and the nature of evil, influenced by Hannah Arendt (Eichmann in Jerusalem: A Report on the Banality of Evil, Viking Press 1963)

Chp. 22, pg. 290, Willie's speech, influenced by Winston Churchill's speech "We Shall Fight on the Beaches" - a common title given to a speech delivered by Winston Churchill to the House of Commons of the Parliament of the United Kingdom on 4 June 1940.

Chp. 22, pg. 295, inspired by Emiliano Zapata Salazar (8 August 1879 – 10 April 1919) was the general of the southern Mexican revolutionary army. Also, the main leader of the peasant revolution in the state of Morelos, and the inspiration of the agrarian movement called Zapatista. *"I'd rather die on my feet, than live on my knees."*

Chp. 23, pg. 302, re: Ethics in regards to exploiting a broken system, Chris Hedges: Corporate Totalitarianism: The End Game (2018) - https://www.youtube.com/watch?v=ZBcOyv8LZ8s

Chp. 23, pg. 302, as influenced by Ayn Rand and Nathaniel Branden's "The Virtue of Selfishness: A New Concept of Egoism"

Chp. 23, pg. 302, John Maynard Keynes ("Economic Possibilities for our Grandchildren" *Essays in Persuasion*, London: Macmillan, 1931, pg.370) *"When the accumulation of wealth is no longer of high social importance, there will be great changes in the code of morals. We shall be able to rid ourselves of many of the pseudo-moral principles which have hag-ridden us for two hundred years, by which we have exalted some of the most distasteful of human qualities into the position of the highest virtues. We shall be able to afford to dare to assess the money-motive at its true value. The love of money as a possession — as distinguished from the love of money as a means to the enjoyments and realities of life — will be recognized for what it is, a somewhat disgusting morbidity, one of those semi-criminal, semi-pathological propensities which one hands over with a shudder to the specialists in mental disease."*

Chp. 23, pg. 307, The "Great Jubilee" inspired by David Graeber ("Debt: The First 5,000 Years", Melville House, 2011)

Chp. 24, pg. 314, influenced by Jean-Paul Sartre, re: the freedom to dismantle capitalism.

Chp. 24, pg. 316, "Trickle Down Economics" inspired by "Reaganonimcs" (US President Ronal Regan)

Chp. 24, pg. 316, Maurizio Lazzarato ("The Making of the Indebted Man" pg.164) *"The fight against the debt economy and above all against its "morality" of guilt, which, in the end, is a morality of fear, also requires a specific kind of subjective conversion... We must recapture this second innocence, rid ourselves of guilt, of everything owed, of all bad conscience, and not repay a cent. We must fight for the cancellation of debt, for debt, one will recall, is not an economic problem but an apparatus of power designed not only to impoverish us, but to bring about catastrophe...The financial catastrophe is far from over, since no regulation of finance is possible. Its regulation would mark the end of neoliberalism."* (pg.245) *I call "laziness" political action that at once refuses and eludes the roles, functions, and significations of the social division of labor and, in so doing, creates new possibilities. Why bring back laziness from the limbo to which the workers' movement had relegated it? Because it allows us to think and to practice the "refusal of work" starting from an ethical-political principle that will perhaps lead us out of the enchanted circle of production, productivity, and producers ("we are the true producers!").*

Chp. 24, pg. 317, influenced by Paul Lafargue (The Right to be Lazy, 1880)

Chp. 24, pg. 318, re: "money restricting freedom" and the existential idea of "bad faith" influenced by Jean-Paul Sartre

Chp. 24, pg. 318, Voltaire (Candide, 1759) *"Work keeps at bay three great evils: boredom, vice, and need."*

Chp. 24, pg. 319, Adolf Hitler (David Nicholls. Adolf Hitler: A Biographical Companion. Santa Barbara, CA: ABC-CLIO, 2000, p. 245.) *'The capitalists have worked their way to the top through their capacity, and as the basis of this selection, which again only proves their higher race, they have a right to lead.'*

Chp. 24, pg. 319, David Harvey ("The Seventeen Contradiction and the End of Capitalism" pg. 292) *"The arrogance and disdain with which the affluent now view those less fortunate than themselves, even when (particularly when) vying with each other behind closed doors to prove who can be the most charitable of them all, are notable facts of our present condition. The 'empathy gap' between the oligarchy and the rest is immense and increasing. The oligarchs mistake superior income for superior human worth and their economic success as evidence of their superior knowledge of the world (rather than their superior command over accounting tricks and legal niceties). They do not know how to listen to the plight of the world because they cannot and willfully will not confront their role in the construction of that plight. They do not and cannot see their own contradictions."*

Chp. 24, pg. 320, Joseph Schumpeter ("Capitalism, Socialism and Democracy" pg. 198) *"A considerable part of the total work done by lawyers goes into the struggle of business with the state and its organs. It is immaterial whether we call this vicious obstruction of the common good or defense of the common good against vicious obstruction. In any case the fact remains that in socialist society there would be neither need nor room for this part of legal activity. The result saving it nor not room for this part of legal activity. The resulting saving is not satisfactorily measured by the fees of the lawyers who are this engaged. That is inconsiderable. But not inconsiderable is the social loss from such unproductive employment of many of the best brains. Considering how terribly rare good brains are, their shifting to other employments might be of more than infinitesimal importance."*

Chp. 24, pg. 321, David Harvey ("The Seventeen Contradiction and the End of Capitalism" pg. 294) Ideas for Political Praxis

Chp. 25, pg.327, influenced by Howard Zinn (History is a Weapon, "The Problem Is Civil Obedience" November 1970)
https://www.historyisaweapon.com/defcon1/zinnproblemobedience.html

Chp. 25. Influences pg.331-341:

Joie Pena ("Reasons Why Las Vegas Is the Worst Place Ever" Vice)
https://www.vice.com/en_us/article/dpwwbx/reasons-why-las-vegas-is-the-worst-place-ever-821

Megan Koester ("I went to Las Vegas alone and was totally depressed" Vice)
https://www.vice.com/en_us/article/5gky9a/las-vegas-is-the-most-depressing-place-on-earth-to-be-alone

Heart Attack Grill – Las Vegas (https://www.heartattackgrill.com, 450 Fremont St #130, Las Vegas, NV 89101)

Niki Goffin ("Top 11 Reasons Why Disney Land/World Sucks!" Kid 101)
https://kid101.com/top-11-reasons-why-disney-worldland-sucks-bonus-disney-cartoons-that-make-me-burf/

Chp. 25, pg.335, David Graeber ("The truth is out: money is just an IOU, and the banks are rolling in it" The Guardian, 2014)
https://www.theguardian.com/commentisfree/2014/mar/18/truth-money-iou-bank-of-england-austerity

Chp. 25, pg.336, Henry Ford (The American Mercury in 1957, How Internationalists Gain Power), *"It is well enough that people of the nation do not understand our banking and monetary system, for if they did, I believe there would be a revolution before tomorrow morning."*

Chp. 25, pg.336, David Harvey ("Marx, Capital, and the Madness of Economic Reason" pg. 40) *"Banks leverage their deposits to lend out a multiple of the assets they actually possess. Their loans can be three times or in periods of 'irrational exuberance' as much as thirty times the assets they have on deposit. This is money creation over and beyond that needed to cover current value production and realisation. This money creation takes the form of debt and debts are a claim on future value production. an accumulation of debts is either redeemed by future value production or devalued in the course of a crisis. All capitalist production is speculative, of course, but in the financial system that characteristic is heightened into a supreme fetish. The financier, says Marx, has the 'nicely mixed character of swindler and prophet'. Fictitious capital may or may not be realised through valorisation and realisation at some later date. At the apex of the world's financial and monetary system sit the central banks armed with seemingly infinite powers of money creation no matter what the state of value production."*

Chp. 26, inspired by "Fight Club" Novel by Chuck Palahnuik (1996), Film Directed by David Fincher, starring Brad Pitt, Edward Norton and Helena Bonham Carter, Fox 2000 Pictures (1999)

Chp. 26, pg.342, inspired by David Mamet's "Glengarry Glen Ross" (1992), Directed by James Foley. Ricky Roma (played by Al Pacino) *"All train compartments smell vaguely of shit. It gets so you don't mind it. That's the worst thing that I can confess. You know how long it took me to get there? A long time. When you die you're going to regret the things you don't do."*

Chp. 26, pg.342, David Graeber, "Hope in Common" (Infoshop, September 7, 2019) http://www.infoshop.org/hope-in-common/
"Hopelessness isn't natural. It needs to be produced. If we really want to understand this situation, we have to begin by understanding that the last thirty years have seen the construction of a vast bureaucratic apparatus for the creation and maintenance of hopelessness, a kind of giant machine that is designed, first and foremost, to destroy any sense of possible alternative futures. At root is a veritable obsession on the part of the rulers of the world with ensuring that social movements cannot be seen to grow, to flourish, to propose alternatives; that those who challenge existing power arrangements can never, under any circumstances, be perceived to win. To do so requires creating a vast apparatus of armies, prisons, police, various forms of private security firms and police and military intelligence apparatus, propaganda engines of every conceivable variety, most of which do not attack alternatives directly so much as they create a pervasive climate of fear, jingoistic conformity, and simple despair that renders any thought of changing the world seem an idle fantasy... What is debt, after all, but imaginary money whose value can only be realized in the future: future profits, the proceeds of the exploitation of workers not yet born.

Chp. 26, pg.343, Joey Chestnut, Competitive Eating Champion and World Record Holder. Nathan's Hot Dog Eating Contest, annual 4th of July eating contest held in Coney Island, Brooklyn, New York City.

Chp. 26, pg.347, Albert Camus ("The Sea Close By" in Lyrical and Critical Essays,1970) *"Knowing that certain nights whose sweetness lingers will keep returning to the earth and sea after we are gone, yes, this helps us to die."*

Additional Influences, Shout Outs & Further Reading/Viewing:

Alex Gibney ("Enron: The Smartest Guys in the Room," 2005
American documentary film based on the best-selling 2003 book of the same
name by *Fortune* reporters Bethany McLean and Peter Elkind, 2929
Entertainment)

Andrew Stanton ("WALL-E", Andrew Stanton - Director, Screenplay, Story,
2008, Walt Disney Pictures, Pixar Animation Studios, Produced by Jim Morris)

Aristotle (Concept of the Good Life)

Charles Ferguson ("Inside Job," 2010, Academy Award Winner for Best
Documentary Feature, Distributed by Sony Pictures Classics)

Charlie Chaplin ("Modern Times," 1936, United Artists)

Christian Marazzi ("Capital and Affects: The Politics of the Language
Economy," Semiotext(e) 2011)

Daniel Goleman ("A Force for Good: The Dalai Lama's Vision for Our World,"
Bloomsbury, 2016)

David Harvey ("The New Imperialism" (2013), "A Brief History of
Neoliberalism" (2003), "A Companion to Marx's Capital Volume 1" (2010), "A
Companion to Marx's Capital Volume 2" (2013), "The Ways of the World"
(2016)

Fritz Lang ("Metropolis," Film, 1927 German expressionist science-
fiction drama film directed by Fritz Lang. Written by Thea von Harbou in
collaboration with Lang, stars Gustav Fröhlich, Alfred Abel, Rudolf Klein-
Rogge and Brigitte Helm. Erich Pommer produced it in the Babelsberg
Studios for Universum Film A.G.)

George Orwell ("Animal Farm," 1945, "Nineteen Eighty-Four," 1949, Secker and
Warburg)

G.K. Chesterton ("The Napoleon of Notting Hill," Bodley Head, 1904)

Jacob Kornbluth, Robert Reich ("Inequality for All," 2013 documentary film
directed by Jacob Kornbluth presented by American economist, author and
professor Robert Reich, based on his 2010 book *Aftershock: The Next Economy and
America's Future*.)

Joseph Stiglitz ("The Price of Inequality: How Today's Divided Society
Endangers our Future," W.W. Norton & Company, 2013)

Jim Bruce ("Money for Nothing: Inside the Federal Reserve," written and directed by Jim Bruce, narrated by Liev Schreiber, Liberty Street Films 2013)

Michael Lewis, Adam McKay ("The Big Short," 2015 film directed by Adam McKay. Written by McKay and Charles Randolph, based on the 2010 book *The Big Short: Inside the Doomsday Machine* by Michael Lewis)

Michael Moore ("Capitalism: A Love Story," 2009 American documentary film directed, written by, and starring Michael Moore, Dog Eat Dog Films)

Michael Winterbottom, Russell Brand, Melissa Parmenter ("The Emperor's New Clothes," 2015 documentary film directed by Michael Winterbottom and starring actor/activist Russell Brand, StudioCanal UK)

Richard Adams ("Watership Down," Rex Collings Ltd, 1972)

Yanis Varoufakis ("And the Weak Suffer What They Must?" Talks at Google: https://www.youtube.com/watch?v=P2Zpkz7lK-s Greek economist, academic and politician. Minister of Finance from January to July 2015 under Prime Minister Alexis Tsipras. Varoufakis, member of the Hellenic Parliament for Athens from January to September 2015; he regained a parliamentary seat in July 2019.)

Made in the USA
Monee, IL
09 December 2019